PRAISE FOR KAI

"*Original Sinner* is a sizzling hot, irreverent, and seductively enthralling read. Lucifer is guaranteed to become your new morally gray book boyfriend addiction."

— Abigail Owen, #1 *New York Times* and *USA Today* bestselling author of *The Games Gods Play*

"Kait Ballenger is a treasure you don't want to miss!"

— *New York Times* and *USA Today* bestseller Gena Showalter

"An extremely promising high-voltage start [. . .] Readers will savor strong characterization, steamy animalistic sex scenes with Dom/sub subtext and an interesting series arc."

— *Publishers Weekly* Starred Review for *Rogue Wolf Hunter*

"This story has it all . . . The chemistry is electric, and the spicy banter is terrific."

— Fresh Fiction for *Cowboy Wolf Trouble*

"Hits all the sweet spots of paranormal romance. Recommend to readers of Nalini Singh and Maria Vale."

— *Booklist* for *Cowboy in Wolf's Clothing*

"Adventure, intrigue, and a super sexy premise!"

— Terry Spear, *USA Today* bestselling author for *Cowboy in Wolf's Clothing*

"The romance is sexy, and a fast-paced, rollicking plot will keep readers engaged."

— *Kirkus Reviews* for *Wicked Cowboy Wolf*

ORIGINAL
SINNER

OTHER TITLES BY KAIT BALLENGER

Seven Range Shifters

Rogue Brotherhood

ORIGINAL SINNER

KAIT BALLENGER

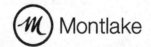

Published by Montlake, Seattle

www.apub.com

Amazon, the Amazon logo, and Montlake are trademarks of Amazon.com, Inc., or its affiliates.

ISBN-13: 9781662528873 (paperback)
ISBN-13: 9781662528866 (digital)

Cover design by Caroline Teagle Johnson
Cover art by Christian Bentulan
Cover images: © VALUA VITAL, © Yellow Cat / Shutterstock; © Alisa, © Protsenko Dmitriy / Adobe Stock

Printed in the United States of America

To the women who felt shame and still turned the page . . .

Good girl.

AUTHOR'S NOTE

Dear reader,

Thank you for picking up a copy of *Original Sinner*. I'm so thrilled this sexy, irreverent story has you intrigued. *Original Sinner* is the book of my heart. I wrote it as a rebellious act of reclaiming my writing joy, as a fearless and unapologetic way to do whatever the hell I wanted on the page, without limitations. Like all my work, it's an exorcism of my own demons, but also an homage to every dark, delicious thing I love in a story, and as such, the contents may not be suitable to all readers.

Original Sinner is a dark, sexy paranormal fantasy romance featuring a villainous, morally gray billionaire who coercively blackmails his employee into dating him. As a main character, Lucifer is exactly as seductive and horrible as you would expect him to be, and his love interest, Charlotte, while traumatized by her fundamentalist religious past, is no withering wallflower.

As such, this book contains heavy themes of religious trauma with frequent references to shame, sex, virginity, self-worth, body image, body shaming, purity culture, the concept of sin, and the role those assigned female at birth are expected to play in the fundamentalist Christian church. It has frequent references to previous emotional, physical, and sexual abuse that is parental, religious, and spousal in nature and occurs mostly off page. It shows manipulation, stalking, references to drug use, alcohol abuse, forced confinement, and the nonconsensual drugging of a secondary character. It references forced marriage and forced pregnancy, contains graphic violence and murder, and, of course, has a healthy dose of swearing.

Readers who are sensitive to this content, take heed, and prepare to be seduced by mythology's ultimate bad boy . . .

THE ORIGINALS

Lucifer—Pride

Azmodeus—Lust

Mammon—Greed

Belphegor—Sloth

Satan—Wrath

Leviathan—Envy

Beelzebub—Gluttony

CHAPTER ONE

Charlotte

At least the villains show you who they really are.

I stare up at the entrance of The Serpent, the neon lights from the club's open doors spilling out onto the darkened street. The line I'm standing in wraps around several blocks, which in Hell's Kitchen means you're not likely getting inside unless you're a celebrity, but still we've been standing here for the better part of an hour, listening to the music inside the club thumping. The air outside is close. Humid and sweaty. Hot enough I'm struggling to breathe. But I don't need to see inside to know exactly what waits for me.

Lucifer owns this city. Along with everything and everyone in it.

Ever since he and the other Originals arrived topside nearly a decade ago, his brother's viral nightclub has been marketed as a den of sin, sold to the digital masses as a place to fulfill your darkest fantasies.

Sex. Drugs. Fornication. Idolatry. No matter what you call it, pick your poison and you'll find it inside The Serpent's walls. The obsidian building looms over me, glittering in the nighttime lights of the city like a dark, sinful promise.

God's judgment won't find you. Not in this godforsaken city.

But my own fantasies are a far cry from here.

I shift my weight where I stand, more than a little anxious. This date is only beginning, and already I can tell the sex will be bad. Awful, really. If we even manage to get that far, which according to Jax—my bestie—I need it to. Just a few more one-night stands to get all the "purity culture bullshit" ingrained by my family out of my system and I'll finally be able to enjoy myself for real, or so Jax keeps telling me.

The ghost of my newly lost V-card hangs like a shackle around my neck, weighing me down, a constant reminder that I don't belong here. New York may be the Big Apple, but ironically even before the Originals turned the world upside down, to me, it's always been forbidden fruit.

Sin incarnate.

The line moves slightly, but only because another group has finally called uncle and given up their spot. I keep to the shadows, uncomfortable with the gazes that scan me head to toe.

Back home, my virgin status made me valuable, cherished. Here, my limited experience marks me as *other*, exactly the wrong kind of novelty. One I'm trying to do something about. If you can even call a few minutes of unlubricated penetration in the dark an *experience*. Which Mark did, apparently. I didn't even come, but who's counting?

To be fair, keeping the lights off was my idea. My stomach twists at the thought. Moving past the way I was raised is a constant struggle, but that's exactly why I'm here, I suppose.

Hoping the devil will save me.

Suddenly, the line moves forward, which leaves me and my date for tonight still standing half a block from the entrance. Shit.

I sigh. Just my luck.

It's not Blake's fault he's a douche, really, even if he did lie on his dating app profile and say he majored in both finance and accounting. But ask and ye shall receive.

I wanted a bad boy, and that's exactly what I got. A horndog frat boy majoring in business administration with a minor in sports management, a questionable future, and a not-so-hidden agenda. I *wanted* bad.

I just didn't expect him to be so . . . predatory.

Blake's hand snakes its way onto my lower back, drawing perilously close to my ass. My heart skips a beat, but not in the way I'd hoped for. We only met one another an hour ago, and the conversation since has been limited, to say the least. A mixture of sports I don't care about and recollections about parties I'll likely never attend.

Blake's made it crystal clear since we started at the back of the line this evening that there's only one thing he's interested in, and it has little to do with my brain and a lot to do with somewhere he can stick his dick before night's end. I'm not sure he even cares if I'm willing.

Isn't he supposed to try and work for it?

Or maybe I'm being naive. This city is still new to me.

"Please don't," I say as his hand dips closer to groping me. I step to the side a little, placing myself just out of reach.

Blake frowns, but this time, he doesn't try to bully me. Though if the past hour holds true, that doesn't mean he'll take the hint. Not by a long shot.

I sigh again and step further into the shadows, half-tempted to lean against the building like if I slump hard enough, I'll somehow manage to disappear inside its walls. These heels are killing me, and I'm tired of standing here with my asshole date, even if this *is* exactly what I chose. But what other options were left for me?

My father would say I'm asking for it, standing here dressed in a too-short minidress with a neckline that dips almost to my navel and shows off my cleavage generously. A shameless hussy, that's what he'd call me. A jezebel. Maybe worse.

Not the most original, my father.

But I've worked too hard to get here to turn back now. Sacrificing myself on the altar of an arranged evangelical marriage before I even hit my midtwenties isn't my destiny, and I have no intention of returning to the life I escaped. Not now. Not ever.

A bouncer prowls past us, scanning the line, probably for some B-list celebrity. He gives me and Blake a once-over.

His eyes lock onto me.

"You," he says, surprising me as he hitches a thumb over his shoulder toward the velvet ropes. "You can go in."

"M-me?" I sputter.

Before I left our apartment, Jax told me I looked "fucking fierce" tonight, and the tarot card she pulled said something major was about to happen, but it's not as if I actually *believed* her. It's her borrowed dress I'm wearing, after all, and while I may have run from my messed-up religious family, a small part of me still believes in God, though I doubt He'd speak to me through a deck of cards.

He doesn't exactly speak to anybody these days, considering he up and abandoned us all.

Now Lucifer and the others are in charge.

The bouncer waves me forward, and I grin, moving to cut the queue.

Blake starts to follow, but the guard blocks his path quickly with a meaty hand.

"Not you." The bouncer looks directly at me and tilts his head. "You go. He stays."

I try hard not to look as relieved as I feel.

"Seriously?" Blake moans as I step away from him.

I glance over my shoulder. I should feel bad about ghosting him, about cutting in line in front of all these people, especially when they've been waiting longer than me. Coming here was Blake's idea, after all. Not that I needed much convincing. Lucifer and this club have intrigued me since long before I ever moved to this city.

Who *wouldn't* be intrigued by a man who's equal parts myth and mystery?

But for the life of me, I can't bring myself to feel bad for Blake.

I shrug. "Sorry." I say it with all the I'll-pray-for-you kindness I was raised with, which means I don't exactly mean it.

The club's bouncer follows me.

"Bitch," Blake mutters as I step past him.

My stomach churns. I shouldn't be surprised that's all it takes to make Blake turn nasty, but the hate in his voice still sends my pulse racing. Tears threaten at the edge of my eyes, the confrontation instantly triggering me, but I don't bother to glance over my shoulder again as the bouncer releases the velvet rope. I rush into the club, quickly making my escape. I don't want to give the bouncer a chance to change his mind, and if I really *do* decide I want to take someone home tonight, I can find that someone here easily.

Someone who's not Blake.

Someone who lives up to my fantasies.

The inside of The Serpent is everything I anticipated. Dark, modern, brooding, if you can even call interior nightclub decor "brooding."

Gluttony's club is decorated in all lush, dark colors and red neon lights, the inside packed with so many sweaty, writhing bodies, I instantly feel as if the walls are pressing in on me, which only makes the tears that threatened before an actual problem. I scan the ground floor, searching for the restroom. Somewhere, anywhere I can get my shit together, but the line to the ladies' room is practically as long as the one where I left Blake, so I ditch that idea.

I move my way through the crowd, swiping at my eyes, no doubt making my mascara a hot mess as I go. I'm not really sure why I'm crying, but I'm fairly certain it has little to do with Blake and a lot to do with why I'm here in the first place. It's not as if my own father hasn't called me a hell of a lot worse. The way supposedly godly men can treat the women they keep trapped under their thumbs can be . . . fucked up, to say the least. One of the many reasons why I left home, though this isn't exactly home, either, is it?

It's that exact thought that makes it so I'm crying twice as hard now, hard enough that the club's music rings in my ears, and I'm definitely having an anxiety attack, because I can't seem to breathe. My vision blurs, and I stumble my way through the crowd and up what must be a set of interior service stairs. A closed door waits at the top.

A promised escape from everything.

I wrench it open and duck inside. The moment it seals behind me, I sink against it and sigh in relief, more than a little grateful that the hallway I'm in is blessedly dark.

And empty.

The club's music thumps distantly.

I pull my phone from the clutch I'm carrying and hammer out a quick text to Jax.

This was a mistake. I don't belong here.

Her response comes instantly. As if she anticipated my breakdown even before I did.

That's not true. You've worked hard for this.

This being the celebratory night out I'm supposed to be enjoying before my life changes irrevocably. Before I sell my soul to the devil in the form of a competitive internship at his company.

Out of thousands of applicants, they somehow picked me.

It doesn't matter that I've come this far. Running away from my family and living it up in NYC for a few weeks is one thing. Working for Lucifer himself is another. It's the one decision I've made in the last few weeks that I can't recover from with any kind of certainty, though I doubt I'll even see him. Dodging photos is the Prince of Darkness's specialty, after all, and what would an intern matter to the billionaire CEO of a multinational conglomerate, let alone *the* fallen angel?

"It's not as if I'll even work with him personally," I mutter to myself.

Though I doubt that detail would matter to my father.

"And who might that be?" a distinctly male voice answers from the dark.

It wraps around me like a warm coat, its charm made of velvet and sin. It's a voice meant for unspeakable things, things I've only begun to learn about within the last few weeks, and yet it . . . does things to me.

I clench my legs together, parts of me softening even as my shoulders become stiff, rigid.

"Who's there?" I whisper, half hopeful and half freaking terrified I'll receive an answer. Hearing voices where there are none is exactly the last thing I need.

But if I'm *not* hearing things, I'm in deep, caught alone in the dark in a club famed for its unlimited vices. There are no rules here. Nothing to protect me.

What would my father say to me?

"I could ask the same," the voice answers back.

Whoever he is, he's moving closer now, quickly closing the distance between us.

In the darkness, I can almost make out his shape. A large shadow of a silhouette that doesn't just blend into the darkness, he *becomes* it. As if it were a part of him.

My heart races, adrenaline overtaking me.

The hairs on the back of my neck rise on end.

"Stay back," I hiss, lifting a feeble hand.

As if that will protect me.

I sound pathetic, even to my own ears, but I'm running out of choices. I have no clue whether the door I came in locked behind me, and even if I could find the handle without stumbling around like I'm drunk in the dark, I'm not risking moving.

I'm frozen.

In the face of a predator, I will always be prey.

That's what my father's gifted me.

"What brings you here, little dove?" The flash of a lighter sparks as he burns a cigarette, briefly illuminating his face.

I only get a quick glimpse before his lighter goes out, but he's just as gorgeous as I expected he'd be. As gorgeous as that luscious voice sounds. With looks that could kill and cheekbones so sharp they're almost cutting. He's wearing a suit that, based on how well it fits him, looks like it cost a small fortune, at least to me.

My one-room flat in Chinatown isn't much, but it's something.

Whoever he is, he must work in the offices here. He's an employee. He's too at home not to be, though I doubt he's one of the waitstaff.

"I'm waiting with bated breath, darling," he says, smirking at me.

I can't see the expression. Not clearly, anyway, but I can hear it in his voice. Feel it. It slithers through me, leaving a wicked trail of goose bumps in its wake.

I don't know what causes me to answer. Fear, maybe? But I don't bother to think.

"Confirmation that I'm supposed to be here, I guess." I glance down at my still-glowing phone. "Among other things."

"Mmm," he grumbles, as if my answer is uninteresting.

Though he doesn't leave. Not yet.

The orange end of his cigarette pulses as he brings it to his lips again. The shadows around him move with it, illuminating a mouth I have no doubt has sinned.

For one brief, insane moment, I can't help but wonder what it would be like to have lips like that pressed against me, whispering to me in the dark. But the moment I think it, I drop my chin, shame filling me. Whoever—*what*ever—this man is, he's a stranger. A mystery. A potential threat, though he hasn't done anything to me. Yet.

What is *wrong* with me?

"If it's love you're searching for, you won't find it here." He says it as if he can see right through me, though I know in the dark he can't make out my features any more clearly than I can see him.

"And what *will* I find?" I ask before I can stop myself.

Those wicked lips twist. "Pain. Pleasure. That's all anyone here can offer you. Even me."

"Isn't love a kind of pleasure?"

He huffs. "No," he says quickly, as if his word is resolute, sacred. "True love is ferocious, vicious, destructive. True love is costly, and humanity knows little of it. It's a price few are willing to pay. You all want the feeling of love without any of the work that goes into it. It's an irrational, self-destructive impulse disguised as joy."

My breath hitches. "Speak for yourself."

At that, he chuckles, like I've finally said something amusing. "So, tell me, little dove, if love's what you desire, do you belong here? Will you find what you're seeking?"

Heart pounding, I take the out for what it is and seize it.

"No, I . . . I don't think I will."

He steps closer.

Dangerously close.

Without warning, I throw myself toward the door, praying I find the handle. My hand connects with it instantly—*thank God*—and seconds later, I'm barreling down the service stairs back into the fray of the club, the strobe lights overhead flashing.

I don't bother to look behind me to see if anyone is chasing me. Though I swear that even when I reach the street, I can still hear that deep velvet voice, laughing like he did when I fled down the stairs. I don't stop until I'm in a taxi, which miraculously pulls over for me. I wrench the door open and throw myself inside, sealing the haunting sound of that dark laughter behind me.

My heart is still racing as I mumble a vague direction to the driver, terrified of what this means, because whoever he was, if what he said is true, love doesn't sound as dark and wicked as it should be. If love is vicious, if love isn't kind . . .

It sounds like power.

And somehow that's not at all terrifying.

CHAPTER TWO

Lucifer

It took no more than a glimpse to know the doe-eyed beauty who just fled my brother's club doesn't belong in this city. That alone should have been enough to make me ignore her. I have little interest in those who aren't tempted by me, but ever since Eve, I've found easy targets difficult to resist, and as of late, I've had a particular penchant for cruelty.

"It's unkind to toy with them, don't you think?" Astaroth's amused voice cuts through the din, finding me where I lurk in the shadows.

I lift the last of my cigarette to my lips, allowing the smoke to fill my lungs until it calms me. The orange ember glows generously, flaring through the dark. It's my godforsaken duty to tempt those who are weak willed and vulnerable, to feed off their desire, their lust for power. I am the voice in their ear, tempting them into this city's underbelly, and make no mistake . . .

I fucking revel in it.

"Cruelty is what you make of it." I flick the ashes and stub out what's left of my cigarette beneath my Armani shoe. The sound of the club's music thumps below stairs. A reminder of exactly how little I care for humanity. So little I allow my siblings to offer them all their destructive pleasures at humanity's own expense, their money given as an offering to me.

The vices inside my brother's club are the luxury rope with which they choose to hang themselves, but I can hardly bring myself to give a shit.

Not when they make it so easy.

"You know that's not what I mean," Astaroth says, joining me.

If there's such a thing as friends in hell, Astaroth is as close as I'll ever get to having one.

He's loyal, which is all I need any demon to be.

I release a long sigh, ignoring Astaroth's prodding as I stare at the now-closed door where the little doe fled, nothing but the sound of my laughter chasing her.

It's been a long time since any human has tempted me. Since I've *wanted* to toy with one. But whoever she was, she was more lamb than human, an innocent creature brought to slaughter, and I've always had more than a passing taste for blood.

Though tempting her inside my brother's nightclub is a little cliché, even for me.

"You've been distracted," Astaroth says, drawing my attention once more. He fishes out a cigarette of his own and lights it. "It doesn't suit you."

My gaze snaps to his, and he flinches slightly. It's a dangerous accusation. One which, if uttered by anyone else, would mean they'd suffer my wrath just as quickly as my gaze snapped to Astaroth. If they even lived long enough to see morning. But Astaroth is *allowed* to annoy me, only because he's earned it with a millennium of loyal history.

"Have I?" I lift a brow, knowing exactly what Astaroth means but refusing to acknowledge it. Humility has never been my strong suit.

"Gabriel's return draws near." He brazens it out, like he always does.

The mere mention of my brother's name irks me. Like a splinter under the skin.

"And?" I sneer.

He says it as if I don't know. As if it isn't the sole thought that consumes me.

"And it weighs on you," Astaroth says, taking a long drag. "Clearly."

"I'm as ready as I'll ever be," I say, perhaps a little too defensively, but I refuse to admit any vulnerability. Even to Astaroth.

It's for that same sinful reason that I rule this city. Thanks to the gauntlet my Father has thrown down for me. In the scheme of the universe, it's a blink of an eye, the time we've been given.

Whoever rules NYC's dark underbelly upon Gabriel's return gets a free pass for all they've done to humanity. A heavenly get-out-of-jail-free card, as it were. It's been ten years since *He* sent his angelic errand boy to offer the opportunity.

To my brothers. To Lust. Envy. Greed. All six of the other Original sinners respectively.

All of them *except* me.

And I've never much appreciated being left out.

Astaroth lets out a low whistle, reading the anger in my voice easily. "With a look like that, things are likely to get messy," he says, as if the cold war we've been waging since we got here isn't *already* messy. But I know as well as he does, this round is different.

The stakes have been raised considerably.

"Of course they will."

In fact, I anticipate it. I may own this city, but each of my siblings rules their own corner, holds their own reach, which is exactly what places them at war with me.

It's only a matter of time before one of them tries to make a move. One last attempt to dethrone me before dear old Dad returns. It's one small part of the wicked games we play.

Among other things . . .

As if on cue, the club's music is cut suddenly. Abrupt silence follows, and I glance down, waiting expectantly before the walls are rent by the sounds of screams. In the span of a moment, the mood below stairs shifts from seductive to startling.

Astaroth sighs, exchanging a grim expression with me as we both move toward the door. "Who's your bet on this time?" he asks halfheartedly.

"Envy," I wager, rolling my eyes. "It's always fucking Envy."

"Or Greed." Astaroth shrugs. "She's been on a particular bender as of late."

The moment the service door opens, the screams grow louder, doubling in intensity. It fills me with a little more fucked-up glee than I care to admit, and a smirk twists my lips despite the rage that courses through me.

I've never cared for humanity, and their fear pleases me.

Astaroth and I descend into the chaos, fighting against the current of patrons trying to escape the club. I should have expected they'd strike while I'm here. Tonight. My siblings aren't exactly known for their subtlety, and while The Serpent may not be Gluttony's most financially lucrative investment, it's by far the most popular, the most public facing.

The one most likely to stir the paparazzi.

It's a pathetic attempt to cause a blow to my pride, to get my face in the papers. They know me all too well, my siblings, but what they fail to understand is they cannot damage what's already been stolen from me.

What our Father has already taken.

I fight my way through the crowd at first, but the patrons soon part easily, sensing the something *other* that separates Astaroth and me. They may not recognize my face, but I am not human. Not like them.

Though I'm no angel either.

It takes only a handful of minutes for us to reach the club's second floor. A glittering array of lush cushions and darkened alcoves lit beneath soft neon-pink lighting meant to mimic an erotic version of the second ring of Hell, or to give the humans an impression of it, really. The dead man lying in the middle of the club's floor isn't exactly a surprise to me.

The cleanup here come morning is hardly pleasing. There are no rules in this club, and thanks to my less-than-subtle influence in NYC's politics, there are no laws within these walls either. Finding dead bodies on any of The Serpent's seven floors is commonplace. Expected, even.

What *isn't* commonplace is the bullet hole that pierced the man's skull.

His blood seeps onto the marble flooring, pooling in a macabre sort of halo as a distant camera flashes. Not a usual sight on this floor, which means . . .

"Not Envy."

"Nor Greed," Astaroth agrees.

No, the man's naked form and still erect penis say it all.

Lust has finally made his move against me.

CHAPTER THREE

Charlotte

"You picked a hell of a day to start."

I struggle to keep pace, thanks to the cheap heels I'm wearing, as I follow Imani, my new supervisor, through the lavishly decorated high-rise. She's a fiercely dressed Black woman, who stands nearly a full head taller than me, and she's wearing a blazer with a sleek, pin-striped romper that complements her model-like figure perfectly. Her outfit, along with her designer heels, likely costs more than my rent, and as the director of public relations for Apollyon Inc., Lucifer's multinational holding and conglomerate specializing in luxury goods, she's as intimidating as she is posh.

Striding down the hall ahead of me, she commands her designer Jimmy Choos with the kind of runway-worthy stride I can only dream of.

"You'll be responsible for some of our smaller online and social media communications, which coordinate with a lot of our affiliate branding." She glances over her shoulder toward me as I stumble. I glance down at my knockoff heels, my face heating at how uncomfortably underdressed I am.

She shakes her head a little, smiling like I'm amusing—a child playing dress-up in Mommy's clothes—before her brows lower and her expression turns serious. "And the devil wears Versace. Not Prada. Make a note of it."

Versace, not Prada, I type into the note app on my phone before pausing.

"Why not Prada?" I lift a brow.

Imani comes to a stop in front of a corner office before she rolls her eyes. "Girl, don't ask." She pushes open the glass door and leads me inside.

The office is filled with natural lighting from the floor-to-ceiling windows that overlook the city. The Upper East Side, if I'm getting my NYC geography right, considering we're standing on the sixteenth floor. In the early morning hours, with Central Park in the distance, it's a generous view. Breathtaking, really. A brand-new iMac embellished with Apollyon's logo—a serpent, of course—waits on a glass desk. A seriously plush desk chair and a few potted plants complete the room. It's big, unexpectedly private, and has a view any intern would envy. Must be her office.

"You'll work here," Imani says.

I step further inside, gaping a little. "Are you . . . are you sure?"

She places a hand on her hip. "You don't like it?"

"No, no, of course I like it. It's just . . . I'm only an intern, so I expected less. That's all."

Imani frowns like I've offended her. "Lucifer takes care of his own."

I nod, understanding quickly.

As the director of public relations, Imani's solely responsible for Lucifer's image, so I guess I shouldn't be surprised she's defensive of him, especially since I'm a newbie. She has a reputation to uphold, and she's good at her job. Damn good. Only a true PR genius could somehow turn the devil from a fallen angel feared by the masses to an A-list billionaire celebrity in under a decade, and I've done enough research to know Imani's been working for Lucifer from the start.

Ever since he came topside.

"I'm sorry." I lower my gaze before I peek around the office some more. "I didn't mean that he wouldn't. This is just . . . all so new to me."

Imani nods, like she somehow gets it. "Well, you better get used to it real fast, because we have a meeting in"—she checks her watch—"fifteen minutes."

My eyes widen. "We?"

I'd thought it was generous she offered to give me an office tour, especially since she's an executive-level hotshot. She no doubt has at least a hundred employees working under her who could have onboarded me, and to be honest, I figured I'd be fetching coffee orders and making copies. Isn't that what an intern is supposed to do?

I never expected I'd get to work with her directly, and the idea leaves me more than a little starstruck. I've seen Imani on the news plenty of times before, speaking at Lucifer's press conferences in his place. She's always seemed competent and confident. Beautiful, worldly. The kind of woman I've always wished I could be.

"My assistant just went on maternity leave, and I'm not sure she's coming back." She waves a hand. "I don't have time to search for a replacement, but I need someone to fill the role while she's gone, and your résumé's as good as any. I'll put in a request to HR to bump up your salary, of course. You good with that?"

"Yes! Yes, of course."

She smiles.

From the glint in her eye, she knows I'm getting the better end of this deal. She's giving me a major career glow-up, but I can't help but wonder if I deserve her kindness.

Or if I can even do the job well. I'd better make sure to earn every penny.

"It's just . . ."

I turn away from her then, trying to hide my growing concern as I glance around the office. The sky outside is a bright cerulean blue, and Central Park is full of lush summer trees. Glittering high-rises pepper the Manhattan skyline, and yet with each passing moment, my heart drops a little.

In the window's reflection, Imani quirks her head.

"Why me?" I ask as I turn to face her. "Why me when you have dozens of other employees who would kill for this opportunity?"

Imani's smile widens, showing off influencer-white teeth as she shakes her head. From her designer heels to her perfect smile and flawless complexion, she's pure New York City, and it shows. If Jax were here, she'd be screaming at me to shut my mouth and accept what the universe has given me, but all of this is happening so fast—my move to NYC, the internship, and now what is essentially a huge promotion, and on my first day, no less.

I can't possibly be this lucky.

Imani shrugs. "I'd rather train someone new to meet my needs than have to break in someone who's already set in their ways. And my help ain't free." She looks me over, sizing up my worth. "You'll have to work hard to keep up. Be available. Long hours. Weekends."

"Yes, ma'am," I say.

She scowls. "Call me ma'am again and you'll have a one-way ticket back to Podunkville. I'm not old enough for that." She fluffs the natural curls of her hair a little before her gaze rakes over me. From the grin on her lips, she's teasing, but I know better than to dismiss even a subtle warning.

Imani's the boss here, the one calling the shots, and if I expect this to last, I'll need to work my ass off to impress her at every opportunity.

"Where you from, anyway?" Her gaze flits over me.

I'm wearing my best business casual, a white blouse and navy-blue pencil skirt you could find at any Middle America Target. My cheeks flush pink.

I don't belong here, and that's as obvious to her as it is to me.

"Kansas," I answer. "Topeka."

She laughs like I've just said something hilarious. "Well, child, you ain't in Kansas anymore."

"Yes, Imani," I say, correcting my earlier mistake.

I want to show her I can learn quickly.

She smiles. "Better. We'll work on it." She glances at her watch again, then back to me. "I'll give you a few minutes to settle in, then I'll be back to get you for the meeting. Be prepared to take notes." She turns to leave.

She's almost to the doorway when a nervous thought grips me. "Imani?"

"Hmm?" She turns back to me, one sculpted brow lifted.

"You said I picked a hell of a day to start, but . . . I'm not sure what you mean."

Imani scoffs, shaking her head again. "Lesson number one of working in publicity." She reaches for a glossy magazine tucked into a hanging mail folder outside the door and tosses it onto my desk. "Read the damn papers." She grins before taking her leave.

For a long moment, I just stand there, still awestruck. This is an amazing opportunity. One that feels too good to be true. Finally, I inhale a deep breath, fortifying myself a little. I can do this. I'm a hard worker. It's one of the few good things my upbringing taught me.

I make my way over to my desk, smiling at the idea of any part of this glittering building being *my* anything. Releasing a happy sigh, I grab the magazine. I didn't even know people still read physical magazines anymore, and the idea amuses me. But my grin quickly fades as I scan the bold lettering. My stomach drops instantly.

Murder investigation: influencer shot dead when Lucifer attends famed nightclub.

My eyes widen.

What exactly have I gotten myself into?

CHAPTER FOUR

Charlotte

Imani returns ten minutes later, finding me mostly as she left me. Only, now I'm up to speed and prepared to tackle what we're facing. I can see why today of all days would be like jumping into the company shark tank with both feet. Even in a rag mag, a headline like that will go viral and no doubt create a media shitstorm, one that's unlikely to blow over anytime soon. Not without some serious reframing. Thankfully, with all the accusations constantly surrounding my father's congregation, I've gotten rather good at that.

Burying.

Maybe I'm not so unqualified for this, after all.

Imani summons me with the curl of one manicured finger.

I snatch an iPad and the stylus I found inside the desk and hurry after her. As we stride down the hall, someone's desk phone rings nearby, and I hear the rhythmic whirr of a copy machine.

"Do we . . . have to help the cops figure out who did it?" I ask as I struggle to keep up with her.

I'm breathing hard. This woman walks faster in heels than I can jog in sneakers.

Imani doesn't look at me. "Girl, who do you think you are, Nancy Drew?"

I shake my head, but she stops abruptly, her dark eyes turning as sharp as a hawk's. "You *did* sign the NDA agreement already, didn't you?"

I nod. No way could I forget that.

It was absolute hell getting through a document of that length. Let alone buying enough ink for my cheap at-home printer. Typical NDAs are only a few pages long, but Apollyon Inc.'s was a nearly one-hundred-page monster I would have needed a never-ending supply of espresso and a law degree to fully comprehend.

I might have skimmed it a little.

"Good." She turns away, and we're walking again. "Then you might as well know that Lust did it. Lucifer wasn't involved, of course."

I force an exaggerated smile in agreement. *Of course.*

"Lust?" I lift a brow.

"You know, Az. Azmodeus? Lucifer's brother. Try to keep up."

An elevator dings, and someone's fingers tap across their keyboard.

When I don't respond, Imani stops again, causing me to nearly crash into her. "You do know who Az is, don't you?"

I sputter, uncertain what to say without making myself look naive. "I . . . knew the other Originals existed, but I guess I didn't realize they were *all* his siblings?"

I smile apologetically.

Imani looks at me as if I've grown a second head, one that's not nearly as flattering as the first. "Did you live under a rock out in Kansas, or something?"

I shrug, eyes downcast. "Something like that."

She shakes her head like she can't believe me before waving a dismissive hand like she doesn't have time for this little education session. Considering the PR nightmare waiting for us, I know she doesn't. Creating a narrative is one thing. Controlling a narrative that's spinning like a tornado is another. It's one of the few things growing up in the shadow of my father's pulpit taught me. *Refocus. Reframe. Redirect.*

Until the truth becomes muddy.

"By tomorrow I expect you to have memorized all of NYC's major power players, A-list celebrities, and billionaires, particularly the ones who have any relationship to Lucifer."

"Yes, Imani."

"Good." She brushes herself off. "Now try not to gape at him or, God forbid, say anything while we're in there."

"You mean, he's actually going to *be* in the meeting?"

Imani sighs, rubbing her index finger and thumb over her temple like I've already put her at her wit's end before she's even had her coffee. "Don't tell me you thought you'd come work for the devil and never have to be in the same room as him. I don't tolerate that kind of nonsense."

I shut my mouth, stopping myself just short of admitting I had thought exactly that. When she says it that way, it *does* sound ridiculous, but I expected to be an intern, not the temporary assistant to the director of public relations for company headquarters.

She places her hand on the handle, pausing just outside the boardroom door. Glancing down at me, her eyes soften for a moment, like for the first time she's seeing exactly how young and green I am. "Look, at the company-sponsored parties, he's the one who smokes like a chimney. You can't miss him."

"He smokes? Like regular cigarettes?"

It's a surprisingly human habit for a man who, for all his faults, is a fallen angel.

"I've told him he should quit. It's better for the image. No one in luxury smokes these days." She shrugs dismissively. "He says it reminds him of the brimstone in Hell."

I blink. "I . . . guess even the devil gets homesick?"

At that, Imani laughs like what I've said is hilariously funny before she pushes open the door, leading me into the meeting.

The conference room looks like every executive-level boardroom in every megachurch I've ever been in. Neutral colors, modern fixtures, electrical outlets for technical equipment, and a rectangular wooden conference table with plush leather executive seats and employees in professional business attire. Their company-branded leather portfolios line the table, and the smell of coffee and lemon-scented cleaning supplies hangs in the air.

I try not to let my eyes wander as I follow Imani to two open chairs midway down the table. A pair of steaming disposable coffee cups from the Starbucks down the street wait for us, but my gaze stays glued to Imani's back. If there's one thing I'm good at, it's following directions, doing *exactly* as I've been told.

My father worked hard to cultivate that particular skill in me. Much to my own detriment.

Silently, I start to take my seat against the wall with the other interns, but Imani soon waves me to the big table. As I take the seat beside her, the fine hairs on my arms prickle into an array of goose bumps that's all too familiar. I don't need to look up to know Lucifer's here. To feel him. The awareness hits me like some long-lost instinct.

But the sensation isn't new to me. It's familiar and not in a good way.

Slowly, my gaze creeps upward, just enough to sneak a peek, part of me knowing and fearing what I'll find there.

The man from the club. The one whose sinful lips haunt my dreams.

I stiffen, my pulse racing.

Casting my eyes low, I try not to look at him, just as Imani told me.

Though calling him a man isn't exactly a fair description. True, he looks like a man, without a doubt, but "man" implies something normal, something mortal and human, and while Lucifer may *look* like a man, he's no doubt something other.

I feel that otherness combing over me.

Touching. Caressing.

Like he can see right through me.

I keep my eyes down, letting the strands of my hair fall forward a little in hopes of covering my face. It's a pathetic attempt to make sure he doesn't notice me, though I doubt he'd remember me, even if he did.

Why would he? I look worlds different from how I was dressed the other night, and the hallway he caught me in was ridiculously dark, blessedly so—the only light that either of us could see by was the passing neon of the club's strobes and the ethereal orange glow of that damned cigarette. Our interaction was nothing special, meaningless, really.

And yet . . .

I wasn't exactly wrong about him. My first impression held true. He *is* a danger to me, and I have no doubt that it's more than his mouth that's sinned. Except now that I know he's my boss, the full danger he poses is even clearer.

Lucifer owns me.

My gaze drifts up, and I steal another glance, my palms sweating before I force myself to sip my coffee and prepare my iPad to take notes. The coffee is so hot it nearly scalds me, but I don't dare show my discomfort or glance up again, even though I'm tempted to. He's just as droolworthy as I expected he'd be, even more so than I realized when we were alone in the dark, with dark hair and even darker eyes that cut through me.

He's stunning.

It seems like an odd thing to think about the devil, that he's beautiful, but it's not really, at least not when you consider it biblically. Lucifer once stood at God's side, his most cherished angel, and there's a freaking reason he tempted Eve. I'm all too familiar with the story. Only now, he represents everything I've ever been tempted by.

Everything that's forbidden to me.

Or *was*. Until recently.

I'm not sure why that thought makes my pulse race even harder as I grip my company stylus. We only shared a handful of words, but those words left an impression on me. *He* left an impression on me. One I haven't been able to escape since.

Someone clears their throat, cuing the meeting to start, and I open my note app. I keep my head down, though my heart is still racing.

Even here in a room full of people, it feels as if his dark laugh is still chasing me, though he hasn't so much as glanced in my direction.

Quiet falls over the boardroom as the smart lights lower. Lucifer sits at the head of the table, one long leg propped over the other, as a person to his right, who going by their gender-nonconforming look might be nonbinary, activates the soundbar's voice recognition and fires up the interactive smartboard.

A video clip waits.

I instantly recognize the man on the screen from the magazine Imani gave me. Unlike Lucifer, his face is all over the internet and on every television screen these days. Azmodeus "Az" Apollyon. Prince of Ruin. Lust himself, if you follow his frequent sexual exploits in the media—which Jax and every other normal twentysomething certainly does—and, according to Imani, the Original responsible for this morning's gruesome headline.

Lucifer's brother.

A chill claws through me.

The employee to Lucifer's right taps their tablet, and the clip starts to play. The sound of the paparazzi shouting Azmodeus's name from where he walks on the red carpet fills the room.

"Az! Az! Azmodeus! Az!"

Their shouts war with one another until someone manages to shove a mini-microphone into his face. "Care to comment on the events at your brother's club last night? On Lucifer's unexpected appearance there?"

Azmodeus's gaze rakes over the reporter, feeding the cameras exactly what they're craving, the raw lust that he's so aptly named for, and even knowing what I do now, I might be pregnant just from looking. He's stunningly beautiful, so much so he's almost painful to look at.

A fairer-haired version of the dark king that sits on his throne before me.

Even in the morning light of the boardroom, the shadows seem to bend toward Lucifer. Eagerly.

"A tragedy, really." Az smiles a devious, playful grin. "Too bad Lucifer isn't more of a lover than a fighter."

For the cameras, he plays the comment as lighthearted teasing, but to anyone who knows the truth, it's anything but.

He's just deftly laid the blame at Lucifer's feet.

Without further comment, Az steps away from the microphone, continuing down the carpet with some gorgeous woman on his arm as the paparazzi shout his name again. Someone pauses the clip, and the boardroom's fluorescent lights brighten.

The smooth voice that follows chills me. Its deep velvet-and-sin cadence that had me hot in a few words the other night is now mixed with a cold, cutting rage. Lucifer doesn't raise his voice, but the effect it has on the room is all the same.

"Does anyone want to tell me why the fuck my brother was interviewed before me?"

I feel myself stiffen as every gaze turns toward Imani. I shrink in my chair a little, but somehow, *she* manages to look calm, poised even. I can't say the same as I fight the urge to squirm.

"We've been through this, Lucifer," she says. "It takes time to set up a press room with no cameras in it. It's the digital age. You want the first interview? Show your face. More than some hazy paparazzi-snagged profile. Until then . . ." She shrugs, as if she said what she said, and she's daring Lucifer to contradict her.

From the unsurprised looks in the room, I get the feeling it's not all bravado. She's earned Lucifer's respect, enough of it to speak to him that way.

If I thought Imani was impressive before, I didn't give her nearly enough credit. It takes more than a little bravery to be the woman who reins the devil in.

How the hell am *I* her assistant? Temporary or otherwise.

"And as *I've* made clear time and time again, Imani . . ." He tents his fingers together, his elbows propped on the arms of his chair, and even when seated he appears tall, towering over most of the employees at the table. "I enjoy my anonymity too much to give it away."

The moment the words leave his lips, I have to stop myself from scoffing a bit.

Do you, really?

What would the devil know about being a nobody?

I think the words silently, but still Lucifer's gaze snaps toward me. As if somehow, he managed to hear me.

Did I say that out loud? Or . . . oh my god . . . Maybe he really *can* see all the dark thoughts inside our heads.

Just like the papers say.

The idea causes me to blush instantly, my face burning with heat.

"You," he says, those dark eyes piercing me, and I jump a little. "What do you think?"

Now every person in the room is watching me almost as intently as he is.

My eyes grow wide. "I . . . I don't know," I manage to choke out. "I'm just an intern." My response is barely more than a whisper, though I've likely already gotten myself fired on my first day.

Just my luck.

I can feel Imani's gaze drilling holes in the side of my head as if to scream that if I know what's good for me, I'll shut up and shut up now. But if I really *did* know what was good for me, I wouldn't be sitting here in the first place, and in truth, I find it way too freaking hard to control myself while I'm pinned beneath Lucifer's gaze like a butterfly on a display board.

Something in him brings out the . . . wickedness in me.

Imani leans forward, clearly prepared to save me. "I'm sorry, Lucifer. She's my new assistant. She's filling in for Rebekah, and—"

He lifts a hand, silencing her as he continues to stare at me. "No, by all means," he says, speaking directly to me. "Enlighten us."

He smiles then, the sharp tips of his canines showing, and even that normally pleasant expression appears dangerous, violent even.

My pulse races, and I try hard not to swallow, but the lump that's formed inside my throat makes it nearly impossible to speak. If my hands weren't thoroughly planted in my lap, I'm pretty certain they'd be shaking, but I didn't come this far to back down at the first sign of a challenge, and I've already drawn Lucifer's attention.

What's one risk more?

"Well . . . do you . . . do you really enjoy anonymity?" I ask, daring to lift my gaze toward him. "I mean, you're *you*. It's not like you can be all that anonymous. The paparazzi stalk you constantly. Your side-profile alone gets nearly as much media attention as your sibling's faces, so you don't truly know what it's like to be a nobody. Not really. And if your brother being interviewed first pisses you off, then is that dubious anonymity honestly worth the effort?"

I mean for it to appeal to his pride, his desire for attention, but the moment the words leave my lips, I realize it's done the exact opposite.

I've pointed out a flaw in his system. A weakness. In my very first meeting.

God help me.

He tilts his head to the side, examining me curiously. His dark gaze spears through me, causing my breath to hitch and reminding me of every desire that's ever plagued me, all the ways that I've sinned. As if his singular talent isn't simply *being* the worst among us, it's bringing out the worst in us, in me.

"I guess I'm just saying a little self-reflection goes a long way, that's all." I glance down at my iPad again.

The room is still for a long beat. Painfully still.

Finally, Lucifer moves, one hand falling from where it lingered near his lips, before he breaks into a deliberately slow clap. The blatant humiliation is so embarrassing that I can't help but wince.

My face turns crimson.

"Well done, Imani," he says viciously. "Where *exactly* did you find this one?"

"Like I said, she's filling in for Rebekah. It's temporary." Imani casts a frustrated glance toward me. If I still have a job, I'll be paying for my honesty in spades later.

Fuck. My. Life.

Lucifer cocks his head to the side, still watching me. "Make it permanent."

My stomach drops.

A few murmurs break throughout the room.

Imani sputters, which I'm fairly certain is a first for her. "I'm sorry. What?"

His gaze swings toward her then. "If she has the balls to speak to me that way on her first day, maybe someday she'll be nearly as useful as you."

I know I shouldn't look at him, that I should keep my eyes glued to the table, but somehow, I can't seem to stop myself from staring.

Even as I read the words for the major insult that they are.

I am nothing. A no one. Barely useful.

And Lucifer has the power to make or break me.

He doesn't need to think twice about my bratty behavior, no matter how he coerced it from me, because to him, I'm not even worthy of the brief attention he's gifted me.

Not yet, anyway.

He makes a point to stare directly at me, those dark eyes never leaving me as he speaks. "Malachi, do whatever you can to be cooperative with the police. We want to show them we're being particularly transparent throughout their investigation. So transparent we'll parade them through the office if we must. And Imani, draft up a press plan to deal with this hellscape, along with a strategy presentation for your little *suggestion* that I debut to the press, and make sure your new assistant takes the lead." He finally glances toward Imani, and suddenly I can breathe again. "We'll see if she warrants the attention she's so desperately seeking."

I can't help it as another embarrassed flush flames through my face, but it's not his humiliation that stills me. It's the words he chooses, coupled with the way he looks at me, that dangerous grin twisting into a devilish smirk. That single look stops my breath short, sending the memory of that dark velvet voice in the club echoing through me.

Will you find what you're seeking?

Temptation grips me.

I shake my head a little, watching as he rises from his seat, causing everyone else in the room to stand and begin to leave. It's only once Lucifer is well and truly gone, and Imani summons me, that I realize I'm the only one still sitting, and worse, he's just confirmed my greatest fear. He *did* recognize me, right from the very start, and the next thought that occurs to me is the most dangerous of all.

Perhaps that's not as terrifying as it should be.

CHAPTER FIVE

Charlotte

"You didn't?" Jax's jaw falls open.

"What else was I supposed to say? He practically cornered me." I've just finished recounting the full events of this morning's meeting, sparing only a few key details. Mainly, that I'd already met Lucifer in Gluttony's club a couple nights earlier. I'm not sure why I skipped that particular part, but somehow it feels private.

Like something meant only for me.

I spear another forkful of lo mein, shoving the noodles into my mouth. The garlic, ginger, and soy sauce form a delicious blend. The Chinese takeout container clutched in my hand is still fresh and warm, carried only a few feet home to our tiny one-bedroom apartment from the restaurant downstairs, but I would have eaten it with just as much gusto if it were cold and days old anyway.

They don't make it this good in Kansas. Not even close.

I abandon my fork in the container and cover my mouth with my hand while I lick some oyster sauce from my lips.

I swallow another bite before I cast Jax another helpless expression. "You're looking at me like I'm crazy."

"You *are* crazy. White-girl crazy. This is the same as thinking a mountain lion is a cute kitty and trying to pet it."

I groan. "I don't know why I said it. The truth just sort of . . . slipped out."

Jax gestures for me to continue, her chopsticks still in her hand. "So, you mean to tell me that you called out the owner and billionaire CEO of the whole damn company for not being 'self-reflective' enough in your very first meeting, and *somehow* you still have a job?" She gapes before using the utensils to grab another bite of sticky rice while she mutters something in Vietnamese. "White-girl privilege at its best. I think you're insane. Lucky, but insane."

"You and Imani both." I try and grin a little, poking at my dinner. "But what else was I supposed to do when he called me out in front of everybody like that? *Lie?*"

Jax lowers her brows at me. "Yes," she says, the sound muffled through her chewing.

"Lie? To Lucifer?"

She swallows then. "Lie. Bend the truth. I don't know. Maybe anything except damaging the pride of the devil?" She shakes her head, still watching me like I'm flirting with trouble, which only causes me to deflate further.

"He took it all right from Imani," I mumble. That sinking feeling that I've royally messed up claws its way inside my chest again. "And what is he paying me for if not for my opinions? That's half of public relations, anyway. Opinions crafted into stories." I drop my fork into the box like it's disappointed me. That was a weak argument, even for me.

Jax points her chopsticks toward me. "But Imani's earned her place, you haven't."

"I know. I *know*." I let out a groan, sinking farther down into my chair. "Now I need to help Imani come up with a plan that's going to blow him away on top of all the mess we're dealing with. And how exactly am I supposed to do that when he already hates me?"

"Does he though?" Jax lifts a brow suggestively. "Sounds to me like you got away with murder." She smiles playfully.

She's fishing for gossip about today's headlines, and we both know it.

I shake my head. "You know I can't talk about that. Especially not after that meeting." I grab at one of her containers to distract her, only for her to swat my hand away with a mumbled "Get your own wontons, bitch," making us both laugh.

Side-eyeing me, she uses her chopsticks to expertly drop one of the wontons onto my plate and winks, watching me for a long beat.

When I still refuse to answer, she sighs. "Fine. Don't tell me. I get it. You signed that crazy NDA, I know."

"There's not much to tell at this point. Besides, I think there's more to it, anyway." I stuff the wonton into my mouth before she can take it back.

Jax bats her lashes, her new teal eye shadow glittering. "Oh? Do tell."

I shrug once I've finished chewing. "I can't help but think it's only the start, or at least it feels like that."

She places her plastic soup container on the table, setting her utensils down beside it. "What do you think he gets out of all this, anyway? Coming topside, I mean?"

"Hell if I know. A chance to play God?"

"I think it's more than that." She looks up at the spiritualist altar she placed on our dingy living room wall when she first moved in, her eyes going momentarily dreamy like she's seeing something I can't. Jax is a psychic. In her words, a lightworker or a sixth-generation shamanic healer, as she calls it. At least professionally.

She's also an aspiring Broadway actress, the kind of fun-loving party girl I'll never be.

"What do you mean?" I steal another wonton from her when she isn't looking.

She plays with the black and blue ends of her hair a little, her expression still dreamy. "I mean, an influencer who has a known beef with Lucifer's brother shows up dead when Lucifer's at the club, and, well, it doesn't really seem like a coincidence, does it? There's a lot that's going on there behind closed doors. That's all I'm saying."

I stay quiet then, falling silent under the guise of chewing. I was careful to leave out any details that would violate my NDA when I told Jax about the meeting, but she's perceptive as hell. Maybe clairvoyant, depending on which of her clients you ask. But I have no doubt that spilling the tea about who exactly facilitated the murder at Gluttony's club, even to my bestie, would be a violation of the terms of my employment, one that'd get me fired immediately.

My shoulders slump, and I curl in on myself, still poking at my food. I don't like keeping secrets from Jax, and the distance it creates between us bothers me. We've been friends since I first arrived in the city, and while it may have been only a handful of weeks that we've been living together, already she feels like a sister to me, the best friend I've ever had.

I trust her. Unconditionally.

Can't say that about anyone else in my life.

"Hey, don't look so down on yourself." She places her hand over mine and gives it a reassuring squeeze. "I'm sure whatever you and Imani come up with will blow him away. Think of it as an opportunity to impress your boss. That's all."

I nod, turning back to my lo mein. "If you say so," I mutter halfheartedly.

I want to tell her everything that's plaguing me, but each time I open my mouth, that dark laugh comes back to haunt me, reminding me of all the ways I'm unworthy, of all the ways I don't belong here.

And to all the lengths I would go to make certain I no longer feel that way.

"So, I've been thinking . . ."

Imani groans from where she's seated at her desk several feet away. Somewhere amid all the chaos, it just became easier for me to hole up and work at the spare table in her office rather than us running down the hall or pinging emails at each other constantly. "I'm not certain I like where this is going."

It's been four days since that initial headline ran, and the surrounding media nightmare has been relentless, to say the least. Imani and I have been working together around the clock, the task of rerouting this narrative consuming my whole first week. She wasn't lying when she said I'd need to be available. On call, almost twenty-four seven . It feels as if we've fielded interviews and made statements every hour to every major news company within the Western Hemisphere. LA, Chicago, London, Paris—even Tokyo and Beijing. *Everyone* wants to know what Lucifer has to say about the murder in his brother's nightclub.

Or better yet, if he's responsible.

The gossip magazines are going crazy, and even some of the more conservative congregations, like my father's, have announced this is another sign of the second coming. Leave it to evangelicals to somehow make someone *else* dying about themselves. I try not to roll my eyes at the thought. It's no laughing matter, really. The victim was a famous ragmag journalist and flamboyant media personality known by the stage name Paris Starr, who'd apparently had several well-known and, more importantly, very recent altercations with Lucifer's brother Azmodeus in the days preceding his death.

Imani and I have attempted to drop subtle hints about Az and Paris's feud in the media's direction nonstop, but it's no use. No one's nearly as interested in Az's culpability as they are in the possibility of Lucifer's, and I've rehashed the details so many times with so many different reporters that at this point, I'm pretty sure I could recite it all in my sleep. I even had to talk myself out of spending the night in my office last night.

In my defense, it hasn't taken me long to learn that NYC commutes are a nightmare.

Hell embodied.

The angle Imani and I have taken with this story is that it's all an unfortunate tragedy, a random coincidence that no one could have predicted. The sort of coincidence that's sure to happen when you make your living in NYC's exclusive VIP scene, where everybody knows everybody. After all, NYC may as well be a small town, if you know the right people.

Never mind that, according to all the details Imani's told me, we know without a doubt that Azmodeus is to blame. There's hardly a more subtle calling card for a man who's literally Lust personified than ensuring his victim dies naked and with a still-throbbing penis, though thankfully those all-important details haven't leaked to the press—yet— which is a whole other part of mine and Imani's job. Aiding the police investigation in any way possible, providing them any information they may need.

The rest remains a mystery to me.

Pointing fingers would only make Lucifer look more guilty. Instead, we've gone out of our way to accommodate both the media and the investigation, as well as the victim's family. Imani even had me contact the victim's partner and his parents to offer to pay for the funeral, but that seems to be the approach of anyone with money, really.

Pay who you can to keep quiet.

Together, we managed to get the family to make a statement absolving Lucifer of any responsibility, saying how Paris loved to frequent Gluttony's many clubs, particularly The Serpent, and it was a sheer coincidence Lucifer happened to be there that evening, especially since his appearances at his siblings' clubs are so rare. We've even commissioned an honorary gold-and-diamond-lined remembrance plaque with Paris's name on it to be placed outside one of Gluttony's other clubs. I'm not even sure whether Paris Starr ever set foot inside any of Gluttony's other businesses, but that's the story we're telling.

Not that it's done us any good.

The rag mag and influencer conspiracy theories keep spiraling. To the point that one of the nastier ones even ended up with a full-page spread in *Entertainment Weekly.*

Something *has* to give.

"Just hear me out. Please?"

Between all the late-night hours and the early morning calls, Imani and I have developed a close working relationship quickly. She's fierce and brilliant and willing to listen to my ideas, no matter how new to this I may be. To a point.

"You have two minutes before I've got another call from Hong Kong. Make it quick," Imani grumbles from behind her fourth coffee.

That's all the permission I need.

"What if what we need isn't a good way to spin this, but a distraction story?"

At that, Imani perks up a little. "I'm listening."

"Lucifer finally showing his face."

She rolls her eyes. "Girl, we've been through this."

"I know. I know. I get that he gave the project to me as a fool's errand, but hear me out. What if we don't treat it that way?"

Imani's brow lifts like now she thinks I'm truly crazy. "You want *more* work?" She rotates her desk chair away from me, shaking her head in disbelief.

"No, not more work. *Less* work. Once this is all behind us, that is. What if we approach the plan to Lucifer showing his face in a fresh way? I know you said he's shot it down every other time, but at this point, what have we got to lose?"

Exasperated, Imani flops her head onto the back of her chair. "Other than more sleep?"

"It'd be the perfect distraction from this," I offer.

"What *exactly* are you proposing?" Her hand goes to her temple, her tell for when she's quickly losing her patience, but I haven't lost her attention just yet.

"We treat his image like we do any other luxury good. Limit access. Create exclusivity."

She rotates her chair enough to look at me skeptically. "Go on."

I close the screen of my laptop, directing all my attention toward my pitch. "Instead of a free-for-all press release or appearance, what if we make it like an exclusive launch party? But instead of a new product, it's a new start to the company's branding. One with Lucifer finally in the public eye."

She purses her lips. "Rebranding is a classic move of the guilty."

"But it works. We could even pair it with the launch of a new product."

"The Giovaldi account?" Imani quirks a brow like I've piqued her interest.

"Yes, like the Giovaldi account." I smile widely. "Or maybe even the start of a new philanthropy foundation? Nothing looks better than giving back to the community."

My father's congregation taught me that.

They fell for his games every time. Hook, line, and sinker.

Imani nods thoughtfully, at least considering it. It's one of the many qualities I admire about her. She may be an executive hotshot, but you'd never know it from the way she treats me and the other staff she works with.

She's quiet for a beat before finally smiling. "I don't know if it's me or the four cups of coffee talking, but I like it. Why the hell not?"

I squeal excitedly, clapping my hands a little.

Imani shoots me a pointed look. "Don't get too excited. We'll still need Lucifer's approval. Do you think you can pull a presentation for it together before tomorrow's meeting?"

We've been working toward tomorrow's all-hands meeting the whole week, preparing to detail all the ways we've protected the company's brand amid the media chaos.

I glance at the table that's temporarily become my desk. Messy, scattered papers cover the surface. The air smells like our recently finished coffee, and I still have several hours of work to complete, but I'm not stupid enough to miss an opportunity when it's been given to me. Not one like this. "Yeah, I think I can manage to get something together by tonight." I gather the papers and start to arrange them into neat little piles.

"Good," Imani says. "After this call I'll leave you to it. I've taken enough damn interviews. I'm taking the rest of today as PTO. It's time I got some sleep."

I make a mock salute with my hand. "I'll hold down the fort, boss. Promise."

Imani nods appreciatively at the same time her desk phone buzzes, a sign of the downstairs secretary attempting to connect her overseas call. She picks up the receiver on the first ring. "One second, Jeanine." She presses down the mute button before she turns and looks at me. "Good work on this, Charlotte. I mean it." She smiles at me, giving me all the encouragement I need before turning back toward her desk.

I grin like a fool, organizing my papers before quickly returning to my work. I settle into my seat and straighten my posture, filled with a newfound determination to prove myself. For once that determined feeling stays with me as I work, keeping me grinning even as the sun fades from early morning into the long-darkened shadows of the night.

CHAPTER SIX

Lucifer

"Did you really have to drag me out of bed for this?"

My brother sits across from my desk inside my office, his displeased grumbling carrying to where I stand at the floor-to-ceiling window. It's taken nearly as long to get him here as one would think—several days, actually, considering Bel does everything and everyone on his own time. But what else would you expect from Sloth?

Outside the window, the evening smog obscures what remains of the sunset, the colors blending into an amalgam of orange and red before me. Like hellfire, only tamer, though little else is in this city, yet Hell's not the particular part of my origin story that I miss.

Not entirely.

I take a sip of my whisky, the amber liquid burning as it makes its way down my throat. "You and Az have been rather cozy as of late." I finally glance over my shoulder.

Bel shrugs unapologetically as he sprawls back in his chair. Ever the lothario. One would think he'd be unfit, considering he's known for inspiring others to remain lazy, but these days, the laid-back, cut-abed, surfer-boy persona is working for him.

"What's there to say? You know I don't like to get caught up in the family politics." He waves a suntanned hand dismissively, like he's flicking away a rather irritating fly. "It's not worth the energy." He shrugs before he sips from his own drink, a whisky and tonic.

I take mine straight.

My unamused huff in response doesn't faze him, though I don't expect it to. It's not exactly a lie that he doesn't join in our family's little reindeer games, but it's not entirely true either. Bel may *pretend* he doesn't care what happens in the scheme of, well, everything, particularly when it comes to our family feuds, but that's only true so long as he's allowed to play the field in whatever way benefits him. He's slow to act of his own accord, but quick to switch loyalties when it suits him. Only if it requires minimal effort, of course.

Bel does everything in half measures, refuses to take life seriously.

I bury my hands in the pockets of my suit coat, taking stock of my middle sibling. Everything about Belphegor is leisurely, relaxed in a way I never will be. All the way from his shaggy hair to his sandal-clad toes. If I didn't enjoy the fucked-up life I've carved for myself in this city, Bel's carefree nature would make me more than a little green. Though Levi would lose his shit if he ever heard me mutter that particular turn of phrase. He's hated it ever since Wrath coined it for him when we were barely more than cherubs.

But old habits die hard, I suppose.

I cross the room toward Bel, coming to a stop at my desk where I lean against its edge. "Usually, I'd be inclined to agree with you, if Astaroth hadn't already told me you were with Azmodeus that evening." The look in my eyes shifts from cordial to don't-fuck-with-me in an instant. "Try again, brother."

Bel swears. "Fucking Astaroth." He drags his fingers through his bleached blond hair, casting me a halfhearted sneer. "He works too much, if you ask me. Enough that he's got a permanent stick up his ass." He raises his voice on those last few words, clearly hoping that Astaroth, who's standing sentry outside the door, can hear.

My gaze doesn't falter from where I've pinned Bel beneath it.

Bel slumps in his seat, pouting over the fact that I refuse to let this go.

"You're deflecting, Belphegor." I use his full name whenever it suits me. "I wouldn't think that's your style."

Bel quirks a lazy brow.

I grin viciously. "Doesn't it take more effort to lie?"

The bite in my words is little more than a thinly veiled hiss.

"Fine," Bel grumbles. "So I was with Az that night. What of it?" He shrugs, spreading an arm over the back of the chair once more. "You know he and I have business together."

Az's investments reside mostly in the porn industry, while Bel's are in a mixture of television—specifically, streaming services that promote binge-watching—some off-the-book involvement in the drug trade, and a few unconventional connections to Big Pharma he'd rather the media not know about. Naturally.

"And what exactly is Az's business with Gluttony's club?" I say, not bothering to beat around the bush.

Bel shrugs again. "I find it too tiresome to say."

Meaning he's not going to offer me any information for free.

Normally, I'd play the game with him. Throw him a bone or whatever it took to get him to talk, but I don't have the time nor the patience for his bullshit today, not with the company's stockholders already irritating me. Without hesitating, I snap my fingers, and not even a second later, two of my demons burst into the office, prepared to do my bidding. Namely, torturing Bel in whatever twisted ways I deem necessary until he's finally willing to talk. Of all our siblings, Bel's always been the easiest to manipulate. It's tragic, really.

He doesn't even put up a proper fight.

"Okay, okay," he says, throwing up his hands as if we were children again. He calls uncle before the guards even reach him. He waves them off before making a point of straightening that god-awful Hawaiian shirt he's wearing. "You never did know how to take a joke, Luce."

I scowl at the nickname, one that another of our numerous siblings coined for me.

One I'd be hard pressed to consider family these days.

"Leave Michael out of this," I sneer.

Three days of the company's board members bitching about how stocks have dropped has left me shorter tempered than usual.

Bel sighs. "Az is opening up a new club," he confesses finally. "One that's supposed to compete with The Serpent."

I quirk one dark brow. "Really?"

The news is anticlimactic, even for me.

Which means there's no doubt something more to it.

But if Bel knows anything, he doesn't show it.

He brushes off his shoulder, baring his teeth toward one of the guards in a halfhearted attempt at menace. "I told you it was uninteresting." He rolls his eyes.

"What good will opening a new club possibly do for him?" I mutter the question more to myself than anyone else, but Bel still answers me.

He shrugs. "I suppose someone will have to fill the void once you're gone."

Bel suddenly has my attention now, my gaze cutting to him.

"Pardon?" I lift a dark brow.

Bel makes a get-outta-here face like I can't possibly mean what I'm asking. "Oh, come on, Lucifer. Don't be naive. *Someone* will have to fill your place here once Gabriel returns and dear old Dad lets you get out of that demon-infested prison for good."

I hold Bel's gaze for a prolonged beat, my face expressionless.

I have no intention of leaving. Not now. Not ever.

Bel laughs like we're sharing an incredibly funny joke, but the moment he realizes I haven't joined him, his laughter dies quickly. "You . . . don't actually think you can have it all, do you? To stay here, rule Hell, *and* get Dad's redemption?" He scoffs. "It doesn't work like that, Lucy."

My lack of response tells him everything it needs to.

Bel swears violently. "Fuck me. Of course you do. *Of course* you would think you'd get to have your cake and fucking eat it too. You were the one who thought it was a bright idea to challenge Dad and get us all kicked out, after all. Lucifer—"

"Are you finished yet, Bel?" I mutter coolly.

The ice in those words is enough to give him pause.

I didn't become who I am simply by being the first of us to fall. My brothers may have built Hell alongside me, but whether they like it or not, I will always be the worst among them, their leader.

No matter how much they resent me.

"Yes, yes, I think we're done here," Bel replies.

"Good." I push off my desk, rounding the obsidian surface to stand beside the executive seat. I pin my brother with a menacing glare. "Then crawl back into your quaint little Hampton beach house and stay there—quickly."

Bel turns to leave, clearly understanding the dismissal.

He's almost at the door before he turns and says, "You're making the same mistake all over again, you know."

I lower both hands onto my desk, using my arms to support my weight. I don't bother to look at Bel as he continues.

"You don't get to have it all, then or now. That's not how it works, Lucifer. You're the only one among us who never accepted that."

My gaze snaps toward him. "Get out," I snarl.

Bel hesitates but doesn't say anything.

It's only once the door closes behind him and I hear his footsteps retreat that I allow the full extent of my anger to take hold. Abruptly, I shove the contents of my desk to the floor, taking out all the office supplies in one fell swoop. Several items clatter onto the carpet, breaking instantly, but it's not enough to satisfy me. Not truly, and not because I believe Bel is right.

But because, for once he saw straight through me.

CHAPTER SEVEN

Charlotte

I run so hard I can feel my heart pumping, though I don't know what exactly I'm running from. The space between my legs aches, a painful steady throb, and my feet scrape against the gnarled roots of the forest floor, a forest that should feel familiar.

But it doesn't.

Someone is after me.

Suddenly, one of the raised tree roots rears up, catching my ankle. I fall victim to it easily. Like prey, I'm captured, but instead of the harsh impact of mud and earth I expect, a rough pair of hands catches me, holding me close in the dark.

"Charlotte," I hear that velvet-and-sin voice hiss.

I lean into it, melting further into the shadows, until there's nothing else left but the stars overhead and the dark's embrace. My breath swirls like smoke in the cool night air, the ache between my legs intensifying at the sight of those full, sinful lips.

"Charlotte," I hear that dark voice whisper again. Only this time more serpentine.

Nearly as harsh as I expect he would kiss.

Charlotte!

I wake with a jolt, quickly realizing I fell asleep on my laptop in Imani's empty office, and I've been drooling onto the keys. Horrified, I straighten and swipe at my mouth.

"Burning the midnight oil already?"

I let out a startled shriek.

Swiveling in my chair, I find Lucifer leaning against the doorway, his arms crossed over his chest and his dark eyes fixed on me. Like I conjured him straight from my dream.

I sputter a little. "Imani went home."

"Did she?" He grins, mocking me, those sharp canines flashing. His gaze darts toward a nearby clock.

It's nearly one in the morning.

Oh God.

My face heats. "I . . . was just finishing up a presentation for tomorrow's meeting. That's all."

"And did you?" He watches me for a long beat. "Finish, that is?"

My flush deepens.

There's no way he means what I think he means, and yet . . .

I squash the thought before it can truly begin. He's my boss, plain and simple. That's all he'll ever be. That's all I *want* him to be. No matter how my dreams say otherwise.

"Yes, sir," I whisper. My gaze drops to the floor.

When I glance back up, those wicked lips twist. "Good girl."

I freeze, even as his praise turns me molten. Those two words do things to me that they shouldn't.

And he knows it.

His smirk widens. "Make sure you head home before security locks up."

Without another word, he turns to leave.

Finally free, I sigh and sink down in my chair.

No longer having those dark eyes on me *should* feel like a relief, but the moment he's gone my mind turns hazy. Lucifer's presence feels like a gravitational pull, powerful enough that it lifts me from my body, makes me forget myself, and the sudden loss of his attention is so intense, so acute, it leaves a gaping void in me, an endless space so empty that before I know what I'm doing, I'm on my feet, standing beneath Imani's doorframe.

"Mr. Apollyon?"

He turns back toward me, his hands in his suit coat pockets. "Lucifer, if you will, or sir . . ." Another smirk twists his lips. "If it suits you."

Is he . . . ? No. He couldn't be.

I can hardly breathe, but I lower my gaze before I dare step forward. "About the other day . . ." I glance up at him through my lashes.

He watches me for a long moment, those dark eyes piercing through me. The color is so dark they're almost black, save for when he moves. Then there's a glint of amber there, like he keeps some of that burning hellfire locked up inside him, a monster barely leashed.

I'd do well to remember that.

I glance down at my hands again, suddenly realizing I'm wringing them together. "In the club, I . . ."

"You don't need to offer an explanation about what you do with your free time, Miss—?"

"Bellefleur," I offer. "Charlotte Bellefleur."

"Miss Bellefleur." He nods, dismissing me as he turns to leave again.

"Did you mean what you said? In the club, I mean?"

He stops abruptly, not bothering to look toward me, though something in his voice shifts. "Unlike my Father, I make a habit of *only* saying the things I mean."

At the mention of God, a chill runs down my spine, filling me with an awareness of all the ways Lucifer is *other*, unlike me, yet when he's standing there, dressed in a suit that fits him like a love letter to the male body, I find it way too easy to forget.

It's one small part of why he's a danger to me.

"I understand."

"Will that be all, Miss Bellefleur?" He glances over his shoulder, clearly ready to dismiss me.

"Yes, sir." I nod, refusing to meet his eyes. "Though I . . . think you'll like the presentation Imani and I came up with for you."

He nods curtly. "Till tomorrow, then."

I watch him leave, feeling my phone buzz in my pocket just as he reaches the elevator doors. I don't have that many friends in NYC yet, and at this hour, a text could only mean one thing. I pull out my phone and glance down at it.

"Shit," I mumble.

Lucifer's voice reaches toward me. "Pardon?"

"Sorry." I shake my head, waving him on. "It's nothing. It's just . . . my friend got really drunk, and I need to go save her, I think. That's all."

One minute I'm resolved to keep my business to myself and the next thing I know I'm babbling like an idiot. That's what he does to me.

Lucifer tilts his head, watching me curiously. "Do you make a habit of playing savior to all your friends?"

I frown. There's a subtle judgment in his words I don't appreciate.

"She's my roommate." I don't mean for it to sound defensive, especially considering this man's my boss, but somehow it comes out that way. Though from the flat expression he returns, Lucifer doesn't exactly appear fazed.

Instead, he looks intrigued.

It's irritating, really. How collected he always is.

Always controlled.

I turn back to my phone, starting to text a reply message to find out where the hell Jax is and let her know I'm on my way, but before I know what's happening, I *feel* Lucifer beside me, like a burning heat. He stares over my shoulder, towering over me as he takes in the drunken texts and accompanying picture.

A shiver prickles down my spine, a welcome awareness thrilling me.

"That's one of my brother's clubs," he comments.

Az, he means. Though I'm too distracted at how close he is, how that deep velvet voice feels like a thrum against my skin, to worry what he thinks of that, as if it's any of his business.

"What's your friend doing there, little dove?"

The nickname, the reminder of our interaction the other evening, irks me, and suddenly, my protective instincts kick in.

I step away, placing some distance between us, more than prepared to defend Jax, even to my boss. "She doesn't know anything, if that's what you mean . . . sir." I tack the address on at the end like an afterthought. I mean for it to keep things professional, to soften the interaction, but all it does is show that he's rattled me, and he knows it.

His lips curl wickedly, like he has a secret he'll never share, but before he can say anything more, I grab my purse from Imani's desk and brush past him, heading for the elevators. Everything about him is *designed* to tempt me, to draw me in.

I need to remember that.

"Where are you going?" Lucifer's still watching me, his eyes sparkling with a twisted curiosity.

I'm not sure which is more terrifying, his fleeting interest in me or how much I crave it.

Talk about delayed rebellion.

I glance down at my watch, trying to look like I'm in a hurry, which I *am*. I don't know exactly which one of Az's clubs Jax is at, or even how to get inside, and she's not responding to any of my follow-up texts. "I need to catch the train to Brooklyn if I expect to find her, and get her home, and still get enough sleep before tomorrow's—"

"I'll take you."

He says it so suddenly, I think we're both a little shocked by it.

"It's on the way," he says, though that's a blatant lie, and we both know it.

His response is so collected, so controlled, I almost convince myself that I imagined his momentary surprise. This man does *nothing* without a purpose, without a plan.

That much is clear to me.

He joins me beside the elevator, placing a hand there to stop its sliding door from closing.

This is a bad idea.

I shake my head. "You don't have to—"

"You're right. I don't." Those dark eyes spear through me, promising something way more tempting than a favor, something far more unholy. "But I'm offering."

There's more to his words, or so it seems, and it makes me understand how he tricked Eve, but as soon as the idea sparks inside me, I stomp it out, ending it before it can become anything. Just like that damn dream.

I'm being ridiculous, reading more meaning into this than there is.

What's the danger?

We're colleagues, after all. That's all we'll ever be.

Besides, I could use the help.

"Okay." I nod. "Okay."

He steps inside the elevator, leaning against the far-side handrail to wait for me.

But still, I feel myself hesitate.

"Shall we?" He lifts a dark brow.

At his prompt, I hurry inside, coming to stand beside him as the elevator doors close. The elevator makes its way down into the darkness, descending for what feels like an eternity until we reach the ground floor. The doors open once more, and we exit together, though Lucifer doesn't bother to so much as look at me. But no matter how I twist this, I can't shake the feeling there's more to his words than a simple favor.

And I've just foolishly taken the fruit he's given me.

CHAPTER EIGHT

Lucifer

I don't know why I insisted upon helping my new employee retrieve her friend from Azmodeus's club, but the moment the words left me, my pride wouldn't allow me to take them back, even if I'd wanted to. She sits beside me now in the back of my Lincoln Town Car, trying hard not to fidget uncomfortably. The window partition separating Dagon, my driver, from where we sit is sealed shut, leaving us painfully alone. As we were in my club the other evening.

The lights from the city's nightlife flash past the window, illuminating the candlelit undertones in her dishwater-blond hair. There's nothing particularly remarkable about her. She's of a medium build, on the short side (good for kindling, as far as Hell's concerned), reasonably pretty, and yet undeniably plain. With soft, freckled features, an adorably upturned nose, and wide doe eyes that appear hazel at first glimpse, a dull color, really, but when you look closer, the amber encircling the irises takes on the shape of a fucking starburst.

A goddamn starburst, for fuck's sake.

It's disgusting, truly. Like she's some innocent, ethereal faerie, though such things are little more than myth, even to me. I don't know what exactly it is about this woman that intrigues me, but something about that doe-eyed innocence brings out the predator in me, and it's been a long time since I've wanted to tempt someone for sheer amusement's sake.

The idea thrills me.

"She's not always like this, you know. Jax, I mean," she says, breaking the silence suddenly, as if she's uncomfortable with how long it's been stretching.

Astaroth tells me mortals find it distressing. The quiet, that is.

If you ask me, it's because it leaves them alone in their own mortality. With thoughts I know without a doubt are filled with wicked deeds.

Exactly as I warned my Father they would be.

Glancing toward her, I try to see inside that pretty little head of hers, spread her darkest sins open for me, but for once, I find nothing, exactly as I did during that damn meeting.

I scowl, instantly pissed off.

What kind of witchcraft is this?

I've never been unable to see inside someone's head before, never been barred from exploring their darkest sins, their cruelest fantasies, and the thought that she might not have any irks me.

"I'm not sure why I'd feel the need to explain it to you though, even if she were." She laughs a little, though there isn't much humor in it. She's nervous and chattering, though I haven't entirely been listening. "It's not as if you'd judge her for it."

I huff, my expression unmoving. "Make no mistake, Miss Bellefleur. I've already judged humanity long ago and, as I'm sure you remember, I famously found you all wanting."

"Right." She nods, falling silent for a moment. "I . . . guess what I mean to say is that you . . . sort of promote these things, right? Sin, I mean."

I don't try to mask the irritation I feel.

She's no different than the rest.

Though the second I think it, something about that thought doesn't exactly ring true.

"Do I?" I twist my head toward her, capturing her gaze with my own.

She flushes instantly.

I try once more to see her true nature, a subtle push inside her soul meant to bare her darkest sins, but once again, I come up empty.

Nothing.

I frown, and her eyes widen slightly, confused by whatever flash of violence she sees in me, but I recover easily.

"You all do love a good scapegoat." I turn back toward the front of the car.

I'm deflecting now, but she doesn't notice.

"What do you mean?" she asks.

I look toward her, my voice dropping low. "Is it me who tempts you, Miss Bellefleur? Or do you simply need someone to blame?"

For a long beat, she doesn't say anything.

She simply blinks at me, completely unaware she's been caught in my game. "Both," she whispers boldly. "Honestly, I think it's both."

Even in the darkness, the close quarters of the cab, I see those long lashes flutter as her eyes flit to my lips momentarily. A spark of desire flashes there, one I can't ignore willingly, and my cock stiffens even as she turns away.

Maybe not so innocent, after all.

So why can't I see inside that pretty little head of yours?

"Stop here," I command Dagon. We're half a block away from the club but pulling up in the Town Car will no doubt make a scene. "We'll enter round back."

Charlotte's eyes widen like she hadn't considered the possibility of actually going inside with me, and in that moment, it takes everything in me not to lean over and whisper all the salacious things I've been thinking in her ear, things that would certainly send her running, though once I do get inside that pretty little head, she'll no doubt disappoint me.

They all do eventually.

"You're coming inside? With me?" she practically squeaks, as if the thought terrifies her.

Though I doubt her fear is for the reason *most* humans find me terrifying.

The way she worries her lip every time I catch her glimpsing at me says otherwise.

"You didn't think I'd let you go in alone, did you?" I offer a wolfish grin. "What kind of monster do you make of me?"

I'm not certain what she's been told about how I treat my employees, but if it's that I don't take care of my own, that'd be one of only a thousand disingenuous lies humanity has fabricated about me. I take pride in caring for my people, junior employees included.

And like it or not, this naive, doe-eyed princess is exactly that.

Mine.

Per contract only.

Though I think that could be changed. Easily.

The rules of New York City are whatever I choose them to be.

"I think you're the kind of monster that tempts innocent women with forbidden fruit," she replies tartly, hearkening back to Eve.

There's a spark of challenge in her eyes, and though I know whatever I'm doing here beside this woman can lead to nothing good, that small moment of resistance still thrills me.

"That's where you're wrong, darling." I lean past her under the guise of opening the car door, close enough to allow me to whisper in her ear. "I don't need to tempt them." I pull back, the featherlight touch of my lips brushing against her ear. "They come willingly."

CHAPTER NINE

Charlotte

We're out on the street and in an abandoned alley before I even fully recognize what I'm doing. I'm alone at night with *my boss*, the Prince of Darkness himself, a man who's known for his wicked deeds, and we're about to enter one of NYC's most erotic sex clubs, one that happens to be owned by his famous playboy of a brother, who Imani says murdered a man in cold blood, only to leave his body like a present for the beast beside me.

My poor life choices are catching up to me quickly.

I still don't know what Lucifer's true involvement was in Paris Starr's murder or what exactly that means for me as his employee, but all things considered, I *should* be afraid, terrified even, and yet, I can't bring myself to feel even an ounce of fear.

My heart flutters like a traitorous butterfly, the nervous adrenaline thrilling me.

If ever my father feared my fall from grace, *this* is it.

Somehow, I know that explicitly.

At first glimpse, The Body Shoppe looks nothing like a sex club. Instead, it looks like an abandoned auto repair place, the air rent with the smell of oil and rubber. The echoing sound of a saw whirs from somewhere in the background as we pass an old vehicle. We approach the clerk, a Latino man who stands sentry at the counter, who doesn't say anything. He nods toward us as Lucifer discreetly slips him an obscene amount of money, and the man gestures to the door behind the counter, allowing us entry.

We round the counter, prepared to enter the club, but before we can reach the door, Lucifer pauses abruptly. He turns toward me, and for a moment, I half expect him to tell me to stay close, or maybe to give me some chivalrous warning. Instead, he only casts me a single vicious look, raking over my attire, from head to toe. "Try not to look so desperate, darling."

Embarrassment floods through me, causing me to glance down at what I'm wearing. Nothing about my outfit is suited to this place. What appeared professional in the office looks entirely wrong here, my collared shirt-and-skirt combo paired with my black-heeled Mary Janes making me look like a stuffy librarian.

And *not* the good kind.

Sighing, Lucifer reaches for me, opening the top button of my shirt and mussing my hair a little before I can even breathe. I don't move.

I'm frozen, allowing him to have his way with me.

Though he doesn't touch my body. My skin. Almost deliberately.

When he's finished, he nods. "Better."

I don't bother to say anything or try to defend myself as he turns away from me, and I fall in line behind him, prepared to follow his lead. Normally, I would take major issue with someone speaking to me that way, but from him, I allow it, almost naturally.

What is *wrong* with me?

We enter The Body Shoppe, and the inside corridor isn't at all what I expected it'd be. Instead of something akin to a high-end strip joint, it's posh, the height of chic, burlesque luxury. Like Azmodeus both enjoys human sexuality and aims to mock it.

"What the hell did you get yourself into, Jax?" I whisper beneath my breath.

Though if the tables were turned, I'm sure she'd be asking me the same thing.

Erotic red lights hang overhead, illuminating a pathway that leads to a series of private rooms. To our right, a dominatrix dressed in pink latex passes me a black masquerade mask that feels more like someone gifting me new lingerie than a face covering.

"For anonymity." Lucifer's voice chills me.

I turn just in time to watch as he slips on a mask of his own. It's white and unadorned, setting off the midnight strands of his hair and the olive undertones of his skin. I bite my lip, struggling to look away. He's honestly breathtaking. Looking at him reminds me of the time I was thirteen and one of my church friends managed to find an old copy of *Phantom of the Opera* in her aunt's downstairs cellar. I remember feeling so wicked then, watching it with my friend, though I knew I shouldn't be.

My father would never have allowed it.

When father found out, he beat me for it, told me the devil was in me.

Suddenly, standing beside Lucifer, those words take on a new meaning.

I flush a little.

"Follow me," Lucifer mutters.

I do as he says, not bothering to ask questions. He's helping me, after all. I wouldn't have found this place so fast or have gotten inside without him, but for the first time since I turned in my employment paperwork, I start to wonder if there was more in that contract than there appeared to be.

Something that binds him to me.

Or me to him, really. Something that makes me eager to please him.

It's a silly thought and yet, once I think it, the question consumes me.

It would explain whatever this . . . tension is between us, though something about that answer feels too simple, too easy.

I follow Lucifer through a series of lavish halls and plush, silk-lined alcoves, both of us searching for any sign of where Jax could be. A few of the club's performers pass us in various stages of nudity. People of all genders are clad in tight leather, latex, and lace paired with even tighter corsets, their flamboyant makeup meant both to mock and titillate. To my left, a feminine groan sounds, and I turn to look into the open door of one of the many private suites, only to find a large, masked woman on a dais, completely nude save for her glittering pasties, being fucked by a man.

A sharp breath tears from my lips, drawing their attention to me.

Their heads turn in my direction, the tassels attached to the woman's pasties bouncing each time her partner thrusts into her. "Care to join us?" she asks.

I gape, suddenly frozen.

"She's not for you."

Lucifer stands behind me now, his presence engulfing me as he places a hand on my lower back, gently guiding me away. His touch isn't protective, it's possessive, but still professional. Well, as professional as possible considering where we are, and yet, like everything he does, there seems to be more meaning to his words, to how he touches me. There are hidden depths to the Prince of Darkness, far deeper than I anticipated, and I have a feeling I haven't even begun to scratch the true surface.

We make our way farther into the club, the music in the background growing in intensity. We pass several more viewing rooms, several more couples, throuples, and polycules in various stages of undress. The club's patrons are diverse in age, race, class, and gender, and I never would have been able to imagine many of their . . . creative positions previously, but if Lucifer notices them like I do, he doesn't show it as he continues to lead me.

I feel my pulse race.

Finally, we reach a more open section of the club, the main floor by the bar, away from the voyeur rooms. My heart drops.

"Jax."

I spot her right away. She's passed out in one of the club's booths, some white guy dressed like he's a bartender at a speakeasy leaning over her. I can't see the look on his face, but it doesn't take a genius to guess what he's planning in a club like this.

Separating from Lucifer, I move across the main floor so fast I'm practically running.

I reach for the man's shoulder, wrenching him away from my friend. "Get off her."

"What the fuck?" He glares at me.

"I said, get off her." I shove against his shoulder, making him stumble a little.

Eyes wide, he throws up his hands in surrender, like he suddenly realizes what I'm thinking, though he still doesn't look pleased. "Look, it's not what it looks like. She was like this when I found her. I'm the one who got her this gig in the first place and—"

Lucifer's deep voice cuts in. "If you have any hope of leaving here whilst still breathing, I suggest you make yourself scarce, quickly."

A chill runs down my spine, and the shadows around us seem to move. Lucifer says the words so coolly that for a moment, I almost miss the sharp violence in them, but suddenly, I understand exactly how he came to rule this city.

Lucifer doesn't make threats. He makes promises. Violent promises.

For a beat, the bartender doesn't respond, until finally his pride gets the better of him.

He puffs out his chest, squaring himself up.

But before he can dig his own grave, a sultry voice interrupts him.

"I would have thought threatening my employees is beneath you, brother."

The voice slithers through me, making me instantly regret my decision to come here tonight.

Azmodeus stands on the far side of the club, his eyes fixed on us as that lusty grin of his twists his lips. His shirt is open, and there's red lipstick smeared all over his neck and collar, leading down to his . . . I tear my gaze away. There's a man knelt at his knees. Az is wearing pants, but his open fly does little to disguise what his partner was doing only moments ago.

He waves the other man away, not bothering to button his pants. There's an open whisky bottle in his hand, and he makes a show of taking a generous swig of it before smirking at us like the party is only beginning.

Though he doesn't wear the same burlesque makeup, Azmodeus belongs in his place. Everything about him lives and breathes it, more than any of the performers I've seen.

I glance toward Lucifer, watching his expression turn to ice so quickly that if I didn't already regret coming here, I do now. It doesn't surprise me that Az is here. It is *his* club, after all, but I had hoped, prayed even, that tonight Az would be at literally any of his other venues, or maybe even walking the red carpet with some equally gorgeous person on his arm.

Just not *here*, of all places, seemingly lying in wait to confront my boss.

When Lucifer's sole reason for being here is because of me.

Sometimes it feels like fate has it in for me.

The section of the club's floor where we stand is mostly empty since most of the patrons have already abandoned it in favor of the club's private rooms. Azmodeus crosses the space toward us, and even the way he prowls like a languid jungle cat is undeniably sexy.

Though, he's not nearly as tempting as the devil beside me.

At least to me.

Lucifer is temptation embodied. Humanity's original and greatest sin.

Azmodeus claps a hand on his employee's shoulder. "You're free to go back to the bar, Ian," he says, his eyes never leaving Lucifer's. "Leave my brother to me."

At the word "brother," recognition floods Ian's features an instant before he turns as white as a sheet. He nods before he scrambles away.

Good riddance.

From the booth, Jax lets out a confused groan.

"Jax. Jax." I lean over the seat and shake her, but it's not working, even though her breathing is steady.

A martini glass sits on the table. It's still nearly full of a glittering pink liquid. Jax parties hard, but I've never seen her drink herself to the point of blackout.

Not without someone to get her home safely. This isn't like her.

Desperate, I grab the martini glass and lift it to my nose. There's a very faint off smell about it, beyond the astringent scent of alcohol. It's so subtle that in the middle of a wild party, you'd never notice it, which is exactly what it was chosen for, of course. A small number of extra bubbles coat the drink's surface, and when I lift the glass overhead, holding it closer to the light, I notice some of the pink liquid on the bottom has changed color.

All signs *Jax* taught me to look for.

That thought settles into me, making me uneasy.

I glance toward Lucifer, dread twisting inside my gut. "There's something in her drink," I whisper.

Lucifer's jaw tightens, but it's Az who reacts first. He snatches the martini glass, plucking it from my hand and taking a swig like he's some kind of half-drunken pirate. He smacks his lips at the taste, but something sparks in his eyes then, something like fury, and he sobers instantly. His gaze turns toward me, and I take a small step back.

"And who might you be?"

My eyes dart toward Lucifer, uncertain how to answer. Azmodeus has already proved he's willing to damage Lucifer's image, and I can't think of anything in this moment that would make mine and Imani's job worse than admitting I'm his employee.

I can see the headlines now.

Lucifer frequents sex club with company intern!

How freaking predictable.

And I know better than anyone that even innocent truths can be twisted into their own illicit story.

I glance toward Lucifer again, desperate for help, but I don't find any, and for one brief insane moment, despite that he's done nothing to deserve my pity, all I can think is how lonely it must be to be blamed for every misstep, saddled with every wicked deed.

To have a father who would rather disown you than love you unconditionally, and for some ridiculous reason, I can't help but want to protect him.

Like no one ever did for me.

"I'm his girlfriend," I say, muttering the first lie that comes to mind.

"Girlfriend?" Az echoes, one eyebrow lifting in suspicion.

The moment the words leave my lips, my eyes widen. The onset of my panic must be obvious, but if it fazes him, Lucifer doesn't dare let on. Something in his expression darkens then, almost imperceptibly, and before I can begin to think about how I'm going to play this, suddenly I find a lock of my hair wrapped around one of his fingers as he gently tugs me into his arms. His body presses flush against mine as he holds me from behind.

"Isn't it obvious?" he says to Az.

The heat in his voice blazes through me, and my heart races at how easily he lies. One of his hands clutches my hip as the other snakes its way to my throat, gripping me. My breath becomes heavy, strained from where his hand rests at my neck. He doesn't choke me, though his grip is still tight, possessive.

Tight enough to thrill me.

A spark of interest lights in Az's eyes at the open display of lust, though whether on my face or Lucifer's, it's unclear to me. All I know is that my mind is too clouded by the feel of Lucifer's lean, muscular body against me. The broad span of his chest. How his shoulders shadow me. His hand at my throat.

His darkness seems to envelop me, and I let out a sharp gasp.

But I don't dislike it. Not nearly.

Slowly, he leans down, the heat of his breath whispering across the skin of my ear. "Play along now, Charlotte."

Then he presses one gentle kiss on my cheek. It's nothing but a brush of lips against skin, but that one touch is enough to light an inferno in me.

Like Judas, he's branded me, marked me as his.

"She's a little plain for your usual tastes," Az comments, though there's delight in his voice as his gaze flicks over us. Clearly, Az enjoys watching.

Heat flames through me.

Az quirks his head. "I wasn't aware you were interested in vanilla sex, Lucifer."

I shrink a little at the words.

My background may have ensured I'm not super confident in the bedroom—yet—but I understand enough to know that Az is basically calling me a prude.

My ears flush pink.

"You never truly know who someone is until you see them behind closed doors, do you?" Lucifer whispers against my skin. He's speaking to Az, but somehow, it still feels as if he means to taunt me. "Until you witness their darkest desires."

His lips brush against my neck in another kiss, and I melt against him. Even as my mind screams this is wrong . . .

My body betrays me.

Suddenly, Lucifer releases me, the game he's playing temporarily over, before he nods to where Jax lies, as if he needs to order me to attend to her. It takes a few seconds for me to gather my bearings, and I even stumble a bit as my brain seems to come back online. It feels as if my whole world has been tilted on its axis within the span of a few moments, but then Jax stirs slightly, her long lashes fluttering, and all my senses return.

What the fuck?

I grip her hand, attempting to wake her again, but it's no use.

"I would think drugging my lover's roommate would be beneath you, Azmodeus," Lucifer comments, continuing with my lie.

I don't know where he's going with this, but he's so good at it that if I didn't know better, I'd believe him, without question.

His gaze flicks down at his nails like he's bored before it settles on Azmodeus again. "But you never did know how to keep your business clean."

Whatever Lucifer means, his words find their mark.

Azmodeus's expression changes from lust-fueled greed to carnal violence in an instant. "Do you truly intend to fuck with me in my own club, Lucifer?"

Lucifer sneers. "If the shoe fits."

Jax groans again, and her obvious discomfort tears through me.

"Would one of you help me? *Please.*" The words leave my lips before I can even fully consider what the consequences of either of their "help" will be.

Their attention snaps toward me.

"She needs medical assistance," I mumble.

A spark of amber flickers in Lucifer's eyes. "Fix this," he growls to Az.

"I have an ambulance already waiting." Az snaps his fingers, and suddenly a whole team of EMTs and several of his employees descend on us. A stretcher is rolled up alongside the booth, and a burly leather daddy lifts Jax's limp body, assisting the EMTs. Az or his bartender must have called them before we even arrived.

Not even money can make emergency services get anywhere that fast in New York City.

"I don't tolerate liquid ecstasy in my clubs, and to suggest otherwise is a direct insult to me and my purpose," Az says, casting a furious side-eye toward Lucifer. "She'll be cared for at the nearest hospital immediately."

"Thank you," I say, nodding to him, and I mean it, truly.

Az inclines his head, lifting the whisky bottle in his hand as if to toast me.

"Brother." Lucifer gives a curt nod to Azmodeus, signaling the end of our discussion, before we turn to leave. Lucifer places a hand on my lower back, guiding me. I open my mouth to tell him I have every intention of riding with Jax to the hospital, but Az's sultry voice interrupts me.

"Oh, and, Lucifer," he calls after us.

We pause, turning toward him.

"Before you go, why don't you two lovebirds enjoy yourselves in one of my private suites." Az smiles viciously. "My treat."

CHAPTER TEN

Lucifer

"What are you doing?" The hint of panic in her voice is almost enough to bring out an ounce of pity in me. *Almost.*

"You heard my brother," I answer, as I lead Miss Bellefleur by the hand through the club's back corridor.

The one that connects to the private suites.

"But we can't . . . I mean—"

I stop abruptly outside one of the empty doors, capturing her wrist in my hand to keep her from fleeing, but the shock in her eyes causes her to still.

"It's *your* lie, darling," I growl. "Time to see it through."

I half drag, half lead her into one of the open rooms with me. It's mostly empty, save for one plush-looking chair and some empty hooks for missing kink paraphernalia. I close the door behind us, sealing it shut, before I release her. I cross the space and settle myself into the chair, draping myself across the leather cushion like a goddamn king, which is exactly what I am, after all.

Prince of Darkness. Prince of sin and wicked deeds.

And if she dared think this kind of wickedness was above me, she was foolishly mistaken.

Best get this over with quickly.

"How long are you going to keep me waiting, little dove?" I say impatiently.

She glances between me, the empty room, and the now-closed door, desperately searching for a way out. The door is unlocked, and she can leave anytime, but she's been caught in a trap of her own making, and we both know it.

It's face Az with her lies, or me, and the moment she recognizes the limited choices in front of her, she blushes furiously.

"I . . . I can't do this."

"You can and you will." My gaze rakes over her, lingering. "Trust me."

She laughs a little like I've said something ridiculous. "Trust you?" She blinks, shaking her head at me. "You chose to come here with me tonight."

"I *offered*. You accepted. Try again."

She looks around, like she's hoping for any excuse to help her escape the inevitable. "The door is closed." She shrugs. "He can't possibly know what we're doing in here. We can fake it."

I chuckle at that. "If you think my brother can't *feel* when I make an offering to him, try again."

"An offering?" She blinks.

"Lust. It's his sin," I say. "That's how it works, darling."

Recognition settles over her, and she blanches, the full extent of what she's done dawning on her. It's a situation of her own making, and yet . . .

"But I didn't . . . I didn't mean—"

"The road to Hell is paved with good intentions, Miss Bellefleur," I purr. "You're about to learn that lesson, explicitly."

She glances between me and the door, then back again, to where I'm settled into the chair. She's thinking about running. I can see it on her face, and if she does, I won't bother to chase her. Even *I'm* not that kind of monster, and there's a special place in Hell reserved for those who use their power to coerce sex and intimidate. But for now, if she decides to stay here, she has a choice to make.

"It's your move, little dove," I say, my voice dropping low. The same one she accused me of using upon Eve. "Make your play."

"And if I run?" she asks.

"Don't insult me," I snarl. "I won't fire you, if that's what you mean. You're free to leave if you choose, but if you do, it'll be *your* name in the headlines come morning and by your own doing."

"I was trying to protect you."

I scoff. It's a lie, clearly. No one has *ever* tried to protect me. Humans fend for themselves. Always. They're nearly as prideful as me.

"Foolish girl," I hiss, my voice turning serpentine, tempting. "I don't need protecting. It's *you* who needs protection from *me*." I smirk. "But even your God can't save you from yourself."

She shakes her head. "I don't know what you mean."

As if she's innocent in all this.

I chuckle. "I can see it, you know." I rake my gaze over her. "How you want me." I'm bluffing, baiting her, but she couldn't possibly know that. "I can see *all* the dark thoughts inside that pretty little head of yours."

I try once more then, a subtle push inside her soul, meant to bare her to me, but still I come up empty.

My nostrils flare, the temptation infuriating me.

Her eyes narrow. "You're lying."

"Am I?" My grin widens. "Am I wrong?"

She doesn't answer, but the way her throat writhes as she swallows and those doe eyes fall to my lips says everything. I may not be able to see the thoughts inside her head, but I'm not immune to the desire in her gaze either.

She wants this as much as I do. I'm certain of it.

Slowly, she takes a step toward me.

"Tell me I'm wrong," I demand. "Tell me I'm wrong, and I'll fix this little mess you've created, easily."

For a moment, I think she might lie, both to save herself and me, but then her eyes fall to my lap once more, her voice barely a whisper. "You're not wrong."

A cruel smirk twists my lips. "Then do your worst, darling."

Inhaling a sharp breath, she fortifies herself a little, and I almost expect her to back down, to run, but then she approaches me, the sound of her heels echoing through the silence. "This is wrong."

A dark chuckle tears through me. "I created wrong. Don't preach to me."

She stops, standing just before me. "Yes, sir," she whispers.

We both go still.

Those two words unleash something in me, something far more dark and wicked than she bargained for.

"Say that again, I liked it," I growl.

She drops to her knees before me. "Yes, sir."

It's the best and worst thing she could possibly do, and the second I see her kneeling before me, my cock responds. It strains against the fly of my suit pants, painfully hard, but we don't need to give into temptation, not truly, for Az to have his due, and I only intend to take this as far as she leads it.

She lowers her head.

"Don't be shy, little dove." I lean forward, gripping her chin and forcing her to look at me. "You have my attention now."

CHAPTER ELEVEN

Charlotte

I'm so out of my depth and so turned on that I don't even remotely know what I'm doing. So the moment Lucifer gives me the reins, I flounder. I gaze up at him from where I've knelt between his knees, like I'm his subject and he's my king, but before he can tell me to stand, I feel myself move. I climb onto his lap almost instinctually.

I straddle him, facing him so that my ass hovers over his knees.

That fiery amber flickers in his eyes. "Nothing we do here leaves this room, and nothing changes when we leave. Do you understand me?"

He's making me no promises. No guarantees. Except that come morning, we'll both forget all about this. One night only, and then maybe I'll have gotten whatever this crazy rebellion is out of my system.

It's all the permission I need.

I settle myself onto his lap, and the pleasured groan he releases nearly undoes me.

"Don't play innocent now, Charlotte," he whispers, and my name on his lips sends a rush of heat through me. I feel myself slicken. "Be greedy."

I do exactly as he commands, roughly shifting myself deeper into his lap, my skirt riding up around my waist, until the wet heat of my center rubs against his cock. I gasp. Even beneath the shield of his suit pants and the damp lace of my thong, he's large and thick, likely more than I could take comfortably, but the thought of him inside me, dirtying me, is a cruel, tempting thing, and I feel more than a little breathless.

"Wicked, wicked girl," he purrs. A smirk twists his lips. "If we fucked, would you call me Daddy?"

My eyes widen, humiliation gripping me at how he sees straight through me, to the trauma that brought me here. How many others have pulled this same stupid religious rebellion with him? The embarrassment nearly kills me.

Flushing, I shake my head and start to stand. "I can't—"

"No." He grips my face roughly, forcing me to look at him as he pulls me back down into his lap. "We're not through yet." He holds my gaze for a long beat. "You were made for this. For sin. Take what you came here for, what you need."

I swallow hard, but temptation gets the better of me. I follow his command then, my gaze tracing from the subtle cords of his throat to his lips. It'd be so easy to take what I've been dreaming of since I first met him in his brother's club the other evening, and I can't stop myself from being a bit greedy, a little reckless even.

I surge forward, claiming his lips.

He kisses exactly the way I expect he would fuck, rough and penetrating—a harsh clash of tongue and teeth that stops my breath short. His mouth parts for me, and for a moment, as much as I'm enjoying myself, I think I might end it there, with just a quick taste, but then suddenly, his hands are on me, tangling in my hair as he growls. "Harder."

At his command, I deepen the kiss, and he matches my intensity, his tongue sweeping over my lower lip to part me. He tastes of smoke and whisky, of dark promises and even darker sins, but I'm too caught up in my own desire to fully appreciate what I'm doing.

I'm kissing the fucking devil.

What would God think of me?

At the moment, I can't bring myself to care. Lucifer's kiss feels like a claiming, a new beginning, a harsh punishment against God for all the things *His* people did to me. The revenge and his lips are so delicious that before I know it, I find myself moaning, rocking my hips against Lucifer, desperate for him to be inside me.

The need is so strong that already my pussy pulses, inching me dangerously close to finishing as I grind myself against him, and for a brief moment, though I've never come with anyone else in the same room before, I think I may fall apart in his arms, if he lets me.

But Lucifer must sense the need in me, because abruptly, he grips a handful of my hair, pulling me back by the root of it to break the kiss between us. His lips are a little swollen from where I've claimed them, and the sight leaves me breathless, needy.

"Does that satisfy your curiosity?" His voice is lower than I've ever heard it before, filled with something I'd interpreted as desire.

But he was the one who stopped our kiss, and the realization that he may have only been doing this to tempt me, to save face with his brother, shocks me.

Suddenly, the damp feeling between my legs and my still erect nipples feel all wrong, though the answer to his question is obvious to both him and me.

It wasn't enough. Not nearly.

My curiosity isn't even close to satisfied.

Without another word, I extract myself from his lap, straightening my clothes, though I can tell from the smirk on his lips that it does little good. I look freshly fucked, and I nearly came all over his lap as if I was. All it took was his mouth on mine to do that to me.

How thoroughly could this man ruin me?

I'm in trouble. Big trouble.

Because I was wrong before. He's not a danger to me.

I'm the danger. The way I feel around him is the true path to madness.

"My brother will appreciate your offering," he says, his dark eyes spearing me.

"And you?" I ask. "Did you appreciate it?"

He laughs devilishly. "Run along now, little dove, before you do something to *truly* unleash me."

I hesitate, but then at his dismissal, I turn and leave, rushing out of the club, only this time, that dark laughter doesn't chase me, and I don't have to wonder about all the things a mouth like his could do to me.

I know now, explicitly.

And it's not nearly enough to satisfy.

CHAPTER TWELVE

Charlotte

I wake to the sound of steady beeping, the unnatural noise echoing in my ear. The astringent scent of antiseptic fills my nose, and it doesn't take long for me to recognize I'm still in the hospital. *Jax.* My eyes snap open. Jax isn't asleep as I left her. She's awake. Finally.

"Hey," she mutters.

"Hey." I sit up. "How are you feeling?"

The blue-and-black strands of her hair are messy, and her light-brown skin is a little paler than normal. Her eye makeup from last night is obviously smudged from sleep, but otherwise, she looks a lot like she normally does after a night of hard partying.

Save for the hospital gown.

"Like a freight train hit me," she says, "but I'm okay. I think."

"Good. Okay is good. Lucifer helped me find you, and we were able to get you before—"

"I know," she says, smiling appreciatively. "Ian told me."

I follow her gaze near the door where I see the bartender from Az's club waiting, only this time he's dressed in plain clothes, jeans and a concert tee that look way more this century. He's around our age, midtwenties, with a handsome, easy smile and warm brown eyes that likely earn him a lot of tips.

"Hi." He lifts a hand toward me.

I frown. "Clearly you don't know how to listen to warnings."

The moment the words fall from my lips, it surprises even me how much I sound like Lucifer. Already he's dug his claws into me.

Ian's eyes widen, and whatever he sees in my expression then, I can tell it's not anything close to what he expected from me, but slowly, he lifts his hands in surrender once more. "Like I said, it wasn't how it looked. I'm the one who called the ambulance. I was just checking her pulse, though I do feel guilty since I was the one who got her the gig." He shrugs. "Sorry about that. I have a soft spot for pretty girls, so sue me." He shifts his gaze to Jax and winks.

"It's true," she says, making me feel instant relief. "Ian and I met a few days ago, and he pitched me doing a one-time open reading for the guests at Az's club."

I glance between them then, confused. "Why didn't you tell me?"

Jax makes an apologetic expression. "I wasn't sure if it was going to pan out, and then I was worried it was going to cause a problem, considering . . ."

Considering I work for Lucifer now.

That goes without saying.

I nod, straightening where I sit in the visitor's chair beside her bed. "I wish you'd told me, but I get why you didn't."

It would have caused me to worry, especially after that damn meet—

My eyes widen. Oh no. *The meeting.*

I glance at the clock on the wall. Already, it's nearly nine thirty.

"Shit," I swear.

Jax and Ian both look toward me.

"What's wrong?" Jax asks.

I glance at my phone. "I have to be in that meeting in an hour, the one Imani and I have been working toward, and I haven't even—"

"Go," Jax says, waving me on. "I'll be fine."

"Are you sure?"

I hate having to abandon her so quickly, but I *have* been at the hospital with her all night.

She nods before Ian says, "She's safe with me. Promise. I'll get her home."

I study him and, for a moment, I feel a bit guilty about how I treated him, considering he called the ambulance and all. "I'm sorry I was rude at first. I was just—"

He shakes his head at me. "Trying to protect your friend," he finishes. "I get it. You don't need to apologize. I'd do the same."

I nod, glad we've reached an understanding.

"But if you're looking to repay me . . ." He casts me a teasing grin. "Letting Jax give me your number couldn't hurt."

"Ian!" Jax shrieks, throwing her hospital pillow at him.

It misses and lands on the floor near his feet.

"I'm kidding. I'm kidding." Ian lifts his hands again. "Okay, only a little." He makes a pinching gesture with his fingers. "Unless you and Lucifer are really . . ."

"We're not," I say, shutting that idea down fast. "Though if you could not tell Azmodeus . . ."

He smiles knowingly. "Your secret's safe with me."

"Secret?" Jax's jaw is nearly on the floor, and her eyes are sparkling like she wants me to spill *all* the tea and she wants it spilled now. Or, preferably, yesterday.

"I'll tell you later," I say. "Promise." I glance at my phone once more, then back to her.

I wet my lips. I feel awful leaving her, and I still wonder if she knows who may have spiked her drink, but there's no time to discuss that now.

"Later," she says, reading my expression.

I need to get to that meeting.

"Go. Go." She waves at me.

As I leave, Ian casts me one last grin, his smile the perfect mix of friendly and flirty. I return the look, though in truth, I'm too focused on the meeting to really process what I'm doing. If I play this right, I'm supposed to please my boss.

Just like every delicious thing we did last night.

I'm nearly ten minutes late when I finally stumble into the conference room and already, I can tell I'm screwed. Lucifer sits at the head of the table, his expression grim and his eyes filled with a cold fury I hadn't anticipated. Quietly, I try to slip into the back, unnoticed, as I take my seat next to Imani.

Someone else is in the middle of presenting, but still Lucifer's gaze snaps toward me. "You're late," he says, interrupting the presentation and causing all eyes to turn in my direction.

Those two words hold more meaning than I expected.

As if he were anticipating me. And he's pissed that I'm late.

"I barely missed the train and had to wait for the next one." I glance between him and Imani, who sits to my right.

She lifts a brow at me, but I shrug innocently.

The presentation resumes then, though the other employees' curious glances still dart toward me. I keep my expression neutral, try to play it off, but Lucifer's frustration flusters me, even as the regular flow of the meeting continues. I truly thought I could do as he said, forget what happened between us last night, as unnatural as that would be for me, but every time I deliberately look away so my eyes don't meet his, all I can do is imagine his hands on me, the way they tangled in my hair as his lips and tongue plundered mine like he was a thief.

The best kind of marauder.

Though it's not until that moment that I realize exactly what it is he's stolen from me.

My pride. The confidence that'd slowly begun to build in me.

Whether I like it or not, Lucifer owns that part of me now.

And I gave it to him willingly.

I sit quietly in my seat, waiting for the remaining presentations to finish. With each passing minute, my initial belief in myself wavers, but I'll be damned if I allow him to fluster me. To ruin this. I worked hard on this presentation. To impress him. To impress Imani.

I won't let one stupid kiss destroy it for me.

I may have been a willing participant, but that doesn't change the fact that Lucifer owes me.

He may not see it that way. Hell, he may not even be grateful, but regardless of what he thinks, I single-handedly saved him from yet another blow to his reputation last night. This one likely even more damaging than the first. Not to mention I've worked tirelessly with Imani to reroute the initial narrative that caused all of this.

"Charlotte," Imani says from beside me, drawing me from my thoughts.

I blink, coming back to myself. All eyes in the room are on me.

"It's your time to shine." Imani gives me an encouraging smile, but her voice has an edge to it that is distinctly telling me: *do not fuck this up.*

"I'm ready." I plaster on my best Sunday-morning-greeting face. Tablet in hand, I make my way to the front of the conference room, where Lucifer waits at the head of the executive table.

I set up my iPad on it, syncing the Bluetooth connection with the smartboard, but with each movement, I can feel Lucifer's gaze on me, his otherness washing over me until I'm suddenly fumbling to get my iPad to AirDrop my presentation. Last night when I was staring down Azmodeus, something about Lucifer's otherness made me feel protected, safe even. Now, it simply makes me feel exposed, vulnerable. Like all my thoughts are on display, which if what he said is true, they are. But I won't let him get under my skin.

This is my chance to prove that I belong here.

That I deserve this amazing opportunity Imani gave me.

"Charlotte's taking the lead on this, but she's got my stamp of approval," Imani says, smiling like she's both proud and encouraging me. "Take it away, Charlotte."

I nod, steeling myself as I turn toward Lucifer. I won't pretend like there's anyone else I'm addressing in this meeting. Everyone here knows that what Lucifer says goes. Maybe it'll appeal to his vanity, but that's not why I choose to do it. It's not because I fear him either.

He's watching me intently, his chin resting on his fist as he stares at me.

No, I do it because I know people rarely talk to him this way, one on one, as if they aren't afraid of him, and unlike many, I'm *not* afraid of him. The worst has already happened to me.

Long before I came here.

I meet his eyes then. Suddenly, everything I'd planned for the presentation abandons me, and it's just me and him, talking while we're alone. Like this.

I don't second-guess myself. I just go with it.

"I know you said you don't want to lose your anonymity by showing your face to the press," I say, starting off with acknowledging the elephant in the room. "And you're not wrong. That *is* an asset and your choice."

He leans forward a little, his brow lowering as if that's obvious, but the fact that I've admitted it has intrigued him, at least, or so I think.

"I understand why you wouldn't want to give that up. Really, I do." I glance toward Imani then, and she nods, encouraging me. "But it's my job to convince you why *both* those things, your anonymity *and* your debut, can be an asset to the company." I gesture to the other employees watching us. "Your choice to remain in the background for so long has created a unique opportunity for you."

I swipe left, cueing my first slide, and whispers spread through the conference room as all six of his siblings' faces appear on the screen. Red-carpet-worthy headshots of each one of the Originals, save for

Lucifer. From the ripple of unease among my coworkers, the slide has the exact effect I intended.

"Your siblings gave away their anonymity the moment they came topside and stepped into the limelight, but you didn't," I say. "You knew better than to give away your most valuable asset to the press—yourself—which puts you in a distinctly strategic position." I swipe left again, the next slide showing a graph breaking down a time-specific analysis of how often Lucifer has appeared in the headlines over the past six months in comparison to his siblings. Even with him refusing photos and video interviews, it's not even close.

Public interest in him beats out *all* his siblings combined by a mile.

"None of the other Originals has nearly as much sway with the press as you do because they gave away their most valuable asset, their sense of mystery. That's exactly what stirs the public's intrigue, and they traded it for quick and easy fame. But you didn't."

I tap the next screen, displaying another infographic. "We know the laws of supply and demand. The scarcity principle. Limit access. Create exclusivity, and the value of something increases exponentially. It's a model we use all the time in luxury." My next slide highlights several campaigns Apollyon Inc. has run for their products using the exact same model. Balenciaga. Versace. Ferrari. Among others.

"But what we haven't considered is that we can apply that same principle to you, Lucifer," I say, daring to use his first name.

A hush goes over the room, and for a moment, I worry I've gone too far, but then I realize Lucifer's lifted a hand to pause me. "So, what you're proposing is that the company commodifies me?"

I hesitate.

When he puts it that way, it doesn't sound as promising as I'd planned, but . . .

"Yes," I say, leaning into it. There's no point in trying to lie to him. I know he's a master at it. A true artist in his ability to manipulate. "But you're already a commodity for this company. That's why this . . . *business* at The Serpent has been such a threat to the company's stakes." I choose my words carefully. "You *are* the company. Your reputation, your image is the company and your namesake. We just haven't been using you to your full extent. In fact, we've undervalued you, considerably."

Resuming control, I swipe to the next slide. "We're not proposing what your siblings do now. We're suggesting a different way. Think of the opportunity that doing several limited-access campaigns could create. We could pair it with the launch of a new line like the Giovaldi account or a new branch of company philanthropy. It'd be the event of a generation, the first time the public sees the devil's face. The first time they get an exclusive interview. The press would be falling over themselves to get access to you."

Just like I was last night.

The thought comes to me out of nowhere, and the moment it does, my eyes fall to Lucifer's mouth, and recognition quirks his lips.

He leans back in his chair, crossing one long leg over the other almost lazily. "There's just one problem with this plan of yours, Miss—"

It takes me a second to realize he's prompting me for my name. Like I'm of so little importance to him that he can't be bothered to keep it in his memory, though I'm certain the move is deliberate. Meant to hurt me.

I flush. "Bellefleur," I answer tersely.

"Miss Bellefleur," he says, smirking. "You forgot one key aspect of this little presentation of yours."

The whole room, the whole world seems to hinge upon his next breath.

"Me," he breathes.

Panic floods over me.

"For all your vapid flattery, you forgot to ask yourself what benefit there is to me in all this." Lucifer shrugs dismissively.

Desperately, I swipe forward several slides in an attempt to save face. He's *trying* to embarrass me. I can feel it. "I had the finance department run the projections. The company's profits and stocks would increase exponentially, and the spike in growth would be sustainable. Limiting access over time would mean—"

"You think I truly care about an increase in the company's stock value?" Lucifer's eyes narrow at me. "I already have more money than God. Financial promises mean nothing to me."

"For your pride, then." My words hold a dangerous bite, but I can't help it. He's angered me. "You don't enjoy being bested by your siblings, letting them damage your reputation in the papers. All that stops if you listen to me, to Imani. If you let us help you."

It's the wrong thing to say.

Imani stands as if she's prepared to defend me, but Lucifer raises a hand, silencing her. "That's your fatal error, Miss Bellefleur. The assumption that you can be of any use to me." The way he looks at me then is so flat, so devoid of any emotion, that I can't imagine how I ever mistook him for anything other than the monster he's being. "Let me tell you something about being me." He grips the sides of his chair, leaning toward me.

"Every insult, every wicked deed, every fucked-up thing you could possibly imagine inside that pretty little head of yours and more has been said of me. You humans with your stories and your papers. You can't hurt me. Every unspeakable thing has already been said about me throughout the course of your short, pathetic history, and the worst part is that it's true."

A subtle burn lights in his eyes, and for once I'm not entranced by it. I can see the hellfire there, the pain, the agony, and it stills me.

"Humanity's ire means nothing to me, Miss Bellefleur. *You* mean nothing to me, and the sooner you realize that, the better off you'll be."

My knees go weak, and I feel myself trembling as tears gather in my eyes, but there's nothing I can do to stop it. Not without looking away from him, which I won't.

I refuse to show him exactly how small and vulnerable he's made me.

"Now, if *helping* is so important to you, why don't you head back to the middle of nowhere where you came from, Miss Bellefleur?" he says, driving the final nail in me, with the intimate knowledge I gave him, no less. "Because clearly, you don't belong in New York City."

No one moves for a long beat, and to my credit, I manage to keep my chin up.

To not let any tears fall.

I don't waste my energy giving him a scathing look. I'm too busy trying to stop myself from crying. I won't let him see how he's hurt me, but I hope he hears my thoughts loud and clear.

I hate you, I scream.

And despite all I've been through, I think it's the first time I've ever truly hated anybody.

And what shocks me the most isn't that I think it.

It's that I mean it.

Undoubtedly.

CHAPTER THIRTEEN

Lucifer

"That was uncalled for."

I tear into my office following that godforsaken meeting. Astaroth sits in wait, but it's Imani who's hot on my heels. "I don't remember asking for your opinion, Imani."

Her dark eyes flash with fury. "That girl's got potential, and if she quits because of this, I swear to—" She stops just short of saying something particularly damning, but her anger isn't even close to quelled. It's hard to get anything past her, and though she may not know exactly what happened between me and Charlotte last night, she clearly suspects it.

She knows me, more than I ever intended for her to.

Even though I've never dallied with an employee before.

I wave a hand dismissively. "Potential is a dime a dozen. Potential doesn't interest me. Respect does."

"Respect?" Imani wrinkles her nose. "If you were interested in respect, you damn sure would've fired me a long time ago." She appraises me like she's disgusted with what she sees. "I'm not going to be here to clean up your messes forever, you know."

"Last I checked, you weren't doing me any favors." I round my desk, dropping into my executive seat. "I've been paying you for over a decade."

"True." She steps up to the desk, stabbing a finger onto the surface in front of me. "But if you think for a minute you can get any senior PR employee to pull the kind of hours I do without threatening them, think again, Lucifer. Every workers' union in New York and beyond would be breathing down your neck." She glares at me. "Humanity's growing more and more tired of the Originals by the day. Give it another generation, and things are going to be tough for you. You need me."

I shrug. "Threats aren't above me."

"Nothing's above you." She says it without any judgment. It's merely a fact she accepted when she chose to work for me. "But her presentation was good. The delivery was a little faulty at moments, but the idea was a decent one. I wouldn't have signed off on it otherwise."

"And I'd expect nothing less."

Astaroth lifts a brow from where he's seated, but I shake my head, staying him. I'll deal with him shortly.

"But neither of you are telling me anything new," I say, turning back to Imani.

"Maybe not." She crosses her arms, looking down her nose at me. "But we can't tell you anything new if you refuse to listen to reason, if you refuse to let us do our jobs, which is exactly what that girl was trying to do."

"That woman," I correct her, leaning back in my seat. "She's a woman." I lift my gaze toward Imani. "Let her fight her own battles."

Imani's nostrils flare as she lets out a slow, furious huff. But she knows better than to argue with me when I've dug my feet in. No matter how much she dislikes it. "Are we done here?" she asks.

"You followed *me*."

She stares at me for a long beat.

I nod. "Yes, we're done here."

Without another word, she turns and leaves, barely casting so much as a glimpse toward Astaroth. My office door shuts heavily behind her, just short of slamming.

Astaroth lets out a low whistle. "You pissed her off something fierce."

"She'll get over it. She always does." Uncharacteristically, I prop my feet on the edge of my desk before pressing a hand to my temple.

"You don't normally tempt Imani's anger. She could cause trouble if she wanted."

I scowl. "If you have something to say, Astaroth, fucking say it already."

He doesn't try to stifle his grin. He knows he's pushing me. "I hear you were at Az's club, alone, with the girl last night." He takes in my now-loosened tie and disheveled hair. "She must be something if she's already gotten under your skin."

My scowl deepens. No one gets under my skin. I stand from my chair, crossing the room to lock the office door. As soon as the lock clicks, I turn toward Astaroth.

"I can't see her sins," I say, the words falling into the quiet between us.

Astaroth lifts a brow. "Excuse me?"

"You heard me," I growl. "I can't see them. I can see everyone's, but not hers."

"Fuck," Astaroth mutters quietly, pacing back and forth over a small section of the floor as if he's trying to parse out exactly what I'm saying. Once the idea seems to settle, his face turns deadly. "Why didn't you tell me?"

I wave a dismissive hand. "I wanted to be certain it wasn't a fluke."

"And is it?" he asks.

"No," I say quickly. "No, I've tried more than once."

Astaroth swears loudly. "This is bad, Lucifer. Very bad."

"You think I don't know that?" I sneer.

"The timing means something. You must realize that."

With Gabriel's return so close, he means. It'd be just like my Father, or one of my siblings, for that matter, to attempt to pull the rug out from under me just as we near the finish line.

They've tried as much before.

"I'm aware," I answer tersely. My jaw tightens.

"We can't afford any unexpected setbacks," Astaroth says, giving voice to what I'm thinking.

"And what exactly do you propose we do? Kill her?"

"Keep her close," he says, smirking at me. "It'd hardly be a chore for you."

In other words, fuck her until she's loyal to me.

Even though she's my employee . . .

It wouldn't be the worst thing I've done, hardly, and the idea holds more than a little appeal for me. Despite how I ended things, I enjoyed last night, though I've never made it a habit to dally with humans. On the rare occasions I've indulged myself, I've chosen to stick to demons or the Nephilim.

"And when this is through?"

"Discard her, like the others," Astaroth says, as if the answer is obvious. "It'll be easy."

It'll be easy. His words play in my mind like a refrain.

I nod, agreeing, though something about Astaroth's suggestion doesn't sit well. But for the life of me, I can't begin to place my finger on why it bothers me.

CHAPTER FOURTEEN

Charlotte

My vision is blurred, and I'm crying in earnest by the time I reach my office, but thankfully, Imani doesn't follow me out of the meeting. Instead, the moment we left the conference room, she veered right toward Lucifer, fast on his heels. Likely following him as they decide to fire me.

As if today can get any worse.

As soon as I hear the click of my office door shutting behind me, I collapse against it, sobbing uncontrollably. If anyone comes to the other side, they'll definitely hear me, but I can't stop myself from caving into the emotions ripping through me like a tidal wave, even though I managed to hold it together during the meeting.

I hate him.

I hate him so much I can hardly stand it. So much I feel it vibrating through me.

I stay like that for a long time, crying and furious until I don't have any tears left. My mascara is smeared all over my face, and some of it has even gotten onto my hands. I'll have to clean myself up if I expect to hide what I'm feeling from Imani. Not that she could possibly understand what this means for me.

I *knew* coming here wasn't a wise decision, that working for the devil wouldn't be the best choice, but it was also the one place I knew my father wouldn't follow me. The one place he wouldn't try to hunt me down and drag me back to that godforsaken hellhole of a house where he left me. I never intended for this company, this job, to be my permanent home. Working for the devil is hardly a lifelong goal for someone raised like me.

But I'd also hoped that maybe I could build something meaningful for myself here, in the city. At least temporarily. That I'd finally find some acceptance here.

A home.

The idea that he's taken that from me before I've even fully been given a chance to prove myself settles into me, shifting my emotions from hurt to rage. My hands clench into fists.

He used me.

Fucked me over. All to play his own twisted game.

I don't know how I ever expected anything less.

I can't begin to understand what he had to gain from following me to Az's club last night, but I know there must have been something in it for him.

Something beyond *helping* me.

At the thought of that word, I scowl, my anger heightening. So much, that before I can fully think it through, I cross my office over to my desk and drop into the seat. I move the mouse to wake my company iMac up, typing in my password to illuminate the home screen. I pull up a blank Word doc, my fingers dancing over the keys.

Journaling has always been cathartic for me.

Before my father discovered my diary and took it away, at least. Only after he'd read every page, violated my privacy, just like he violated everything when it came to me. He burned it shortly thereafter. In one of our church's outdoor fire pits. It's only now that I'm safely away from him and in weekly therapy that I've started to reclaim the practice.

I start typing, the words flowing out of me like a torrent, a release. The feeling of letting all my hatred out is so cathartic that I channel all my rage into it, every cruel thought, every hateful word I wish I could say to him, though I don't know exactly who I'm writing to.

There's too many of them. The men who've hurt me.

Lucifer is only one of several.

But I focus all my fury on him, toward what he did to me in that meeting.

I don't know how long I sit there or how many minutes tick by on the clock as my fingers blaze across the keys. All I know is that as I finish typing the last sentence, I feel my anger release like a physical weight from my shoulders, like I've exorcised whatever hateful demon possessed me. I glance over the press release I've created. It's vicious and furious and uncharacteristically damning of Lucifer and his love life, or his lack thereof, but I have no intention of ever sending it.

No, this is solely for me.

Satisfied, I lean back in my seat, scrolling through the work I've done. I'm just about to exit the document and hit delete, when suddenly the door flies open, and Imani's in my office. I minimize the document onto the task bar without thinking.

She takes one look at me, shaking her head like she's unsurprised by what she sees.

I swipe at my smeared makeup, but it's too late. She's already seen the damage.

"Grab your bag," she says. "We're going to lunch, then you're taking the rest of the day off."

I don't bother to argue with her. Without standing, I grab my purse from where I stored it on the shelf behind me as she passes a mono-grammed handkerchief to me.

I swipe my eyes with it, leaving the pink surface dirty. "Thank you," I say.

She doesn't look at me. "Don't thank me. I've been cleaning up his messes for a long time." She gives me a meaningful look then, and I don't know how she knows, or if she's aware of the specifics, but still, embarrassment fills me.

Which means I must not be the first, nor am I likely the last.

My stomach sours at the thought.

I glance down at the floor. "I'm sorry. I know I've disappointed you and—"

"Don't even start with that nonsense," she says. "This isn't a usual company. I knew that when I chose to work here. But listen to me, Charlotte, because I'll only say this once, you hear me?" She gives me a look like I better pay attention if I know what's good for me. "You don't want to get caught up with Lucifer. I've been cleaning up after him for over a decade. Trust me."

It's the most damning thing I've heard her say about him, and I'm not certain how to react to it. "What am I supposed to do?" I pass the handkerchief back to her, and she tucks it away in her leather Fendi before turning toward me.

"Keep your head down and keep working, but remember this is no place for you."

My stomach churns harder. "Are you firing me?"

"No." She shakes her head. "No, I'm not foolish enough to shoot myself in the foot like that. This is a bump in the road, a big bump, but you're still a smart girl, all things considered. I know the kind of background you came from."

I open my mouth to ask how she could possibly know, but the look she gives me isn't one of understanding, it's one of intimate knowledge. Imani has her own demons, though she's not about to bare them to me. "I'm the head of PR. You didn't think I'd do my own digging?"

I'm not surprised she knows my secrets. Just embarrassed.

"I . . . never expected anything less."

Not even Jax knows the full extent of everything that led me here. Not entirely.

"Good, then we're on the same page." She straightens, gripping the strap of that gorgeous Fendi. "Come have lunch with me, and we'll talk about what you'll do *after* you finish working for me. Consider it a favor. Career woman to career woman."

After you finish working for me.

Meaning, she's going to help me pivot to something I'm better suited for.

Something that's not here.

This is only temporary, I remind myself. That's all it was ever supposed to be. A leg up. Lucifer hasn't changed that.

"Thank you." I sniffle, finally standing. "Though honestly, I don't understand why you're doing this for me."

Imani sighs a little, like I'm still being naive. "I've been around long enough that I'd rather spend my time building other women up than shooting them down." She gestures to her dark skin. "There's no love for women who look like me in this industry, and I'm not about to use the bit of power I've gained against somebody. Poor choices aside. I intend to pay it forward, at every opportunity."

"Thank you," I mutter again. It's all I seem to be able to say. "I want to do my best to make you proud."

She scoffs, walking toward the office door with the expectation I'll follow. "Girl, it doesn't matter what I think. It doesn't matter what anyone thinks, so long as you're able to look at yourself in the mirror each morning. That's what working here's taught me."

I nod, understanding. After the past twenty-four hours, I'm certain that working here means Imani has seen a few things that would make others' souls curl, but she handles it gracefully, wearing all her strengths and her flaws like they're precious jewelry.

So I follow her lead.

Because that kind of confidence is all I've ever really wanted for myself.

By the time Imani and I finish with lunch, and I manage to catch the train home, it's already early evening. I key into the apartment, dropping my bag onto the floor as I close the door behind me. Jax stands in our little makeshift kitchen that's really no more than a small stove, a barely-larger-than-mini refrigerator, and a sink.

Counter space is a luxury neither of us can afford currently.

It only takes one look for her to know something's wrong.

We've both been dealt a really shitty hand in the past twenty-four hours, but still, she catches me. Before I can even tell her what happened, she hugs me, gripping me tight as I sob into her shoulder. I'd thought I'd gotten out all my tears back in my office, but clearly, I was wrong. She leads me over to our secondhand love seat, and we sink down onto the cushions beside each other. I rest my head on her shoulder as we both tell each other everything.

The events of last night. The initial meeting with Lucifer.

The details of her gig with Az. All of it.

Fuck the NDA. This is what I need. A friend who accepts me unconditionally.

It's no less than what I'd do for her, and I know Jax would never hurt me. She knows how important this job is to me.

I managed to squirrel away a little money before I escaped my old life, but Manhattan burned through that nest egg quickly. The high price tags here are real, and I learned that fast. I only have enough to see myself through another month, maybe two, if I manage it properly, and that's *with* Jax splitting the rent.

I need this job.

The fact that I got picked for it in the first place is nothing short of a miracle, considering the limited experience on my résumé, which means I have no choice but to see this through. Long enough to have the experience needed to pivot easily.

Exactly like Imani suggested at our lunch today.

"So, what are you going to do?" Jax whispers to me once my tears have dried.

"Exactly what Imani said. Keep my head down until I've gained enough experience. I can't go anywhere else right now without taking a major pay cut."

That's another reason I need this job. If there's one thing I can say for Lucifer, it's that he pays his employees extremely well. Above standard market rate, even in NYC. It won't be easy to find another base-level position in PR that pays what he's paying me, though I've yet to see my first paycheck. But Imani assures me that given some time, and with her recommendation, it'll be easy. I just need to survive where I'm at long enough for her to be able to recommend me to another company.

"And what about you?" I say, easing off Jax's shoulder to look at her. "How are you doing?"

"Better. All things considered. A little queasy, but mainly from anxiety. I don't know who could've put that in my drink, and if you and Lucifer hadn't found me . . ." Her voice trails off and she shudders. "That's something I don't want to consider."

"Apparently you were taken care of, though, considering Ian had already called the ambulance." I nudge her, giving her a small smile.

"True." She nods. "That's one good thing that could come out of this. You and him, I mean." She bumps my shoulder playfully.

I roll my eyes. "He's not for me. Besides aren't *you* interested?"

Jax tends to stay single, happily, but deep down, I think she's just keeping her options open as she searches for Mr. Right. A nice guy like Ian could be that for her. She shakes her head at me. "Nah, he's clearly more into you than he is me. Plus, bartenders aren't my thing. Been there, done that." She waves a hand, referring to her most recent ex.

"His loss. You're clearly way hotter than me." I wink.

Jax grins. We both know it's true, but she doesn't say anything.

Quiet settles between us, the distant sounds of the restaurant below our feet carrying. The city is noisier than I'd ever expected it'd be, but oddly, it's almost comforting. Like a reminder that for all our faults, we're not alone. There's solace in being one of many.

"I think I'm done with men for a while," I say.

She grins. "You're switching to women, you mean?" She teases a smile out of me.

"No, not that there's anything wrong with that." I feel a constant need to be clear about my stance on these things, considering my ultra-religious family. "I just mean this little . . . incident with Lucifer taught me my lesson is all."

"About getting involved with *your boss*, or the devil, not men," she corrects me. "Ian would be a more even playing field, trust me. Besides, you know I say the same thing every time a guy hurts me." From the way she looks at me, she's still convinced all this relationship stuff would be easier if I got past all the hang-ups that are stopping me. She's not wrong exactly.

I just don't know if casual sex is the answer.

She nudges my shoulder with hers. "Just don't write anything off before it can begin, okay?"

"Okay," I agree.

"Now, you promised you'd watch the first season of *Bridgerton* with me. Prepare to feast your eyes on this beauty." She unfolds her laptop, gesturing to the handsome actor on the screen.

I smile, settling in as Jax breaks out her new set of Oracle cards to show me while we watch the show, allowing myself to forget all the growing problems around me.

CHAPTER FIFTEEN

Charlotte

The following morning starts out like any other. The sound of my phone wakes me, and I force myself to get out of bed and get dressed. On the other side of the room, Jax stirs in her sleep. She keeps much later hours than me, considering she's hired to do readings at a lot of late-night parties, and as usual, I do my best not to wake her.

I shower quickly, putting on my makeup once the steam inside our closet-size bathroom disappears. My eyes are still puffy from spending yesterday crying, but it's subtle enough I doubt anyone will notice.

Exiting from the shower, I dress and pull on my heels, not bothering to switch on our little ten-dollar Keurig knockoff and make coffee. I grab a granola bar from the cabinet and decide to treat myself to the Starbucks near Apollyon.

After yesterday, I deserve something to make myself happy.

I take the green line uptown, which takes ten minutes longer than usual, but it's too expensive to go by taxi every day. Whenever I do, the meter ticks by, each mile draining more and more cash. But once my new salary comes in, maybe I'll be able to save enough up to move somewhere farther uptown. I get off at 86th Street then walk to the Starbucks on the corner of 85th and Lexington. Heading inside, I'm welcomed by the fresh scent of coffee. I wait in line and place my order.

A Venti iced latte with white mocha, sweet cream, and caramel drizzle with an extra shot of espresso. Hot is my usual preference, but not in this summer heat.

I can already tell the weather today is going to be scorching.

Order in hand, I make my way toward Park Avenue. It's a few minutes before nine o'clock and I don't want to be late clocking in again. Especially not after the conversation with Imani about laying low. Not that she was blaming me or anything. I was an equal participant in what happened between Lucifer and me, though I didn't share any explicit details.

The way he tore me apart in that meeting was punishment enough. But I'm determined to not let it happen again. As much as it hurts me.

It was stupid to think there would ever be anything between us.

That much is clear to me.

I stop just in front of the building, glancing upward. Apollyon Inc. looms over me, the massive high-rise reaching toward the sky like a glittering behemoth in the morning light. Letting out a long sigh, I shake myself off a little and then head into the lobby, smiling at the downstairs secretary, Jeanine. But it only takes one wide-eyed glance from her for me to recognize something is off.

I brush off the alarmed look she gives me, choosing to ignore it instead of saying anything.

Maybe I'm being paranoid, yesterday's events considered.

It's hard not to feel like I have something to hide. Sleeping with your boss is the kind of office gossip that gets around quickly. Not that we did anything other than kiss, but I know better than to think anyone would believe that.

It isn't until I get into the elevator and two employees from another floor share a look and stop whispering the moment they see me that I start to think something is really wrong.

Did Imani change her mind? Did she tell someone?

But as soon as I think it, my throat feels thick with shame.

Imani's been nothing but kind to me. She's helped me at every opportunity. If word of what happened in the meeting or any speculation about me and Lucifer gets out, I have no one to blame but myself. It'd be my own poor choices that landed me here.

And Lucifer's. He's equally responsible, if you ask me.

I step off the elevator and onto the sixteenth floor, which houses the PR department and my office, and the feeling only gets worse. All eyes are on me, and an eerie hush sweeps across the open floor as I pass the few cubicles and the glass-walled conference rooms that lead toward my office.

Once I'm out of sight, I quicken my pace, hurrying toward my door.

I rush inside, nearly slamming it shut behind me, but I don't catch the break I was hoping for.

Imani's sitting at my desk, waiting for me, her eyes filled with something worse than fury.

Disappointment.

My vision swims, and my knees are suddenly unsteady.

"You couldn't have possibly listened to me, could you?" Her gaze sweeps over me. I'm dressed as I usually am, in my Target-bought heels and pencil skirt, with a matching white blouse buttoned thoroughly to my neck. There's no judgment in her look, but there's a kind of confusion there, like she's not sure what Lucifer sees in me.

Instantly, my stomach drops. "I don't know what you mean."

"Don't you?" she asks. "Don't you, really?" She scoffs and throws a newspaper onto my desk.

It's not one of the usual entertainment mags we frequent. It's the *New York Times*.

But it's the headline that stills me.

Lucifer: lusty loverboy or listless and lonely? it reads.

My hands are shaking as I step forward, staring down at the words. The headline *I* wrote.

All the blood drains from my face. "I . . ."

"Don't bother trying to explain yourself. I already know it came from your computer," Imani says. "The syntax has your voice written all over it. You didn't think I'd recognize your writing in a goddamn press release?"

I shake my head, still in disbelief. "It's . . . not what it looks like."

A knock sounds at the door, and someone opens it without warning. Jeanine. "Lucifer wants to see you in his office. Now."

Imani glares at me, moving to stand, but Jeanine shakes her head, looking a little unsteady. "Not you," she says. "Her." She nods directly at me.

My breathing goes shallow as I desperately grasp for something to hold on to.

Suddenly the floor beneath me bottoms out, or at least it feels that way, and then the next thing I know I'm falling, only this time, there are no hands there to catch me before I hit the floor.

I wake on an unfamiliar couch, my whole body stiffening, but it isn't the feel of the cushions that frightens me. It's the velvet-and-sin voice that follows.

"Thank you, Jeanine."

The vein in my neck ticks as something like panic unfurls inside my chest, and I instantly recognize where I am, though I've yet to open my eyes.

Lucifer's office.

Where else could I be?

The room smells exactly like he tastes, a lingering mix of cigarette smoke and whisky. Like I've suddenly been transported to an office from *Mad Men*, instead of one built in this century. Though mad is a fair description, considering the events that led me here.

I didn't send that press release, but clearly someone else did.

Someone who has it in for both Lucifer *and* me.

I don't open my eyes. Instead, I lie still, listening.

The door closes, marking Jeanine's exit, but another voice fills the room. Imani.

"We need to get out in front of this."

"I'm well aware of that," Lucifer answers coldly.

He's remarkably calm, all things considered.

"Then make certain she agrees." No doubt she means me. "We don't have many other options left. Not with Gabriel's return this close."

Gabriel?

She can't possibly mean . . .

But of course she does.

Who *else* would she mean?

Not for the first time, I realize exactly how far in over my head I am. So far I'm practically drowning, but I've been in worse situations before, enough to develop a fierce survival instinct, and I'll do whatever it takes to get myself out of this.

Exactly like I did when I came here.

"You know me, Imani," Lucifer says coolly. "Miss Bellefleur won't prove a challenge."

I struggle not to grit my teeth.

Like hell I won't.

Imani must nod in agreement or something, because for a few seconds, no one says anything, until finally I hear the brush of her designer heels against the plush carpet as she moves toward the door. Her tone softens slightly. "Just don't hurt her or anything. As a favor to me."

The resignation in her words, like she's powerless to help me, is enough to make my spine as stiff as a board.

"You have my word," Lucifer says.

A moment later, I hear the door to his office open and close again, leaving us alone.

"You can stop pretending now, Charlotte," he says to me.

Another chill rakes down my spine, one that's far too familiar, but I don't bother to ask how he knew I was faking it. I open my eyes and sit up on the sofa, abruptly taking in the office around me. It's massive, taking up nearly half a floor or more, every fixture the height of luxury. Lucifer sits in his executive chair, his black-topped desk poised in front of him. The surface must be made from real obsidian.

The desk is positioned in front of a rectangular conference table, parallel facing, its surface made of the same deep stone. Two modern art pieces—maybe Pollocks—in varying shades of black and white flank the desk, the plush rug underneath giving way to marble flooring that peeks out around the edges of the room.

I sit on the far side, at a corner sofa and coffee table that's clearly meant for casual entertaining. A modern chandelier with glass dripping like teardrops hangs between us, though the space is filled with natural lighting from the floor-to-ceiling windows.

If I thought the view from *my* office was stunning, it's nothing compared to this. At night it must be breathtaking. All the downtown lights glittering at his feet.

I stare at Lucifer, refusing to say anything.

Regardless of what Imani said, I'm not going to make this easy. Not now. The rules have changed.

And not even she can save me.

Lucifer rises from his chair, coming to stand at the edge of the conference table. He crosses his legs at the ankles, placing his hands in his pockets as he looks at me.

It should be a sin how gorgeous he is, but I guess that's the point, really.

"You've gotten yourself into quite the mess, you know." Those dark eyes sparkle.

"Have I?" I tilt my head, questioning him.

My response is bratty, petulant even, but if he expected me to play nice after he embarrassed me in that conference room, he was sorely mistaken.

"The kitten has claws, I see." He smirks.

Something about the way he says it infuriates me.

As if I'm no more than a minor problem to be dealt with.

"Go ahead and do it then, why don't you?" I wave a hand at him. "Fire me. Smite me. Whatever it is you were planning." Best get this over with.

Lucifer chuckles. "Oh, darling, firing you would be far too easy." He grins, showing off those oddly pointed canine teeth. "Where's the fun in that?"

The moment he says it, it's like the rug has been ripped out from under me, and I suddenly can't figure out how to stand. The world seems to tilt for a second, but I try my best not to show it. "If you're not going to fire me, then what are you going to do?"

My vision tunnels, anxiety trying to get the better of me.

That wicked grin of his twists. "That's not the right question, little dove. The better question is: what are *you* going to do for *me*?"

"I don't understand."

What could I possibly have to offer him?

He shifts to standing, coming to his full height as he rounds to the desk where he retrieves a sleek laminated folder. He crosses the room with a predatory grace before he drops it onto the table in front of me.

The folder makes a deafening smack as it hits the table's surface.

I reach for it. "What's this?"

I open the folder, seeing my name written in my own handwriting at the top.

"Your employment contract." He nods toward the file. "First rule of business." He taps his finger on the document. "Read the fine print."

Snatching up the paperwork, I flip through it furiously, searching for the small addendum sections that I previously skipped.

"Article two. Section three," he says, directing me toward the appropriate header.

I scan through the paragraph.

"You can redefine the terms of my position at any time." I lift a brow. "So what?"

Lucifer smirks. "So, I'm choosing to redefine them. Immediately."

My blood runs cold, and something about the way he says it alerts me to what a fool I was. How could I *ever* believe that firing me was the worst he could do?

"What do you mean?"

His smirk widens before he moves toward his desk. "That little press release of yours was hardly the worst thing anyone's said of me, but it wounded me. Truly." He places a hand over his heart, mocking me.

What I wrote didn't hurt him at all.

He's simply toying with me, but I have no choice but to sit here and take it.

"Did you really think I'd sit by and let my pride be damaged by the press so easily?" He's behind his desk again, fingers steepled as he watches me. "I intend to do something about it."

"And what does that have to do with me?"

"Everything, Charlotte." A spark of hellfire lights in his eyes. He holds my gaze for a long beat, neither of us moving, until finally he glances toward the window like we're having a polite coffee chat, instead of him threatening me. "Do you value your job, Miss Bellefleur?"

The change in his tone startles me.

"You know I do. I wouldn't have written that press release if I didn't."

I wasn't the one to send it, but *he* doesn't know that. I play my cards close.

Let him think the worst. For now, at least.

Something shifts in his expression then, maybe at the glimpse of my wounded pride. Like he's a shark prepared to strike at the first sign of blood.

"You embarrassed me in front of the entire board. All the executives. Imani." I shake my head. "I wasn't about to sit by and take that."

"Nor should you," he says.

It's nothing close to an apology. No surprise there.

"But your choice has created a unique opportunity." He echoes my words from the meeting. It's meant to mock and bully me, to embarrass me further, but even as I flush, I force my expression to remain steady.

God, how could I have ever been so naive as to think he'd be capable of caring for anyone? Especially me. And after one stupid kiss.

He doesn't deserve my pity, or my kindness. Or the help I've freely given him.

"Get to the point, Lucifer."

He frowns at me, like I've just taken all the fun out of whatever game this is. "I suddenly find myself prepared to debut to the press."

A brief spark of hope lights in me.

"With you alongside me."

My stomach drops.

I blink, more than a little confused. "I . . . don't understand."

"It's simple, Charlotte." He comes to stand in the middle of the room. "That little press release of yours created an unprecedented interest in my love life, or my *lack thereof*," he says, quoting me.

I wince.

The section I wrote on how a mysterious billionaire celebrity notably hasn't ever been spotted in public with a partner was particularly scathing. It may or may not have included insinuations that the . . . ahem, size of his manhood might be to blame.

Not my proudest moment obviously, considering what I felt pressed against me the other evening, but I never intended for anyone else to read it.

Lucifer especially.

"You're going to fix that for me." He grins.

"How?" Already, I see where this is going, and I don't like it.

Not one bit.

"By playing the role of my queen, naturally. My fake fiancée." He shrugs. "It was your idea originally."

He can't possibly be serious.

"No." I shake my head, coming to stand. "No. Absolutely not."

I turn, heading toward the door.

"Walk out that door and you'll find yourself fired and served for libel before the end of the evening."

My jaw drops.

The audacity of this asshole . . .

But he's not wrong. A press release like that could warrant a lawsuit for libel, especially for someone with such a distinct image. He *is* the company's branding.

Anger roils in my belly. It's my own fault that this comes as a surprise to me. This kind of villainy is exactly what he's always been known for, until the last decade, at least.

I spin to face him. "You wouldn't dare." I nearly spit, I'm so angry. Like a venomous snake. Though not nearly as much as the monster before me.

"Try me," he says, smirking.

For a moment, I consider doing exactly that, walking out the door and washing my hands of this whole thing. But I *need* this job.

More than anything.

It's a miracle I'm even standing here. The odds of me getting this position were akin to lightning striking me. And I don't expect it to strike twice.

It's this or flounder in the NYC job market until my prospects run dry.

It's this or be forced to admit defeat.

If my money runs out, I could end up on the street until my father comes looking for me. Jax would do anything within her power to ensure that didn't happen, but she's nearly as strapped financially as I am. Together, we're barely making rent, but without each other . . .

Her dream ends with me.

It's that single thought that stops me from giving him the middle finger and walking out the door.

I don't care what Lucifer does to me. All my life I've been kept prisoner at the hands of powerful men who attempted to break me. But Jax is the first person who was ever truly kind to me, who saw me for who I am and didn't tell me that there was something broken inside me.

For wanting a normal life. For being human. For not being the perfect picture of evangelical piety.

She took me in without question.

She may not be a Christian, but it was the most Christlike thing anyone has ever done for me. I can't repay her by turning my back on her now. She needs this just as much as me.

Lucifer's smirk quirks savagely like he can see the exact moment I come to my decision.

The exact moment he's broken me.

"What am I supposed to do?" I breathe.

He rises from his chair then, prowling toward me. "There's no requirement for physical intimacy, if that's what you mean."

"Surprise, surprise," I hiss. "I would have expected nothing less but pure evil from you."

Lucifer chuckles like I've offered him some depraved form of amusement.

He moves so fast that suddenly, he's gripping my chin, his thumb coming up to brush my lips as he smears my red lipstick. "Oh, Charlotte, you have no idea how truly vicious I can be." His gaze rakes over me, that amber fire burning, lingering, and it surprises even me that despite all he's done, my body still responds to his attention eagerly.

My nipples pebble beneath my shirt, and a rush of heat pools between my legs.

His lips twist knowingly, like he can smell the fear and desire on me, but abruptly, he releases me. "Astaroth will be in touch," he says, wiping his hands of me.

What's in this for you? I nearly ask, but I can't seem to bring myself to form words, to think. That's what his nearness does to me.

Instead, I nod, resigning myself as I turn to leave with what little shred of my dignity is left.

I head toward the door, the sound of my heels echoing as that velvet-and-sin voice follows, making me soft in places it shouldn't.

"I'll look forward to the next time we meet, Miss Bellefleur."

CHAPTER SIXTEEN

Charlotte

Half a week goes by before I hear anything, leaving me with nothing to do but sulk. Not even Jax or the endless pints of Ben & Jerry's she supplies can console me. Instead, I hole up in our apartment and refuse to get out of my pajamas for several days. I avoid all news sources, mainly my phone, as I watch several old seasons of *Downton Abbey*.

I'm four days in and still wearing the same pajamas from the day before—a pair of heart-patterned Walmart sweatpants and a worn "Keep Calm and Follow Christ" T-shirt from several youth retreats ago—when suddenly there's a knock at the door.

I don't look to see who it is before I answer.

It isn't him, anyway.

Instead, it's a man I've seen by his side in the tabloids countless times. Astaroth. Lucifer's bodyguard. Or close to it.

He takes one look at my pajamas, the bird's nest that's my hair, and my red puffy eyes before he wrinkles his nose. "Get dressed."

I slam the door in his face.

It's petty and pointless, and it's not him I'm angry with, but for the first time in days, it feels good to aim my rage at someone other than myself.

I do as I'm told, though it takes me a while to get ready. Not because I'm doing anything special to make myself look good for Lucifer, but because I haven't showered in two days, and the knots in my hair show it.

By the time I'm fully clothed and feeling almost human, it's nearly an hour later and somehow, Astaroth has managed to let himself into our apartment. I don't bother to ask how he got inside. It doesn't matter, really.

There isn't a place in this city Lucifer doesn't own.

Nowhere is outside his reach.

For that reason, trying to run is useless. I know because I spent the better part of two days seriously considering it. But wherever I go, he'd find me, and that's to say nothing of all the reasons I chose to stay. Better to get this over with.

"I'm ready." I step out of the room Jax and I share.

Astaroth looks up from his phone, giving me a quick once-over, though he doesn't say anything. The cut-off jean shorts and relaxed T-shirt I'm wearing paired with Jax's Converse and a cheap pair of sunglasses from the corner bodega aren't exactly the height of New York City fashion, but he never specified there was a dress code.

"Are we going or not?" I gesture toward the door.

Astaroth grumbles before he silently leads me out of the apartment, pausing for me to lock the deadbolt. Not that it matters, clearly. I follow him down the narrow, aging flight of stairs. Several of the steps leading to our apartment are crooked and droopy, a throwback to this neighborhood's old tenement days, but he navigates the hazard easily.

Outside, the sun shines overhead in mockery. I squint despite my sunglasses, my eyes slowly adjusting.

Lucifer's Town Car waits for us.

Astaroth slides into the passenger seat beside the driver with a grumbled "Get in."

I follow his directions, climbing into the back then relaxing into the plush leather seats. As we drive, a divider separates Lucifer's driver and

Astaroth from me, which I'm grateful for. With early morning traffic, it takes us a while to make our way to midtown. I stare out the car's tinted windows, still refusing to look at my phone.

The number of red notifications on the home screen is wild, but I want to live in blissful ignorance for as long as I can, and though I've had several days for the idea to sink in, I'm still not ready for the reality of playing Lucifer's fiancée. Not just yet.

When we finally reach the Madison Avenue building, Dagon hops out, scanning the street. He opens my door and ushers me inside like I'm some sought-after celebrity, though there's no paparazzi there to greet me.

Yet.

Astaroth joins me in the elevator and inserts a key into the panel, revealing a hidden button. He presses it, and then we're headed skyward. When we reach the top floor, he gestures for me to step into the open foyer beyond. The moment I do, the elevator doors slam shut behind me, sealing him away without even a halfhearted goodbye.

So much for being friendsies.

"Dick," I mutter under my breath, though I doubt he'd care what I think.

I get the impression that, like Lucifer, Astaroth and Dagon aren't exactly human, though if they aren't fallen angels, what *are* they?

I push the thought aside, not allowing myself to linger on it.

The idea is too much. Almost as much as me standing outside of Lucifer's penthouse prepared to play his blushing bride. Ten years ago, only congregations like my father's ever really believed we had to fear the influence of the devil. The rest of us thought we knew better. If only we could have known what was in store for us.

Me included.

A closed door waits on the far side of the foyer, flanked by a table with a decorative art bowl and some potted plants. I sigh and head toward the door, not pausing to knock before I try the handle. To my surprise, it opens, allowing me to slip inside.

When the door falls closed behind me, it echoes so loudly that it feels like I've stepped into another world. One where money is no object, bills never go unpaid, and luxury isn't a privilege that people like me can't afford, but the only true standard of living. My eyes widen as I slowly make my way into a second foyer, one even larger and more open than the first. It has a sleek separate elevator of its own, and I glance inside, gaping a little as I read the numbered buttons on the control panel. Lucifer's penthouse spans five floors.

Holy shit.

Luxury doesn't begin to cover it.

I blow out a long breath as I make my way past the elevator and farther into the space. The ceilings are every bit of twenty-five feet high, and this one room is likely worth more than what most people would earn in ten lifetimes. Easily. I glance around, my breath stopping short as I take in the near-360-degree view of midtown. I can hardly bring myself to breathe, and yet something about it feels like a waste to me.

Or maybe it's *who* it's wasted on.

"What do you think?" Lucifer's voice comes from behind me, sending a sudden shiver down my spine.

"Of your apartment?" I lift a brow as I take in the opulent view. "Is that what you'd call it?"

"You wouldn't?"

I open my mouth a little, trying to find something insulting to say. Anything to hurt him the way he's hurt me, but the penthouse is breathtaking. A beautiful homage to modern art and architecture. It sounds ridiculous, but even being in a space like this feels like a blessing, and yet I can't bring myself to say any of those things.

Not after what he's done to me.

"Seems like it'd get awfully lonely for one person." I shrug.

It's both truth and lie.

I'd trade my apartment for this in a heartbeat, and I'm not ashamed to admit it.

There's no glamour in poverty.

"The claws are already out, I see." Lucifer crosses the room toward me until he stands so close I'm forced to look up at him. "Don't worry, darling. I find a little pain with my pleasure to be thrilling." His gaze brushes over me, and it doesn't matter that I'm fully clothed, I feel as bared as I did when I nearly came all over his lap.

Damn him.

My eyes narrow. "Did you ask me here just to toy with me or do you actually have something valuable to say?"

"Ouch." He grins, circling me like a tiger would its prey. "Tsk tsk, Charlotte. You wound me." He places a mocking hand on his heart.

"What do you want, Lucifer?" I take off my sunglasses and place them on top of my head. "I didn't come here to play."

"Really?" His gaze deliberately falls to my lips, mimicking how I've looked at his a dozen times before. "I would have thought otherwise."

I flush instantly. Having cool undertones sucks.

"It was a mistake." I tear my gaze away. "The other night, I mean. The club's atmosphere got the better of me. That's all."

"Of course. The atmosphere. Naturally."

He steps away, and the breathing room it gives me is a welcome relief as he crosses to one of the windows overlooking the city.

He's quiet for a long beat, watching the cars and passersby. I brace myself, waiting for the other shoe to finally drop as he tells me exactly why he summoned me here, but then he catches me off guard, and says, "Would you like a tour?"

I blink.

At first, I think, *What harm could it do?* But then I pause. I learned my lesson the last time.

There is nothing harmless about Lucifer.

"No, thanks."

"Oh, come now, Charlotte. I don't bite." He grins wickedly. "Not hard, at least."

I glance away, trying to hide how his attention still affects me, but my eyes soon find their way to him again.

He smirks slightly.

Stupid, stupid hormones.

"Fine," I relent. "Lead the way."

The genuine smile he gives me in response is so staggering that for a moment, my anger falters, and I can't feel the floor beneath me.

Is this what it's like to be in his good graces? To earn his praise?

My cheeks burn crimson.

You're not interested in him. Remember? Not anymore, I remind myself.

But with his eyes on me like this, it feels as if the whole universe hinges on his next breath, like *I* alone command his attention, and the power in that is so intoxicating, I feel my vision spin. Exactly like when I straddled his lap.

"Whatever you're doing, stop it," I say.

Lucifer doesn't answer me.

Instead, he simply grins before turning away and releasing me.

The shift in his focus hits me like a cold shock, and it strikes me then that I'd do *anything* to feel that way again. How I felt in the club. In his lap.

It's an addiction, whatever this tension is between us, one I'm powerless to fight, and I'm not certain which is more dangerous, his anger or his approval. Or which I crave more.

But I won't allow him to toy with me. Not if I can help it.

"Shall we?" He gestures to the open penthouse.

Tentatively, I follow his lead as we explore the first floor. He guides me to an open dining and living room with lush modern decor that looks more like art than furniture. The far wall is lined with a thin decorative fireplace and a banquet table that seats at least twenty. The fireplace isn't lit currently, not in this summer heat.

A grand piano sits in the adjacent corner near the wall. A Steinway & Sons. Its black surface is so flawless I'd guess it's rarely, if ever, played. A shame, if you ask me.

I spent a lot of time singing in my church's choir, and music is one of the few parts of my childhood that never hurt me.

"Do you play?" I nod to the piano.

"Naturally." Lucifer smirks a little. "Only the devil's music, of course."

He escorts me up a set of glass stairs to a second floor that's nearly as stunning as the first, with a commercial-size kitchen large enough to feed a small army, a private wine cellar twice the size of my apartment, and a patio lined with ornamental cherry blossoms that overlooks the city. We continue mostly in silence, and it's oddly . . . comfortable being alone in the quiet with him, Lucifer occasionally commenting about the architecture or the penthouse's features as each additional floor reveals new luxuries and amenities so extravagant they leave me speechless.

All told, there are two in-ground pools (one indoor and one rooftop), eleven bedrooms, fourteen bathrooms, a billiards room, several offices, a multistory home library, and an in-home gym that could only be described as a private recreational facility. Each of the closets alone is nearly the size of my bedroom.

It's so . . . *much* that I can hardly bring myself to say anything.

"So . . . ," Lucifer says as we approach the top floor. "What do you think?"

I shrug. "It's missing an in-home spa, but otherwise, it's okay, I guess."

Lucifer snorts, and for once I think I've actually amused him. "Quite the comedienne now, aren't you, Charlotte?"

I open my mouth to fire off some witty comeback, but suddenly, his phone rings, and I almost jump out of my skin.

"If you'll excuse me." He removes his phone from his suit coat pocket and presses it to his ear. "Yes?"

He steps away then, leaving me alone.

The moment he's fully out of sight, I sink against the nearest wall, my legs weak and my jaw slack as I silently let out all the expletives I've been holding back for the past half hour. Prior to coming here, I don't think I could have imagined this level of wealth, and I grew up in a church that was basically Six Flags Over Jesus.

It both thrills *and* disgusts me, and yet I still haven't seen even a glimpse of exactly what I'd hoped to see on this little tour.

The dark truth behind the facade. The man behind the mask.

At first glance, Lucifer is nothing more than a decadently rich billionaire, an A-list celebrity businessman, separate but fundamentally no different from the rest of us.

I don't believe that for a second.

I stand there for a few moments, trying and failing to listen in on his conversation. Around the corner, I can hear his muffled voice deep in discussion. His tone strengthens as he commands whatever poor soul happens to be on the other end of the line. I glance around, and my eyes fall to a single darkened hallway that we haven't explored.

Slowly, I step toward it, glancing over my shoulder, afraid he might catch me, but he told me I could explore. So where's the harm in it?

Steeling my confidence, I stroll toward the hall, surprised when no automated lights flick on overhead. I tiptoe toward the cracked door that waits at the end. A soft yellow glow escapes around the frame's edges, almost like he left it this way on purpose. Like he's daring me to go in.

I wouldn't put it past him.

I place my hand on the door handle, hesitating only for a moment before curiosity gets the better of me, and I step inside.

My heart races as I take in the room before me.

I've never seen anything like it, and yet it doesn't take a genius to know that this is where the *real* Lucifer spends his days.

Lucifer's playroom boasts every kind of kinky toy and contraption I could imagine, not that I've spent much time dwelling on it. But now, as I glance around the room, I picture every sinful detail, every wicked deed. There are several structures and swings that I'm not sure how you would use, but with the rest, it's easy enough to guess.

Hooks filled with kink paraphernalia line the wall, everything from soft, downy feathers to handcuffs, chains, riding crops, whips. A plush armchair sits on a dais in the middle of the room, its black leather making it look like a throne fit for a king.

Or someone with all the power of a god.

"Do you like it?" Lucifer's voice wraps around me, startling me a little.

"It's . . . comprehensive," I say, struggling to find the right words.

I scan the room, trying hard not to imagine all the things he's done here. Things he might do to me if I asked him. I flush. "If you're into this sort of thing, that is."

Which I'm not, I remind myself . . .

Am I?

He tsk-tsks, like he's disappointed in me. "Now, now, Charlotte. There's no kink shaming here."

He follows my gaze to the throne in the center of the room before crossing the space to stand beside it. "The devil's chair." His hands are casually tucked in his suit coat pockets as he glances between me and the dais, a devious grin on his face, as if I've revealed something by allowing my eyes to linger there. "Go on, then." He nods toward it. "Take your place."

Before I can change my mind, I step forward, and the next thing I know, Lucifer's hand is in mine, the energy of his touch pulsing through me as he guides me up and onto the dais.

I settle into his chair eagerly.

I have a clear view of the whole room from here, his dark, sinful kingdom lying at my feet.

"How do you feel, Charlotte?" His words are a hushed, tempting whisper. A literal devil on my shoulder, but he doesn't touch me. He doesn't have to.

His otherness does it for him. It wraps around me, hot and suffocating until my breath becomes shallow, needy.

"I feel . . ." The words tumble from my lips, fully within my control, and yet . . . not. Like he's unleashed some dark part of me I never knew existed. "I feel powerful." My hands grip the chair's plush arms as my gaze darts to his.

There's a fire in Lucifer's eyes, that hint of amber I so rarely see.

But it's his words that taunt me, whispering in my ear and tempting me further into his dark spell. "And what will you do with that power, little dove?"

"I'll use it," I say.

I don't even hesitate.

"Naturally." He grins like that's exactly the answer he wanted from me, but I'm too caught up in the rush of power consuming me to truly recognize that he's the one in control. "Go on then, take it," he whispers. "Take what's yours."

My eyes snap to his, that darkness inside me strengthening.

"On your knees," I command, lifting my chin toward him.

Something dark flashes in his expression then, something like pleasure.

Lucifer grins wickedly. "With pleasure, my queen."

He drops to his knees before me, one of his hands coming to rest on the smooth skin of my calf. The moment his skin touches mine, I turn molten. My legs fall open from where I'd crossed them at the knee until I'm spread wide. One of his hands grips the inside of my thigh, hard enough to leave bruises, but the bite of pain beneath the pleasure thrills me.

"What shall I do now, Miss Bellefleur?" His words take on a dangerous edge, a subtle intoxicating hiss. He dips his head lower, and even through the material of my shorts, I feel the heat of his mouth on me. "What would you do with me?"

The question seems to hum inside me, rattling in my skull, but it's the reminder of what I really am to him that brings me back to myself.

Miss Bellefleur.

I'm no more than a paid employee.

"Nothing." I sneer.

Abruptly, I try to snap my legs closed, but the width of his shoulders stops me.

Casting me a vicious smirk, Lucifer slowly moves to stand, his hand on my thigh brushing dangerously close to my center, so close I can't help but shiver.

I lean toward him, drawn to his touch. Even with the spell broken, the energy between us is magnetic, and the movement isn't lost. To him or me.

And I hate myself for it.

"You're a dangerous little creature, aren't you?"

At his full height, we're nearly eye level now as he looks at me.

I lift my chin. "I scratch and bite."

"You'll crawl and beg, too, by the time I'm through with you." He grips my chin roughly as he takes in my flushed skin, the shallow rise and fall of my chest. "As soon as I get inside that pretty little head of yours."

My jaw tightens, and though I'm not certain what he means, I vow right then and there that I won't give him the satisfaction.

No matter how he tempts me.

"Let me go, Lucifer. This wasn't part of our deal."

"Pity." Lucifer watches me for a beat, his eyes never leaving mine, before he finally steps away, allowing me the space I need to scurry down from the dais.

But as I follow him out of the playroom and back to the main floor, I can't help but glance over my shoulder, letting my gaze linger on his chair momentarily, remembering how powerful I felt there. And for some dark reason, I can't help but think that's exactly what he wanted to show me.

CHAPTER SEVENTEEN

Lucifer

"Why am I here, Lucifer?"

The elevator deposits us on the bottom floor of the penthouse, and I exit first. "Don't tell me you forgot about our little agreement, Charlotte."

"Of course not." She follows me without prompting.

Already so well trained she doesn't even notice how readily she obeys me.

My penthouse is still mostly empty, save for the two of us, most of the limited staff I keep having been dismissed for the day hours ago, and considering the little trick I just pulled inside my playroom, she's acutely aware of it. Her eyes dart around the space as she fights not to wring her hands. As if someone among the staff could save her from me. But I don't intend to hurt her, at least not physically, and there are far worse ways to break a person.

I'm known for my creativity.

"Then surely you know what's in store for this evening," I say.

She seems unaware of the dark turn of my thoughts but, of course, she can't possibly know how restrained I'm being.

I could have pushed her harder in there, bared her soul *and* eaten that pretty little pussy she offered me so willingly. But I'm not done toying with her just yet. I enjoy our game of cat and mouse immensely.

"No, actually. I don't. I haven't looked at my phone for several days."

"Sounds like someone's been neglecting their duties."

"You don't pay me to read the gossip magazines for you anymore."

"You're right. I pay you for whatever suits me." I turn toward her then, stopping abruptly as we reach the foyer. "Which is why you have an appointment here with Xzander Malone in"—I check my Patek Philippe watch—"three minutes."

The penthouse doorbell rings right on cue, and one of my few remaining staff members comes out of the woodwork to open it, allowing a whole team of designers and stylists to flood in.

"Hello, darling." I exchange cheek kisses and rapid pleasantries in French with Sophie, my personal stylist, as the rest of her and Xzander's teams file in. Sophie glances in Charlotte's direction as if she expects me to introduce her, but I wave her off quickly.

The others give us a wide berth the moment they look at me.

"So, this is your plan? To dress me up like I'm some kind of human Barbie doll?"

"Don't be so dramatic. Xzander's an up-and-coming revelation in the fashion industry. You'll love him." I continue to greet each of the staff as they enter. "We're having cocktails tonight. You'll need to be dressed for the occasion."

She scoffs. "Cocktails weren't part of our agreement."

I shoot her an amused look. "Oh, Charlotte, our agreement is whatever I choose it to be."

I'm right, of course, and I watch her eyes narrow in frustration as she realizes it.

So feisty.

Several racks of designer clothes are wheeled past, and her eyes widen a little more with each passing one. I may be richer than God, but no one goes to these kinds of lengths for a simple cocktail hour, not even me, and Charlotte is smart enough to recognize that.

"You took my idea." Her jaw drops. "The foundation opening."

Her gaze sweeps over me, taking in my three-piece Armani suit as she puts two and two together. Claude truly outdid himself this time. The fit is even more stunning than usual.

"You're debuting to the press tonight?"

A pulse of grim frustration courses through me. "Correction: *we're* debuting to the press. Do try to keep up." I look in a nearby mirror, straightening my suit coat and adjusting my cuff links as another one of my staff emerges.

"Shall I have Dagon ready the car, sir?"

I pause for a moment, considering. "I think I'll take the Aston Martin today, actually."

I'm feeling a little more reckless than usual.

I glance toward Charlotte.

He nods, quickly retrieving the keys for me.

"And if I don't play along?"

Charlotte draws my attention toward her again. Her lips are pursed, and she's giving me that defiant little look she gets that makes me want to bend her over my knee.

My cock stiffens.

Oh, I'm going to enjoy breaking this one immensely.

I lift a brow.

"What happens if I don't cooperate?" she repeats.

I step into her space, lowering my voice. "I'm happy to file that libel suit now if you'd rather. Just say the word. My lawyers assure me the statute of limitations is up to a year."

"A year?" Her eyes bulge, making the fucking starburst that encircles her irises even more apparent. "That's how long you plan to keep up this charade?"

I catch a lock of her hair, stilling her instantly. She's like soft clay in my palm, so pliable and eager. "No, Charlotte. You're mine for as long as I need." I release her, nodding to the attendant, who hands me my sunglasses before I dismiss him.

"Don't you think it's fair we agree on an end date?"

I scoff. "I'm the devil. Fair isn't in my vocabulary."

She scowls, clearly done playing games with me. "So, you're just like your Father, then? Keeping people under your thumb with no guarantee of a reward."

My shoulders stiffen.

"Don't get cheeky. It doesn't suit you." My lips tighten into a thin line. Any mention of my Father instantly puts me in a foul mood. "We'll end it at the Met Gala." I brush out the door, heading for the elevator.

I have places to be, and babysitting this little human isn't on the list.

No matter how tempting she may be.

She pauses momentarily, counting under her breath like she's calculating the date before she races after me. "The Met Gala takes place the first Monday of May. That's over nine months from now!"

"Good counting, darling." I wave a dismissive hand. "I'll move it to September this year."

She stops suddenly, blinking. "You'll . . . move it to September?" she repeats slowly.

I shrug. "I'm on the benefit committee."

It's a minor inconvenience, really.

"Of course you are." She buries her face in her hands.

I tilt my head, watching her. I don't know why it's *this* that seems to alert her to the extent of my power, but something about that irks me.

Or perhaps it's that my little trick in the playroom didn't work.

Fate hasn't been favoring me lately.

I press the elevator button, leisurely placing my hands in my pockets as the door opens. I step inside, flashing one last smooth grin at her. "Till this evening, little dove."

She gapes at me. As if I haven't just promised to move one of the city's biggest events of the year on a whim, and for her benefit, no less.

"Where are you going?"

"My brother has a debut present for me." I smirk.

"And what about our agreement? Don't you think we should establish some ground rules?" She catches the door and holds it. "In writing."

I glance at my watch. Already I'm running late, and while there's not a person in this city who wouldn't eagerly wait for me, my brother included, I pride myself on being punctual.

"I would think the house rules are abundantly clear." I lift my sunglasses as I lean into her space, crowding her against the elevator door. My voice drops low as I give her a taste of what she's clearly wanting. *Me.*

She softens for me instantly. It's almost too easy.

"House rules. I tell you what to do. You say 'yes, sir.' Are we clear, little dove?"

"Yes, sir," she whispers, sweet enough it nearly makes me purr.

My cock twitches, even as the corner of my mouth curves.

This human will be the death of me. If I'm not careful.

I pull away, and she shakes her head as if coming out of a haze before she crosses her arms. "You can't expect me to perform well in front of the press without meeting some basic conditions, Lucifer."

I lift a brow, intrigued.

"I want to keep my job. At Apollyon. At least give me that. And no physical intimacy required, at least when we're not in front of the cameras. Like you said."

I can't begin to fathom why she would want to keep her job when I'm already paying her for her current role—quite generously—or why she wouldn't want to sleep with me—that sultry look in her eye when I had her in my chair said otherwise—but I know a good trade in my favor when I see one.

"Done," I growl. "And allow me to make *my* rules crystal clear." I tick off a finger. "One: smile for cameras, darling. Two . . ." I tick off another as I close the distance between us. "Remember you are mine to command."

She bites her lower lip. Like she's resisting the urge to say "yes, sir" again.

We'll be fucking by week's end. I'm certain.

"And three?" she asks innocently.

I lean in, my gaze raking over her, enough to stop her breath short, and for a moment, I make her think I might kiss her again before suddenly I jam my finger into one of the elevator buttons, overriding where she's stopped the door from closing.

"Lucifer!" she shrieks, the door starting to close on her.

"Rule number three." I smirk as I watch her struggle just before the doors close. "Never forget who I am."

CHAPTER EIGHTEEN

Lucifer

"You're late." Astaroth's mouth presses into a thin slash as I approach, making him appear uncharacteristically annoyed with me.

"You're never late when you're the most significant person in the room."

Astaroth scoffs as he passes me a cigarette from where he's leaning against the side of the brick building.

I place it between my lips and allow him to light it before I inhale deeply, the sweet smoke filling my lungs. "I had important business to attend to."

"Toying with your little human?" Astaroth shifts where he stands.

His face betrays nothing, but it's the *way* he says it that alerts me.

"Are you . . . jealous, Astaroth?" I grin wickedly.

Astaroth grumbles as he waves a dismissive hand. "I find her annoying."

"She's a twenty-three-year-old human. Of course she's annoying." My gaze flicks over him. "She'd likely say the same of you."

Astaroth grunts before taking another drag.

"And what you call toying, I call strategy." My grin widens, knowing full well I'm baiting him. "I put her in the chair."

Astaroth perks up, his eyes lighting. "And?"

"It was just a quick taste, really." I take one last pull before stubbing the remainder out beneath my Louis Vuittons, but Astaroth lowers his chin. "A gentleman doesn't kiss and tell, Astaroth."

"In other words, you found nothing."

"Rather bold tonight, aren't we?" I lift a brow, and he looks away then, capitulating as I straighten the cuffs of my suit coat. "I'll have to get more creative, it seems."

Astaroth grumbles once more. "I don't like this. I don't like this at all."

I thump a hand onto his chest. "Save it for our guests tonight. Shall we?" I lead the way toward the door, Astaroth flanking me.

With Charlotte and I debuting, the paparazzi will be out in full force tonight, which means instead of a pleasant little jaunt to the Meatpacking District, where most of my brother's businesses reside, Astaroth and I are outside an old, abandoned shipyard in godforsaken Queens.

We enter through the side, the rusted door creaking from where it now barely hangs on its hinges. The industrial beams of the old building reek of mold and decay, and a single light bulb hangs from an old drop-cap chain atop the ceiling. We make our way deep into the building's belly until we reach the far side, where we exit out into the shipyard again, accessing a part of the yard where several old shipping containers wait. The brine of the sea rends the air.

My brother's men flank one of the containers.

I nod, and one of them pounds on the door for me.

It takes several minutes before my brother finally emerges, his forehead damp and sweaty. He takes the cigarette I offer before he wipes the sweat from his brow with one rolled-up work sleeve. "You know I don't like to share." Gluttony's gunmetal gaze meets mine.

"It would appear so."

I only received the call that Beelzebub's men had managed to get their hands on the hired thug who murdered Paris Starr this morning, but from the looks of it, he's been holding on to the little rascal for far longer.

Z's broad frame is underlined with a brawny kind of muscle that speaks to the long hours he spends toiling away in his many kitchens. The life of a celebrity chef isn't exactly all glamour these days, but the connections it's given him in the food and beverage industry have benefited me greatly.

Though most of his income comes from his large e-commerce investments, anyway.

"You should have called sooner." My gaze flicks over him, taking in his disheveled appearance. It's easy to guess why I'm the best torturer among us.

I've had considerably more practice.

Z takes a long, luxurious drag before exhaling. "It's my club, Lucifer."

"And yet, somehow, it's still *my* name in the papers."

Z grins darkly, as if that amuses him.

For all his many talents and Food Network appearances, my younger brother would much rather exist in the background than have his face in the media regularly. Z's most at home in his kitchens or out on the streets, tempting humanity where they choose to eat and drink. It's that fact that makes him far more insidious than the glitter and glamour of his twin, our beloved sister, Greed.

"Which is why I'm offering to *share* him with you." Z shudders a little at the word before he claps me on the shoulder. "You know that doesn't come naturally to me."

I roll my eyes, stripping off my suit coat and slipping on the leather gloves that Astaroth hands me before I fasten the buckles over my wrists. "In other words, you've had your fill and now I get to dine on your leftovers. Or clean your mess, as it were."

Z's relaxed expression grows tense as I draw near.

"You forget, dear brother, that everything you are, everything you have, belongs to me," I hiss. "Mind your leash." I step back and finish strapping on my gloves, then nod to one of Z's men. "Shall we?"

They glance briefly toward him, uncertain about taking orders from me in front of my brother, but I can hear their rapid breaths, see the beads of sweat on their foreheads.

They fear me.

My brother nods in agreement, and one of his demons white-knuckles the door as he opens it.

I pause, glancing one last time toward Z. "I look forward to seeing what culinary creations you and your staff have in store for us tonight."

My brother inclines his head, lifting the flask he removed from his pocket in acknowledgment.

Astaroth passes my blade to me, and I slip inside the old shipping container without a second thought as he closes the door behind me. I prefer to do my work up close and personal.

It allows me to enjoy it more thoroughly.

The human strapped to my brother's chair has already been worked over for several days, or so it seems. The air inside the shipping container reeks of excrement and vomit, and though there's no physical signs of it, I know he's been tortured. Deprivation of food and drink, Z's signature, among other things. Humiliation. Starvation. Shame.

Torture is an art, and the best among us can do so without leaving a mark.

But I didn't come here to be so restrained this evening.

I pull out the vacant chair Z left, placing the seat so its back faces me. I drop down into it and examine the knife in my hands before I look toward the sweat-covered human. His lips are parched, and from his gaunt face, he hasn't eaten in nearly a week.

But that means little to me.

A vein in my neck throbs. My hatred for humanity runs deep.

"Another well-dressed thug," he rasps.

I grin. "Your words. Not mine."

"I would have thought this is below your pay grade." He looks over my suit.

"I find a personal touch to be most effective, actually." I watch him carefully. "You murdered a man in cold blood. He who casts the first stone and all."

"What are you going to do?" He coughs, finally lifting his head toward me.

"A better question for you to ask would be: 'What can *you* do for *me*?'" I flip my knife about in my hands, its blade glinting in the single fluorescent lantern sitting in the corner. "That kind of initiative puts me in a better mood, you see."

"I don't give a rat's ass what I can do for you or anybody. You're gonna kill me either way." His lip curls.

"See, that's where you lack foresight." I stand from my chair, circling my prey. "You see, what matters now is what I do *before* I kill you, and you'll find I'm not nearly as generous as Gluttony." I round in front of him again and give him a little glimpse of the knowledge he's missing, of exactly where he'll be headed once he and I are through here.

A look at my true face.

His response is pure animal. Making him rabid with fear.

Hellfire tends to have that effect on humanity.

His eyes widen, his nostrils flaring as he begins to thrash wildly, straining against his hold. "Please," he begs. "Please! I . . . I didn't know it was you. I didn't know you'd be involved. I swear it." A fresh sheen of sweat coats his clammy skin.

I tilt my head slightly, considering him.

"Would it surprise you to know that I believe you?" I step closer, using the smooth surface of my blade to forcibly lift his chin.

He slams his eyes shut, refusing to look at me. Like a child hiding beneath their covers in the dark. Though the true monsters answer to me.

"There's few among your kind who'd dare cross me willingly, and you don't strike me as having the kind of ironclad balls required for that." I release him, my blade falling away from his throat, and he whimpers. The smell of fresh piss follows. "So, tell me, Antoine. What exactly did Azmodeus hire you to do?"

He shakes his head vigorously, still refusing to look at me. "It wasn't Az who hired me, man. I swear it."

My blade moves so fast that it comes as a shock to both him and me. Blood pools across his cheek as he screams, bucking wildly. I didn't recognize I cared so deeply about *exactly* which of my siblings is responsible for this little situation—about which of them is using Charlotte as a means to tempt me—until now.

I don't appreciate being fucked with.

"Don't toy with me, or you'll find out how little patience I have for humanity."

"All right. All right," he cries. "Like I told your brother, I'm on Az's payroll. That much is true. But he . . . he didn't hire me to kill Paris Starr, man. I swear it."

"Then who?"

He keeps his eyes squeezed shut, shaking his head at me. "I don't know. I didn't get a name. You know how it works on the streets. They call him the Handler. Said he worked for one of your siblings. Paid in cash. Didn't say who. And Az was already gunning for your place. I needed to move up the ranks, you know? I figured two birds, one stone."

Abruptly, I kick the vacant chair out of the way, and he cowers at the rough metallic screech. "Bully for you." I flip the knife in my hands. "But unfortunately, I'm growing tired of this conversation, and today, I have places to be."

His eyes fly open again. "So that . . . so that means you'll let me go?"

The flicker of hope in his eyes is tragic, really.

I chuckle. "Oh, no. I have no intention of letting you go. At least not while you're alive, anyway."

I move so quick he doesn't have time to gasp or flinch before I have him pinned against the wall by his throat, the chair he's still tied to dangling underneath him as he stares down the end of my blade.

"But whether I kill you now or you die gasping and alone in your bed when you can no longer stand in a mere thirty years' time, what you humans fail to understand is that you belong to me either way."

Antoine screams as my blade bites into the first bit of flesh I plan to remove from him today.

"All I have to do is wait."

CHAPTER NINETEEN

Charlotte

By the time Sophie, Lucifer's personal stylist, has finished with me—several *hours* later—I'm all caught up on the media coverage from the past few days and prepared for the foundation opening. Well, mentally prepared, at least.

No matter how fictional, the news coverage today served as a welcome distraction, considering Sophie has either sugared, waxed, or plucked almost every inch of my body as she attempted to make me over from my forehead all the way down to my toes.

I might have screamed a few times.

To be fair, I didn't even know people could wax certain . . . *places*, and even though it's been hours, well, my asshole still hurts, to say the least, and I haven't even begun to get dressed yet.

"Ne touche pas." Sophie swats my hand for what must be the hundredth time since she first began letting my foils set.

"It itches," I whine.

The chemicals have been sitting in my hair long enough they're starting to irritate, and it's not as if I'm really used to any of this. I was never allowed even basic highlights back home. I was supposed to be happy with what God gave me.

Never mind that God's gift was a boring, mousy blond.

Sophie mutters something rapid to her assistant in French, tsk-tsking and shaking her head, though she does start to remove the foils and wash the excess dye from my hair finally.

"Don't mind Sophie. Pain is practically her love language." The voice comes from a Black man in a brightly patterned outfit.

He's a new arrival. I'm certain.

There's been so many people in and out of Lucifer's penthouse throughout the afternoon that all the faces started to blend eventually, but I would have remembered him. The bright colors he wears make me smile, his outfit and matching eye shadow both joyously camp and chic.

Sophie shoots him an annoyed look. "Beauty knows no pain," she says in heavily accented English.

"Except Brazilian waxing," I say.

Our new guest snorts.

"I'm Xzander." He extends a gloriously ring-covered hand toward me.

"Charlotte." We shake, but I'm careful to keep my fingers spread. My nails are still drying, and Sophie is nothing short of overprotective of her work. "You must be the designer."

I looked up Xzander's work on my phone after Lucifer mentioned him. Though there's been absolutely no sign of my boss-turned-so-called-fiancé since he swept out of here earlier, abandoning me.

Good riddance.

"In the flesh." Xzander gestures to himself. He's wearing a metallic gold eye shadow that catches in the light, and I don't know what it is about him, but I can see why Lucifer chose him.

I like him instantly.

"So how do you want to look tonight, Charlotte? Fun? Flirty?" Xzander wiggles his brows as Sophie begins snipping at the ends of my hair. "Or are we going for sexy?"

Sexy? Me?

Not a chance.

I look down at my lap, taking in my fresh nails and manicured toes that peek out from beneath the black cloth Sophie's draped over me. Sexy is not me. Sexy is a woman who was never forced to wear a "true love waits" ring, and who never struggled to locate her own clit until recently.

For a moment, my breath hitches, and I drop my chin to my chest, though I know from talking with my therapist that the true shame isn't mine.

"Honestly?" I push the thoughts aside.

Xzander nods. "Honestly."

"I . . . just want to look like me."

He grins. "So, like the woman who's ensnared the devil?"

I laugh. *If only . . .*

"More like the woman stupid enough to get herself ensnared *by* the devil," I correct. "Horns and all."

Xzander lifts a brow, though he doesn't prod me for details. He gestures around the penthouse like he's missing something before his gaze settles on me. "And you're telling me you don't want to be here?" He says it as if that's hard to believe.

I move to shake my head a little, causing Sophie to rattle off something in French that I think has to do with me being still. "It's complicated."

Xzander takes a seat on a nearby chair. "Diva, every good story is."

I glance out the window to where Madison Square Park waits below. The last two weeks have felt like I've been living in a dream, or a nightmare, depending on which part you choose. I still don't know who sent that press release, or who would even want to, for that matter.

But I intend to find out.

"I just . . . don't want to be a pawn in his game, that's all."

"But it's more than that." Xzander's eyes narrow as if he can see right through me. "You want to make him squirm, don't you? Regret messing with your heart?"

I snort. *My heart?*

"Something like that," I admit slowly.

"How about this?" Xzander stands, circling me, like he's mentally taking in my measurements. "How do you want to feel tonight? Who do you want to be?"

I glimpse toward the window again, watching the sunset start to fade over the city below as I think back over the last couple weeks. To Lucifer. Jax. Imani. Every person who left an impression on me. To be honest, I've been asking myself the same thing. Every day since I escaped that hellhole where my father left me. And to think that after growing up under his roof, I thought there were no bad choices ahead of me. That things couldn't get any worse.

I simply traded one villain for another.

"I want to be the kind of woman who looks like she belongs. Like I'm not just his arm candy, or a mouse that's not worthy of being by his side," I say softly. "I want to look like I'm formidable, like I'm not just some passive queen."

"Now *that's* something I can work with." Xzander smiles, finally shooing Sophie off, so he can begin his work. "Though clearly you don't play chess, Charlotte."

I lift one sculpted brow. "Why's that?"

Xzander grins mischievously. "Because any good player knows, the queen's the most powerful piece."

It's another two hours before I'm fully ready, but when Xzander finally steps back from the boudoir mirror and allows me to look at myself, I struggle to speak. The black dress I'm wearing is simple and elegant, setting off the golden undertones of my summer tan and making it look as if my skin has been lit from within.

The neckline dips scandalously low, and the dark material hugs my every curve, creating a dramatic silhouette, even as the hem seems to defy gravity. There's a slit up my thigh that reveals a daring glimpse of leg, and the color of the material isn't simply black, it's inky.

Like Xzander harvested a little of Lucifer's shadows just for me.

I brush my hands over my hips, and the fabric seems to move with me, taking on a life of its own. And that says nothing for the magic Sophie's worked with my hair and makeup.

I don't even recognize me.

My hair falls down my back in loose waves, the golden highlights and my new extensions giving it a dimension I never could have achieved naturally. My eye makeup is dark, nearly as coal black as my dress, making me look almost sultry. I still look like myself, of course, but everything about me has been enhanced, dialed up past ten and polished like an uncut gemstone turned into a jewel.

It's stunning.

"Lucifer isn't going to know what hit him." Xzander smiles at me in the mirror, where he stands behind me, admiring his work.

My mouth goes a little dry as I take it all in. "I'm . . . not certain I can do this."

Xzander lifts a brow.

I bite the inside of my cheek for a moment, and the smile I give him is tight as I meet his eyes in the mirror. "Hold my own against him, I mean."

I am nothing if not the obedient servant my father made me.

"That doesn't sound like the woman who wrote that press release." Xzander's gaze flicks over me. "You weren't scared of him then. Why now?"

"I . . . didn't realize how much he owned me," I admit. "How much his attention would cost."

"And now that you do"—Xzander passes me a black clutch meant to be paired with my dress as he smiles encouragingly—"what are you going to do about it?"

I smile weakly.

I have a feeling that question is going to plague me for the better part of the evening.

And maybe even into the days and months ahead . . .

But I don't have time to answer it now, so I nod, forcing another tight smile in gratitude as Xzander leads me out of the room, a light quiver igniting in my stomach.

Our task tonight is simple: make the press believe the story Imani has crafted for them. The one where my relationship with Lucifer started as a hot and heavy affair at Gluttony's club two months ago, shortly after I arrived in the city, which she was certain to mention we were reliving the night of Paris Starr's murder. Complete with video footage of both of us coming in and out of the club that night.

A less-than-subtle media alibi, if you ask me.

Imani is good at her job.

According to the tabloids, the whole thing started long before Lucifer ever realized his company planned to hire me. After all, everyone knows junior employees have little to no contact with the founder and CEO. How could he have possibly known?

And the press release?

Little more than a heated lover's spat. High-profile foreplay, really.

All I need to do is play my part and sell it.

To look like I'm madly in love with Lucifer, and he with me.

I'm less confident about that second part.

I'm not even sure he's capable of it.

Lucifer waits for me at the bottom of the penthouse stairs as I descend to the first-floor foyer, his expression unmoving as he watches me. If Xzander expected a shocked reaction from him, there isn't one, but as I draw closer, something in Lucifer's eyes shifts, making them burn like dark coals, and the shadows on the edges of the room seem to move toward me. It's hard to believe this man knelt between my knees earlier this morning, offering to pleasure me.

No matter how hard I try, I can't seem to forget that.

Or the power it gave me.

"Beautiful," Lucifer murmurs as I approach, his smile slowly building as he sweeps his gaze over me. I feel the otherness that surrounds him like a caress. "You look stunning, Charlotte."

The heat that burns through my cheeks irks me. I don't want to enjoy his praise, and yet, I do. I don't even have to fake it.

A part of me craves his attention.

"Shall we?" He extends his arm toward me, the cuffs of his suit coat revealing the white underneath. But as he steps forward, I notice a small drop of crimson along the inner edge.

I open my mouth, prepared to draw attention to it and ask him if it's what it appears to be, but then suddenly my arm is in his and the moment is gone. So fast I almost believe I imagined it as he leads me toward the elevator.

We ride down to the lobby in silence. Neither of us looking at each other.

I take a deep breath to steady myself.

This isn't a game. This is reality, and it's starting to feel that way to me.

And I'm fully aware of what the consequences will be if I don't play my part.

When we step off the elevator, Lucifer takes my arm again, and the attendant opens the door for us as Lucifer leads me out onto the street. Lucifer's Town Car sits at the curb, Dagon already waiting. Dagon opens the car door as soon as he sees us, but it's the sudden flashing lights that shock me. The presence of the paparazzi where there were none only a few hours ago.

They shout for me, quickly surrounding us. "Lucifer! Lucifer! Charlotte!"

"Eyes forward, Charlotte," Lucifer hisses as he ushers me into the vehicle.

Dagon closes the door behind us, but the lights continue to flash, the crowd of photographers yelling our names, even though we're alone again.

"That's only a fraction of the cameras that will be present at the venue," he says. "Best prepare yourself before we arrive."

I blink, still a little stunned. "I didn't expect them to be so . . ."

"Aggressive? Violent?" he suggests.

He glances in my direction, and suddenly I realize we aren't talking about the paparazzi anymore.

My expression hardens. "I was going to say soulless, actually."

Lucifer smirks, but it's the hellfire in his eyes that really gives him away. He's furious with me. I don't know exactly what I've done to make him so angry, but it doesn't matter.

I *want* him angry with me.

In fact, I crave it.

No matter how fucked up that makes me.

He leans forward, his voice dropping low. "Let's get one thing clear, Charlotte. You're here to play a role. How you feel about that role is of little importance to me."

I lean in, matching his movement. "I never expected anything less from the monster who's imprisoned me."

He huffs. "Quite the gilded cage you're in, no?" This time, his expression is cold as he looks down his nose at me. "Don't blame me for the choices that led you here, little dove. That part was all you."

"And what about you?" I snap as the car begins to move. "You're not innocent in all this."

"I never claimed to be." His eyes narrow.

I don't know why, but his admission shocks me.

Like his words hold more meaning than he's letting on. But I can't put my finger on what exactly.

I don't try to stop myself from watching his face carefully then. The subtle rise and fall of his chest. He keeps his eyes trained toward the front of the car, refusing to look at me, but in that moment, it strikes me that I really don't know anything about Lucifer beyond what the papers and years of Bible study have told me. And until now, I never stopped to question any of it.

If it was true, I mean.

No one ever does.

And there's something almost . . . sad about that, if you ask me.

We continue the rest of the ride in silence, the tightness in my chest that comes with that thought distracting me until finally the car pulls to a stop outside 583 Park Avenue.

My heart pounds hard against my ribs.

Even through the window, the paparazzi are going wild, practically salivating at the opportunity to get a glimpse of the man beside me.

Maybe I'm not the only one in a gilded cage.

"Don't engage with them. Leave that to me," Lucifer says.

Dagon starts to open the door, but I stop Lucifer, placing a hand on his arm as I refuse to break eye contact, and he signals for Dagon to wait briefly.

"So that's it, then? I'm just supposed to stand by your side like a good little pet and do as I'm told?" I don't know what about that makes me so angry. I knew it would be like this, but something about how disappointed I still feel makes me furious.

At how powerless he's made me.

"Isn't that exactly what you want to be? A good girl?" Lucifer tilts my face toward him, bringing my mouth dangerously close to his, and any pity I might have felt for him is lost as his eyes fall to my lips, knowingly making my breath uneasy.

As if to punish me.

"This could be so much more pleasant, if you'd let it be," he whispers.

My mouth waters. My body practically craving it. I have half a mind to give in then. To close the gap between us and just let myself enjoy this ridiculous break from reality. To slip into the obedient role my father trained me for. But I refuse to give him the satisfaction.

"Just tell me what you want me to do, *sir*." My lip curls, and I pull away abruptly.

"That's easy, little dove." Lucifer captures my hand in his own, quickly sliding a black diamond ring onto my finger like I'm a bitch in need of a collar as suddenly, Dagon opens the door, and the lights begin flashing. "Smile for the cameras, darling."

CHAPTER TWENTY

Lucifer

I hate events like this. The lie of human civility. By my hand, half the people in this ballroom could collapse as they choke on the excess drinks they consume, and it would do nothing to tarnish their image of me. So long as I behave as they expect.

I am the monster they made me, after all.

I sip my whisky, not bothering to hide my disinterest as one of the foundation's many donors drones on about the generous donation she gave. It's gauche, really.

The celestial chandeliers cast a starlit glow over the guests. The clink of fine china and the constant hum of conversation mixed with the venue music fills my ears. Every wealthy human donor in this room believes they can buy my favor. Purchase their way out of Hell. A fake escape from their own guilt. From their fear of me.

Funny that it's not me who sends them there.

My attention wanders, and my eyes find Charlotte easily. She's standing on the far side of the ballroom, conversing with another one of the donors, and thanks to the bit of magic Sophie and Xzander worked this evening, she truly is the most beautiful woman in the room.

My brother stands beside her, along with whoever the poor soul is that's currently on his arm. Suddenly, Azmodeus leans over and

Original Sinner

whispers something that's no doubt salacious into Charlotte's ear, and she smiles coyly.

A flash of rage sparks in me.

I may have my doubts as to whether Azmodeus orchestrated whatever this little situation is between Charlotte and me, or the media chaos of Paris Starr's murder, but, like it or not, Charlotte is *mine*, and I won't hesitate to destroy him and half this godforsaken city if Azmodeus doesn't swiftly remove his hand from her—

"She's lovely, you know."

The voice comes from behind me, interrupting my train of thought.

I turn to find my sister grinning at me.

"Your human, I mean." She nods toward Charlotte.

I quickly wave away the donors as I turn toward her. "Greed."

She preens a little at the old name, the pride she takes in it a welcome offering to me, before she steps closer, placing a hand on my arm. "Come now, Lucifer, you know I've always preferred when you call me by my childhood nickname. It makes us feel more like a real family."

A real family? I nearly scoff.

Neither of us has ever known such a thing.

I glance over my sister's voluptuous form. In an emerald-green dress that leaves little to the imagination and barely covers her generous tits, she's come a long way from the neglected cherub she used to be, and she wears her confidence tonight beautifully.

"Mimi doesn't exactly suit you these days." I take another sip of my drink.

"Perhaps you're right. Too diminutive." She waves a hand. "Fine. Mammon, then." She takes my arm in hers, and I allow her to turn us so that Charlotte is in our line of sight once more.

Mammon signals to one of the waiters carrying a tray of canapés.

The waiter hops to and quickly extends the silver tray toward her. She snatches the last prosciutto-wrapped date from the plate and pops it into her mouth, making a delighted, unapologetic noise before brazenly licking her fingers.

"Fetch more of those," she orders the waiter.

Mammon delights in everything, her lifestyle an homage to her true purpose.

It's why, despite dipping her plump fingers into a little of everything, from our brothers' businesses to the fossil fuel industry, she's made such a name for herself with her lifestyle branding. More is better, after all. As the only female among us, the masses both adore and hate her. She and her plus-size figure are a regular media controversy. Because what she sells is an excess of commercial hedonism wrapped in a fantasy of treat-yourself self-love. All of which she's convinced her many followers is necessary, of course.

"Z outdid himself this time, truly," she says of her twin, licking her lips before she turns her attention back toward Charlotte and me. "So, tell me, brother, is it true? Are you really in love with that little snack of a human?" Her gaze flits over Charlotte appreciatively. "She's adorable. I might have had her for myself if you hadn't already called dibsies."

"We're madly in love," I say flatly.

"Are you?" Mammon bats her long lashes at me as she smirks wickedly.

I look away, trying to mask my annoyance with this particular line of questioning. "You know better than to believe everything you read in the papers, Mimi."

"Do I?" Her eyes widen, all faked innocence, before she shrugs. "I'd rather hoped it was true, honestly."

My attention turns back toward Charlotte then, lingering on her momentarily. I don't know exactly what it is about my fiancée that continues to draw me to her, but I intend to make it my business to know.

I'll see the darker parts of her eventually. Given time.

"Fame is a blank check these days," Mammon says from beside me, following my gaze as a devious little smile rounds her face. "One she'll want to cash sooner or later."

I intend to tell my sister that blank check or not, Charlotte belongs to me, but then my fiancée throws back her head, laughing uproariously at one of Azmodeus's jokes in a way that lights up the whole room, and the thought is lost to me.

Something inside my chest constricts, and whatever it is, I don't like it.

Suddenly I find I want to torture my brother, exactly as I did his employee this evening.

Slowly.

"If you'll excuse me." I break free from my sister's clutches and stride across the room.

Charlotte holds a near-empty glass of champagne in her hand. Her third, if I've been counting correctly, which I have. Enough to make her loose lipped and vulnerable, yet not drunk exactly, though at first, she doesn't look toward me.

Her eyes find mine moments before I reach her, as if she can sense my approach.

My hand falls to her lower back, and I pull her in to my side swiftly, reveling in the way she softens against me. It's enough to make any man grin, even me, at the thought of all the wicked things she'll allow me to do to her this evening.

She's practically begging for it.

"Brother," I say, letting a hint of hellfire spark in my eyes as I cast a scathing look toward Azmodeus.

A less-than-subtle warning.

The atmosphere in the group goes cold. Message received.

No one touches what belongs to me.

"If you gentlemen would excuse me, I need to borrow my future bride for a moment," I say tersely.

"Of course." Azmodeus inclines his head toward Charlotte, as he and his partner for this evening disappear into the party's thrall along with the others.

I quickly lead Charlotte away with me.

When we're finally out of earshot, I release her, and she turns to me, swaying a little, as I give her a cold look. "What kind of game do you think you're playing tonight, darling?"

She lifts a brow. "Game?" She steps closer, lowering her voice to a whisper. "I'm playing a role. *Exactly* like you told me."

"And apparently, that role includes batting your pretty little lashes and giving come-fuck-me eyes to my brother?"

She sputters, gaping at me. "I was doing what you said. Smiling for the cameras, remember?" She watches my expression, and suddenly her eyes grow wide, like she's seeing a whole new side of me she wasn't aware existed. "Wait. Are you . . . jealous, Lucifer?"

I scoff. "Don't be ridiculous. You simply need to sell this believably."

She crosses her arms. "And what exactly did you have in mind, *sir*?"

She says it with such disrespect I have half a mind to put her over my knee right then and there. Exhibitionism isn't beyond me.

My voice drops low. "What I expect, little dove, is a tad more effort on your part."

"A little more *effort*?" Her voice goes shrill on the last word. Enough to draw attention. She notices the faces looking at us, smiling at the media personnel present as if everything is fine before she steps closer, muttering through her teeth, "I've been fake laughing at your brother's crude jokes all night, and you expect a little more effort?"

She fakes a grin as a nearby photographer passes, but the fury in her eyes is clear.

I don't know why the fact that she doesn't actually enjoy Azmodeus's humor pleases me, but it sates my wounded pride all the same. I grip her by the back of the neck, drawing her to me. "Yes, I do. If you intend to continue with our little arrangement."

She huffs, shaking her head. "And what do you expect me to do? Follow you around like some lovesick puppy?" She gives me a dazed, tipsy look.

The idea holds more appeal than she intends it to.

"Careful."

"Or what?"

I lower my voice. "We may be in a crowded room, but you're throwing matches at a gas tank, darling. You could get burned easily."

She pulls back slightly, hurt in her eyes. "That's all I'll ever be to you, isn't it? A pawn for you to use?"

I blink. I have no idea where the sentiment comes from, but still, she steps close, placing both hands on my chest like she means to embrace me. The alcohol she's had makes her brazen as she whispers, "You may be able to force me to be compliant, but that doesn't mean you've earned my respect. *Sir.*"

She tears herself away from me with a haughty little huff, gliding toward the dessert table as several members of the press eye me suspiciously.

I curse under my breath.

"Trouble in paradise?" Greed asks, appearing at my side once more.

I stride past her toward the bar. "Fuck off, sister."

Paradise would require she actually care for me.

I order another drink before Astaroth finds me.

"Do you need me to get her under control?" he mutters into my ear. "I could make her behave easily."

I see the glint of one of his blades flash.

"No." I shake my head, my eyes darting to Charlotte once more as I sip my drink. "No, leave her to me." I glance toward Astaroth. He cleans up quickly. "How's our friend?"

"All squared away." Astaroth nods. "He'll send a strong message come morning."

"Good." I watch as Charlotte disappears into the party. "Good."

CHAPTER TWENTY-ONE

Charlotte

My jaw clenches, and I sway a little. I'm filled with righteous fury as I down my fourth flute of champagne. As if having to smile for all the cameras, and Lucifer, as I walked the red carpet on his arm wasn't enough, I've had to fake interest in every dull conversation presented to me. The company I've been forced to endure tonight would be more than enough to make even the most docile of people disgusted.

No wonder Lucifer is such a control freak.

I snatch another champagne flute from a passing tray. My fifth and what probably should be my final, if I'm honest. Everyone who's anyone in New York City is here, all the who's who of the city present to witness Lucifer's debut . . . with me. Despite my silent dismissal of the press as we entered, there's a definite interest in who I am and what exactly I'm doing on Lucifer's arm. Like Xzander said, I'm the woman who ensnared the devil, after all. Or at least that's what the press thinks.

I look around the party dazedly.

I expected to feel a bit more pressure being among the city's glittering elite, but Xzander really did work some magic into my outfit.

All eyes are on me. But not with judgment or censure. It's like I belong here.

At least temporarily.

I sip my champagne, watching the other guests' movements. I'm not usually much of a drinker—my father's church never even used real communion wine—but at the moment, I could use something harder. Though I need to leave here standing up.

I sigh and abandon my nearly full glass, handing it to a passing waiter who nods and whisks it away for me as I begin to search for water instead.

"Already calling it quits?"

A voluptuous blond woman approaches, and though she looks different in person, I recognize her from my Apollyon presentation immediately. Greed.

"You shouldn't allow my brother to get to you, you know. He insists upon controlling everything." She waves a dismissive hand before stepping closer and lowering her voice a little. "I find a bit more freedom to be liberating."

"I'd imagine so." More is Greed's thing, after all.

I take in the full image of her. Greed's body and her outfit are an homage to excess. To overindulging. Making her the perfect mixture of over the top and alluring.

"I don't believe we've had the pleasure of meeting yet." She extends a manicured hand toward me. "Mammon, but you can call me Mimi."

"Mimi?"

"It was Lucifer's nickname for me when we were children, or new to existing, as it were, though he'll never admit it, of course. Not publicly."

It's hard to imagine Lucifer as a child, or a . . . cherub, I guess?

Anything other than the man he is currently.

"He really should be a little more grateful for the things he has, you know."

"I wouldn't expect you to know much about gratitude," I mutter before I can stop myself.

Shocked, I clap a hand over my own mouth, but Greed simply throws back her head and laughs at me. Maybe I *have* had too much to drink this evening.

"Oh, I can see why he's so taken with you." Mammon reaches into the matching emerald clutch she carries, removing an elegant-looking business card. "If you ever get tired of him bossing you around, call me." She tucks it into my cleavage before I can stop her, admiring me appreciatively, and then she's gone.

I blow out a rough breath.

"Don't worry. She tends to have that effect on people." This time, the breathy, melodic voice comes from a dark-haired woman scouring the dessert table behind me. "Dissatisfaction is kind of her brand. There's always more to be had with Greed."

I nod. "Of course."

She glances across the table, extending a hand toward me with a grin. "Evie."

"Charlotte."

She smiles, her eyes lighting up. "Oh, I know. You're all anyone can talk about."

"Lucifer is, you mean," I say, correcting her.

She nods, still smiling at me in a prolonged way. "Oh, well, him too, of course."

I lift a brow, trying to place her. "Are you with the press?"

She shakes her head. "Me? Oh no. My father is one of the richest men in the city." She lowers her voice. "Russian Mafia." She winks.

I blink. I must have misheard her. "Excuse me?"

She laughs, suddenly rounding the table and lacing her arm in mine like we're besties. "Don't look so scared, silly. Everyone's a criminal at these things. What better way to cover up your crimes than charity?" She looks out toward the partygoers and sighs dreamily. "Though you didn't hear that from me." She abandons my side, floating back to the dessert table to pop a chocolate-covered cherry into her mouth. She squeals as she claps her hands. "Oh, that's good."

I quirk my head. "So, if that's true, what brings you here?"

She shrugs dismissively. "My father wants to buy Lucifer's favor, of course. Just like everyone else here. And I'm one of the city's favorite socialites, so he uses me as leverage." She continues to grin, but then her voice loses its dreamy quality. "I'm his pretty little pawn. Though you'd know that if you'd been here as long as they say you have."

She glances over me, appraising me coldly.

Maybe Lucifer was right.

Maybe I *am* failing in my role tonight.

I open my mouth to try and deflect her, but she beats me to the punch.

"What about you?" she says suddenly, her voice taking on that breathless, childlike tone once again. "Why are *you* here?"

I bristle. At first appearance, Evie may appear flighty, but clearly, she sees right through me, and she knows as well as I do that I don't belong here.

"I'm Lucifer's fiancée," I say, mimicking her and forcing a laugh. "Why wouldn't I be here?"

She steps around the far side of the table to join me. "You don't have to lie to me, you know. I know a trapped woman when I see one."

My brows shoot up. "Excuse me?"

"We all have that look in our eyes." She gestures to my face. "I do too. Like I'm desperate for someone to love me. But how can we be desperate for something we've never really experienced? That's the cruelest part of our existence, I think. Women like you and me." She stares wistfully into the distance for a beat before she sighs. "Well, I better get back to the party."

As quickly as she came, she floats away, practically leaving me sputtering.

What. The. Fuck.

"If you're smart, you'll stay away from that girl. She's a lit fuse ready to blow," someone says from beside me.

I turn. Imani.

"And Lucifer isn't?"

Imani shakes her head at me like I'm being naive. Clearly, she's still angry with me. "She may be New York City's favorite it-girl, but her father keeps her under lock and key. Rumor has it he's trying to force her into an arranged marriage. You wouldn't know anything about that now, would you?" She turns a scathing look in my direction.

I open my mouth, half prepared to confess everything to Imani, but then my eye catches Lucifer's, and my stomach churns. "I . . . I think I need a moment. Excuse me."

I make my way toward the ladies' room, only allowing myself to take a full breath once I lock the stall door behind me. I sink against it, my pulse racing.

Is it really that obvious?

What my father did to me?

I glance down at Greed's card, still hot in my hand, her words coming back to me.

If you ever get tired of him bossing you around . . .

I crumple the card in my fist, intending to throw it into the toilet, but then my phone dings, and I abandon it inside my clutch as I fish out my phone instead.

It's an unknown number, but with a New York City area code.

Lucifer. Obviously.

It's not like he ever actually bothered to give me a way to contact him. He'd probably make me call and schedule an appointment with Jeanine. I open the text.

I've got my eye on you, it reads.

I scoff. Yeah. Definitely Lucifer.

I move to shove my phone back into my clutch and snap it shut with a little more force than necessary, but then pause.

If he thinks he can control me that easily, then he really hasn't figured me out at all.

Pulling out Greed's card, I flatten it out and fire off a quick email to her with my résumé attached.

Mimi, It was lovely to meet you. Let's connect.

Satisfied, I slip my phone back into my purse and exit the stall.

The evening continues about how I expected, with Lucifer giving me a wide berth. He only casts occasional intrigued glances in my direction from where he stands on the second-floor balcony, as I do the exact opposite of what I was told.

I flirt shamelessly.

Men. Women. Anyone who comes across my path.

No one is safe from me.

By the time the event's winding to an end, half the ballroom is practically eating out of the palm of my hand, and it wasn't even that hard, honestly.

My father may have groomed me to be obedient and demure, but he also taught me *exactly* how to appeal to the whims of rich and powerful men.

The modern church has plenty.

I've nearly finished my rounds, having introduced and ingratiated myself to every major power player in the city, before finally, Imani taps my shoulder. "Time to go now, Charlotte."

I open my mouth and try to find something to say to her, but . . . nothing comes to me.

Lucifer waits beside the lobby door for me, prepped to make our exit.

When I reach him, he extends his hand toward me. "Shall we?"

To anyone else, he'd simply look enamored with me, but I'm learning to recognize the subtle changes in his expression quickly. If I thought he was furious with me before, it's nothing compared to the way he looks at me now. But I don't care.

Let him hate me.

The feeling would only be mutual, after all.

As we head out toward the waiting press on Park Avenue, Lucifer tucks me against him, leaning down to hiss into my ear. "Don't think your behavior tonight will go unpunished."

A shiver runs through me.

"And what are you going to do?" I sneer. "Spank me?"

His grip on my lower back grows more possessive, more intense. "Don't tempt me."

"Have you ever stopped to consider that maybe that's exactly what I want?" I say tartly. "For you to dominate me?"

If I wasn't tucked so firmly against his side, I might have missed the brief hitch in his step then. He blows out a slow breath as he chuckles like he's amused with me. "If that's the case, you'll get far more than you bargained for tonight, little dove."

I look up and meet his gaze. "Try me."

Hellfire sparks in his eyes. "Smile for the world, Charlotte."

We fall silent then as we reach the red carpet, and the cameras begin flashing. Lucifer navigates the few questions we take from the press with ease, commanding their attention with a natural charisma that even I have to admit is a little intoxicating.

The media is going to be eating this up for weeks. It's not an exaggeration to say this is the news event of the century.

Everyone wants a piece of Lucifer.

Most of the questions are straightforward. Clearly staged, thanks to Imani. And those that are even slightly off topic, Lucifer thwarts easily. That's not to say his debut isn't without controversy, of course. A wall of police officers block off a group of far-right evangelical protesters around the corner on 63rd Street.

I try not to glance toward them, but the sight of one of their signs stops me.

CHARLOTTE BELLEFLEUR IS THE REAL "LITTLE WHORE."

My stomach twists.

I've been so caught up in this situation with Lucifer that I never stopped to consider what those from my old life might think.

Not that they matter to me.

Lucifer's gaze follows mine, noticing the way I tense, and his jaw ticks.

"No more questions," he says then, the confident, commanding tone drawing all my attention toward him.

"What about Charlotte?" one of the reporters in the crowd yells from behind me.

Lucifer turns to address him. "Miss Bellefleur won't be taking any questions this evening."

I smile in fake agreement as Lucifer starts to turn us away, but then that sign catches my eye once more, and suddenly I'm done for the evening.

I'm done being what anyone expects me to be.

Abruptly, I step out of Lucifer's arms and turn toward the journalist. "Actually, I'd be glad to answer some questions," I say, smiling politely.

I don't want to look toward Lucifer to see what his reaction is. But I can't help myself.

The danger thrills me.

His expression is unperturbed and unmoving. He doesn't miss a beat.

But I can practically feel the fury radiating from him.

I take the press questions in stride, answering each one honestly and thoughtfully. Well, as honest as I can be while maintaining our story, anyway.

A few minutes later, as the cameras continue to flash, Lucifer draws me close once more. "That's enough," he hisses into my ear before he addresses the press. "No more questions, please."

We head toward his Town Car, pausing to give one last wave to the cameras as Dagon holds open the door for us. But the pressure of Lucifer's hand on my hip is a little more biting than it was previously.

"Come on, Lucifer! Give her a quick kiss for us, would ya?" someone shouts from the crowd.

I expect him to ignore the heckler, but before I can stop him, suddenly his hands are on me, pulling me to him so that we're nearly nose to nose. "You think you have what it takes to play games with me, little dove?" he growls.

I stiffen. "I'd say I already am."

"You underestimate me."

"Or maybe you're the one underestimating me."

He chuckles wickedly, stroking the back of his hand over my cheek in a way that makes me shiver. The press is going to eat their fill of this and then some. They'll be begging for seconds.

But all I can think about is the monster in front of me, the way his large hands grip the back of my neck and his fangs flash as he brushes noses with me. "You want to burn, Charlotte? So be it." He tightens his grip on me. "I've always liked to play with fire."

He kisses me then, and it's different from before.

Rough and untethered, and it ignites something dangerous in me.

The cameras go wild, and I can hardly breathe against the mixture of pleasure-pain that floods me. My lips. My chest. My body. All the way down to my center. His kiss consumes me.

But it isn't until he pulls back and releases me, smirking devilishly for the cameras, that I bring a shaky, unsteady hand to my mouth.

Only to realize there's blood on my lips where he bit me.

CHAPTER TWENTY-TWO

Charlotte

I expect Lucifer to drop me at my apartment, but instead he takes me back to his penthouse for the night. The silence builds between us, the tension so thick that by the time an attendant opens the door for us and we're standing in his foyer, I regret baiting him.

No matter how much it thrilled me.

I follow him inside, uncertain of what sort of punishment waits for me. He hasn't said so much as a word since we left the foundation opening, and the anticipation is killing me. I can still taste the salt and iron of my own blood on my lips. Where one of his fangs nicked me. Or where he bit me intentionally.

Honestly, I'm not sure.

It isn't until the penthouse door falls closed behind us with a cruel echo that he finally addresses me.

"What sort of game do you think you're playing here?"

"Excuse me?"

He turns toward me, hands in his suit coat pockets. "Don't play coy, darling. You heard me."

"We've been through this."

"Lest you forget, Charlotte, I'm the devil. Punishing humanity is my oldest and greatest pleasure. You didn't think there would be repercussions to defying me?" His eyes darken.

I shake my head. "You won't hurt me."

But even as I say it, I'm not certain it's true.

Lucifer is a true monster. When he chooses to be.

"You want to play, little dove? I'll bite." His gaze falls to my mouth. "But don't come crying to me when you can't walk come morning." He steps past me, heading toward his home bar as the words register.

"Is that a threat?"

He uncaps the crystal whisky decanter and pours himself a finger, returning it to the shelf more roughly than necessary. "It's a promise, darling. That's what you're here for, after all. A little religious rebellion against Daddy."

"No." I look away as the inside of my throat thickens with shame.

"Don't lie, Charlotte." He says my name like a hiss. Like the poisonous snake I know he can be. "Your self-righteous victim act is growing tiresome, quickly."

My jaw drops. "Self-righteous? You're the one who—"

He rounds on me then, the look of contempt in his eyes enough to stop my breath short as he circles me like a predator does its prey. "The press isn't here now. Cut the bullshit. You walk into my brother's club searching for me. You apply for a job at *my* company. You foolishly place yourself in *my* path at every opportunity and then, when you get exactly what you bargained for, you turn down your pretty little nose at me. You think that because you grew up in the church, you're better than me? Try again."

I shake my head. Heart racing. "I never said that."

"Didn't you?" A hint of hellfire sparks in his eyes, and he scoffs before he stares down his nose at me. Like what he sees there isn't impressive, and it infuriates me how small it makes me feel. "I see you for what you truly are, Charlotte. But it isn't me that disgusts you, is it? It's your own desire."

"Lucifer," I say in warning.

"You're exactly what your father would have wanted for you. Sanctimonious. Self-righteous. So disgusted by your own needs that—"

"I am *nothing* like him!" I shriek.

He falls silent then. My chest heaves, from where I'm panting suddenly, and I realize then he's already done it.

He's broken me.

He barely even had to try.

"Perhaps you're right." He glances down at the city before he smirks at me. "He's a prideful man, your father. One of my biggest supporters, you see."

The words land like a blow. Exactly how he intended.

But I've always known that my father was a monster.

A self-aggrandizing hypocrite. It isn't news to me.

We're both quiet for a beat, the weight of his words slowly poisoning my insides, before I finally manage to say, "You're one to talk."

Lucifer goes still. A predator caught unaware by its prey.

"You're a hypocrite too, you know."

His eyes narrow. "I beg your pardon."

But I don't allow him to interrupt me. "You want to call me out for being self-righteous? For using you to rebel against my father? Fine. But you're no better than me." My gaze rakes over him, taking him in from head to toe. "That's why you did it, after all. Started this eternal war you have with humanity. All because Daddy didn't love you enough."

The glass in Lucifer's hand shatters.

"You know nothing of what you speak, human," he snarls, holding one of the shards in his hand to my throat.

But he won't hurt me.

I think . . .

"Don't I?" I hold his gaze for a moment, the adrenaline sending my pulse racing, even as the danger thrills me. "You don't get to criticize me for not listening to you, for rebelling against my father, when you're the world's original rebel. The first black sheep." My gaze flits over him as

I scoff. "You don't like who I am because deep down you're exactly like me. At least I have the balls to admit it."

The shard at my neck pricks against my skin, enough that I feel blood run down my neck.

"That's where you're wrong, darling." Lucifer drops the shard, and his hand is at my throat, gripping me. "I am nothing like you, and the sooner you recognize that, the safer you'll be."

I don't know who kisses whom first, but suddenly his mouth is on mine.

We tear into one another, each of us so unleashed and starved it's like the other holds the key to our last breath.

This isn't gentle. It's a hate fuck. Or it's going to be.

Neither of us is powerful enough to stop it.

"Breathe, Charlotte," Lucifer growls as he releases my throat.

I suck in a harsh breath of air, practically choking as it burns on the way down.

"Can't have you passing out on me, can I now?" Lucifer sneers. "Not until I'm through with you, anyway."

I want to ask what he plans to do to me, but then his mouth is on mine again, and all my thoughts are lost. We clash against one another, each one of us scratching and biting as we tear the clothes from each other's bodies, both fighting in a bid to gain the upper hand.

Lucifer lifts me into his arms as my mouth clamps down on the soft part between his neck and shoulder, and he snarls at me, claiming my lips as I turn molten.

It isn't until a moment later, when my back slams against the cool metal of the elevator, hard enough that the wind is knocked out of me, that I realize where he's taking me.

His playroom.

Finally.

Seconds later, the elevator deposits us onto the fifth floor, and by the time we reach the soft glowing outline of the door, he's already torn my dress from me.

The lingerie I'm wearing is new. Courtesy of Sophie.

Or Lucifer, so it seems, from the way his gaze rakes over me appreciatively.

"Does Daddy know what a dirty little slut you can be?"

I pull back my hand and slap him. Hard.

Hard enough to make his head rear to the side.

I expect him to be furious, but all he does is let out a cruel, vicious laugh as he throws me over his shoulder, bringing his hand down on my ass and pussy so hard I scream and then soften for him. He rips the crotch of my underwear aside, his fingers probing me as his thumb circles my clit furiously until I can't help but squirm at what he's doing to me.

My gown lies in a heap on the hall floor behind us, and for half a second, I think it's a shame for such a beautiful creation to go to waste. But once you reach a certain level of celebrity, there's no such thing as wearing an outfit twice, and I'm pretty sure I reached that level tonight. Lucifer ensured that for me.

I'll never have true anonymity again, thanks to him, and the thought sends a fresh round of hatred coursing through me. I glare at him as he stops fingering my pussy and looks down his nose at me from where he's deposited me into his chair. The power of it wraps around me, and for a moment, cast on the wall behind him, I think I see a pair of dark, shadowy wings before I blink, and then they're gone. As quickly as any hint of kindness he shows me.

Lucifer swipes a hand over his lips, lapping at where I drew blood. And for the first time ever, I notice the end of his tongue is forked. At least, when he wants it to be.

"Spread your legs."

He doesn't hide his contempt for me as he says it, but still, I do what he says.

I spread my legs wide, baring myself to him, my sheer lace panties hanging on by a thread.

"Already soaked for me, I see," he says, running a finger over the seam of my wet pussy lips in a way that makes be shiver. "Do I need to repeat the house rules for you, or are we clear?"

I nod, nearly breathless. "We're clear."

"Show me you understand."

"Yes, sir," I whisper.

"Louder."

"Yes, sir," I snarl.

Satisfied, Lucifer takes a step back, circling as he surveys me. "The safe word is inferno."

"And if I use it, you'll stop?"

He chuckles darkly. "You think so little of me?"

Punishment indeed.

I hold my breath. Fear flashing in my eyes.

"Now you're starting to understand, Charlotte," he says, as he comes to stand in front of me once more. "We'll use the stoplight method. Green means your pleasure, yellow means slow down, red means stop. Do I make myself clear?"

I nod, swallowing.

We're both chasing the edge of pleasure and pain, riding the line between cruelty and enjoyment. But like in Azmodeus's club, I trust that he won't allow us to cross it.

Not without permission from me.

Lucifer drops to his knees suddenly, lifting my ass and ripping my panties off so he can feast on my cunt, but with all the power from his chair thrumming through me, I can't imagine a universe where I don't allow him to do whatever he wants to me. The pleasure is overwhelming.

Fuck.

"God help me," I whimper.

"You won't find my Father anywhere near here tonight," Lucifer purrs as the fork in his tongue meets the softest parts of me. "Not even He can save you, I'm afraid."

He plunges his tongue into me, and I practically come off the chair from the delicious shock of it. None of my previous partners ever came close to putting their mouths on me, and the feeling is so wicked, I . . . I think I might die.

Though whether from pleasure or embarrassment, I'm not certain, really.

I feel a flush creep through my chest.

"Fuck, you taste like sin," he growls against me.

I curse as the fork in his tongue massages circles around my clit.

"Trust me, I'd know." He chuckles darkly.

The thought of sin in this moment, of Heaven and Hell, of good and evil, feels a little absurd, and yet, it's all I can think of as I start to laugh hysterically. My muscles go limp.

I am fucking the devil.

Or I'm about to be.

Lucifer's tongue flicks over me, his movements deliberate and certain. Like he's an expert in my pleasure. And I think for one insane moment that he might be.

That's what he does, after all.

Tempts us to be our most wicked selves.

"Lucifer, please," I keen, practically coming out of the chair as I buck against him, his tongue lapping and thrusting into my cunt in such a delicious rhythm that I can hardly think straight. Spots line my vision. "Holy fuck," I breathe.

"There's no place for anything holy here tonight. Only pleasure. And pain. You'll see." He dips one of his fingers inside me, curling it in a way that strokes a spot deep, deep inside me that nearly makes me come undone.

I arch forward, moaning.

"Come for me, Charlotte."

"I . . . I . . . can't." I pant like a dog in heat, taking everything he gives me.

And I can't help but want more. *More, more, more.*

My whole body aches for him.

"Don't tell me no one's ever touched you here before." His eyes hold a hint of fury.

I shake my head. On his lips, it sounds damning.

Like he wants me to be a slut.

Like he values that side of me.

"Good," he purrs. "Virgins are of little interest to me. Now, come all over my tongue like a good girl."

"I . . . can't . . . I need . . ." I bite down on my lip, nearly drawing blood this time as I nod down to my swollen, aching pussy. "Not while . . . you're watching me."

He chuckles like my embarrassment is amusing, licking his lips. "All right, Charlotte. I'll grant you this, but the next time you come tonight, you *will* look at me." He meets my eyes from between my legs. "What's the point in fucking the devil if you can't take me horns and all?"

Without warning, he flips me onto my stomach, shoving my face into the chair's cushion as he tongue-fucks me. His mouth and his hand find a delicious, greedy rhythm.

But it's his hand in my hair and the brush of his cock outside my entrance a moment later, when he stands and pulls my head back by my roots that nearly undoes me.

"Come for me, Charlotte," he growls as he thrusts into me. *"Now."*

And I do.

I come all over his cock as he drives into me, filling me to the hilt until I feel his balls slap against me.

"No longer Daddy's little girl now, are we?" he purrs as I shudder and seize, struggling to adjust to the size of him mid-orgasm.

He twists my head back to look at him, turning me only enough that he can stay inside me for a few more thrusts before he unceremoniously finds his own release. He pulls out before he shoves me back down again. This time, to the floor.

"Now crawl to the rack on your knees for me."

CHAPTER TWENTY-THREE

Lucifer

She submits so sweetly, her ass bared to me as she crawls at my command.

If she were any other woman, I'd take her there before evening's end. In that tight, unpenetrated bud. Or perhaps give her a little jewel to wear for me. But even though she's no virgin, Charlotte is, and always will be, more Madonna than whore, and while I plan to push her, I have no intention of hurting her. At least, not beyond what she agrees to.

Her submission is a gift. One I do not take lightly.

When she reaches the rack, she sits back on her knees for me, waiting for my next move.

"Daddy trained you well, I see." I smirk.

She bristles at the mention of her father, but it's her rebellion she's seeking here tonight. With me. A two-fingered fuck-you to the way she was raised. One I find I'm able to appreciate.

Despite her hatred for me.

"What would you like me to do now, *sir?*" That single word is filled with all the bratty hate and desire she feels. But the steady rise and fall of her chest gives her away.

She's eager for it.

"Stand and face the cross for me."

She does as she's told, silently rising as she gazes up at me prettily. She doesn't speak, but her eyes say it all.

Prince of Darkness. Prince of wicked deeds.

It's like a silent prayer.

This was always what she wanted from me.

I make my way toward her, drinking her in as a light, embarrassed blush coats her cheeks. Despite everything we just did.

Despite how I can still taste the sweet nectar of her pussy on my chin.

"You'll look perfect spread open for me."

I grip one of her wrists in my own, bringing it up and over her head to place it into the first shackle of my custom free-standing Saint Andrew's cross. Her eyes widen, a look of fear and panic there as she shivers at my touch. But she has her safe word, and she doesn't use it. So I keep going.

The danger thrills her. That's more than apparent to me.

I repeat the same action on her other side before I move to do the same at her ankles, each movement causing her breath to become shallow, needy. I pause momentarily at her feet. I want to feel her legs wrapped around me as she comes apart.

Though kindness isn't what she expects of me. Not tonight.

Only my punishment will do.

"Spread your legs, little dove."

She follows my command, and I shackle her ankles quickly.

She nods, swallowing as I watch the delicate lines of her throat move. "What are you going to do to me?" she asks, her voice barely more than a whisper.

"Tell me, Charlotte," I say as I begin to circle the cross's frame. "How would your father punish you? What would he do when you'd been a wicked, wicked girl?" I slip my hands between her legs, parting the lips of her pussy until I find her swollen clit and circle, roughly.

She sucks in a harsh breath, trying and failing to buck against me. But I'm the one in control here. That's the power she's gifted me.

"He . . . he'd beat me," she pants.

"And how would he beat you?"

"With his belt." I push two fingers inside her, and she lets out a sharp hiss at the sudden intrusion. "With his hand."

"And how many times would he beat you?"

"It . . . depended on how sinful I'd been," she mutters quickly, her eyes tracking me like she can't possibly understand where I'm going with this. "God forgive me."

She'll learn. Given time.

I smirk. "And how sinful have you been tonight? How sinful were you when you came all over my cock, milking me like a good little slut?" I retrieve a belt from my array of toys on the wall, cracking the leather between my hands with an audible snap before I run the smooth leather over her skin. A little impact play to start. Just to see how she takes it.

She lets out another hiss as she shivers. Trying and failing to move toward me.

Always toward. Never away.

"Does this mean I'm going to Hell?" she whispers.

Tears gather at the corner of her eyes.

"No, darling. Though why wouldn't you want to? After all, I'm king." I circle in front of her as I stroke my hand over the head of my cock.

Her eyes fall there, almost greedy.

She watches as I make a meal of it, stroking myself several times from base to tip until her tongue unknowingly darts out to wet her lips at the sight of the moisture that beads on the crown.

"So needy," I purr, continuing to circle her. "So eager. Do you know what my chair does, little dove?"

She shakes her head at me, her eyes tracking my every movement.

"It allows me to see your darkest desires. What you truly want." I stand behind her now, whispering into her ear. "And tell me, what did you truly want this evening?"

"You," she breathes.

I touch her, and her pussy is practically dripping for me.

"I wanted you," she whispers. "Your attention. The power it gives me."

"Bad enough you were willing to misbehave for it?"

She nods, whimpering as I paint the head of my cock over her seam.

"Foolish girl. If you wanted me inside you, all you had to do was ask." I thrust into her, claiming her as she cries my name. I pump several times, enjoying the way her pussy strokes me. She takes my cock like a dream. "I could have stayed buried in you all night," I whisper, "but now I have to punish you."

I pull out of her. Depriving her of the very thing that makes her scream my name. Abruptly, I draw back the belt and gift her the first lash. She cries out in a mixture of pleasure and pain, the skin where the belt hit burning a bright, blushing red.

"Next time you want to fuck, Charlotte, you will ask for it."

"Y-yes. Yes, sir."

"Not sir. Not this time. Say my name."

"Lucifer," she pants. "Yes, Lucifer."

I continue working her. Until she chants my name like a poisoned prayer.

Each lash bringing her closer to ecstasy.

Five lashes. Ten. More.

"Give me a color," I growl.

"Green," she pants, practically keening.

I watch as her world condenses to a single point, reveling in the power she's gifted me. Until I know all she can think—all she can feel—is me. Until I am a tool for her divine will. A channel for her power. Her restaging.

Then, and only then, do I take her.

She cries out, my cock filling her as I grip her now-red bottom and spread her open for me. Already I can feel how close she is. How thoroughly she's lost herself to me.

I twist her chin up, forcing her to look into my eyes at the very last second.

"Come for me, Charlotte. Come for me, darling."

Her pleasure rolls through her like fire, burning and singeing us until we're both coming apart. I empty myself into her, nearly coming out of my skin as I find a kind of release I didn't know I had in me, until suddenly, I'm standing over her, holding her where I've broken her shackles free from the rack to wrap her legs around me.

"More," she mumbles, almost incoherently. "I need more."

She's talking about the punishment I gave her. I know that instinctually.

I stare down at the place where we're still joined, the last shudders of my orgasm rolling through me. At the human woman in my arms, my cum dripping from her pussy. And for the first time in my long existence, I feel . . . I squeeze my eyes shut.

Humbled. By her beauty. By the trust she's placed in me.

By the way she *wants* me to hurt her. Beyond what's necessary.

Instantly, I go still.

Her eyes flutter slightly, the incoherent pleasure of subspace clearly overtaking her as her eyes search for me. "I'm sorry, Father," she breathes.

Something lodges inside my throat.

I don't know whether it's to me, my own Father, or to some distant memory she speaks, but the knowledge that she still believes she is wrong, sinful, nearly undoes me.

"You were never the one in the wrong, Charlotte. It was his shame. Never yours." I whisper it to her without thinking, no longer used to the sound of kindness on my lips. It feels foreign. But in this moment, with her, it pours out of me. Almost naturally. "You're such a good girl, Charlotte. Always such a good girl."

At my fevered whispers she comes apart in my arms, this time, in a different way, crying in big heaving sobs that shake the small mortal frame of her body. I release her from what remains of the rack as she crumples against me, and for the first time in a millennium, I'm . . . uncertain what to do, but then almost instinctually, I wrap her closer, cradling her to my chest as I carry her out of my playroom.

"Let it out now, little dove," I whisper to her. "You're safe here. You're safe here."

I whisper it over and over again as I lay her down in my bed, even long after she's fallen asleep, uncertain whether the words are for a long-forgotten part of myself . . .

Or for her.

CHAPTER TWENTY-FOUR

Charlotte

Someone cradles me. A respite from harsh hands.

I feel those harsh hands then. The terrified thud of my pulse as he lifts his hand to me. His palm across my cheek will sting. Skin against skin. But the smack and the pain that follows don't reach my face.

I surge forward. My bottom stinging as someone holds me.

Softer. Gentler.

"Hush, Charlotte," he shushes me. "You're safe here."

I can't see him, but I relax back instinctually, eyes closed, rocking gently.

A moment later, soft sheets engulf me. Cool hands, and an even cooler balm, soothe my aching skin. Someone trails a warm cloth over my forehead, my breasts, my lips. Little pleasures, little touches that make me sigh and shiver, make my muscles unwind.

Finally, the cloth settles to where I feel his cum leaking from between my legs as he cleans me.

Did Mark ever clean me?

That thought causes me to thrash.

No. No, I can't give him this. Anything but this.

She'll suffer the same fate.

"Charlotte," someone says, a serpentine hiss, but I can hardly stand it. *The fear that threatens to hold me in place.*

So I run. I run until I reach the forest.

Where the shadows wait . . .

My eyes fly open, desperately searching for the shadows as I take in my surroundings. Not a forest, but a bedroom. One filled with early morning light.

Sun streams through the window overlooking the city, and the bed I'm lying in feels heaven sent. But I'm not in Heaven. I couldn't be.

Lucifer.

I sit upright, covering my naked body with the sheets. My eyes comb over the furniture, searching for any signs of movement, for the shadows that sheltered me in my dream, but the room is painfully still, and bright.

He ditched me.

I flop back down into the sheets, trying hard not to cry as I sort through exactly how I feel about that. Unable to escape the sinking feeling inside my chest. It's not as if I expected last night would change anything, but I guess I'd hoped for a little . . . tenderness, after.

I scoff at the word. Tenderness and Lucifer don't even belong in the same sentence, but . . .

A memory tugs at me.

Large hands in smooth circles over red skin.

I roll onto my side, glancing at my bottom to see if he really did rub some of that cooling balm on me, clean and care for me so gently, but if he did, there's no evidence of it. My heart shrinks once more.

Suddenly, my phone pings from where someone deposited my clutch on the bedside table. Beside it, a red rose waits. I smile. A jolt of hope shoots through me. That's something, at least. Grinning like a fool, I reach for it, but when I try to pick it up, one of its thorns pricks my finger.

"Fuck." I curse and drop it onto the mattress as I look to the spot where it drew blood. A crimson drop pools on the tip, and I can't help but laugh a little at the cruel, cruel irony of it.

Did I *actually* think Lucifer would do something kind for me?

I should know better.

Abandoning the rose, I reach for my phone instead, finding a small gold key placed on its surface. I turn it over in my hands, its unique shape familiar from when Astaroth opened the elevator for me. The note beside it, written in a perfect, flawless script, reads:

Come and go as you please.

I swallow. It's only practical, considering our situation, and not exactly as romantic as flowers would be, but I still can't stop my foolish heart from skipping a beat.

Stupid, stupid hormones.

I pocket the key, placing it inside my clutch, before my phone pings again, and I finally glance at the screen. My mouth falls open, and my worries fall away as I stare down at my social media icons.

Holy shit.

The red notification numbers seem to have topped out somewhere in the hundred thousands, but when I open one of the apps and glance at the views of my latest post, one from nearly two weeks ago, I immediately drop the phone.

Nine million views. In a single evening.

And climbing.

I take a slow, measured breath, uncertain what to do. I'm the same person I was only moments before, but somehow this changes things. Xzander's words from last night come crashing back to me then, mixed with the fury in Lucifer's eyes when I spoke to the press.

The queen's the most powerful piece.

Maybe I'm not just a pawn in his game, after all.

Or at least, I won't allow myself to be.

Snatching the rose off the nightstand again, this time I hold it gently, careful not to hurt myself with any of its thorns. I inhale its scent, using the prop to my advantage as I pull the sheets up to my chest and position the early morning city backdrop in the background for a selfie. I take several, picking my favorite, before I stare down at the photo I've chosen.

The woman in it looks sexily mussed, confident, sophisticated, and wealthy.

Influential.

She's nothing like me.

Perfect.

I quickly post the photo with the caption "From my king," which honestly makes me gag a little it's so sappy, but Lucifer's fans will eat it up. I add on a few hashtags for me and Lucifer that have gained popularity recently, confident it will go viral. Satisfied, I flop back onto the bed, even though I'm still a little sore.

It may not stop Lucifer from manipulating me, but it gives me my own kind of power.

The weight of public opinion.

I glance at the screen one more time. It's not as if I want the whole world to know that Lucifer and I have slept together. And I don't even care if they think the feelings behind the post are real—*which they're not*, I try to tell myself, ignoring the pang of guilt in the back of my throat—but based on the comments on my last post, a picture Jax took of me before my first day at Apollyon, the viral masses already think both those things, and the sooner they believe our love story, the better.

The sooner I can go back to being me.

Even if I'm not entirely certain who that is.

Sure enough, the comments start rolling in. Everything from fangirl stans to religious trolls to the occasional political grandstander. There's even some speculation about how high the thread count is on Lucifer's bedsheets, and honestly, I can't help but snort a little at that as I glance around his room, marveling at my newfound celebrity.

To my surprise, the penthouse's master suite isn't anything to call home about. No more or less than any of the other rooms, anyway. The view is better, the lighting darker, and the color scheme more . . . relaxed in a way that reminds me a bit of Gluttony's club, but in a more upscale, sophisticated way. But what sparks my interest the most is that there are actual signs of life here, more than any other room Lucifer's showed me.

A pile of sheet music sits on a table near the glass door that leads out to the balcony, the margins filled with furiously scratched notes and music symbols like Lucifer must have scribbled them sometime late in the middle of the night. It's an original, I think.

I rise from the bed, wincing a little as I walk toward where the sheet music rests before I pick it up. I hum the notes to myself.

It's haunting and sparse with a melody that feels otherworldly.

It's . . . heartbreaking.

I place the composition back where I found it, uncertain what to make of it as a large carved trunk at the end of his bed catches my eye. The symbols that cover the surface are written in some kind of ancient language, what I can only guess is Aramaic. Maybe Angelic?

I run my fingers over the leather strap-protectors that hold it closed along with the heavy iron lock. The metal is cool to the touch, and I half expect it to rattle or some supernatural entity to suddenly pop out at me, but it doesn't.

It's just a regular trunk. Ancient and beautiful, but . . .

Uninteresting.

Giving up on my snooping, I return to the bed and my phone, trying not to wince at how swollen and tender I feel.

I scroll through the incoming comments for a bit longer before I close the app and turn my attention to another matter entirely.

Last night's media coverage.

The articles and video clips take a while to comb through. CNN. FOX. MSNBC. Every major news network in the Western Hemisphere has a piece about Lucifer and me.

It's exactly what I anticipated. All the focus on our media debut. Not a single mention of Paris Starr. Not in connection to Lucifer, anyway.

Imani will be pleased.

Imani.

I glance at the clock. It's a quarter past seven and I'm supposed to be at Apollyon by nine, but I still need to shower and get ready.

But since I'm already here, I might as well have Dagon take me.

I quickly scroll through the other news notifications on the home screen. When Imani told me to memorize all the city's power players, I went home that same evening and, with Jax's help, placed alerts on my phone for each of the Originals.

The articles about Lucifer's siblings are expected. Speculation about the current state of Az's love life. A mix of body-positive praise and misogynist hate for Greed, and the highlights of Wrath's latest feud with some high-ranked political figures in the military.

Wait. Greed.

I pull open my email. Sure enough, I find a reply message from her at the top of my inbox. From the time stamp, it only took a few hours for her to respond to me.

Charlotte,

Of course! Let's indulge! After all, we're practically sisters now.

Yours,
Mimi

I can almost see the catlike grin on her face as she typed her reply to me. She's probably giddy that I reached out to her. That I'm eager to be free of Lucifer.

Aren't I?

I glance down at my still nude body and the mussed bedsheets.

Something inside my chest tightens.

The thought of abandoning Lucifer to go work for his sister makes me feel a little guilty. Especially after last night. But I'm being too sentimental, that's all. Getting inside my own head again. I've never been good at separating feelings from sex, in the short time I've been sexually active, anyway, and this is my chance to practice exactly what Jax has been preaching to me.

Lucifer definitely will.

I look to the reply line and see that Greed's cc'd her assistant to schedule a time and date before I glance down at the bed where I'm lying. At my naked, bruised skin.

What am I doing?

I exit my email app, not bothering to respond to Greed with my availability just yet, before I strip off the sheets. I pull on one of Lucifer's white dress shirts from the nearby closet. It's long enough to mostly cover me, and as I button it, I stand at the door to his closet, taking in the scene. The rumpled bed. The scattered clothes the staff most definitely found downstairs.

The things we did last night in his playroom were the best kind of terrible. Or the worst kind of wonderful, depending on who you're asking. I blush at the thought and the memory it leaves on my lips, and elsewhere . . .

And yet, for the first time in a long time, I feel . . . lighter.

Free. From my own shame.

Lucifer gave that to me.

"It doesn't change anything," I say out loud to myself.

Maybe if I say it enough, I'll actually start to believe it.

With that thought, I frown, heading toward the bedroom door. I'm suddenly in a much worse mood than when I woke up a few minutes ago, and I traipse through the penthouse, unsurprised when I don't encounter anybody. Lucifer keeps his staff to a minimum.

It takes me a while, but I find the guest bedroom Xzander and I used to get ready for last night's philanthropy gala on the fourth floor, and sure enough, there's a whole wardrobe full of clothes waiting for me. I take another selfie with the walk-in closet's generous contents in the background.

This time with the hashtag #Blessed.

My new followers will eat it up. This little glimpse into mine and Lucifer's reality. That's what they want to see, after all.

What we eat. What we wear. What we do with our time. How we indulge.

The fantasy we're selling.

The one where my poisoned lips are stained red with lipstick rather than blood.

Not reality.

Pushing that thought aside, I browse through the closet's contents, seeing what selections the style team left for me. Dior. Chanel. Louis Vuitton. It feels like I'm living in a dream.

It's more than anyone could ever ask for.

I finally settle on a chic, business-casual Dior dress and matching heels. It looks like something Imani would wear, and that thought sends a fresh wave of confidence through me, along with a tiny sting of loss. She and I are still not okay, but I'm going to fix it somehow.

I shower quickly, surprised that even after I blow-dry, the sleek sheen of my hair stays the same. Whatever treatment Sophie gave it yesterday afternoon, it still looks nearly as good as it did last night. Though more casual. I watch a video tutorial on how to style it. I suck at the first few tries, but in the end, the way I tie it up is a mix of fun and flirty.

I grin at myself in the mirror, feeling more confident than ever.

Money really *can* buy anything.

Satisfied, I make my way downstairs to find a full breakfast waiting. But Lucifer is still nowhere to be found.

"Guess it's just me," I mutter to myself.

I eat alone and watch the bustle of the city streets as I continue to glance at my phone. Midway through stuffing my face with some delicious French pastry, another news notification pops up. This one with Az's name and the cupid emoji I assigned him. It seemed like a better choice at the time than the tongue, heart, and sweat emojis I chose originally, or God forbid, the eggplant-peach combo Jax suggested.

I tap through to the article, though it isn't about Az specifically.

Instead, it's about a man who worked at one of his clubs briefly, several years prior, whose body was found floating in the East River this morning, all the skin flayed from his corpse. An unexpected chill rolls down my spine.

Suddenly, I'm no longer hungry.

"Is everything to your liking, Miss Bellefleur?"

The new voice causes me to jump, and I turn to find one of Lucifer's staff members, a middle-aged Indian gentleman, watching me. I think his name is Ramesh, though so many people were around me yesterday I could be wrong.

I struggle to find the right words, my mind still reeling from the news I just read. "Uh, yes. Yes, it's great. I'm just . . . not as hungry as I expected I'd be."

I don't know what it is about the article that bothers me. Beyond the normal sadness that anyone feels at a loss of human life. But . . .

My mind flashes to the spot of blood near Lucifer's cuff link.

No.

Immediately, I shake my head, willing the thought away.

I can't even be certain of what I saw, let alone accuse him of anything. I'm jumping to conclusions. Seeing connections where there aren't any. Not beyond my instincts.

Instincts that, after living under your father's roof, you've learned not to ignore.

The little voice in my head sobers me.

Unaware of the dark turn of my thoughts, Ramesh says, "Of course, Miss Bellefleur. Though I'd recommend taking a scone to go. You have a long day."

Now he has my attention.

"I do?"

"Mr. Apollyon arranged several meetings for you this morning."

I lift a brow. "With who?"

"I believe some potential brand sponsorships, Miss Bellefleur."

I feel lightheaded. "Brand sponsorships?"

I glance toward my phone once more. My notification numbers are going crazy again, and, sure enough, several major luxury companies and labels have started following me overnight. I quickly change the settings to no longer display the notification numbers.

I guess business moves fast these days.

But my devilish "fiancé" moves even faster.

I can't allow Lucifer to get the upper hand in this fucked-up game we're playing. Not when we're straight out of the gate.

Ramesh turns to leave, but I stop him.

"Actually, Ramesh, could you please let the sponsors know that my plate is as full as I like today? I'll need to reschedule for another time, and please tell Mr. Apollyon that I'll be taking charge of my own schedule. Effective immediately."

Ramesh nods. "Yes, Miss Bellefleur."

"And could you . . . also have Dagon get the car ready for me please?"

Internally, I cringe at the words. At how pretentious they sound. I sound like *him*, but this is my life now. At least, temporarily.

"I need a ride to Apollyon headquarters. For work," I add with a smile. "Please."

"Of course." Ramesh turns and leaves. He doesn't seem fazed by my behavior.

My phone pings again, and I let out an annoyed huff. The constant notifications are going to be a problem. But this time, it's a text message. I read the preview across the home screen.

Don't think you can hide from me.

I roll my eyes. Lucifer. Obviously.

Unlocking the home screen, I let out a pissed off grumble and text back.

I'm not hiding.

I pause for a moment, debating my next move, before angrily typing out:

You're the one who wasn't here when I woke up this morning.

I hit send. It sounds a little more hurt than I wanted it to, but there's no turning back now.

A moment later, three dots appear across the screen like he's going to respond, but then they disappear.

Nothing.

I jab the button to turn off the home screen and silence my phone. If he thinks he can control me that easily, he clearly didn't learn anything from the cocktail party last night.

CHAPTER TWENTY-FIVE

Charlotte

It's nearly an hour later when I walk into Apollyon, well past nine o'clock, considering Dagon had to take several unnecessary detours to shake the paparazzi. But Dagon assures me that, based on his years of experience working for Lucifer, there's no such thing as being late when you're a celebrity, and I have no intention of arguing with a demon.

Or someone who I'm pretty sure is one, anyway.

I'm already late, to the point that there's no reason to scan my security badge to clock in, if I'm even supposed to do that anymore, and as I stroll through the door, Jeanine, the downstairs secretary, takes one look at me, her eyes flying wide before she practically dives for her desk phone. I don't think she plans to remove me from the building. That'd cause too much of a stir with all the cameras currently positioned outside, and Lucifer isn't *that* furious with me over the stunt I pulled last night.

Not if what happened after in his penthouse is any indication.

More likely she's letting him know that I'm here.

I make a mental note that Jeanine is pretty much Lucifer's eyes and ears inside the building as I head to the sixteenth floor, ignoring the wide-eyed gazes and not-so-murmured whispers. The mail carrier openly gapes at me, and a senior financial exec drops half his portfolio papers the moment we make eye contact.

I stroll into Imani's office confidently.

She glances up from where she's on a video call before she says, "Anderson, I'm going to have to call you back." She exits the meeting screen before she assesses me, taking in my new look from head to toe. "Well, you sure took to fame like a duck on a june bug."

I rear back a little. "What's *that* supposed to mean?"

The snipe doesn't surprise me. It's how badly it hurts.

If I didn't admire Imani, the offhand remark wouldn't matter. But I *do* admire her, and I'd have to be a fool to not hear the judgment in her voice.

She shrugs. "It means you haven't wasted any time getting cozy in your new role, that's all."

The words smart, landing like a hornet's sting. That familiar shame my father instilled in me twists inside my gut again. But suddenly, Lucifer's voice is there, inside my head, whispering to me. *It was his shame. Never yours.*

Did he really say that to me last night?

I . . . can't remember.

I shake away the thought. I was so caught up in the high of everything we did that I can't exactly remember all the events that followed. But I knew when I came here to expect a fight.

I just didn't expect it to be with Imani.

"What happened to building other women up rather than shooting them down?"

Imani rotates her desk chair, reaching for her coffee as she refuses to look at me.

When she doesn't answer straight away, I place a hand on my hip. "Well?"

She casts me a scathing look. "That was *before* you complicated my job for me."

I frown. "Well, I'm about to uncomplicate it."

Her gaze falls to me, and I give her an earnest look.

"I didn't send that press release, Imani."

She watches me for a beat, and for a second, I think she might believe me before she finally huffs and says, "Save it. We've been through this. I found it on your computer. IT even traced the original file there for me."

"I said I didn't *send* the press release. Not that I didn't write it." I close her office door. The last thing either of us needs is anyone overhearing this. "But I'm going to find out who did."

"You really won't let this Nancy Drew shit go, will you?" She rolls her eyes.

"Think about it. Why would I send that press release? Sure, I was angry when I wrote it, right after he humiliated me in the meeting. But why would I choose to get myself wrapped up with Lucifer like that, or worse, fired? You know how much I need this job. What it means for me."

Imani sighs, rubbing at her temple. "Suppose I did believe you, then what? You expect me to believe that someone just happened to break into your office, log on to your computer, and send an already written press release you had open and waiting?"

I drop my hands to my sides. "Stranger things have happened."

Imani shakes her head. "I'm not buying it."

I stomp one of my Louboutins. "Our boss is the freaking devil. If someone had told you you'd be working for him eleven years ago, would you have believed them? I know we haven't known each other long, but I do know you're a good judge of character, and you've gotten to know me. So, I would hope you'd have a little faith in me right now. You said yourself this isn't your usual company." I gesture to the Apollyon serpent on her portfolio. "Obviously."

Imani falls quiet, staring up at me from her desk chair, jaw clenched, before finally she says, "You really didn't send it?"

My shoulders sag in relief. I latch on to that tiny thread of hope and pull.

"Why would I? I'd already gotten more than I'd ever expected from this job. From you." I gesture between us. "More than I'd ever hoped for, actually. Even if you hate me, I'll always appreciate what you did for me. How you tried to help me."

She lifts a brow. "And that's what you're here for? To ask me to help you again?"

"No. Not exactly." I inhale a long breath, stopping myself short of pacing. "I told Lucifer I wanted to keep my job, to continue to work for you, and he agreed, but . . . I want to stick to our original plan. Gain experience working under you so I can pivot easily."

Imani scoffs. "You play your cards right, and with the kind of fame you stumbled into, you'll never have to work again a day in your life."

"We both know that isn't true." I shake my head. "Or what I'd want, for that matter. As soon as Lucifer's done with me, it won't take long before I'll be old news, a celebrity's washed-up ex. Then where will that leave me?"

Imani goes quiet for a moment, considering.

"So, will you help me?"

She lets out a long sigh through her nose, her eyes combing over me.

But whatever potential she sees in me, for now, it must be enough.

"I'll treat you the way I treat any other employee. That's all."

I press my hands together like a prayer, bringing them to my lips to express my gratitude. "Thank you, Imani. I won't let you down. I—"

"But none of this press release nonsense." She wags a finger at me. "You keep whatever shit you have going on with that and Lucifer far, far away from me. You hear me?"

I nod. "Of course."

"Good. Then let's get to work." She settles into her chair. "Everything's gone to hell in a handbasket around here. We've got our work cut out for us now that the gloves are off and you're both in the public eye. You thought we were busy before? This is a whole new level of media frenzy."

"Use me however you see fit. I'll do whatever you ask. I swear."

I spend the rest of the day working with Imani in her office, taking interviews and doing everything exactly as she directs me before she finally clocks out for the day, leaving me alone for the first time all afternoon.

Gathering my paperwork, I make my way back to my own office, locking the door behind me as I enter. It's empty and not yet personalized, other than a neatly folded handkerchief Imani must have left on my desk the morning she discovered the press release came from my computer. I pick up the pink silk only to find it monogrammed with a prettily embroidered CB. There's a small handwritten note on pretty stationery tucked into it.

Charlotte, Don't let him knock you down, girl. Keep going.

She left this for me?

I hug it to my chest, my heart feeling full. The thought that she planned to give me this after Lucifer embarrassed me in that presentation meeting brings tears to my eyes, but I swipe them away quickly. I'm going to work hard to repair that relationship at every chance I get. To prove myself worthy. To restore Imani's respect for me.

And for myself.

I read the note once more, the words of encouragement warming me.

Keep going.

"Oh, I plan to," I mutter, both to myself and an absent Imani.

I set my papers down on the desk and begin examining. *Everything.*

I open every drawer, explore every nook and cranny. I even attempt to look for some sort of hidden door in the wall or empty bookcase turned hallway, but in the end, all I have to show for it is a slightly messier office and a pair of uncomfortably clenched teeth.

I soften my jaw, flopping down into my desk chair as I look at the computer screen. My company iMac is locked, and I'm not even sure if my passcode works anymore. Technically, I wasn't fired, but when I walked out of Lucifer's office last week, I don't think anyone expected me to return here.

Least of all me.

I start to enter my password, to check and see if it still works, when a thought grips me.

The iMac is password protected, which means . . .

Whoever sent the press release was an Apollyon employee.

Or someone with access to my login information, anyway.

The thought makes me freeze, and I sit there for a moment, torn between keeping this news to myself and the nearly irresistible urge to run out into the hall and scream that it was another employee who did this to me. Who betrayed Lucifer.

Someone who had it in for both him and me.

Ultimately, reason wins out, and I decide to keep quiet and get back to my work. Not that I'm dropping it.

I smile. Nancy Drew's got nothing on me.

Suddenly my desk phone rings.

Jeanine.

I pick it up, and the call syncs with my iMac through the company cloud. "Hello?"

"Miss Bellefleur?" she says, her voice coming through the iMac's speaker.

"Yes?"

"Mr. Apollyon asked me to pass on a message to you."

"He did?" My pulse races, though whether from excitement or frustration, I'm not certain.

I haven't heard from him all day, other than that random text, and *this* is how he chooses to contact me?

"Yes, he said to inform you that he'll be picking you up for dinner tonight. Seven thirty. A private tasting menu in Les Salons above Le Bernardin. He'll send a car for you."

We're having dinner.

That's news to me.

He didn't even bother to ask, but I guess he doesn't have to, does he? That's what he's paying me for, after all. And no one says no to Lucifer.

Least of all me.

Plus, who would pass on dinner at one of the best three-star Michelin restaurants in the city? I guess I'll have to face him sooner or later.

"Thank you, Jeanine."

There's a scuffling noise as Jeanine moves to hang up the receiver, but then at the last second, I nearly shout, "Wait! Jeanine?"

"Yes, Miss Bellefleur?" she answers, a little more exasperated than she was a moment ago.

I'm not sure how to phrase it, so I just ask her outright. "Why didn't Lucifer just text me?"

"Text you?"

"Yes, text me." I nod, though we're not on a video call, so she can't see me.

There's a brief pause, then . . .

"I'm sorry, Miss Bellefleur, but Mr. Apollyon is extremely busy, and to the best of my knowledge, he doesn't text. All his communications are filtered through me."

Which means . . .

My eyes go wide.

"Of course," I mumble. "Thank you, Jeanine."

I hang up the phone, quickly reaching for my new Fendi purse. One even sleeker than Imani's. My cell phone waits in the inside pocket, and my stomach drops as I open the home screen and glance at the text message with Lucifer's name followed by the grinning devil emoji. The number is foreign to me. But if it isn't Lucifer who texted me . . .

Then who did?

CHAPTER TWENTY-SIX

Lucifer

The knock near the elevator door is unexpected, but when I turn to find my new, human fiancée entering my office, it couldn't be better timing.

"Charlotte," I say, casting her my most devilish grin as she enters. "What an unexpected surprise. Please. Come in, darling. The detectives were just leaving."

The two officers from the NYPD seated in the office lounge area exchange tense glances, coming to their feet as the woman on the right, who's clearly in charge, nods. "We'll be in touch if we need anything further, Mr. Apollyon."

"Of course." I nod amicably, still grinning.

They head toward the elevator.

The moment their backs turn, my smile fades while Charlotte and I watch them go.

Leaving us alone together.

"I didn't expect to see you until this evening."

She waits until the elevator doors close behind them before she faces me. "They think you're responsible for the murder of Paris Starr."

She says it like it's a matter of fact. No hint of question in her voice.

As if she, too, might believe it.

I don't try to hide my distaste for that as I turn to the office bar to pour myself a whisky. It's not the sort of greeting I anticipated from her, not after last night, but I'm coming to learn that my fiancée is anything but predictable.

Not now that she's proved her willingness to defy me.

Not that I mind.

All the more reason to punish her.

I practically invented brat taming.

"Of course they do. You can't exactly blame them now, can you?" I lie. I pour myself two fingers of a rare black Bowmore. "I am the devil, after all."

"And did you?" she asks, those deceivingly innocent doe eyes staring up at me. "Have anything to do with it, I mean?"

I shake my head. "Careful, Charlotte. I may have been forgiving of the detectives for doing their job, but you . . ."

"I'm your fake fiancée," she says.

I look toward her, my gaze raking over her in a reminder of everything we did last night. There was nothing *fake* about that. She submitted herself to me. Praised me. Both body and soul.

"Yes, well, you're another matter entirely."

Her cheeks flush pink.

I down the rest of my whisky, throwing it back before I turn away. "What brings you into the office today? I wouldn't have expected you'd be up and walking so quickly."

I round the far side of my desk, just in time to see the blush in her cheeks creep lower. No need to tell her that I already know she had to beg one of my staff for an Advil before she came in today, or that I'm certain she's reminded of how I felt inside her with every step. She may not have been a virgin previously, but my fiancée is undoubtedly new to kink.

And I am not a gentle lover.

Though I take pride in my partners' pleasure. Greatly.

"It was a mistake," she says. "We shouldn't do it again."

I can't help but scoff. "At my brother's club or at my penthouse?"

The question catches her off guard.

"Your mistakes are starting to rack up, Charlotte. What's next? You trip and your mouth falls onto my cock?"

She flushes even deeper. "I hate when you do that." She wraps her arms around her middle like she means to protect herself. "You don't need to be cruel."

But I can't help myself.

Not when it comes to her.

"And what exactly am I doing?" I say, smirking at her in a way I know makes her weak in the knees. It did even *before* we slept together.

"Toying with me. Like my emotions are a game to you."

I sober instantly. "I assure you, your emotions have *never* been a game to me."

Her mouth pops open in surprise.

I let that rare admission sink in as I return my attention to my desk. Contrary to popular belief, I'm actually quite busy.

Hell doesn't run itself. Even if I only pop down there occasionally these days.

She pushes back her shoulders as she steps forward. "So that's it? You just get to manipulate me into playing your fiancée, and then fuck me until I can barely see straight, and then call it a day?" She says it like it hurts her. "You don't get to have it both ways."

"Would you like things to be different?"

She blinks. "Excuse me?"

"You heard me," I say. "Would you like for things to be different?"

I wait for a long moment as she sputters.

"Wh-what kind of question is that?"

"Let me make myself abundantly clear, *Miss Bellefleur*." I use her surname in the way that it suits me, the way I know without doubt provokes her, as I round my desk once more, leaning against the front edge. "In a span of a little over a week, you've gone from being a glori-fied intern to being the world's most powerful woman. You have fame, fortune, celebrity. Everything your heart could desire, thanks to me. So, if you happen to also get thoroughly buggered in the process, who cares? So long as you're enjoying it, darling."

She gapes at me. "Is that . . . is that how you see this?" She gestures between us. "Is that what you think you've done for me?"

"Isn't it?"

"I . . ." She shakes her head, lifting her hand toward me. "I can't deal with you right now, Lucifer."

"So, it was a lie, then? Your desire for me?"

She freezes, and when I look at her, I know she's wet for me. I can smell it. Her need so intense I can practically taste it.

"What did you say?"

"I said, the way you go still every time I look at you. The way you melt into my touch." I prowl toward her. "The way you beg for me, crawl for me. The way even now, you wish for me to tell you you're a good girl, especially when you take my cock. Isn't that what you want to hear?" I stop in front of her. "If that's all a lie, then tell me."

"Stop," she whispers.

I pause where I've reached for her, but then she leans in, stepping closer.

"Stop what, Charlotte?"

"Making me feel this way," she exhales.

I reach out and stroke a single knuckle over her cheek.

She shivers and leans into it. "Like there's an ache inside me and the only answer is you."

I growl, my cock stiffening as I lace my fingers through her hair, gripping her as if I mean to kiss her.

Her lips part. Anticipating. "This was supposed to be fake."

"I assure you, it's fake. It's *all* fake. Everything but this." I take her hand and press it to my aching erection before I kiss her, claim her with tongue and teeth.

When I release her, the sight of her swollen lips flips a switch inside me, and I use the bit of leverage I have from her hair to push her down and onto her knees. "Now suck my cock like a good little slut and maybe I won't put you on the rack this evening."

CHAPTER TWENTY-SEVEN

Charlotte

I drop to my knees, and what shocks me is that it's not because I was ordered to or because I'm obedient like my father trained me to be.

Like everything with Lucifer . . . it's because I *want* to.

The power in that admission fills me, lighting me up with wet need as I kneel before him, fumbling with the buckle of his pants. I have the power here, in every sexual encounter between us, because he gave it to me. Gifted it to me with our safe word.

My chest feels light, buoyant in a way I didn't know it could be as my mind churns with the possibilities.

I don't even know if he could truly understand what that means to me.

Lucifer stares down at me from where he leans against the edge of his desk, watching. A smirk pulls at his lips as I expose him, and my eyes go wide.

He's hot and thick and ready for me.

And I haven't even begun to touch him yet.

I stare up at him, long lashes fluttering as I stroke a reverent hand over his cock, tracing a visible vein there. Like steel wrapped in velvet. "I did this," I whisper. "I did this to you?"

He quirks his head. "You're surprised?"

"You could have any woman in the world."

"I could," he says confidently. He looks at me, brows pinched inward, like he's not certain where I'm going with this.

"And yet, you chose me."

The pride that swells in my chest at that thought is intoxicating. And I know without a doubt he feels it. My offering.

His smirk widens. "Now, you're speaking my language, Charlotte."

I tighten the grip of my hand, licking my lips. "Just this once. This is the last time. Promise me."

"I'll promise no such thing," he growls as his head falls back at how I stroke him. I focus on the sensitive head before trailing down his shaft, trying hard to get him to moan for me.

But he sees what I'm doing and a spark of amber lights his eyes.

"Don't try to top from the bottom, little dove. No one likes a dishonest addict. Own your pleasure or leave."

"Fine," I say, pressing a soft, slow kiss over the head. "Until we end things at the Met Gala, then."

"It's your fantasy. I'm simply enjoying the scenery." His gaze combs over me. "Now suck my cock like a good little slut and don't *ever* make me ask twice again."

"Yes, sir," I whisper.

I trail a slow lick over him, playing and lapping until I wrap my lips around him.

But Lucifer grips the back of my head, shoving me down on his shaft far enough I almost choke, my eyes watering as he growls, "Drink deep."

It's half an hour later and my lips are still swollen from where I drank Lucifer clean.

I'm not sure whose desire we were really chasing this time, if I'm honest.

Maybe it was for us both.

I sit on his desk, watching where he stands by the window, a lit cigarette in his hand. Even with his tie loosened, the sleeves of his three-piece suit rolled up to his elbows to reveal his sculpted forearms, and his dark hair ruffled from where he tied me up with his belt and fucked me on top of his desk after, he looks like perfection. More delicious than anything I could ever imagine. Especially now that I've finished with him.

Only he and I know what's changed between us.

How I please him. And him me.

And how the power that's given me has ruined me for all others.

"Best be on your way now, Charlotte. You don't want people talking." He smirks.

"You did it, didn't you?" I whisper, still watching him. "You killed Paris Starr."

He chuckles at me, like he's genuinely amused. "Quite a hefty accusation, considering how you just guzzled down my cum."

I finally stand. "It's not an accusation. Just a question."

"One I'm not inclined to answer. Not without my lawyers present."

"Why not?" I cross the room to stand at his side, pulling my dress on as I turn the open zipper toward him.

He brushes my hair from my nape slowly before he zips it for me.

"Even if I told anyone, it's not as if they'd believe me." I glance over my shoulder.

He stares down at me, amber eyes lighting. "I didn't kill Paris Starr. I was with *you* only moments before. Remember?"

Another spark of pleasure thrums through me. At the memory of that first night.

Of how he tempted me. Even then.

His expression is calm, serious even. But I already know he's particularly talented at lying. "There. Happy?" he asks. He turns away, but not before I think I see . . . hurt in his eyes.

But I can't allow it to deter me.

I face him. "How do I know you're not lying?"

"You don't."

"That's . . . comforting."

"I've been up front with you from the beginning. Can you say the same?" His gaze combs over me, taking in my dress, my shoes, my now ruined hair. "What brought you into the office this afternoon?"

I pluck the cigarette from his hand, cool and collected, until I inhale and immediately start coughing. He lets out another low chuckle.

"Not my thing, I guess."

I pass it back to him, and he brings it to his lips.

"I told you. I want to keep my job at Apollyon."

He exhales. "I wasn't aware your position included fellatio expert." He grins, clearly joking with me, and there's something oddly . . . nice about being casual with him like this.

"You think I'm an expert at it?"

"Your technique could use a little work, but what you lack in experience, you make up for in enthusiasm." He waves a hand. "Now what, exactly, did you come here for, Miss Bellefleur?"

"I was . . . trying to find some answers, actually."

He lifts a brow.

"About who sent the press release . . ."

"Really?" He glances around us like he's checking that we're alone, like we're sharing some dirty little secret. "I thought I was already looking at her."

I glance down at my hands. "I know you won't believe me, but I didn't send it, Lucifer. Sure, I wrote it. When I was angry with you. So angry. But even after you pushed me away in the meeting, I never would have intentionally hurt you like that. I—"

He lifts a hand. "Don't get sentimental now, Charlotte. It's one of my least favorite traits in humanity."

And just like that, whatever spell that seemed to soften him momentarily is gone.

I sigh. "I think it was an Apollyon employee. No one else would have had access to my computer. Or could have gotten past the building's security."

"An interesting theory." He steps away. "One I'd be more inclined to entertain if I didn't have other places to be." He checks his watch.

"So . . . you believe me? That I didn't send it."

He shrugs back into his suit coat, the one he stripped off while I had my mouth on him, before he straightens his now-loosened tie. "Do you have any reason to lie to me?"

"No, I . . . guess not."

His eyes darken. "Good. Keep it that way."

I cross my arms. "What's that supposed to mean?"

Lucifer looks toward me. "It means that if you know what's good for you, you'll stay far, far away from this and Paris Starr's murder. Trust me."

It takes a moment for me to absorb what he's said as he heads toward the elevator, but then . . .

"Wait, are you saying that the press release and the investigation are somehow *connected*?"

Lucifer grins at me. "I said no such thing."

"But you suggested it."

He adjusts his cuff links. "Humanity interprets my mere existence as a suggestion, but that hardly makes their accusations true. I would assume you'd know that by now."

"And are they?" I ask as he steps onto the elevator. "Are they true, I mean?"

He grins deviously. "Would it matter to you if they weren't?"

He smiles at me as he says it, but there's . . . something almost pained in his eyes that guts me. The elevator door closes a moment later, finally leaving me alone in his office.

Lucifer's words play on repeat in my head long after he leaves.

Would it matter?

I'm . . . not certain that it would.

But that doesn't stop me.

I get to work quickly, combing through his unlocked laptop, every file I can find, any shred of a record that might help me locate what I came here for. When I'm finished, I sit at his desk, staring down at the city below me, a file with all the names and information of Apollyon's employees now saved to my iCloud. It's not remotely a smoking gun, but it's a start.

I glance toward the elevator and my heart twinges painfully.

What if I was wrong? What if he isn't the monster who trapped me?

What if he's just as caught in this wicked game as I am?

I look toward the ashtray, where the last of his half-burned cigarette remains. I pluck it from the tray, tossing it onto the carpet and watching where a little hole burns before I stomp it out beneath my heel. Whoever did this needs to suffer.

To pay for what they did.

To both him and me.

CHAPTER TWENTY-EIGHT

Lucifer

The theater is empty. Dark too. Save for the single spotlight that illuminates my brother and the actress he's currently running lines with on stage. I hate this section of this city. Broadway. Times Square. It reeks with the scent of human filth and the unrefined taste of the tourism industry.

"I love you," Azmodeus says, reading his line. "God forgive me, but I do."

The actress places a dramatic hand on his cheek. "Then God forgive us both, Lance."

Abruptly, the lights come up, and I clap slowly as I make my way down the center aisle, breaking their scene. "Lovely. Nauseatingly lovely."

The actress shrieks, covering her bare breasts with her hands before she flees center stage.

Azmodeus curses, raking a hand through his hair before he gestures after her. "Now look what you've done. She was going to blow me."

I scoff. "Naked *Camelot*. That's a new low even for you."

Azmodeus rolls his eyes. "What do you want, Lucifer?"

"Peace, quiet, and a private plane to Majorca, but we can't all have what we want now, can we?" I reach the stage, pausing in front of it as I nod to the script in his hand. "I didn't think these were the kind of lines you like to do."

Azmodeus snorts. "Who says they're mutually exclusive?" He sniffs, swiping away a bit of powder left on his nose as he smirks at me.

My brother is the consummate party boy.

The lusty playboy with an unforgiving twist.

"She's a bit bashful for you," I say flatly, nodding backstage to where the actress fled.

"She's gone now." Azmodeus waves a hand. He doesn't appear to be too disappointed in that. My brother has lovers aplenty. "What brings you to my neck of the woods?"

"Paris Starr," I say, placing my hands in my pockets and rounding the front of stage right to climb its stairs. "We both know we have to discuss it eventually."

Azmodeus retrieves his shirt from where it's been cast onto the floor, shrugging at me, though he doesn't bother to dress. Az wouldn't know shame if it bit him.

Though humans are oddly . . . prudish when it comes to nudity.

"What's there to say? You've already decided it was me, considering how you flayed one of my employees before the launch party last night." He glances toward me, lifting a brow. "The East River? Really, Luce? You couldn't have dumped him somewhere more invigorating?"

"I needed to get your attention. I would have thought you'd be pleased."

Azmodeus picks up the script his Broadway actress cast aside and places it on the nearby stool in the middle of the stage. "Who says I wasn't?" He smirks at me. "Antoine was a decent fuck—all my employees are—but he double-crossed me. I may enjoy polyamory among my lovers, but in business, I find monogamy suits me better."

"As you should." I nod.

His gaze flicks over me. "So, if you know Antoine had gone rogue, what brings you here, exactly?"

I cut to the chase. "The Handler."

Azmodeus's face goes from surprised to amused within seconds, like I've said something hilariously funny. "Right," he says. "I should've known."

"Something tells me you know something I don't, brother."

Az shakes his head. "Now you're just kissing up. Trying to get on my good side. It may work with Beelzebub, and even Belphegor, but me?" He saunters toward me, poking a single finger against my chest. "That kind of flattery is below me. I know what you've been up to lately. Fucking around with your little human." He smiles appreciatively, turning away and calling over his shoulder as he walks off stage left. "I can feel the sexual frustration from Fifth Avenue all the way down to 57th Street."

I growl, following him toward the dressing rooms.

"No frustration. Only pleasure," I say, once I locate him again.

Azmodeus flops down into a makeup chair, the soft lighting of the boudoir mirror casting shadows over his handsome features in a way that would have his followers salivating for days.

He's the media's favorite heartthrob. Nearly as handsome as me, and unapologetically queer in a way the media eats up these days. Men. Women. Nonbinary. Trans. It doesn't matter.

My brother isn't choosy.

"Except for the fact that she hasn't given you what you truly want, has she?" He sneers. "The affection you've always longed for. Not very good for your pride, is she?"

I have Azmodeus by the throat and halfway out of his chair before he can so much as blink. My voice drops to an inhuman register. "Speak ill of Charlotte again, and I won't hesitate to drag you back down into the bowels with me." Hellfire blazes in my eyes. I can feel it.

"Okay, okay." Az chuckles as if this is all in good fun. "Jeez, Luce."

Abruptly, I release him, and once he's back in his chair, Azmodeus grins wickedly. "Easy, brother. You wouldn't want me to think she's got you pussy-whipped, would you?" He brushes off his shoulders, smirking at me.

Another snarl. Another warning.

"Touchy-touchy today, aren't you?" Az's eyes narrow. "Is that why you're here? To ask if I can work a bit of my lust-lovin' mojo and make her fall in love with you?" He shakes his head. "You know better than anyone it doesn't work like that. Lust's my thing. Not love. I find they're best kept separate." He turns away from me, adjusting his hair in the dressing room mirror.

"And your clubs? Are they best kept separate?" I ask tersely.

Azmodeus's expression turns dark. "What are you saying?"

He looks at me in the mirror's reflection.

"I'm saying you're going to help me find the Handler, or there will be hell to pay."

Azmodeus shakes his head. "You should know by now that threat doesn't work on me. After all, I helped you build it."

I nod, capitulating to that minor truth. "Just as I helped you build your many clubs."

They're one of my brother's key sources of power in this city.

His lust-fueled lifeline. Now that we're topside.

Azmodeus snarls. "If you're threatening me, don't be a coy little bitch about it."

"Then allow me to spell it out for you." I lean down, placing a hand on the back of his chair as I meet his gaze in the mirror. "You *will* locate the Handler for me, or else you'll find the NYPD suddenly has a new-found interest in cracking down on your glorified prostitution rings."

"They're virgin auctions," Azmodeus growls defensively, instant fury in his eyes, as if the mere suggestion of anything otherwise sullies their sanctity. The words have no doubt been rehearsed many times before, both with his lawyers and his media team. "There's a difference. We auction off the participants' time, never their bodies. All consensual."

"Naturally." I sneer.

I don't care what the fuck my brother does in his free time, so long as he's there when I need him to be.

"And what do I get out of all this?" Azmodeus twists toward me. "You can't expect me to work for free."

"Why, my undying gratitude, of course," I say flatly.

Azmodeus scoffs, turning away as he reaches for some eyeliner, and I recognize that I need to play my ace. The one Bel gave me.

"And my place on the throne, when I leave."

My brother goes still, those lust-filled eyes watching me.

I don't bother to tell him I have no intention of leaving this city.

Lying comes naturally to me.

And Azmodeus desires far more than the copious amounts of sex he receives. He's nearly as complicated as I am. If a bit horny . . .

"Baa!" he says, jumping suddenly as he slams his fist down on the dressing room table. "I really had you going there for a minute. You can't have expected for me to actually fall for that, did you? I already know you have no intention of leaving."

I grumble. "Belphegor already got to you, I see."

"He always did prefer me to you."

My lips draw flat. "Fine. An undetermined favor, then."

"An undetermined favor?" Az's eyes light as he considers it for a moment. "Done," he says, his voice echoing as the celestial contract seals between us. "This little human of yours has really gotten under your skin, hasn't she?" He lifts a brow.

"You have no idea," I admit.

He can't possibly understand what Charlotte means to me or what I'd be willing to risk in order to keep her safe.

Not because I care for her, but because I need her to stay with me.

Until Gabriel's return, at least.

CHAPTER
TWENTY-NINE

Charlotte

By the time I see Lucifer again, it's already early evening. I climb into the Town Car beside him, while Dagon holds the door for me, and we ride from Apollyon to the restaurant together in silence. The quiet is oddly comfortable, reminding me of how it felt when we toured his penthouse the other day.

When we arrive, the host leads us up to the second-floor Les Salons venue, which is empty, except for the two of us. Lucifer likely booked the full room.

A patterned metal structure covers the far wall. The adjacent wall is lined with glass, giving the space a modern, trendy feel. The tables are all decorated with lush summer flowers, and hundreds of floating candles cast a romantic, ethereal glow.

It's stunning.

"The chef will be with you shortly," the host says before he turns and leaves.

I sit across from Lucifer at a table for two, staring.

"So, this is how you live?" I ask, making a poor attempt at conversation. "Every day?"

Lucifer quirks a brow. "I'm not certain what you're asking, Charlotte."

I gesture around us. "The penthouse. The cars. The clothes. The food. All the luxuries."

His eyes narrow. "Yes, I *am* the founder and CEO of the world's leading luxury conglomerate." He says it as if he's suddenly concerned for my intelligence, but I keep going.

"And you're also the Prince of Darkness," I say. "Or the king of Hell, I mean." My brows pinch together. "Is there a difference?"

Lucifer's expression goes from confused to annoyed. "Where exactly are you going with this?"

I shrug, trying to keep the discussion going. "It's just . . . I have some questions, that's all."

"Questions?" he repeats, brow lifted.

"Yes, questions. About how you live. And you know, your role and everything."

He watches me skeptically. Like he's trying to assess what's gotten into me.

"All right," he says finally, surprising me with how easily he agrees. "Go on, then."

I blurt out the first thing that comes to mind.

"Do you always have a forked tongue or is it just when you fuck me?"

The waiter chooses that exact moment to appear at our table, and I can't help but notice his eyes go wide as the previously steady water in his hand wobbles slightly. He clears his throat, resuming the image of professionalism like a mask. "Water for the table," he says, refusing to look at me. He places the decanter on the table and pours two glasses of white wine, leaving the bottle to chill at the table before muttering, "The chef will be out shortly." He makes a hasty exit.

Peeking between my fingers from where I've buried my face in my hands, I'm still too mortified to say anything as I glance toward Lucifer, only to find his lips pressed into a thin line as he attempts to stifle his snickering. A fresh wave of embarrassment rolls through me.

"It's not funny," I snap, flicking my napkin at him. "And you didn't answer me."

He sniffs, dropping his hand before he reaches for his wineglass, his expression darkening. "I can be whatever you like, Charlotte."

My heart flutters.

But that's the only answer he gives me.

"And do you . . . you know." I gesture toward his back. "Have wings?"

He pauses midway through lifting his wineglass, setting it down again as he looks at me. Clearly, this question is a bit touchier, and Lucifer's moods are mercurial. Or so I'm learning. "I find this line of questioning to be tiresome. I'd much prefer a different lesson in anatomy." He grins at me.

"Such as?"

The tenor of his voice drops low. "Come here, darling," he purrs.

My heart skips. "Yes, sir."

I stand and cross to the other side of the table where he's sitting, and suddenly, he tugs me down and into his lap. I let out a surprised eep.

He sits me between his legs, facing me toward the table, my lap out of view beneath the tablecloth. He runs a smooth hand over my hip, then down the length of my thigh before he's spreading me, his hand doing delicious, wicked things beneath my skirt.

"What are you doing?" I hiss, attempting to cover myself where my skirt's lifted. "The waiter will be back any minute."

But he doesn't allow my wiggling to deter him.

His other hand falls to my neck, gripping me hard enough my breath grows shallow.

I still instantly.

"Unless you have a different idea, I plan to enjoy you along with my meal."

"You can't . . . I mean, I can't . . ." I gesture to my lower half. "We can't do *that* while we're here, okay?"

"And why the hell not?" he asks, clearly annoyed with me.

Lucifer isn't used to hearing no.

"Because we're in public," I hiss.

He lifts a brow. "And?"

"And it's . . . I don't know. It's indecent."

He chuckles. "Now you sound like my brother, Michael. He was always such a prude."

"Michael? As in the archangel?" I blink. He plunges a finger inside me, and I moan a little. "How many siblings do you have, exactly?"

Lucifer doesn't get the chance to answer, but from the look in his eyes when I glance over my shoulder toward him, the message is clear. I'm doing the annoying human thing.

The chef arrives at our table a moment later and acts like it's perfectly normal for a couple to eat in the same chair.

Even as Lucifer purposefully licks the finger he just had inside me.

I listen to the chef's description of our tasting menu, trying to enjoy all the intricate attention to detail, but I can't help but notice how Lucifer's hand grips my thigh, how close it is to where I want him to be, and with each passing minute, I'm more ready for him to touch me. The anticipation is killing me.

Maybe I'm a little more daring than I give myself credit for.

When the chef finally leaves, my need must be obvious, because Lucifer chuckles at me, nipping at my ear with one of his fangs as he pulls me deeper into his lap and hikes up my skirt.

"I hate you," I breathe, my head lolling back onto his shoulder from how he touches me.

"You and most of humanity," he purrs into my ear. "But I think what you really hate most, little dove, is that you actually love me. In the proverbial sense, of course."

"I do *not* love you."

He chooses that moment to part my pussy with his fingers, finding my clit, and I let out a loud, breathy moan. "Whatever you have to tell yourself to sleep at night, Charlotte." I can hear the amused smirk in his voice. Clearly, he's enjoying the way I gently rock my hips to chase his touch.

I let out another needy moan, dying to feel him inside me, before he releases my throat, placing his hand over my mouth.

"No noise. Not here. Your sounds are *only* for me."

It takes only a few more strokes, his fingers dipping inside me, in and out, then circling my clit in a delicious, steady rhythm, before I'm coming, the sound muffled as I bite down on his hand.

My orgasm crashes over me, the mix of desire and the fear of being caught heightening everything.

I come so hard that for a moment, I think I see stars.

When I'm finished, Lucifer releases me, allowing me to stumble on now wobbly legs back to my side of the table as the waiter returns with the first course of the tasting menu. A warm scallop caviar that tastes so good that this time it feels like it's my mouth that's coming.

"Fuck me, that's good," I say, swallowing the single forkful. I glance between Lucifer and the empty restaurant around us. "This is insane. Everything about this is insane."

He makes a show of licking his fingers clean of me again, which only causes me to bite my lip and feel like I'm ready for round two. I'm not sure I can wait until we go back to the penthouse later, and I'm already so wet for him, I can feel the dampness soaking the crotch of my thong.

"Do you mean me? You? The orgasm I just gave you, or the food that nearly made you have another one?" Lucifer's wicked gaze darts to my empty plate, and I flush a little. But he instantly makes it better when he says, "I brought you here for a reason, Charlotte."

"That reason being . . . ?"

"My brother tells me shellfish is an aphrodisiac."

It takes a moment for me to realize he's joking, but when I do, I throw back my head and laugh hysterically. I laugh until I'm nearly crying. At the absurdity of this whole situation. At how luxurious I feel eating this food when some people have nothing, and how ridiculous it is that I'm dining with the devil. And, more importantly, that I'm enjoying it. Thoroughly.

We're boss and employee.

Enemies and lovers.

And now, reluctant friends, it seems.

That thought sobers me, and I fall quiet then, noticing how Lucifer's studying me curiously. We eat in silence after that, and I try not to make it obvious how I'm watching him from across the table. Each movement is fastidious. Smooth and controlled. But no one's charm comes that naturally. It's the image he's cultivated. Carefully.

But I want to see the man beneath. The true soul. Not what he's made himself.

The waiter brings the second course a few minutes later, and only then do I finally regain the courage to speak.

"Do you . . . have any friends, Lucifer?"

His dark eyes narrow. "What kind of question is that?"

"An honest one. Humor me."

"Astaroth," he says. "If you must know."

"And your sister? Greed?"

"What makes you mention Greed?" His brow wrinkles like he can tell I'm up to something.

And suddenly this whole getting-under-his-skin thing is harder than I expected.

"Just wondering." I brush off the comment.

He returns his attention to his wine.

"Would you consider . . . *me* a friend?"

Lucifer chokes, nearly spitting some of his wine back into his glass. "What the fuck has gotten into you this evening?"

I scramble for an excuse. "I . . . guess I'm just trying to be more relaxed with you, that's all."

"Relaxation isn't my wheelhouse. That's Bel."

"Bel?"

"Belphegor. Sloth. My brother." He rakes a hand through his hair, leaving it a bit more disheveled than it started. "What the fuck am I even paying you for?"

I ball my napkin in my hand. "To keep sitting here, even when you act like an ass."

He leans forward, bending over the table toward me. "And what would you have me say to you, Charlotte? That we're friends? If that's what you need to tell yourself to feel better about the fact that we're fucking, then so be it."

"If not friends, then what would you call us?"

He waves a dismissive hand. "I don't see the point in entertaining this line of questioning."

I toss my napkin onto the table. "I think it was a mistake for me to come here tonight." I stand and head for the stairs.

I almost reach them, and for a moment, I think he might actually allow me to walk out before suddenly, he says, "Charlotte."

I pause.

"I will answer your questions," he says tersely. "No matter how frivolous." He wrinkles his nose at the word before he gestures across from him. "Please. Sit."

I feel my lungs expand and I stand a little taller. I have to work hard to keep myself from smiling then.

I've won.

At least, for tonight.

I return to my seat, and the chef joins us with the third course of our tasting menu. A warm lobster carpaccio with a squash-herb salad and Thai curry-lemongrass bouillon. Lucifer's face remains expressionless, not showing whether or not he enjoys the food. Meanwhile, I have a hard time not moaning like a cat in heat with every minuscule bite I take from the small, delicate plate.

"Must you do that?" Lucifer says eventually, gesturing toward my face. "Enjoy it so thoroughly?"

I lift a brow. "Don't you?"

He doesn't answer. Just takes another sip of his wine.

We're both quiet for a beat, but then . . .

I drop the verbal bomb I've been holding.

"Have you ever been in love, Lucifer?"

He goes still for a moment. Preternaturally still.

I tense, fully expecting him to lash out at me, like he always does whenever I get too close, but then something in his eyes softens, and when he looks toward his drink and then me, he appears almost . . . lost.

And suddenly I know what I need to do.

I'm going to make Lucifer fall in love with me.

Or learn that he's capable of caring for someone, at least.

I've been going about this whole thing the wrong way, trying to be like him when what I really needed to do all along is to be more like me. Beautifully human and flawed in every way.

To show him we're worth saving.

"I'm . . . not certain I'm capable of it, if I'm honest," he says softly, the words a low, tormented whisper. He swallows hard, moving his napkin from the table into his lap then, as if suddenly remembering himself. His voice turns cold. "Though I don't know exactly why I'm telling you any of this."

"Maybe because you trust me."

"Or perhaps because you're one of the few decent humans I've encountered." He swirls his wineglass before he looks at me, and I think it may be the most meaningful compliment anyone's ever given me. "Take that as you will," he says. "I find humanity often disappoints me."

"But I don't?"

"You wear your desires on your face, Charlotte. Yet somehow, you still surprise me."

I smile. "Maybe I'm more complicated than you think."

He huffs. "Yes, well, I'd know if I could see inside that foolish little head of yours."

"What do you mean by that?" I ask. "You've said it more than once now, but I've . . . never been certain what you mean."

He sighs, abandoning his fork next to his plate. "It means that when I look at humanity, I can see your greatest sins. It's what I use to punish you."

What a sad, awful existence that must be. Always seeing the terrible. No wonder he thinks the worst of us.

"And with me?"

"But with you, I . . . find I cannot."

"What does that mean?"

His nose flares. "It means it doesn't work with you."

"Why?"

"I don't know exactly." He shakes his head.

My mouth goes dry. "That . . . can't be good, can it?"

The waiter chooses that moment to return with the fourth course of our tasting menu, and our conversation pauses.

"I know you're not exactly the sharing type, but why not tell me this from the start?" I ask once the waiter steps away.

He shrugs a shoulder. "I didn't think it was relevant."

"Lucifer." I meet his gaze. "Be honest with me. For once. Please."

Reluctantly, he nods. "I needed to be certain you weren't involved."

"Involved in what?"

His eyes darken. "In whatever wicked game my siblings are playing."

My eyes grow wide. "Why would your siblings plot against you?"

He traces the rim of his wineglass with his finger before he looks at me. "Gabriel's due to return shortly, and when he does, whoever rules New York City will receive a heavenly get-out-of-jail-free card from my Father. Total redemption. It's why we're here."

"Total redemption?" I breathe. "What does that mean?"

"Access to Heaven. Our wings, of course." Lucifer swirls his wine. "Among other things." But he doesn't elaborate further.

"But why here?" I gesture to the window, to the city that waits below. "Why New York City?"

"If all the world's a stage, New York City is the center spotlight. It's simply the arena, the haven of vice we've been given."

"And Gabriel's message," I say uncertainly, "you're . . . you're certain it's true?"

He quirks a brow. "You think I wouldn't have done my due diligence?" I blush slightly at the insinuation, but continue to hold his gaze until finally, he sighs. "Only my Father is capable of opening the gates of Hell, and Gabriel is bound to the truth as his messenger."

"And the reason? That . . . that God let you out?"

I'm almost too terrified of the answer to ask, honestly.

"For fun? The apocalypse? Who the bloody fuck knows?" Lucifer snorts. "Your guess is as good as mine, darling."

I suck in a harsh breath, feeling more than a little unhinged that even the Originals don't know what God's plan for all this might be.

They're just as in the dark as the rest of us are.

"Okay, so that's . . . a . . . much bigger deal than I was expecting. But I'd say you basically have that in the bag, wouldn't you?"

"The winds of public opinion and celestial battles shift quickly, and I can't afford to lose." Hellfire sparks in his eyes. Bright and terrible.

Though this is the most unguarded I've ever seen him.

I mean to ask him why, but the waiter returns to refill our water, and I . . . think I already know the answer. I would give anything to have my father's love. His approval. It doesn't matter what he did to me, or how much I hated him, then or now. When that's something you've never had, a part of you will always crave it.

And Lucifer would move Heaven and Earth to reclaim even a piece of it.

The waiter returns shortly with the fifth course, and when he leaves, Lucifer catches me unprepared when he says, "How about you, Charlotte? Have *you* ever been in love?"

I pause, lowering my eyes toward my plate.

"Once," I answer honestly. "Or I thought I was. But that . . . dream came crashing down quickly." I set down my fork a moment later, the darkness of my own past catching up with me. "I'm sorry, but I'm not hungry anymore."

"Come." Lucifer beckons me.

He takes me by the hand and leads me from the restaurant then, leaving the waiter a more-than-generous tip before thanking the chef personally.

It isn't until we're alone in the car and he turns that handsome devilish grin on me that I finally ask, "Where are we going?"

"You'll see."

When we pull up outside 172 Madison Avenue, the building that includes his penthouse, my heart sinks a bit. But then he grabs my hand and, instead of heading to his penthouse, he leads me to a separate part of the building. One I haven't seen previously.

A few minutes later, we're standing on the rooftop, the stars overhead twinkling above the lights of the city. The view is breathtaking, and it feels as if I could reach my hand up to the heavens and scoop some of the stardust from the sky to keep.

"It's gorgeous," I say, staring out at the stars and the night sky, the city laid out at my feet. "Is this what you wanted to show me?"

Lucifer smirks. "No, Charlotte. Have a little faith."

He turns his attention toward the sky, and the shadows around us move suddenly, and then, before I can draw my next breath, the sky above us is bursting with color. Green. Blue. Purple. Pink. The aurora borealis. Over New York City.

I gasp, momentarily speechless, and then I'm laughing, laughing with all the joy that fills me as the lights sweep over us, painting me in their glow.

I turn toward him, breathless and uncertain what to say.

"You asked about my role," Lucifer says, stepping toward me, an amused, sad grin on his lips, as if the massive upheaval in nature and magnetic physics he created doesn't even faze him. "I'm the Lightbringer. Or I used to be."

I'm uncertain what I say in response, or if I even say anything at all. If I do, I don't remember, at least. I'm too shocked by the revelation that it isn't the shadows Lucifer's been moving.

It's the light.

God, it's so obvious now.

It bends toward him in every room. Seeking him, almost naturally.

A short while later, he drops me back at my apartment for the evening, having reluctantly agreed to let me go when I insisted that I needed to go home. As soon as I close the apartment door behind me, I go straight to the bedroom, trying to be quiet so I don't wake Jax, but also because I need to be alone. I collapse onto my bed, unable to stop myself from crying.

I cry for him first.

For myself second.

And then for the world.

For the secret, buried parts of him. This beautifully broken divine being that no one else will likely ever get to see.

CHAPTER THIRTY

Charlotte

"And then can you believe that asshole tried to short me on payment?" Jax says.

I scan through the numbers in front of me, searching for a duplicate.

"Charlotte? Charlotte, are you even listening?"

I glance up from the stack of papers in my lap. The phone numbers of all Apollyon employees. I've cross-checked them three times now with the number that's been sending me texts, but none of them are matching.

I look vaguely toward my best friend. "What?"

Jax cocks her chin to the side before she shakes her head at me.

"Sorry. I'm just so—"

"Distracted by this whole Lucifer thing," she finishes for me. She grins knowingly before she flops down onto our couch beside me. "He's really gotten inside your head, hasn't he?"

I shrug. "I guess so."

It's been ten days since Lucifer cast the aurora borealis over the city, an event that sparked all sorts of speculation and debate in the news about what could have possibly caused such a massive disruption in nature. The ideas were . . . creative, to say the least. Everything from aliens to Christ's second coming to even a fear that the Earth's magnetic poles might have somehow shifted.

In the meantime, Lucifer and I have fallen into this strange kind of rhythm. One where I spend my weekdays working and learning from Imani, but my evenings and weekends belong to him. Carriage rides in the park. Private theater previews. Fine dining. I know it's all supposed to be for the cameras that now follow us both endlessly, but I can't help but wonder if certain parts of it are real, or if . . .

Maybe he feels the same way as me.

I swallow hard, not fully prepared to admit the truth of how I feel about him to myself, or especially out loud yet. *Maybe we're both just lonely,* I try to tell myself.

But I'm falling, hard, and the look Jax gives me says she already knows it.

It's written all over my face.

I groan, covering my face with my hands. And here she went and warned me to keep my feelings and sex separate.

"I know. I know. It's just . . ."

"You can't help but see the good in him." She peels one of my hands away and laces her fingers through mine, squeezing softly. "You always do. You see the good in everyone. It's part of what I love about you." She smiles like that's somehow a good thing, rather than a sign that I'm naive, before nudging shoulders with me. "Plus, I'm sure it doesn't hurt that the sex is mind blowing."

I flush, laughing a little as I duck my head lower to hide my face again. I'm still not entirely comfortable talking about my sex life with Lucifer just yet, even with my bestie. With all the twisted religious trauma in my background, I'm not sure I ever will be. "I also really need to figure out who sent that press release," I add, attempting to change the subject.

Jax sighs. "I know you want to figure out who sent it, for, well . . . closure, I guess. But why does it matter, anyway? What's done is done, right?"

"I guess I just have a feeling that whoever sent it wanted to hurt Lucifer."

"And if they did, that would mean it's a good idea to stay out of it. Lucifer's a big boy. Or angel. Er, whatever." She flaps a hand in a who-cares gesture. "He can handle himself."

"I just really want to know, okay?" I lean my head toward her, giving her my best puppy-dog, please-don't-be-mad-at-me eyes.

"Okay, okay." She lifts her hands in surrender. "I get it, and you know I'm here for you. Have you told him about the texts, at least?"

I sigh, already anticipating another argument in the making. "No, I haven't."

"Charlotte, you need to tell him!" Jax shrieks. Her brows draw together. She's been on me about this for the last several days, ever since I told her. "We'll get this figured out, and I'm sure everything will be fine, but if you don't tell him, how is he supposed to protect you? You're worrying me."

"It's not his job to protect me, Jax. Even from some stupid text-message creeper." I stand and stalk toward the kitchen, grabbing the remainder of the matcha smoothie I had for breakfast from our minifridge.

"But it's *your* job to protect *him?*" She throws me a look that distinctly says *bitch, please* before rolling her eyes at me.

"Okay, point taken," I grumble, returning to the sofa as I stab my reusable straw into the lid of my smoothie.

Jax sighs. "Look, all I'm trying to say is that if you got yanked into this against your will, and he has the power, let him use it to keep you safe." Her voice softens, a hint of pity in her eyes. "And since you're not sure if things between you are real or fake, well, maybe cool it on all the hearts in your eyes, okay? I just don't want to see you get hurt."

I nod. "I know."

She pulls me in for the kind of comforting hug only your bestie can give after she's basically told you she doesn't approve of your life choices, but she still plans to love and support you, anyway. That's what true friends are for, after all. Calling you on your shit and making you a better person, while still loving you at the end of the day, flaws and all.

"How about you come out with me tonight?" Jax casts me a hopeful grin. "I'm meeting some theater friends at The Sapphire Lounge, and Ian's coming with. It could be a fun change of pace."

Another one of Gluttony's clubs.

I'm not exactly thrilled about the idea of missing out on an evening with Lucifer, no matter how fake our relationship may be, but Jax always takes me to the trendiest places, and it could be a good photo opportunity. And truthfully, I've missed the "high vibes" and laid-back positivity of my bestie. Hanging with Jax is easy. We could use some time together.

I give a halfhearted smile. "Sure, why not?"

Jax lifts her water bottle in the air, the one with the peeling sticker that reads "Virgos do it best," dancing a little as she pretends it's a stiffer drink. "Yas, queen!"

I laugh as she stands and heads toward our shared bedroom.

"Plus, Ian's been dying to see you, you know." She wiggles her brows over her shoulder at me.

I roll my eyes, following her. "Even if I was interested, you know I couldn't start anything with him until this whole thing with Lucifer is over. We still have another two weeks before the Met Gala."

She stands in front of the body-length mirror at the foot of her bed, holding up a strapless gold dress she snagged off a nearby hanger. Our apartment is small enough we don't even have a proper closet, so we split the bill for a standing clothes rack.

The word "rack" brings up a fresh memory that makes me blush a little, and I turn away, busying myself with searching for an outfit of my own so Jax doesn't see where my thoughts were heading. Maybe I can take her to the penthouse with me, and we can raid my closet there.

"I still can't believe he moved the freaking Met Gala for you." She tosses the gold dress aside, trading it for a cerulean blue one. Like a lot of aspiring Broadway artists, Jax is an amateur fashionista. No doubt she'd appreciate all the details more than me. "It's the biggest fashion event in the city. I mean, who does that?"

"Lucifer, apparently." I shrug. "He made it sound easy."

"Maybe for him, but for the rest of us peons?" She scoffs.

"What do you have against him, anyway?" I place a hand on my hip, but I drop it as soon as she turns to me. She isn't trying to be a bitch. She's just concerned for me.

If the roles were reversed, I'd do the same.

She crosses the room and places her hands on my shoulders, a worried expression on her face. "I just don't want to see you get tied up with someone who's emotionally unavailable, that's all. You're still so new to this whole dating thing."

I force a smile, not loving the reminder of my old life, even as I place my hands over hers to reassure her. "I know you're just looking out for me, but I'm in this at least until the Gala, okay?"

She doesn't realize that I'm doing this, at least in part, for her.

She nods, understanding, even if she doesn't agree. "If you say so." She flits back to the other side of the room, this time heading for the mountain of heels she keeps piled on the floor in one large heap. There's a slim, creaky door to contain them that's probably *supposed* to be the closet but is really more of a crawl space turned shoe storage than anything.

Jax lived here first, so I didn't hesitate to cede the space to her.

She owns more shoes than me, anyway. Well, she did *before*, at least.

"What about you?" I ask, trying once again to change the subject. "Have you . . . had any insights into who might have put something in your drink?" It's only been seventeen days since then, and I don't want to bring up something so touchy, but we've hardly seen each other lately, and I also know she'll need to talk about it eventually.

Even though Lucifer and I found her before the worst could happen, being someone's target in that way changes you.

She shrugs, returning to the gold dress. "Not really. But I did have this dream where I was back there. At Az's club, I mean." She glances over her shoulder. "But you and Lucifer were there, standing in front of me. You were . . . trying to tell me something, but I couldn't hear you over the sound of the music, I guess, and there was this, this man standing in the background, watching over you, like he knew you, but he was cloaked in shadow, so I . . . couldn't see his face. He reached out a hand toward you and Lucifer, and I tried to warn you. Of what, I don't know. I just knew I had to tell you, but the drugs were already in my system, and I . . . I couldn't move." She stares off into the distance for a moment, that glazed look she gets sometimes during her tarot readings. "And then I woke up." Her attention snaps toward me.

Silence presses between us.

Jax waves a hand, forcing a smile. "I'm sure it's nothing."

I nod, forcing a grin in return, but as I glance toward my phone, looking down at the unknown number and the cryptic string of texts I've been receiving, I can't help but picture a shadowy figure, coming for both Lucifer and me.

CHAPTER THIRTY-ONE

Charlotte

I stop by the office later that afternoon to let Lucifer know I won't be joining him for whatever outing he's planned for us that night. I figure it's a small courtesy, rather than ditching him over the phone. I've even rehearsed what I'm going to say. *I think it would be good if I was seen out with my friends.* Or maybe, *even real couples need to spend some time apart.*

But neither of those really work for me.

Yet when I arrive at the front desk of Apollyon, Jeanine tells me he isn't there.

"He had to . . . you know." She makes a gesture and points to the floor, like Lucifer might be somewhere underneath. "He said to let you know he'll be back later this evening."

I blink.

Okay. So Hell is a legit place, and apparently, he still goes there.

Noted.

I blow out a rough breath, trying not to look like that's new information to me. "Thanks, Jeanine." I turn to leave.

In truth, I feel a bit . . . odd about the fact that he ghosted me tonight, even if I was planning to do the same, but then Jeanine says, "Oh, and he also said to let you know that the penthouse is at your disposal."

I glance back in time to see her wrinkle her nose, like she's more than a little jealous of me, and delivering the message pains her.

I flash her my bitchiest grin. The one Jax taught me. "Don't worry, I already have a key."

With that, I head out toward the street, smiling to myself as I watch her mumble something under her breath in the reflection of the building's glass doors. I'm out near the curb, the late-summer sun shining down on me before I release the breath I've been holding. It's supposed to be my day off, and Jax and I already have plans for tonight, but . . .

I whip out my phone, balancing it in one hand with my PopSocket as I text Jax.

How about some retail therapy?

Grinning, I glance at the skyscrapers above me as I wait for her response. I'm twenty-three years old, and for the first time in my life, I have unrestricted access to a penthouse, a driver, and the company credit card Lucifer gave me, and I'm in New York freaking City.

What could possibly go wrong?

An hour later, Jax and I are half a bottle of champagne deep, and we've been in and out of half the shops on Fifth Avenue. I don't even need the company credit card. The clerks recognize me. I simply point at what I want, and the attendants put it on Lucifer's account.

The fun doesn't stop there.

By the time we're supposed to head for the club that night, the penthouse is trashed. Pool floaties. Champagne spray. Body glitter. Well, as trashed as a place that freaking ginormous can be from only two people, and Jax and I are thoroughly sloshed.

Lucifer's Bowmore doesn't make a half-bad mixer.

Dagon drops us outside The Sapphire Lounge a few hours later, trying not to show his amusement at how Jax and I stumble toward the entrance, giggling. He smiles at the doorman, nodding as if he knows him personally, and we skip the line that wraps around to the next block.

The Sapphire Lounge isn't as popular as The Serpent, or as dangerous, so we don't have to sign any waivers or anything. Entry isn't nearly as sought after, but it's got a fun, less-intense sort of vibe to it.

Ian and several of Jax's other theater friends join us shortly.

Erin. Riley. And Taylor. And a person who introduces themselves as only Avery.

Avery. Just Avery. Emphasis on the no last name.

I'm pretty sure they use they/them pronouns, but I haven't had a chance to ask yet.

By the time we all get our drinks, mine and Jax's pregame buzz is starting to wear off, and we're ready for round two.

"Why aren't we dancing?" she whines, bumping into Ian as she slides into the booth where we're sitting. The blue lights over the dance floor create a gorgeous sheen over her skin, highlighting her best features, and the body glitter we're both wearing gives us an almost otherworldly glow.

"I don't know how to dance," I shout over the music.

"How come?" Ian shouts back to me. He's still sober, though he won't be for long, at the rate we're all going, and he watches Jax and me in that amused way people do when you're drunk and doing something funny.

Though I don't know what I'm doing to make him look like that.

The beat of the club's music pulses.

"Her dad was like an evangelical minister or something," Jax yells too loudly. Loud enough a server passing by our table gives us a funny look. Jax sways slightly. "Dancing was probably the devil's deed or something, right, Charlotte?" she says, making air quotes with her fingers over the words "devil's deed," then throws back her head and laughs.

I don't really find it funny.

"It'sss . . . complicated," I say, slapping a slow, surprised hand over my mouth as I realize I'm slurring.

Jax leans forward, wiggling her brows. "She and Lucifer have this whole Dom-Daddy thing," she shouts to the table.

"Jax—" I hiss, swatting my hand at her.

"What? There's no shame in it, or anything. Get you some, girl." She makes a mock little spanking motion with her hand, and a round of laughter fills the table, before she hesitates. "Though . . . he *is* following the normal rules for it, isn't he?" She quirks a brow, like it's just occurred to her to be concerned about this. It's not as if I have a ton of experience.

I scoff, giving her a coy smile. But I don't answer.

Like Lucifer would *ever* play by human rules.

Ian glances down at his lap as he flushes then, looking adorably bashful considering the topic of conversation. He seems like a genuinely nice guy. "I wouldn't have thought you'd be into that sort of thing, ya know, with your background and everything."

My brows draw together as I try to concentrate on not sounding as totally hammered as I feel. "It . . . makes sense when you think about it, actually," I shout over the music, echoing one of the many conversations Lucifer and I had recently.

Ian lifts a brow.

I screw up my face as I attempt to focus, but instead, I end up word-vomiting at him as I yell over the music. "The modern church is full of that kind of . . . imagery. Especially if you're a woman. You're supposed to love God above all else. You're taught that submission is what it means to be a good woman, and . . . to seek His wisdom in all things. You're supposed to submit to God's authority, and to your husband's, but never question, never doubt. To have faith in Him. For He'll provide everything you need." I make a dramatic pointing motion at the club's ceiling.

"And when you don't do those things, the punishment is . . . well"—I laugh, letting out a small hiccup, as I sway—"majorly fucked up. Eternal damnation, unless you beg for his forgiveness and repent. And to repent, you're supposed to deprive yourself of all the things that might have tempted you in the first place. Things He created, mind you. Almost as if he *wants* to tempt you into punishment. So, in that way, I guess . . . God is really just the ultimate Dom." I flop back down into my seat.

The table goes quiet for a long beat, before finally Erin yells, "I think I'm going to need another drink." She moves to push her way out of the booth.

"I'll go with you." Ian.

He casts a furtive glance at me.

Avery soon follows.

Riley makes no excuse. She simply points to the bathroom and signs something before she does a dance with her hands between her legs, mouthing that she needs to pee.

We likely couldn't hear her well over the music, anyway. She has a cochlear implant that makes her pretty soft spoken.

It's like they're all worried sitting next to me will get them smited, or something.

I bury my face in my hands, slumping down into my seat at the realization that I stupidly made everyone at the table feel uncomfortable. Maybe I'm no longer cut out for this life.

Or maybe I never was in the first place.

Partying has never really been my thing.

"So, maybe less on the God is everyone's Dom-Daddy thing?" Jax makes a pained yikes face at me.

"I don't think I'm up for this, actually." I move to scoot out of the booth, but Jax quickly stops me.

"I thought things were going really well, up until then, I mean." She nods to where her other friends now wait at the bar before she gives me a sympathetic look. "But if you don't want to tough it out, it's okay."

"I . . . think it'd be better if I wait and try to socialize again after I'm through with this whole Lucifer thing. He's sort of invading my mind these days." I've crossed over from comfortably buzzed to the sad side of drunk, and I'm starting to feel it.

"You want me to call an Uber for you?"

I shake my head. "No, I've got it." I brandish my phone before I pull her in for a hug. "I had fun. Make an excuse for me?"

She gives my hand a quick squeeze. "Always."

I grab my purse, abandoning my drink as I make my way toward the exit, relieved once I'm outside and the cool night air hits me. The atmosphere inside the club was starting to feel . . . suffocating. I unlock my phone and I'm texting Dagon to ask him to come and get me when someone comes up by my side and says my name. "Charlotte Bellefleur?"

I turn and the paparazzo's camera flashes at me, barely inches away from my face, so close it nearly sends me down and onto the pavement.

I stumble, temporarily blinded, but someone catches me.

"Hey, get out of her face, asshole!" Ian.

Gluttony's bouncers notice the altercation then, stepping in to place a little space between the camera and me. They haul the paparazzo a safe distance away.

Though the flashes continue.

According to Lucifer, taking pictures isn't a crime. Even if it is invasive and annoying. He had to pay off the press for years to keep his face out of the limelight, apparently.

I don't even want to know how much he had to spend to accomplish that.

"Thanks," I say as I turn toward Ian, who helps me remain steady. As soon as I can stand on my own, he releases me. "I'm still not entirely used to them." I nod toward the camera.

"I'd imagine so." Ian shoves his hands in his pockets as he grins at me.

Jax is right. He *is* cute. Even if it's in a plain, average guy sort of way.

Lucifer's spoiled me for all others.

No one could ever compare.

As if he can read my thoughts, Ian says, "So, I don't mean to pry, but I thought you said it was just for show? You and Lucifer, I mean."

I glance between him and the nearby paparazzo, who's now been joined by a few others, trying to decide what I'm willing to share. "It is . . . well, sort of. But you . . . didn't hear that from me."

Ian's gaze flits over me appreciatively as he rubs at the nape of his neck. "So, does that mean I still have a chance?"

Whoa, boy. He's definitely flirting, but . . .

It does nothing for me.

I place a gentle hand on his arm. "You're a really nice guy, Ian, but I . . . don't think you and I would work, to be honest." I give him a soft smile, trying my best to turn him down easy. I am *so* not used to having problems like this. "But thanks for saving me."

"Sure, anytime." He returns the expression, but it's dimmer than it was only moments ago. Rejection tends to do that, I guess. "Just do me a favor and get home safe, will ya? I'd hate for another repeat of what we went through with Jax."

He seems to mean it earnestly, and he waves and starts to leave.

"Hey, Ian. Wait." I grab hold of his jacket.

He turns toward me, a look of hope in his eyes that I hate to disappoint.

"That night at The Body Shoppe. You . . . didn't see anything, did you? Like a shadowy figure or whoever it was that spiked Jax's drink?"

"A shadowy figure?" He chuckles, raking a hand through his hair. "Now I *know* you've had too much to drink," he teases before his expression turns serious. "But no, I didn't see anything. Though I did catch a glimpse of one of Lucifer's guys, that Asta-figure or whatever."

For a moment, I think maybe he might mean Azmodeus, but I'm pretty certain Ian would know the name of his own employer, even if he's already had a few drinks.

"Astaroth, you mean?"

"Yeah, that's the guy. Lucifer's bodyguard."

"Astaroth?" I ask again. Just to be sure.

He nods. "That's the one. Wasn't anywhere near Jax and the table where she was doing her readings though. Didn't even order a drink."

I make a mental note to mention it to Lucifer at a later date. "Thanks, Ian. Really. For everything." I place a friendly hand on his biceps and give it a squeeze.

He gives me a mock salute. "See you around, Mrs. Lucifer."

He ducks back inside the club a moment later, leaving me alone on the street. I glance down at my phone. I never hit send on my text to Dagon. Guess I'll hail a taxi.

But as I raise my hand, attempting to flag one down, my phone lets out a ping as the screen begins to glow through the dark.

I glance down at it, trying not to hyperventilate as I read.

You can't run from me forever, Charlotte.

CHAPTER THIRTY-TWO

Lucifer

Hell was particularly chaotic this evening.

I'm alone in the penthouse, all the staff having been dismissed for the day after they stayed late to clean up the mess Charlotte and her friend made. I don't begrudge her the indulgence. After all, I created temptation. Though debauchery is more my brother's wheelhouse these days. I roll my shoulders, noting the muscles are tense and sore.

Suddenly, the door to the penthouse flies open, and Charlotte comes racing inside.

I can tell something's wrong from the moment I look at her, and she's clearly been drinking, but the question that burns on my lips leaves me long before I have a chance to rein the hellfire in.

"Tell me," I snarl. "Who do I need to gut this evening?"

She stops in her tracks, blinking at me like for the first time since we've known each other she's . . . frightened of me, before she shakes her head, fortifying herself, and rushes forward, throwing herself into my arms.

I catch her, instinctually.

Everything with Charlotte comes down to instinct.

The way she laughs. The way she smiles. The annoying little way she revels in every mediocre bite of food she eats. Something about this woman bewitches me, and I'm . . .

Powerless against it.

I hate it.

The spell she's cast over me is a wicked one. Unusually cruel.

I hate every waking moment of it. The need it creates in me.

A need for things I no longer believed I was capable of. Until recently.

And the thought that someone may have hurt her . . .

Well, that creates an entirely different kind of need. The sort I'm intimately familiar with.

Some might call me bloodthirsty.

"I said, who do I need to gut tonight?" My voice is barely human, like it's been dragged over hot coals then forged in iron.

She doesn't answer me. In fact, my human fiancée doesn't say anything at all.

She simply sniffles against my chest, her small shoulders shaking, until I have no choice but to stand there and hold her, while battling the nearly irresistible urge to punch something.

To punish whatever or whoever did this to her.

I will raze this city to the fucking ground if that's what she asks of me.

"There's . . . something I've been meaning to tell you, Lucifer," she snivels finally.

"Tell me," I growl.

Whatever it is, little in this world shocks me.

Other than how she makes me . . . feel.

Is that what this is? Feeling?

No one else has ever made me feel before.

Her voice shakes as she speaks. "I . . . I've been getting these . . . text messages for the last couple of weeks."

It's the truth, I can tell. Lies have a distinct taste. Charlotte's most especially. Ridden with guilt and a self-deprecating hate that speaks to her upbringing, but that's . . . not the whole of it. Not entirely.

"Texts?" I prompt her further.

"Yes. From an unknown number. At first, I thought they were from you, but then they . . ."

"Give me your phone, Charlotte."

She shakes her head, placing her hands onto my chest as she pleads with me. "It's no big deal. I'm just sobering up from being a bit tipsy, that's all, and I'm probably just being dramatic. But they—"

"I said, give me your phone, Charlotte."

She stares up at me, lip quivering like she isn't certain she wants to let me see, but then she nods finally before she presses her unlocked phone into my hand.

I scan the messages quickly. One look is enough.

"You will go nowhere without Astaroth or one of my demons tailing you. Do you understand? And that's final." I turn and head for the bar, suddenly in need of a stiff drink.

Though human alcohol has little effect on me.

And even I'm aware enough to recognize it will never be enough.

"Okay, *Dad*," she says sarcastically. She backs away from where I held her, swiping at her mascara-streaked tears. "You can't keep me locked up like a bird in a cage."

"Watch me," I snarl, my fear for her getting the better of me as I glance over my shoulder. "Do I need to put you on the rack again? Teach you to behave?"

Her jaw drops as if I've slapped her. "Are you . . . blaming me?"

The glass in my hand buckles beneath my grip, the shards starting to press into the palm of my hand at what she's insinuating. "No, Charlotte. Don't be ridiculous."

"You *are*, aren't you? Isn't that what you're trying to say here? That this is somehow *my* fault?"

My hand shakes from the fury I've barely leashed as I pour myself another glass in a different tumbler, the movement almost imperceptible thanks to my control. My concern for her should be apparent. "I would *never* cast blame on you for someone else's deeds, but you should've come to me with this immediately."

"So, you could do what? Murder whoever's sending it?" She falls quiet for a beat, glancing out the darkened penthouse window. She rubs her exposed forearms, hugging them around herself. But when she looks at me, for once, her voice is devoid of emotion. "However big of a monster they may be, you'll always be an even bigger one, won't you?"

The words still me.

And I think that perhaps, since my fall, she's the only person who's ever truly managed to hurt me. Damaged my pride.

And that thought makes me furious. With her and me.

A flush of heat rushes through me, even as my voice turns cold, and the look I give her then makes her eyes go wide with fear.

A true predator will always be recognized by its prey.

"If it's a monster you want, Charlotte, then fine, so be it. I'll play your villain." I step closer, crowding her space. "But remember this is what you asked for, darling, when the danger no longer thrills you."

CHAPTER THIRTY-THREE

Charlotte

"Lucifer," I whisper as he steps toward me. "Lucifer, don't. Please."

I stick out a hand as I try to stop him, but I have my safe word, and I don't use it, so my cries mean nothing. He prowls toward me, roughly taking me by the wrist as he leads me toward his playroom, not stopping even when I beg him to let go of me.

Even though we haven't negotiated this scene like we have the others recently.

Even though I'm shaking with fear.

When we reach the playroom, he shoves me onto the floor in front of his devil's chair and forces me to my knees.

"If it's a villain you want, then it's a villain I'll be for you, Charlotte."

His voice is colder, crueler than I've ever heard it, and for a moment, I have the insane thought that this is the voice people hear when they arrive in Hell, when the torture begins.

As they drown amid the sounds of their own screaming.

"This punishment's for you, after all. To teach you a lesson. For fucking around with your own safety."

I'm crying now, but I don't exactly know why. He hasn't done anything to hurt me yet, at least not physically.

But the fact that I've disappointed him this much, hurt him this much, destroys me.

I open my mouth, trying to speak, but the emotions constricting my throat make it difficult to swallow.

"Who hurt you to the point you need to push me away like this?"

I sniffle as he returns from the rack that houses his dungeon tools and other kink paraphernalia.

But I already know the answer.

He holds a long, red satin ribbon in his hands that's clearly intended to bind me.

"Who hurt *you* to the point that you enjoy endangering yourself needlessly?" he roars, clearly furious. The hellfire flickering in his eyes makes me flinch. "You're lucky I haven't gutted that bloody father of yours."

A sudden feeling of cold ripples through me. A tingling discomfort.

If I was smart, or maybe had more self-preservation like he wants me to, I would keep my mouth shut or simply mutter a quiet "yes, sir" and hope I could convince him to treat me like I'm still the good girl I want to be. But I'm not smart, and I'm not a good girl when it comes to my own self-preservation. I'm a brat.

And the knowledge that he's right thrums in my pulse. A flush of fury.

I open my mouth, half-tempted to tell him that it wasn't my father who hurt me, not like this, that there are still things he doesn't know about me, but I bite down on my tongue at the last second, holding it in.

The truth will only make his punishment worse.

Best save it for another day.

"Place your hands together," he says.

I cup my hands, where I'm still kneeling on the floor before him, as he growls, "Like a prayer."

I press my palms flat, raising them above my head as he starts to bind me. Some weirdly beautiful, intricate shibari that I'll never be able to get out of on my own. I've done my research. After the first time he played with me.

With each wrap of the ribbon, the smooth silk tightening against my skin, I feel his disappointment in me. The way I've hurt him.

And worse, the way I've risked hurting myself.

For no other reason than my own immaturity.

As soon as he's finished, he releases me and climbs onto the dais, dropping down into his chair. His earthly throne. I lift my head toward him, swallowing at the sight of how that cursed chair makes him look. Draped over it like he is, he looks the part then. Like a dark, indolent god. Or a wicked king.

Prince of Darkness. Prince of wicked deeds.

He turns his head toward me, and even that small movement is predatory, otherworldly. "Come here, Charlotte," he growls to me.

I rise with a bit of difficulty, thanks to the fact that my hands are bound, swallowing down the lump of embarrassment in my throat as I stumble up and onto the dais, standing like a subject before my king.

From my king. That's what the caption on my post after the first night we spent together read. Even then, I don't think I could have known how true it would be.

Lucifer's shirtless—he must have stripped off his suit coat and vest at some point while he was binding me—and he undoes his belt buckle now, the devious look in his eyes reminding me a little of when I first met Azmodeus at his club.

Vicious. Animalistic.

A monster barely leashed.

"Are you going to use your belt on me?" I whisper, voice shaking.

"No, but I should." His eyes hold a dangerous mix of desire and fury. "But for this, only my hand will do."

The thought instantly embarrasses me, my face, neck, and ears flaming ridiculously hot.

Like I'm a child who needs to be punished.

But that's exactly how he means for me to feel, isn't it?

Because that's exactly what I was being . . .

A child who refused to recognize her own limits, her own capabilities, to the point that I risked my own safety. All I had to do to protect myself was be honest with him.

I drop my head, defeated, nodding before I whisper, "Yes, Daddy."

Clearly there's still a little bit of a good girl in me.

Lucifer beckons.

I sit down on his lap then, my now naked bottom positioned on top of his knees while my hands remain bound at my front. My wrists are wrapped up like a present. My dress is long gone. He tore it from me somewhere along the way to the playroom, but he'll buy me another, easily.

He'll buy me anything I ask for. Give me anything I want.

Only if I behave . . .

With my hands bound, he makes quick work of putting me over his knee, my ass tilted skyward like he's baring it and my pussy toward the heavens.

"Do you know what I do to punish brats, Charlotte?"

I'm not sure whether he means here in his playroom or in Hell, and I don't have the courage to ask, honestly. So I shake my head as I whisper, "No, sir."

"Well, you're about to learn, darling." He rubs a reverent hand over me, making me spread my legs more. Until I'm eager. "The answer isn't what you'd expect it to be. I don't force them into submission." His finger dips inside me, smearing my juices over my already swollen pussy. "I enjoy breaking them, you see." He whispers it so close to my ear I feel his words shiver through me. "So that they *want* to be punished. Feel they deserve it."

Exactly like he's done to me.

"Now, you're going to count the number of days you lied to me. The number of days you needlessly risked yourself." He rubs the flattened palm of his hand over my behind, both a threat and a promise of the pain and pleasure he'll give to me. "Your safe word is inferno," he reminds me.

But I don't use it.

He's right. I did put myself in danger.

By not telling him someone was threatening me.

So I let him. I let him do it.

"One," I whisper.

His first blow comes down onto my ass, hard, sending me careening forward as I tense to keep my balance steady. It smarts and stings. Bad enough I almost yelp, but I know from experience now it isn't the first blow that's the worst.

It's the last.

The final strike before he has his way with me.

The pain turns to heat, slowly radiating outward until I feel my pussy grow impossibly wet. In anticipation.

"Two," I breathe.

This time, the sting deepens, the flush making my skin red. Even as my pussy slickens more. In preparation for what I know follows. In aching need for it.

"Faster, Charlotte," he demands. "Don't stall on the recovery."

"Three," I mutter through clenched teeth. Bracing for the third blow.

Now it's *really* starting to hurt.

"Four," I gasp hurriedly, my heart racing as I try to clench for the impact and fail.

"Five." Now my ass is fully burning, and we're not even halfway through. Already, my pussy is aching, dripping for him.

"Six," I whimper.

It's somewhere between six and eight that I lose the ability to speak, and he takes over counting for me, each number more damning than the last as they fall from his lips.

"Nine."

By the time he's nearly finished, I'm crying, but still, I don't use my safe word.

He's right. He *has* broken me.

I crave this. Crave him.

No one else will *ever* be able to care for me this way.

Be both my lover and tormentor.

Exactly like I need. Like I want.

I'm shaking by the time he reaches the last count, my body vibrating with the euphoric high of the pain. With the peak of pleasure I know follows.

The delicious feel of his cock as it presses against my entrance. The way he fills me. Until there isn't any room left. Only him. The powerful thrust of his hips, each plunge making me clench, tighter and tighter until he gifts me his permission and sends me careening over the cliff into the abyss. The pleasure as his cum paints my insides so deep that I sometimes think I might die from the delicious torture of it, even as darkness swirls through my vision, even as I see stars.

But when he delivers the final blow, my body lurching forward with the momentum of it, my desperate cry going unanswered, he strokes a single finger over the outside of my pussy, bringing it to his lips as he whispers, "A shame you'll be alone tonight."

He casts me from his lap, like I'm not worth anything to him, giving a quick tug at the ribbon that binds my hands.

It falls away from my wrists as he stalks out of the playroom, leaving me alone.

I curl in on myself then, going quiet and still. A despair too deep to fathom ripping through me. As I lie there unmoving, in my mind I scream into the playroom's empty void.

Not because he hurt me.

And not because he decided to torture me like this.

But because I know, without a doubt, I've just undone all the progress I'd made with him.

All within a single evening.

It isn't until a few hours later, once I've showered and tended to myself, that I start to get legitimately angry. Not because he didn't sleep with me. Even the devil deserves the right to decide whether he wants to have sex. But because he tempted me into submission, only to cruelly rip my pleasure away.

To leave me to my own guilt. And without aftercare, for that matter.

A particularly dickish move, even for him.

This is the most callous he's been toward me in days, the first time he's threatened to punish me in nearly a week. Even though I enjoyed the last time, not to mention all the other activities we've tried in his playroom over the last couple weeks, I'm so frustrated by how our stupid argument derailed all the headway we've made that I can't help but want to scream.

My therapist would call this progress. That I've learned to recognize victim-blaming, even if I should have told Lucifer sooner. It's not my fault some stalker is targeting me, and, more importantly, I refuse to believe those kinds of oppressive lies about myself.

No matter who's saying them to me.

Though Lucifer played no small part in that recognition.

The words he whispered to me, or at least what I think he did, that first evening we slept together, lessened my own shame in a way that felt like he'd somehow absolved me. The feeling was only temporary, of course. Not even sex with the devil can heal the years of physical and religious abuse I endured from my father, and, more importantly, the *other* trauma that led me to flee here in the first place, but that doesn't mean I've learned my lesson. Not fully.

So even though I know Lucifer is hurt, concerned for me in his own twisted way, I pull out my phone and open my email.

> Greed, I'd love to meet. Below you'll find my availability.
>
> Best,
> Charlotte

CHAPTER THIRTY-FOUR

Lucifer

I'm out on the rooftop, nursing a drink and a cigarette alone by the pool, when Astaroth finally locates me. The orange glow of my cigarette pulses as I lift it to my lips, the sound of his footsteps approaching. I already sent word to him about Charlotte's stalker several hours ago, as soon as I left the playroom, and my demons move swiftly. Whoever the perpetrator is, if they're in this godforsaken city, I *will* find them, and by daybreak, I'll have torn them apart, limb from limb.

Antoine's death will prove little more than child's play by comparison.

"Nothing yet," Astaroth says, ensuring my already foul mood has no chance of lifting.

"Find them," I snarl. "None of you rest until you do."

Astaroth nods, used to dealing with me and my moods. "The doorman says you have a visitor."

I lift a brow.

"Azmodeus."

I wave a hand, flicking the ashes over the building railing. My brother picked a poor night to come here. "Send him up."

Astaroth turns to leave then, but my next words give him pause.

"What were you doing at Az's club? The night Charlotte and I were there?" A slightly deflated unicorn floatie droops nearby, one that the staff must have missed from when Charlotte and her friend used the pool earlier this afternoon. I toe it into the water with my foot.

I haven't spoken to her since I left her alone in the playroom earlier, but she made her feelings about my punishment abundantly clear, when, rather than tell me herself, she sent the information as an angrily written note through one of the staff.

She's furious with me.

Let her be.

Half the world already is.

Astaroth lifts a brow.

I wave a dismissive hand, lying easily. "She mentioned it before she fell asleep. Apparently, one of Az's bartenders told her."

He nods patiently, though I don't usually ask such frivolous questions. "Gathering intel. On Az, among others," he says without missing a beat.

But Astaroth is anything but patient. Even with me.

And most especially when it comes to the "little human" I now keep by my side.

"Of course." I nod, dismissing him, as I always have, in a way that shows how I've trusted him for over a millennium.

But for once, I let myself wonder if perhaps that trust might be misplaced.

My brother arrives on the deck a moment later, brandishing a thick, black dossier at me. "You have no idea how many people I had to fuck in order to get this."

I'm not certain if he means it in the literal or proverbial sense, but it matters little to me.

He tosses the information onto the pool chair in front of me before flopping down into the one beside it. "I had my demons do some digging on the Handler."

"And?" I pick up the dossier, flipping it open to the first page as I balance my cigarette between my lips.

Azmodeus may appear to be nothing more than the ultimate fuckboy, but what most fail to realize is that pillow talk is often rife with secrets.

And Azmodeus deals in them.

They're his stock in trade that will never lose value, unlike human currency.

"Our beloved sister is the one who hired him to kill Paris Starr, of course. Greedy bitch that she is. Though she's not the only one he's working for, apparently."

I lift a brow.

"A human organization. Call themselves the Righteous. Fucking unoriginal, if you ask me. They don't like our being here. They're causing quite a bit of a stir in the right-wing evangelical community."

"Mmm," I mutter, uninterested.

"And I also found a little something on your human queen," he adds, grinning ruefully.

I don't need to snarl to threaten him.

The light around us moves, suddenly casting a shadow where my wings used to be. The shadows unfurl like they used to before my bloody Father stole them from me.

"Sheesh. Relax, Luce." Azmodeus lifts his hands. "I'm not threatening her. Just doing some digging. Like any concerned brother would. For research, that's all."

That hardly puts me at ease.

"When it comes to Charlotte, fuck around and find out, brother." I pin him with the weight of my gaze before I thumb through the dossier he delivered, already done dealing with him for this evening.

"All right. You win. I'll leave," he says, throwing up his hands. "But there's . . . something you should know, Lucy."

My shoulders stiffen.

I tell myself it's the use of Michael's old nickname that sends my blood boiling, and *not* the way I feel about the human woman Azmodeus speaks of as he says, "I hate to break it to you, brother, but . . ." He grins wickedly. "Our dear Charlotte is already married."

CHAPTER THIRTY-FIVE

Charlotte

I agree to meet Greed at the headquarters of her lifestyle brand, Zest, the following morning. A massive skyscraper on Bond Street in the NoHo neighborhood of Lower Manhattan. The modern furniture inside the lobby is decorated in bright, eye-catching colors that speak to Mammon's over-the-top personality, while the walls reflect the muted beige, cream, and bamboo furnishings that've become associated with the self-help community.

The reception area smells of lavender and patchouli, and there's a large quote painted as a mural on the wall behind a fountain that I'm pretty sure is supposed to be shaped like a woman's vulva. The mural quote is from some celebrity, I think. It reads:

"In a society that thrives on self-doubt, liking yourself is a rebellious act."

I scrunch up my face as I read the quote, trying to decide what to make of it. Not because I don't like it or because I disagree, but because the woman who owns this building and her lifestyle brand make a living from the exact opposite. Greed's followers buy more, more, more of her latest trending new-age products in a constant quest for holistic perfection.

Maybe that's the point, really.

"Charlotte." Mammon's voice comes from behind me, and I force a smile. It doesn't surprise me that she came down to the lobby to greet me personally. After all, in her words, "We're practically sisters."

Not that I really believe she feels anything for me.

"Let's head to my office, shall we?" She takes my hand in hers like we're best friends and leads me to the elevator, as her secretary hops up from the lobby desk and generously presses the button for her.

"Good morning, Ms. Apollyon," chimes the secretary.

It's only the *Ms.* that lets me know she's talking to Mammon and not me.

Lucifer and I aren't even married and already some people have started referring to me as Mrs. Apollyon.

Mammon nods to the other woman, releasing my hand as the elevator doors close, and we rise skyward. "So, do you *enjoy* fucking my brother, or is your arrangement more . . . practical?"

My mouth pops open, the question leaving me momentarily speechless.

"I wouldn't judge you, if that's what he's paying you for, of course. I love money even more than the next woman, really," Mammon says quickly.

I blink at her, still shocked, the words nearly knocking me off my feet, or maybe it was the sudden jerk of the elevator. I grip the handrail as we race toward the twenty-fifth floor.

"I'm sorry?"

"Oh, don't look so put out, Charlotte. I don't particularly care why you and my eldest brother are sleeping together, but inquiring minds want to know, of course." She lifts her phone and gives it a little wave. "My followers are curious, you see."

Of course.

Greed's even more active on social media than I am.

I glance back toward the elevator door, trying not to panic as I'm caught between telling her the truth and lying. Isn't childishly getting back at Lucifer supposed to be what I came here for?

But that's not entirely true, if I'm honest.

I didn't forget his lesson, and I likely won't anytime soon, but maybe if he'd smoothed things out afterward, it would have stuck better.

I did contact Greed out of anger initially, but what I said to Imani in her office was also true. I need to look out for my own self-interest once my relationship with Lucifer ends, and no one is going to do that for me. Least of all him.

Not unless I grab life by the horns whenever the opportunity presents itself to me.

I aim for neutral as I cast Mammon a teasing grin. "I think my sex life with Lucifer should stay between us, don't you? Especially if we're going to be family."

Mammon smiles like she knows I'm giving her the same sort of answer I'd give to the press, but she's not bothered by my evasion. "Enjoyment, then," she murmurs. "Interesting."

The elevator stops, and we step out into the sitting area outside her office.

"Bjorn, hold my calls," she says to her secretary, a giant Nordic man who, based on his appearance and the covetous way he looks at her, is probably sleeping with her regularly.

He nods obediently and says in a deeply accented voice, "Yes, Miss Mimi."

Mammon closes the door behind us a moment later and says, "I do so love hearing him say that. Don't you?" She laughs, placing a hand on my arm like we're sharing secrets before she rounds to the far side of her desk and takes a seat. She gestures for me to sit across from her. "So, Charlotte, tell me. What can I do for you?"

I take a second to gather my thoughts as I lower myself into the wooden chair across from her desk. The chair's shaped like a hand with a flat eyeball carved in the middle that I think is supposed to be the evil eye or something. Jax would definitely know.

I smile my best Sunday-morning-greeting grin, trying hard not to wring my hands together, no thanks to the nerves currently making my blood race. I expected Mammon to take the lead in this discussion, and I'm not exactly prepared for how familiar she's being with me. Already this interview is different from any other I've ever given.

So I start with the truth.

"You said to reach out to you if I got tired of Lucifer controlling me."

"I did." She preens. Almost giddy.

Apparently, she's going to make me say it.

"And, well, I guess this is me reaching out." I shrug. Like it's no big deal.

She smiles knowingly. "And what do you get out of this little arrangement with my brother, Charlotte?" She runs a finger over an amethyst sculpture on her desk that I'm pretty certain is supposed to be Artemis and Callisto. Or maybe Sappho and one of her many female lovers. "I'd like to know if you expect me to make a counteroffer, you see."

Her reasoning makes sense, I guess, so I use a bamboo pen and a pad of heart-shaped recycled sticky notes on her desk to scribble down how much Lucifer is paying me.

I write the number I'm hoping to make beneath it, underlining it with a flourished line. It's a stretch given my experience, but if there's one thing working for Lucifer has taught me, it's that to the ultrarich like him and Greed, money is no object. Even if it's life-changing for someone like me. And with Imani's guidance, I know to own my worth.

Mammon looks at the figure on the note and grins. "That's all?"

I don't let her taunting deter me. "My interest and experience are in public relations and marketing," I say, also just like Imani taught me. "With specialization in social media management."

"And that's what you'd like to do for me? Here at Zest?"

I nod. "Yes, I think I could be an asset to you. Once I'm done working at Apollyon."

"And are you? Done working there, that is?" She quirks a sculpted blond brow at me.

I shake my head. "Not until after the Met Gala."

The disgust in her expression is immediate. Though I don't fully understand it. Maybe she expected me to be able to start straight away?

"It's two weeks. Standard notice," I say, trying to get our discussion back on track.

But I've already lost her interest. Or so it seems. "And what makes you want to work for me as opposed to one of my brothers?" She stands and crosses to the window, glancing down at the people on the street who look like they're the size of ants. "Any of the lot of them, really." She waves a dismissive hand.

"My therapist says I . . . have a lot to learn about self-love and self-care, and that's kind of your thing here at Zest, isn't it? Part of your brand?"

Pseudoscience aside, anyway.

She laughs. Like what I've said is meant to amuse her. "I suppose it is," she says, turning her attention back toward me. "Here's what I'm going to do, Charlotte." She rounds to the front of her desk suddenly, sitting upon its front edge, so close that our ankles are almost touching. She stares down at me, batting those long lashes, and my mouth goes a little dry. She really is just as beautiful and intimidating as any of her brothers. "I'll file your employment paperwork for you and hire you as soon as you're ready. But first you need to do something for me." She grins.

I'm silent as I wait for her to tell me. I need the security this job will provide more than she could ever understand.

But what she says next makes the breath rush from my lungs.

"End things with my brother."

"Excuse me?"

Mammon's gorgeous face turns wicked. And it's the first time I've ever noticed any resemblance between her and Lucifer. The Originals vary in everything: race, gender, size, color. Like God wanted us to know that sin comes in every flavor, I guess.

"You heard me. End it. Before the Met Gala." She smirks at me.

I shake my head as she rounds the far side of her desk again. "I'm sorry, but I don't understand."

She sits across from me. "My dear, sweet, summer child, you don't think Lucifer is with you because he truly wants to be, do you? Everything he does is for his pride, you see. To win this ongoing race for redemption between our siblings. Especially now that the final stretch is within reach." She casts me a pitiful look, the true color of her mouth showing from beneath her mauve lipstick as her lower lip pops into an overexaggerated pout. "And what better way to get humanity to focus upon themselves, to heighten their pride, overinflate their collective egos than to let them entertain the idea that the devil could fall in love with a human nobody. A human nobody who's exactly like them."

My stomach drops as she drives the final nail in.

"You're simply a pawn in his game, Charlotte." She shoots another sad, pitiful expression at me. "And that's all you'll ever be to him."

CHAPTER
THIRTY-SIX

Lucifer

It's less than a week before the Met Gala, and once again, Charlotte and I are on the red carpet. This time, the event is one I've chosen for her specifically. A philanthropic auction in which the proceeds benefit abused women attempting to reclaim their lives after escaping the religious and physical abuse they suffered at the hands of their zealous husbands, but if she notices the less-than-subtle hint that I know the true secret that brought her here to New York City, my fiancée doesn't say anything.

Instead, she seems distant. Like her mind is elsewhere.

She's been like that for the past few days, really.

Though, for once, I can't bring myself to ask her what exactly she's thinking.

If perhaps she's as hesitant for our arrangement to end as I am . . .

It isn't until the auction and accompanying after-party is over and we begin to take our usual questions from the press that she perks up slightly, playing her role admirably for the cameras. But unlike when we're alone, her smile is fake. Forced. I recognize that now, and the subtle change in her demeanor ends abruptly when a reporter from *Vogue* magazine asks, "Charlotte, care to comment on the recent remarks from your father?"

Charlotte's nails dig into my Versace suit sleeve. "Excuse me?"

"That's enough questions," I say, attempting to shut down the interview and usher her away, to save her from the circus that's no doubt about to ensue. But the media's sharks are ever relentless, and Charlotte remains frozen in place.

"According to our sources," the journalist says, "your father is the minister of the controversial Christian megachurch New Life Nexus, and when he was asked recently about what he thought of your engagement, he shared a verse from the Bible, Proverbs five, lines three through four, and I quote, 'For the lips of an immoral woman are as sweet as honey, and her mouth is smoother than oil. But in the end, she is as bitter as poison, as dangerous as a double-edged sword,' and then when asked to comment in his own words, he said, and I quote, 'May she burn for how she has forsaken me and our Lord and Savior Jesus Christ.'"

The crowd of onlookers falls quiet, sensing fresh blood in the water as the journalist shoves a pink mini-microphone into Charlotte's face and says, "Care to comment?"

"I—"

"*I* have a comment actually," I growl, struggling to keep my voice even.

Charlotte's gaze cuts toward me. "Lucifer—"

"You do?" The reporter's brows shoot up as she turns the microphone in my direction, stepping back a little at the sight of the hellfire in my gaze, though it doesn't deter her.

Bottom-feeders, the whole lot of them.

"I do, in fact." I look toward the camera then, ignoring Charlotte's silent plea for me to stop, how her grip on my arm tightens to where it nearly draws blood as I stare directly into the camera. "You can tell Charlotte's father, and every other worthless, hypocritical piece of religious shit who uses my Father's name to justify their hate, that I will see them in Hell." I sneer. "And I look forward to greeting them personally."

It isn't until we're back at the penthouse, alone again, that Charlotte deigns to address me. She throws up her hands in an I-give-up gesture, her red lips pinched.

"What were you thinking?" she says. "You can't fight my battles for me, Lucifer."

I shrug, hands still in my suit coat pockets. "I don't particularly see why not."

"Because they're my battles. *Mine*," she says, pointing toward herself defensively as she charges through the foyer. "They have nothing to do with you."

I cross to the bar and pour myself a whisky, falling into our usual routine with ease. "I'd say this one has quite a bit to do with me, if that quote holds any meaning for you."

"Ugh!" Charlotte drops her hands to her sides with an audible thwap. "I can't . . . I can't deal with you right now, Lucifer. I just . . ." She grips the roots of her hair before she heads toward the elevator, stripping off her Saint Laurent heels as she goes.

"Is that what he'd do? Quote Bible verses to you?" I call after her, causing her to freeze. "Use my Father's poorly translated, shoddily transcribed, and frequently misinterpreted and misapplied messages in order to get you to behave?" I scoff. "The modern Bible might as well be a record of a poorly played game of human telephone."

Charlotte shakes her head, refusing to look at me. "I don't see how that's relevant."

"Of course it's relevant," I say, my voice undercut with frustration in a way that causes her to face me. "You and I were forged the same way, Charlotte. Cut from the same cloth. Don't you see?"

"Don't try to make this about me." She frowns, clearly still angry. "I am *nothing* like you."

"I think you are," I call after her, as she tries to walk away once more. "And that thought terrifies you, doesn't it?"

"Just stop it. Just stop it, okay?" She whirls toward me, chucking her heels onto the floor in front of her, and shock fills me at the sight of the tears running down her face.

At how they somehow . . . pain me.

She inhales a deep breath.

"I can't . . . I can't deal with you playing the provocateur right now, Lucifer. Just please give me some space. For tonight. That's all I'm asking of you." She sighs heavily before making her exit, leaving me standing alone beside the piano.

The one that guests often beg me to play.

But there's only one human whose requests I'd willingly entertain these days.

I take another sip of my whisky, suddenly finding I can't stomach the taste I craved only moments before. I abandon the nearly full glass on top of the piano instead of shattering it. The thought's tempting. Nearly as tempting as she is. I run my fingers over the piano before closing my fist and pressing down onto the keys. It's at times like this that I find I most wish I could see inside her head, know exactly what she's thinking, sinful deeds or no, but I suppose if it worked like that, she and I wouldn't be here in the first place.

I don't know how long I stand at the window, staring at the passing cars and the city below, before Az arrives. Time works differently for immortals. Moves more quickly. But I can feel his approach even before I hear the subtle sound of his steps. I've asked more than once that he not simply *appear* inside my penthouse.

It doesn't take wings to fly or to step through time and space, as it were.

But all the skyscrapers in New York City make it a bit trickier these days.

"Don't you have anything better to do?" I snarl, turning to face him as he steps out of the ether.

"Than fuck around and annoy you?" Az makes a face as if the question is a particularly ludicrous one before he casts me his signature sparkling grin. "It's one of my favorite activities these days. Ever since you've gone soft for your little human."

"I have *not* gone soft," I snarl.

"Says the man sulking by the window." His eyes dart between me and the glass of $75,000 whisky I just abandoned on the piano alongside the open bottle. He shakes his head at me. "There isn't any shame in celes-*ty*-al dysfunction, you know," he says, replacing *erectile* with *celestial*.

Emphasis on the *I*.

I don't bother to respond.

My brother tilts his head toward me curiously before picking up the Bowmore bottle to examine it. "You know, if you really are that far gone for her, Luce, you could simply tell her? Though that would seem like an entirely anticlimactic end to this little charade you've been putting on." He sets the bottle back down again.

"Even if I did, it wouldn't matter." I turn away.

Sulking, like he said, I suppose.

But unfortunately, I can still see Az's reflection in the window's glass.

Azmodeus's jaw drops, like he's just now realized that this isn't all a game. "Fuck me. You really *do* care for her, don't you?"

I let out an annoyed growl in response.

I don't have the energy to argue with him, and the way I feel for Charlotte is a . . . complicated matter these days. No matter how frustratingly perfect she is or not, how I feel for her is irrelevant.

However big of a monster they may be, you'll always be an even bigger one . . .

Her words echo through me, tearing me apart.

She's right, anyway. More than she could ever fathom.

If only she knew the whole of it.

Az claims my abandoned whisky for himself, taking a sip before he swirls it about in the tumbler. "Why not simply wait it out?" he says, shrugging unhelpfully, as if he's suggesting a change in the furniture. "It's only a matter of time before she says it first, anyway. Humans are so disgustingly sentimental about these things."

"Says what first?"

Az casts a pointed look at me.

My mouth goes dry, and I grumble in understanding, turning away from him again as I shove my hands into my pockets. "I don't think she's going to say it, in any case."

"Well, why the fuck not?" Az says, gesturing wildly at me, like my mood has somehow ruined his whole evening. Or the fun he's currently having at my expense, at least. "I may be your brother, but if I weren't, anyone with eyes can see you're perfectly fuckable. Not to mention this is the single most exciting thing that's likely to ever happen in her whole miserable existence."

"It's not miserable," I snap. "Her existence, I mean."

Az offers a knowing, mirthful grin.

I release a heavy sigh. "It has a purpose. I . . . just haven't surmised what exactly it is yet."

Az's eyes go wide. "Careful, brother, or you might start to sound like Father."

But Azmodeus couldn't possibly begin to guess how much I've begun to reconsider my stance on humanity these days. On what they mean to me.

Or at least, one human, in particular.

CHAPTER THIRTY-SEVEN

Charlotte

It's the middle of the night, several hours later, when I wake from my dream. Not the one where Mark chases me into the forest, into the shadows of the trees that shelter me, hide me from view. I've been reliving that memory-turned-nightmare since long before I ever met Lucifer, though the shadows now take on a new meaning.

No, this time, the dream is different.

When I reach the forest, the darkness no longer feels threatening.

And instead of the gnarled shadows cast by the moonlight chasing me, I see a small, fresh-faced little girl.

"I forgive you, you know," she says to me, giggling.

Though I can't begin to place where exactly I know her from.

"He would have made a horrible daddy."

It's only then that I recognize the similarities in our features.

Suddenly, she disappears, the uncanny sight of her there and gone instantly, leaving my womb feeling unexpectedly gutted and empty.

In her place, a familiar figure steps forth.

Her dark skin seems to blend into the night so that the whites of her eyes and teeth gleam viciously, and when she speaks, her voice sounds like a shrieking chorus of a thousand furies made one. Of every woman who's ever been scorned.

"His is not your child to bear. Daughter mine. Bride of Lucifer."

Her head snaps to the side like someone's calling her.

"Lilith," I hear a sharp, echoing voice hiss.

I wake with a start, rolling onto my side as I place a shaking hand over my belly. Hoping I don't find a generous curve there.

But there's no curve. Other than the normal slope above my mons.

I heave a huge sigh of relief. Grateful that, now that I'm on birth control, when someday I do get pregnant, for the very first time, it'll be by my own choice.

With someone I *want* to spend my life with.

Not someone who's been forced on me.

Even if that . . . *woman* in my nightmare continues to haunt me.

She's a figment of my own guilt, my own fear, I guess.

I glance over to the other side of the bed, searching for Lucifer, but in all the weeks I've been with him, fake relationship or not, I've never once seen him sleep.

At least, not beside me.

It isn't until a moment later that some deep instinct tugs at me, urging me from the bed. I tell myself it's in search of food, but that's not really the whole truth. I grab the silk Ralph Lauren night-robe I now like to use from where I left it at the foot of the bed after my shower and wrap it around myself. The halls of the penthouse feel particularly dark and eerie in the middle of the night, and none of the automatic lights switch on for me, thanks to their programming.

It isn't until I reach the second floor and have my head buried in one of the many industrial-size fridges in the kitchen that a noise carries to me.

The distant sound of a piano.

Casting a wistful glance at the leftover piece of chocolate cake I was about to devour, I head toward the sound. The soft melody seems to lead me.

Silently, I pad toward the first floor, trying not to alert him that I'm here.

I want to hear Lucifer play, unaware that I'm listening, for as long as I can.

By the time I reach the first floor, I recognize the song.

The sheet music. The composition he was writing.

There are more layers to it now, though it's still just as haunting and desolate as when I hummed the notes that first morning. The first morning after we'd slept together.

I can't help but hope that maybe there's a bit of meaning in that.

I tiptoe closer as he plays through it a few more times, looping it and changing some of the notes slightly, like he still hasn't gotten it exactly how he wants it.

But to me, it's perfect.

Even more so because of the voice that accompanies it.

Lucifer sings like an angel, his voice deep and throaty. He doesn't hold anything back as he belts out the words, though they're . . . in a language that's unrecognizable to me. But my heart understands it clearly.

This is the language of his Father.

The tongue God speaks.

Goose bumps prickle across my arms, raising the fine hairs on the back of my neck. It isn't until he's finished, his hands coming to rest on the final chord before he releases the keys, that I step out of the shadows, clapping quietly.

"I thought I felt you there," he says, the shadows that hid me for only a moment twisting around me like a caress before they slowly retreat.

But I know now that it's really the light he's moving.

The shadows are only the result of it.

He pats the bench beside him, and I sit down tentatively.

"Do you play?" he asks.

I shrug. "A little. But I sing. In the church choir. Or I used to, anyway." I glance down at my hands. "I'm sorry I hurt you. Tonight, and that day when you left me alone in the playroom."

"You never need apologize to me, Charlotte," he says.

Not acknowledging if what I said holds any truth.

But I don't need him to say it to know that I hurt him. Deeply.

He may be a former angel, but Lucifer's far more human than he gives himself credit for.

"Will you play it again?" I nod to the keys. "For me?"

"You like it that much, do you?" He smiles, an amused little grin.

"Yes. Very much."

"I wrote it about you, you know."

The admission surprises me, so much that I feel tears well in my eyes, but I can't bring myself to ask him to translate what any of the lyrics mean. My heart already knows.

Lucifer's eyebrow lifts as his face scrunches into a look of confusion. "Why are you . . . crying, Charlotte?" He says the word as if he recognizes the emotion that accompanies it, but he . . . doesn't fully understand what it means.

I can't imagine he would.

He and the other Originals strike me as being, well, a little emotionally repressed, if I'm honest. I think it's a part of being a celestial being. I can't imagine God is the most present of parents, considering how he up and abandoned us all recently.

Lucifer most especially.

I sniffle, embarrassed by how I must look to him. My eyes sting. I swipe away my tears. "I'm just . . . happy, that's all."

But it's not the whole truth.

Not even half of it. It's not even close to what I really want to say.

I don't want this to end.

I don't say it out loud, but something in the way he looks at me, his dark eyes softening, makes me think he feels it too.

The words that we've both decided are best left unsaid.

"I . . . don't particularly care for when you cry," he says softly.

Which only forces a garbled laugh out of me. "Lucifer, I—"

"You don't need to tell me, Charlotte. I already know."

But we can't possibly mean the same thing.

I don't bother to tell him that before I lean forward and kiss him.

It's soft at first. Nothing but a gentle brush against lips.

But then I deepen it. Teasing his mouth open.

And suddenly, he's unleashed.

He tangles his fingers in my hair, gripping me and pulling me to him, as we both lay siege to each other's mouths. Tongues and lips feverishly searching, like we'll find both our last breaths there. A few moments later, he breaks the kiss between us, only to pull back and look at me. The fire in his eyes this time is different, unfamiliar. Unguarded and new.

And more terrifying than any hellfire I've ever seen there.

"Charlotte." He whispers my name like a prayer.

I place a gentle finger over his lips as I slowly stand. I lead him by the hand toward the elevator with me. Once we're inside together, he moves to press the button. For level five. The floor to his playroom.

But I block the button with my hand as I whisper, "Inferno."

Lucifer's gaze cuts toward me, and for a moment, he appears almost lost again, like he isn't certain what to do, and I see the scared, abandoned angel he might have once been then, when he was cast from Heaven. "Please," I say.

I hit the button for the floor where his bedroom's located, taking him by the hand again. I lead him gently once the elevator doors open. I don't stop until we reach his bedroom, where I seal the door closed behind us, releasing his hand.

"Charlotte," he says again.

Soft and uncertain.

I step toward him and place another gentle finger to his lips. "You don't need to say anything."

He shakes his head, capturing my hand in his as I drop it from his lips. "I'm . . . not certain I know how to touch you like this," he admits, swallowing hard.

Without restraints to keep my hands from straying. To keep me from seeing the vulnerable parts of him he doesn't want me to see.

I place my hand on his chest, above where his heart beats.

Immortal and unending.

"Then let me teach you."

We fall into bed together a short while later, my hands still roaming and exploring as we kiss feverishly. I don't think I could ever get enough of touching him like this. Exploring him of my own free will. Even if what we do in his playroom is also my favorite thing.

I have him naked and pressed back against the headboard, arms spread wide, as I climb on top of him, seating myself on his hard length. He slides into me with ease.

Both our breaths hitch.

"Whatever am I going to do with you, little dove?" he breathes into my mouth between kisses, the rise and fall of his chest slowly increasing. He brushes a reverent hand over my cheek. "You've ruined me."

"Why do you call me that?" I whisper back. "Little dove?"

He smiles before he flips me onto my back suddenly, swallowing up my excited little squeak as he kisses me. He brushes my hair from my cheek. "Because it was a dove that brought Noah the olive branch. To show him he still had something to look forward to when my Father's floods receded." The longing in his eyes stops my breath short. "You're that dove for me, Charlotte."

He sinks himself inside me again.

Filling me with all the unspoken emotion he feels for me.

And as I come apart, the sound of his name like a chant or a prayer on my lips, I see a pair of shadowy wings cast on the wall behind him.

But this time, he doesn't try to hide them from me.

CHAPTER THIRTY-EIGHT

Lucifer

It's sometime later, once Charlotte is already asleep, that I finally find the strength to leave her. I could watch her sleep for hours. Days, even. Time passes in a blink for immortals. And tonight, she's more at peace than I've ever seen her. I can't help but think that's at least in small part thanks to me. And I take a deep pride in it.

How she feels for me. It's perhaps the greatest thing I've ever accomplished.

But I can't help but wonder if she still will. Feel that way for me, that is. Once we reach our ending.

Astaroth joins me as I pour myself a drink beside the piano. I've never played as poignantly as I did while Charlotte was listening tonight.

I'm uncertain if I'll ever be able to replicate it.

"We've found him. The Handler." Astaroth scoffs a little at the nickname.

I turn toward Astaroth. "Good," I say. "Put him on ice for me."

Astaroth nods, then exits, once again leaving me alone.

I can't help myself as I glance toward the sky once more, the taste of my whisky bitter on my tongue and my heart pounding as I address my now-absent Father. "This is only the beginning." I take a sip of my whisky. "You'll see."

CHAPTER THIRTY-NINE

Charlotte

The following days pass in a blur, the dates on my iPhone calendar drawing closer and closer to the Met Gala. Not even what Greed told me can ruin it for me. Even if it's true, that's not the whole picture between Lucifer and me.

Or at least, that's what I keep telling myself, anyway.

I'm not certain I'd have the courage to face each morning if I didn't.

We're two days out from the event and the city is already buzzing with energy. The fall leaves on the trees in Madison Square Park and along Fifth Avenue create a feeling of abundance, even as an autumn chill fills the air. It's Friday, and I'm due for the final fitting of my Gala costume at Xzander's studio this afternoon. Evie's going to accompany me.

She reached out a few days ago, clearly trying to strike up an advantageous media friendship, and Imani advised me to go ahead and take her up on her offer.

Before I made my first appearance on Lucifer's arm, she was the city's favorite it-girl, a known "virgin" and celebrity good girl kept on her daddy's tight leash, and, according to Imani, she wasn't lying. Her father really is Russian Mafia.

Which means Evie holds more than a little bit of power, especially down in Brighton Beach. I could use a few powerful friends like her.

Plus, she's not all that bad, really.

Once you get used to the whole dreamy, sunshine persona. I still wonder whether it's legit or if it's all for show . . .

My phone pings, and I glance down from the style chair I'm sitting in and groan. "Ugh. I thought I'd already put it on silent."

Evie makes an adorable little hmmm sound as she acknowledges me. "Change your settings so that it doesn't start your ringtone again after so many calls," she recommends, waving a manicured hand at me as she searches through one of the many racks of clothing that fill Xzander's upstairs studio. "That's what I do when my father and brother won't stop calling me."

Her brother is set to take over her father's place soon, or so I've gathered from her doublespeak.

"I would, but I'm trying to keep tabs on what the other Originals are up to."

Especially Greed.

I glance down at my phone, but this particular notification isn't about one of Lucifer's siblings.

It's about me.

Curious, I click on it, opening the article.

Immediately, my stomach feels like it drops to my feet.

Sensing the sudden shift in the atmosphere, I hear the sound of Evie's heels click across the studio's concrete floor toward me.

Xzander ducked outside only a few moments ago to take a call, leaving us alone.

"What's wrong?" she says, her normally breathy voice taking a stronger tone than usual as she glances over my shoulder at the screen.

She stares down at the headline.

Charlotte Bellefleur or Charlotte Davis? Queen of the
damned already married!

"Oh," Evie whispers. "Well, that's unfortunate." She shrugs like it's
no big deal, heading back toward the rack she was examining. "Though
'queen of the damned' has a nice ring to it, even if there was that awful
old vampire movie." She wrinkles her nose.

"I . . . think I'm going to be sick."

"Hair back, sweetie. Aim away from the costumes," she calls over
her shoulder, as I lurch forward, retching the contents of my stomach
onto the floor.

A moment later, when I've recovered, I turn to find Evie taking
selfies.

"Oh, don't worry, I didn't position you in the background or anything." She says it like that's supposed to reassure me.

As if the whole story I just created with Lucifer didn't just bottom
out from underneath me. As if my old life hasn't finally caught up with
me.

"How do you do that?" I ask.

She quirks her head at me, smiling adorably. "Take such perfect
selfies?"

I shake my head. "No, compartmentalize that way. Smile like the
whole world isn't burning and I'm not vomiting in the corner."

Her expression fades then, and she steps toward me, careful to
tiptoe near where I vomited like she's afraid of getting her strappy
Balenciaga heels dirty.

"Let me give you a bit of advice about living in our world." She
places her hands on my shoulders, turning me so that I'm forced to
look at her.

She has the same stunning features as her mother, who, based on
my Google image searching, was a famous Moroccan model, with a soft
jawline, high cheekbones, wide brown eyes, and long lashes that would
make even the most confident woman green with envy.

I'll never be a permanent fixture in this glittering fairy tale like she is, and Evie will always be infinitely prettier than I'll ever be, thanks in part to the life of luxury she leads, but despite her financially privileged existence, underneath the glamour, I think . . . she might be just as terrified as me.

And she's much too kind for the company she keeps.

"Listen, there's always going to be some scandal or somebody who hates you or someone who wants to see you taken down a peg, or even killed, for supposedly screwing their boyfriend." She shrugs like she's speaking from experience. "Whether it's the media, Lucifer, his family. Hell, even me. But what you can't do is try to hide from it or make yourself small, because if you do, then you let them win."

"So, what do I do?" I ask, eyes searching her face for answers.

"You hold up your head like you're a motherfucking queen." She pinches my cheek, scrunching her nose in a way that's supposed to be affectionate as she says in her breathy, childlike voice, "Now go get your man and give him a good enough blow job he'll take care of it for you. Sometimes all you can do to not scream is keep moving. Or get on your knees, in this case."

Keep moving.

I nod. I think I can do that.

I take Evie's advice, for what it's worth.

She may not be a sage, but she no doubt has more experience with this kind of thing than me, considering she grew up in the public eye, and I . . . think she might be a lot smarter than she appears to be. She'd have to be, to not only survive but thrive while being kept under the thumb of a violent man like her father. Her situation is all too familiar to me.

But as I grab my purse, muttering my hurried goodbyes to her as I rush from Xzander's studio, I see it. The look in her eyes she spoke about when we met that first evening.

Like I'm desperate for someone to love me.

Both in the reflection of the Town Car's tinted windows as I climb inside, and in the haunted look she gives me as she watches me leave.

I arrive at the penthouse twenty minutes later, not even sure if Lucifer will be there or in a meeting. His work schedule is kind of insane. But the paparazzi that stalk us constantly have practically taken up permanent residence outside Apollyon headquarters, and now is *not* the time I want to see them.

Not until this whole thing blows over, anyway.

If, I remind myself. *If this whole thing blows over . . .*

Lucifer will no doubt be furious with me.

Keep moving. Or get on your knees. Evie's voice comes back to me.

In this case, it's not half-bad advice, actually.

To my surprise I'm in luck, and I find him in the wine cellar in a deep discussion in fluent Italian with his sommelier. Lucifer and the other Originals apparently speak every language known to man, and then some, considering the Angelic tongue I heard him singing in the other day. When I rush into the cellar, probably still a little green, he pauses midsentence, looking at me. He scans my face and then the rest of me, from head to toe, clearly recognizing something's wrong, before he waves the sommelier away.

"Charlotte," he says, turning to fully face me. "I wasn't expecting you back for another few hours."

I've practically been living in the penthouse with him these days.

Ever since the night he played for me. Made love to me.

I haven't been to my own apartment in over a week. Jax has been texting me.

"Have you . . . seen the news today?" I ask slowly. Like if I slow the pace of the words, that'll somehow soften the blow.

He quirks a brow. "I don't make a particular habit of it. Why? Is there something I should see?"

"No," I say quickly, shaking my head.

Too quickly, based on the lift of his brow and how his eyes narrow on me.

I start to pace, picking at my fingernails as I refuse to look at him. "It's just . . . there's something about my past that I . . . need to tell you." I chance a glimpse toward him.

He places his hands in his pockets. "Well, go on, then," he says, encouraging me. Like it's no big thing.

Like I'm not about to destroy everything we have in a single sentence.

My mouth feels so dry I stutter over the words. "I'm . . . already married," I manage to choke out.

I close my eyes, bracing for the impact of his rage the moment the words leave me.

But it . . . never comes.

I peek one eye open.

Lucifer tilts his head at me curiously, sighing a little, as he says, "Oh, that."

"You knew?" I practically screech, my voice echoing through the narrow walls of the cellar. "You knew and you didn't tell me?"

Lucifer returns the bottle he and the sommelier were discussing to the wine rack. "I didn't find it to be of any particular relevance, considering it's *my* bed you're sleeping in each night. I supposed you would tell me. When you were ready, that is."

"I'm . . . not ready. Not in the slightest." I shake my head.

"All right," he says.

My thoughts race. Heat floods my face, and the desire to flee is nearly overwhelming. *Why* is he being so . . . so reasonable about this? He has no idea how pissed off that makes me. The guilt and self-loathing have been eating away at me for weeks.

Or maybe he does know, based on how he's smirking at me.

"You knew," I repeat again, stabbing an accusatory finger at him as my muscles start to quiver. "You knew and you didn't say anything."

He examines another one of the bottles on the rack, blowing a bit of dust off its surface. "Neither did you, but you don't see me making any hasty accusations now, do you, Charlotte?" He lifts a brow at me as if to say *See? I'm learning.*

I can be whatever you like, Charlotte. His words come back to me.

Clearly, he's taken that to heart.

"You're not . . . I mean, you're not—"

"Angry?" he finishes for me.

I nod helplessly.

He grins at me, closing the distance between us before he pulls me into his arms. I collapse into him, staring up into his face like I'm broken in two. He's so beautiful that sometimes it feels like he uses it as a weapon against me.

"Well, whoever your *former* husband is to you, little dove," he says, "honestly, I feel bloody bad for the man, considering he'll no doubt be compared to me."

The confident way he says it is so . . . ridiculously narcissistic I can't help but want to kiss him while at the same time, I want to scream.

Instead, I throw my arms around his neck, burying my face deeper into his chest. He allows me to stay there for a moment, silent and still, burrowed safely into him as I slowly allow the relief to seep through me. When I finally come up for air, he tilts my chin toward him, and I start to kiss him. Over and over again.

Anywhere and everywhere I can reach.

"Did I say something particularly arousing?" He smirks like he's the cat that's just caught the canary, one he didn't even know he was on the hunt for.

"No." I swat at him, tugging a little at the base of his hair. "Now, shut up and kiss me, you fool."

"Pushy, pushy," he teases.

We end up naked on the cellar table, and then in his bedroom sometime later, as he finishes aftercare for me, before he finally whispers, "So, are you going to confess your sins to me now, Charlotte?"

I sit up in bed, taking his hand in mine as I say, "You really want to know my greatest sin? The worst thing I've ever done?"

Amber lights in his eyes. Though I'm not sure if he means for it to.

"Desperately," he whispers.

"When I was sixteen, my father decided I was going to be married. To a man named Mark, who was nearly a decade older than me."

Lucifer lets out a serpentine hiss, his eyes narrowing into snakelike slits.

I place a soft finger to his lips. "Shh. Let me finish, please."

He stills, molars clenched, though he nods reluctantly, capitulating as he gives me the space to tell my story.

"I . . . managed to convince my father to hold off on the wedding—for the negative press it'd create—until I was in my twenties, but that was always what he had planned for me. Marriage and babies. Mark was an up-and-coming deacon in one of our sister churches, and marrying him would form a sort of bridge between our congregations."

I trace small circles with my finger over the palm of his hand, unable to look at him. "For a long time, I viewed the marriage as a sort of escape, I guess. I wanted to get out of my father's house so desperately, even if I wasn't ready for the idea of being a wife and everything that comes with it." I grip Lucifer's hand, and he goes so still that for a moment I think I can hear my own heartbeat. "But it wasn't even a full day after I married him that I realized my father would never choose a nice Christian man for me. Instead, he'd chosen someone just like him. Only worse."

Lucifer's lip curls as he lifts onto his elbows beside me, amber eyes still watching me. The calm before the firestorm.

"I was only with him a few weeks before I . . . couldn't do it anymore. Couldn't be who my father wanted me to be. Live the life he'd chosen for me. So, I . . . ran."

"What caused you to run, Charlotte?" Lucifer's voice is inhuman.

Fueled with a righteous fury.

For me.

Because someone hurt me.

"He . . . mentioned something at dinner with his family one night, about . . . about me getting pregnant shortly, now that we were married. That's the goal in evangelical marriages, to . . . to show your devotion to God by being fruitful. You know, the whole 'go forth and multiply' thing? And I . . ." I struggle to breathe at the weight of the memory that presses down onto my chest. "I just imagined what it'd be like to have a little girl with him. A little girl who looked so much like me, and I . . . couldn't stand the thought that she'd be forced to suffer the same abuse that I had. So, I ran. I snuck out of his house in the middle of the night, and I ran into the forest, where the shadows waited for me." I glance toward Lucifer, wondering if he could possibly know the role those shadows have now taken on in my dreams.

Prince of Darkness. Prince of wicked deeds.

And now . . .

My vicious protector, it seems.

"I stole the key to our church from his office and I went there while he was asleep. I stole all the offering money from that week before I came here. It wasn't a lot. Not compared to the bank accounts most megachurches keep, anyway, but I . . . still felt like I was wrong for it. Like I was stealing from God. Even though it was only a fraction of the reparations my father would have to pay if he . . ." I look toward him. "If he ever admitted what he and the church did to me. To me and so many other women."

Lucifer remains quiet for a beat before he says, "He'd forgive you, you know. My Father. He may be a right bloody arse when it comes to me, but in this, he'd support you. It's exactly the sort of thing he wouldn't blink an eye over."

I give him a small smile. I know he means for it to comfort me, and I don't think he could ever know how much those words mean to me, even if I don't fully believe him.

Not even Lucifer can speak on God's behalf.

His guess is better than mine, but even he can't know for certain what his Father wants. Nor can anyone else, really. Especially these days.

Humans are just guessing.

I shake my head, glancing up toward the penthouse's ceiling. Like God might somehow still be up there. "I broke my vows to my husband. I stole from the church. I—"

"My Father doesn't care about any of those things." He says it with such conviction that for a moment, I can't help but want to believe him. "Not so long as you love Him. More than you love me." At that, he smirks, like he suspects that's no longer true for me, but the hurt in his eyes undermines it. "That's His gift to you, after all. Eternal salvation, should you deserve it. Though He . . . never offered the same for me or my siblings. Not until now, anyway. All while He sits back and watches this little competition He's created."

"Lucifer, I—"

"I will take care of this for you, Charlotte," he says, kissing me. Like that's the end of our discussion. "Have a little faith in me."

I open my mouth, but I stop myself as soon as he adds, "Please." The words are a tortured plea. "He certainly never did."

The emotion in the back of my throat makes it hard to swallow.

"Okay." I nod. "Okay."

Lucifer leaves me there, alone in his bed, smiling until his face shines like he's just accomplished some massive feat. He doesn't return until a few hours later, and I end up dozing almost the entire time he's gone. Not wanting to wake until he's there with me.

I don't want to face the world or the endless questions from the media that I know are coming. The looks from the staff. From the employees at Apollyon.

Though none of them matter to me.

The only person that matters has already forgiven me.

Even though it's him that the truth likely hurt the most.

I smile to myself where I lie snuggled in Lucifer's bedsheets. I'd never dare tell him this, but I . . . can't help but think there might be a little more of his Father in him than he'd like there to be.

Lucifer returns to me sometime later, gently sitting on the side of the bed like he's trying to be careful not to wake me. He kisses me and somehow must sense I'm awake, even though my eyes are closed. "It's done," he whispers to me. "I've taken care of everything."

Though I don't know exactly what that means.

It isn't until I wake the following morning and see the hastily signed, court-ordered divorce certificate on the nightstand, the one document that officially sets me free, that I turn to his side of the bed to thank him.

Only to find he's already gone.

CHAPTER FORTY

Charlotte

It's the night of the Met Gala, and not even the string of texts I receive from my stalker can worsen my anxiety.

You filthy slut.

I've got my eye on you.

I'm coming for you.

Don't think you can hide from me.

With each text my stomach tightens like a rock, my anxiety sky-rocketing until even the quiet noises and low lights of the penthouse are too loud, too bright. I don't respond or engage with any of them. Exactly like Lucifer's told me. He still hasn't located the sender, a fact that's made him particularly short-tempered, but I've already changed the settings on my phone to never display my location or show if a message has been read or received.

In the interim, Astaroth and Lucifer's other demons have been tailing me for days, and honestly, I'm more than a little grateful for them. I'm . . . afraid to be alone.

The Gala starts at seven, so Lucifer picks me up in the limo at seven thirty.

So we can arrive at our designated entrance time.

We sit and wait in the line of limousines that spans several blocks, all the way back to Lexington Avenue. Like all our evenings together, tonight is about appearances, but I'm finding it hard to stay still.

"When on earth are we going to move?" I complain, for what's likely the hundredth time within the past half hour. I roll down the window and poke out my head, the cold autumn breeze fanning my face.

"You humans have little patience," Lucifer says to me.

He's in a particularly nasty mood, and for some reason it . . . pains me.

I glance toward him, and images of what could be flash through my mind.

Even as I try to convince myself that tonight won't be our last.

We haven't made any promises or even spoken about it, but the other night changed things.

It changed everything.

"Finally, we're moving," I say, rolling the window back up.

I didn't allow Xzander to put me in the bizarre headdress he initially showed me to match tonight's theme, but the way Sophie decorated and pinned my hair to match my sparkling leather Marc Jacobs dress is almost as elaborate.

I much prefer Lucifer's getup.

An all-black suit with a camellia-flower-lined velvet cloak and sharp silver fastenings that make him look even more like this city's vicious king than he already does. The black guyliner he's wearing tonight definitely does it for me.

I sigh as we pull to a stop again, less than a block from the museum. Time seems to be moving faster than I can process, though we're still stuck here waiting. "What's taking so long?"

"True celebrities are never in a hurry, Charlotte," Lucifer says to me, causing me to narrow my eyes and glare at him.

The limo inches forward.

"Do you think it'd be tacky if I took pictures inside the fashion exhibit?" I ask thoughtfully. "I know we're supposed to turn our phones off, but I never got a chance to go to the museum before I met you, and I've always wanted to see one of the Gala's exhibits."

"Who cares if it's tacky?" he says, grumbling. "Give it a week, and anyone who speaks ill of you will already be focused on whatever other scandalous things we're doing. Or better yet, buried six feet under." He waves a dismissive hand, then pauses like he's just realized something.

I quirk a brow. "What's with you? Why are you being so mean?"

He doesn't answer me.

"Lucifer, you can't make empty threats against innocent people like that, they—"

"They're not empty. Nor innocent, for that matter."

"What?" The fury in his eyes causes the fine hair on my arms to lift in warning. "What are you talking about? Lucifer—"

"I'm sorry, Charlotte. I can't do this. Not tonight." He's out of the car and striding down the street toward the Gala before I can even blink.

The air in my lungs feels trapped, and for a moment, all I can do is watch in shock until my brain comes back online.

No. No, not yet.

I race after him. As best as I can, anyway, considering I'm in heels.

Lately Imani's been giving me walking lessons. Apparently, she used to be a runway model back in the day, before she worked for Lucifer. But I still haven't quite mastered the skill. I have to run for nearly half a block before finally I manage to catch him midstride. Lucifer's well over six feet. And I barely top out at a measly five seven, in four-inch heels.

"Lucifer!" My breasts are almost bursting from my dress as I try to catch my breath.

"I can't do this, Charlotte. I'm sorry," he says, whirling toward me.

I'm suddenly dizzy as the worst-case scenario flashes through my mind.

Do what?

We're close enough to the Gala now that a few of the paparazzi have started to notice us, and the cameras begin flashing.

I lower my voice. "What are you talking about?"

"This." He gestures between us. "Our little charade."

I flinch, shuddering as I struggle for any excuse to avoid what I know is about to come. "You mean . . . our relationship? But I thought you said . . ."

"No, darling, the *other* charade," he hisses. "The only charade that's been of any importance this entire time. The one where we pretend you've somehow changed me."

Something shifts in his eyes then, and the way he says it stills me. Reminds me of Greed.

My mouth goes dry. "Lucifer, what do you mean?" I try to reach for his hand, but he pulls away from me, raking his fingers through his hair.

Spots line my vision as an overwhelming feeling of dread nearly knocks me off my feet. Adrenaline shoots through my system.

"Lucifer, what does that mean?" I repeat. Harder now. More desperate.

"Ask me who sent the press release, Charlotte," he says softly, like he can hardly bring himself to say it. "Ask me who sent the press release."

My eyes go wide in disbelief as I watch him, my limbs heavy.

Because he's already told me the answer the moment he asked me.

I see the truth in his eyes. For the first time.

He had all the means. All the access. The opportunity.

I shake my head, my mind reeling. "No. No," I hear myself saying, refusing to believe he's manipulated me so thoroughly.

A lump forms inside my throat as I suddenly begin to connect all the dots. All the little pieces of information I've gathered over the last few weeks.

That only an Apollyon employee would have had access to my computer. That they would have needed to get past security. That they would've had to have known I was angry with Lucifer, eager to hurt him. That they would've needed to know where my office was. Would have needed a reason to want to manipulate me.

Greed's words come rushing back. Both prophecy and warning.

You're simply a pawn in his game, Charlotte.

My brain scrambles to find a logical excuse as I struggle to breathe.

And that's all you'll ever be . . .

I'm shaking when I finally bring myself to glance toward Lucifer.

But it's the look of . . . self-loathing in his eyes that stills me.

"I poison everything I love."

My lungs constrict, even more spots clouding my vision.

How could I not have known? How could I not have realized this whole time that . . .

The true monster was standing right in front of me.

However big of a monster they may be, you'll always be an even bigger one.

My own hurtful words come rushing back. Said in anger. Like somehow, no matter how naively hopeful I was that it wasn't true, some deep part of me knew.

And still, I was foolish enough to fall in love with him anyway.

My heart seems to slow for a beat.

How could I have been so blind?

"I . . . don't think I can bear another moment of your silence, Charlotte. Please say something." Lucifer's sneer feels so at odds with his words, I feel tossed about in a storm. Then it hits me that the hate in his eyes isn't aimed toward me. It's for himself.

For the monster he always told me he'd be. Right from the very start.

"And the threatening texts?" I say, glancing toward my phone. "Were those from you too?"

"No," he says. "No, I would *never* threaten you. Not the way *they* have. You belong to me."

Slowly I start to back away, shaking my head repeatedly as a fake, nervous laugh escapes me. As if that could somehow make it all better.

"But I don't," I whisper, still barely able to draw breath. "I don't belong to you, Lucifer. You used me. Manipulated me," I mutter before I finally bring myself to glance up at him, my words choppy. "But what I can't understand is why."

"Gabriel's return," he says. "Initially." His expression hardens.

Already making me regret everything.

Everything that I thought we shared.

It was a lie. All a lie.

And the only one who didn't know it was me.

A dull weight presses against my chest, until I'm incapable of filling my lungs completely. "And now?" I ask, my voice quivering.

"And now I . . . find my motives have taken on a different target entirely."

My eyes snap to his face before I glance toward the crowd in the distance. To the protest signs out in full force this evening.

I would never threaten you. His words play in my head almost obsessively.

Not the way they have.

"The Righteous?" I breathe. "That new far-right hate group?"

"Your father's, actually."

A wave of nausea rolls through me.

He smiles, though there's no amusement in it as he shoves his hands in his pockets, adopting a languid pose, but his gaze never leaves me.

Like he's determined to see this through.

As if he's doing this all for me. For my benefit.

Waging war against humanity.

But . . . to what end?

I feel the throb of my own heartbeat in my temple, my apprehension making me lightheaded, but instead of asking him, all I manage is, "You aren't the only one with secrets, you know." I say it as much to shock him as to hurt him.

Like he did me.

Though nothing I do to him could ever compare.

No matter what's happened to me, I'll never be as broken as he'll always be.

Never as vicious. Never as pure animal as . . .

The snake who tempted Eve.

And now . . .

Pain ignites in my palms from where my fingernails dig into my skin.

Me.

How could I have been so fucking blind?

"I met with your sister," I say, my voice turning cruel. I glance toward the few paparazzi sneaking their way nearer to us, the emotions roiling in my belly vacillating between disbelief, hurt, and rage as I try to hide how . . . exposed I feel. "Accepted a job at her company."

Though the second part is a lie.

Anything to try and hurt him as much as he's hurt me.

Lucifer's jaw tightens almost imperceptibly, and if I didn't know better, I'd say he was furious. But now I *do* know better. I know *him*, intimately.

Another lie. Another thing he's kept from me.

"You knew," I say. It's not a question but a statement. "You knew, didn't you?"

He shrugs. "My sister proved a worthy distraction. Exactly as I allowed her to be. Even if she hired someone to kill Paris Starr for her own twisted means."

The shock of Greed murdering Paris Starr barely registers amid all the other emotions I'm feeling as a burst of cold twists my insides.

I force myself to tune everything around me out. Everything except Lucifer's words.

"And us?" I say, shaking my head at him as I shiver. Almost too afraid to say it. "Was that all a lie too?"

He steps forward.

And I can't stop myself from taking a small step back.

"I told you from the start that it was fake, Charlotte. It was all fake. Everything but this." He snatches me toward him, and I have all of two seconds to try to jerk away before he kisses me, silencing my uncontrolled whimpers as he smashes his lips against mine, and for the first time, the bittersweet taste of his smoke and whisky turns to ash on my tongue.

But still, I melt into him.

Another shiver rakes through me, this one bringing a fresh feeling of weightlessness and heat. Warmth infuses my body, filling my heart, my soul, until it feels like it's singing, humming at the realization that he still wants me. Within seconds, my worry starts to lift, and I feel like I've been swept up in a tide of emotions of my own creation and I'm being carried away.

Like every pain and concern has left me.

Desire sparks, low and deep, making my belly warm and my hands practically itch with the need to touch, to explore him. Like I'd endure any suffering, any hardship if only it allowed me to get closer to him.

And even after everything he's done . . . I . . .

Can't help but want to forgive him. To love him.

Worship him.

Suddenly, he breaks the kiss between us, leaving me breathless and panting.

"And what now?" I whisper as we trade breath. Even as my mind screams that I should push him away, my body betrays me. I'm his, completely. "You're just going to throw that all away? Like I never meant anything to you? And for what? To punish your Father? The people who hurt me?"

He's shaking his head at me, like I can't possibly understand. "That's where you're wrong, darling. I never had any intention of letting you go." He tears another fierce kiss from me as his grip on my shoulders tightens, almost painfully. "I tried to warn you, little dove," he whispers against my ear. "I would burn this world for you. Now you're about to bear witness to that."

Abruptly, he releases me then, shoving me only for me to stumble back into Astaroth's waiting arms.

My thoughts flash to what he told me that very first night in Gluttony's club.

True love is ferocious, vicious, destructive. True love is costly, and humanity knows little of it. It's a price few are willing to pay. You all want the feeling of love without any of the work that goes into it. It's an irrational, self-destructive impulse disguised as joy.

Speak for yourself, I'd whispered.

But he already was. Even then, he was trying to warn me.

To tell me what his love would cost.

"You truly expected me to sit back and allow them to hurt you? To not punish those responsible for your suffering when it serves my purpose so perfectly?" He sneers like he finds the whole of humanity beneath him. All of them, except for me. "Your fatal mistake," he says, his voice dropping low as his gaze rakes over me, "was that you forgot rule number three." He leans down, placing one last kiss on my cheek as he whispers, "Never forget who I am."

He turns and leaves me then, standing there on the corner of the street. Astaroth holding me.

"Lucifer! Lucifer, don't!"

Astaroth starts to drag me back toward the limo.

But I refuse to go easily. I thrash and kick, struggling against him.

"Don't allow her anywhere near here," Lucifer orders. Our distant onlookers appear even more intrigued and confused than usual, but none of them intervene. Try to save me.

"Don't worry," Lucifer says, casting one last glance over his shoulder at me. "You've already ensured my Father will forgive me come sunrise. I'll see you shortly."

I watch him go, screaming and fighting against Astaroth, uncertain whether it was always going to end this way. Or whether he's exactly the monster I made him.

The moment I made him fall in love with me . . .

CHAPTER
FORTY-ONE

Lucifer

I stalk the rest of the way to the Met Gala, my long strides eating up the pavement now that Charlotte no longer trails me. I'm unable to bring myself to look back as Astaroth forces her into the limo. Though I want to. I could look at her for an eternity and never tire of it.

I regret nothing.

Punishing those who ever dared hurt her. It comes naturally.

And even if she hates me come sunrise, letting her go would only make me weak.

Already, loving her has made me soft. Irreparably damaged me.

But I will burn this city to the fucking ground before I ever let her go or allow any of her kind to go unpunished for what they stood by and allowed their brethren to do to her.

The flash of the cameras increases, going wild as I draw near the waiting crowd. I make my way onto the red carpet, muscling past a small circle of journalists huddled together at the foot of the stairs as I make my way toward Greed. My sister looks particularly wild and indulgent tonight, wearing a couture Givenchy that makes her appear nude save for hundreds of crystals, a too-tight corset, and a pair of massive faux angel wings that are meant to be a statement piece, though that thought only makes me want to throttle her even more.

My hand is at her throat, the crowd gasping as I lift her off her feet.

Mimi struggles to breathe. Her round face goes from cream to pink.

"I warned you," I hiss, my voice particularly serpentine. "I warned you to stay away from her." Abruptly, I release her, casting her aside like the celestial trash that she is, down onto the red carpet.

The crowd gasps again as she hits the steps hard, hard enough to crack the concrete beneath. As soon as she lifts her head toward me, she laughs wickedly. "Don't worry, brother." Mammon grins, her white-toothed smile turning nasty. "The bitch is loyal to you, you know. I quite enjoy her, actually."

I step toward Mammon, fully intending to take her on for another round. My immortal sister is more than capable of handling herself, but one of her bodyguards steps in. A massive demon who goes by the name Javon, at least when we're topside, who's wearing the body of a large, muscled Black man. "The humans," he hisses to me. "They're watching, sir."

He means for it to appease me.

To acknowledge the fact that even among my siblings, I'm king.

But unfortunately, it inspires the opposite.

"Let them watch." I turn my gaze toward the crowd.

The onlookers. The journalists. The paparazzi. Every one of them who bore witness to Charlotte's suffering and refused to lift a finger to save her. Her and every other innocent like her.

"Is this the best humanity has to offer?" I shout, causing the onlookers to stir a little. "Here for the show, aren't you? The spectacle?" I call to the now-silent crowd.

A few of them start to look a bit uneasy.

Though not as uneasy as they'll be once I'm through with them.

Once I've made them feel every bit of pain they chose to put her through. Every bit of self-hate I now know she felt as they all stood by, silent and disengaged, as her father, a man many of them would call a leader, used *my* Father's good name in order to control her, hurt her.

And for what?

Because they didn't care enough to risk themselves?

To call out hypocrisy when they saw it?

They'll regret the day they ever turned a blind eye. To her and every other innocent.

But despite their cowardice, still, they don't run. Don't turn their back and flee from me.

Exactly like I showed my Father with Eve.

They're vicious creatures. More ruthless to one another than I could ever be to them.

"Well, if it's a show you want," I say, gesturing toward the red carpet like I'm the ringmaster of this whole bloody circus they've created, "it's a show you'll get." I cast one last malicious glare down at my sister before there's a stir in the crowd suddenly.

And that's the moment I realize I've miscalculated.

I came here tonight with the intention of striking first.

Making them pay for what they did to her.

But I forgot one key thing.

Humanity will always be more wicked than me.

Lest they start to fight for their own salvation.

"Lucifer, down!" Mammon shouts from where she now crouches on the red carpet, where Belphegor and several of our other siblings have come to bear witness to the climax of our little game.

I don't bother to question her. I drop to the floor, covering my head and ears.

Just as a bomb goes off inside the Met building.

CHAPTER FORTY-TWO

Charlotte

Astaroth slams the door of the limo, only able to wrestle me inside the vehicle after he was forced to restrain me. The rope cuts into my wrists, tighter and more painful than anything Lucifer's ever used to bind me. I watch as Astaroth rounds to the passenger side, sliding into the seat.

Just then, a bomb goes off.

A second follows shortly after. The sound rings in my ears, even through the car's closed doors. I stare down the block toward where the red carpet waits, to where fire and chaos now reign outside the Gala, listening to the sounds of the screams. People run in every direction, women, men, even a few children, all trying to escape. But it's only a few moments later that I realize that one of those screams is coming from me.

Lucifer.

Was this his plan all along?

All those people. All those innocent people.

How many are hurt? How many of them are dead because of me?

All because I let my stupid pride convince me that I could somehow make the devil fall in love with me. That I was somehow special enough to change him.

God, how could I have been so naive?

Astaroth swears loudly from the front seat, like this isn't at all going how he expected it to. He pulls the gun he keeps at his hip, aiming it toward Dagon's head as he growls, "Drive."

Dagon glances toward the other demon then, seeming to realize only seconds before I do that Lucifer isn't the only one who's been lying.

And if this *was* part of Lucifer's plan, Astaroth didn't know it . . .

"No," Dagon snarls to Astaroth, the look in his eyes telling me everything it needs to.

This wasn't Lucifer's doing. At least, not this part.

And apparently, even demons can show loyalty.

In the next second, the burst of Astaroth's gun follows, and then I'm screaming again.

Blood and other viscera paint the windshield, and Dagon slumps against the steering wheel, his head turned to the right. Dead. His eyes turn cloudy, and I have all of two seconds to process his death before his skin starts flickering like a light bulb going out, causing all his veins to show. Suddenly his body is jerked upright with an unknown force. A cloudy black mass pours from his slack mouth with a demonic roar and smashes through the driver's side window before dissipating.

Astaroth opens the driver's side door and shoves Dagon's lifeless body out onto the pavement as I struggle to process the insane question of whether demons are sent back to Hell when they die or whether they just sort of . . . end. And what the fuck that black mass was.

Exactly whose body was Dagon even wearing in the first place?

I shake like a leaf in the wind, my hands still painfully bound behind my back as Astaroth slides into the driver's seat. He swipes a bit of the blood from the windshield, enough that he can see, and maneuvers the car up and onto the curb, nearly hitting dozens of screaming pedestrians fleeing the Gala. A third bomb goes off just as he manages to finagle us out of the still-waiting line of limousines. We speed in the opposite direction.

Lucifer.

"Why?" I whisper, more to myself than anyone else. "Why would he do this?"

I don't mean Lucifer.

But Astaroth still chooses not to answer me.

He pulls to a stop outside an alley a few blocks over. "He didn't, you stupid cunt," he says, nodding back toward the Met as the sound of another bomb echoes in the distance. "Hellfire's more his thing. Think Sodom and Gomorrah, only worse."

My mind is still processing. Still making connections.

Because if none of this is Lucifer's doing, then . . .

I don't manage to say anything in response before the door to the limo is ripped open and, instead of the cruel eyes of my father that I expect, it's Mark's hateful face staring down at me.

"Hello, wife," he growls as he grabs me.

CHAPTER FORTY-THREE

Lucifer

It takes a moment for my ears to quit ringing, and I pick a bit of bloody shrapnel from my cheek before the familiar chorus of humans screaming fills my ears. Another bomb pops off, the burst of sound creating an additional round of shrieks and agony. But this time, their screams don't belong to me.

The Righteous struck first. Already two steps ahead.

Which means . . .

I'm on my feet, eyes combing through the chaos that now ensues. I'm used to this. The sight of bloodshed. The sound of the tortured and dying.

But by my hand.

Not by someone else's doing.

I stagger forward, laughing a little at the sight of the zealots' flag as it unfurls atop the front of the Met building. A pathetic attempt to claim my city as their own?

"Don't tread on me?" Azmodeus is at my side now, grinning wickedly as he downs the glass of champagne that's still in his hand and reads the words on their godforsaken flag. "Who do they think they are? Fucking Metallica fans?" He cackles with bloodthirsty glee.

It'd take a lot more than a few poorly placed bombs to destroy my siblings and me.

The effort is quaint, really.

My eyes comb the fleeing crowd. "Where's Charlotte?"

"You sent her away," Gluttony reminds me. "Or so I heard." He reaches down and helps his twin, our wretched bitch of an only sister, to her feet. "I saw Astaroth shoving her back into the limo."

"You and half of fucking New York City," Mammon snaps, as if to say *And your point?*

"But that's not nearly as interesting as what happened after." This from Belphegor.

I look toward Bel, who's now joined by our other siblings. Wrath and Envy. He's wearing an all-black, see-through lace dress that covers a pair of metallic boxers that somehow manage to be camp instead of garish.

"What did you see?" I snarl.

"Nothing worth all the fuss," Bel says, waving a lazy hand like he's thoroughly enjoying needling me. "Just how he dumped Dagon out of the vehicle shortly thereafter."

No.

I'm already moving, the shadow of my wings unfurling as I step through the ether, landing only feet away from where I left Charlotte, not far from the vehicle.

The crowd of still-fleeing onlookers shrieks even louder the moment I appear.

Dagon's abandoned body lies in the street.

I glance down to find Charlotte's cracked iPhone on the pavement, picking it up only to find the screen still glowing. My vision warps.

This wasn't a part of the plan, which means . . .

I snarl, entering the passcode to open Charlotte's phone, not pausing even as the small slivers of glass cut through the flesh of my thumbs.

I open her favorite social media app, pressing the button to go live as I lift the screen to my face and address her many followers.

I intend to reclaim this city. And the woman who's mine.

"Find her," I say, snarling at the camera in a way that demands they now work for me. In a way, I suppose they always have. "Find your queen."

CHAPTER
FORTY-FOUR

Charlotte

I wake sometime later, the pressure pounding inside my skull.

With a groan, I open my eyes. Try to lift my head. But the room is spinning and everything's blurry.

Everything but the face of my scorned ex-husband.

My vision begins to clear, and I can make out the hateful, ugly lines of his features. I should have known it was him who sent those threatening texts. The contempt he feels for me is clear.

I can't believe he was ever inside me.

Not that consent ever really played a key part in what he did to me.

He steps toward me. The air smells like fish and sea brine, making me think we're on one of the city's abandoned docks, or not far from there. Mark's hateful expression twists to something sinister as he smiles at me like he's pleased to see I'm awake, but he doesn't show any kindness to me. He never has.

Him? A "righteous" man? Turn the other cheek?

Never.

"You made a fool of me," he says, leaning down so the heat of his breath warms my face. Garlic and cheap gin. And a bit of decay I can't help but think is his soul. "Cuckolded me, and with the fucking devil, no less."

I stare at him, refusing to look away from his generic white face. He could be any man in the whole of Middle America. Someone's father or brother. His eyes filled with hatred.

And I can't stop myself from laughing then.

Laughing at how foolish and small this man once made me feel.

But this whole time, he was really the one who was afraid.

Afraid of me. Afraid of my power. Afraid of every woman who ever made him feel small or want for anything. God forbid he be held responsible for his own feelings, his own temptation.

That's all I'll ever be to him. And to every man like him.

I am both Madonna and whore.

And I won't fucking let him lord power over me. Not anymore.

Not now that I see it's always been mine to take.

My shoulders relax, and for once my breath comes easy.

"What are you going to do?" I wheeze through my laughter. At the fear in his eyes as he looks at me. "Fuck me? *Rape* me?" I shake my head. "You've already done that."

And still, he couldn't break me.

"So, what is it?" I ask, lifting my gaze toward him. A snake prepared to strike. "What are you going to do to me?"

He doesn't answer.

My lips pull back, teeth bared.

"I said, what are you going to do to me?" I shriek, eyes filled with every ounce of hate I feel for him. I don't hold any of it back. The poison. The spite that fuels me.

A gift from Lucifer.

He grips the arms of the chair he's tied me to, leaning down toward me. "I'm going to do you one worse." His nose wrinkles in mock disgust, but he licks his lips appreciatively as he scans me head to toe, still wanting what was never his to have, to take. "I'm going to end that vicious beast you've been fucking."

I throw back my head and laugh at him then. True amusement now.

I laugh until tears fill my eyes, my senses narrowing as he starts to beat me.

I laugh at how he doesn't realize it's his own pride that's already destroyed him. Long before he ever hurt me.

CHAPTER FORTY-FIVE

Lucifer

It takes a few hours before Astaroth returns to me in my office, making a few piss-poor excuses about how Charlotte was snatched out from under him, captured by her own father's fucking lackeys. I don't believe a single word of it.

Gabriel is soon hot on his heels.

For once, my angelic messenger of a brother is a sight for sore eyes. Though the all-white suit he's wearing, which contrasts all too readily against his dark-brown skin, is a little too on the nose, even for me. Must he really dress the part, just to rub it in all our faces?

"Lucifer," he says, by way of greeting.

"Now?" I snarl. "Really, Gabriel? Per usual, your timing couldn't be any more bloody inconvenient."

Gabriel shrugs. "Dad sent me," he says. "His orders. Before He left, anyway."

"Of fucking course He did." I wave a hand, downing the rest of my whisky. The drink burns as it goes down, but it's not nearly fiery enough to appease me. To remind me of home. Back when it was all hellfire and deserving screams, and things were quaint. Simple. Not nearly this level of fucked. "You don't do bloody anything unless it's by His orders, do you?" I ask, pointing toward the ceiling with my middle finger. I phrase it as a question, though we both already know the answer.

Normally, I'm not nearly as unhinged as this, but being unable to locate Charlotte has driven me more than a little mad. It's been several hours since my live video went viral, but thus far, her followers have failed me. Wherever her father's chosen to hold her, she must be unconscious, knocked out or sleeping, because I can't find her.

Even inside the ether.

My pulse races. My power barely leashed.

If any of them lay so much as a finger upon her head, I will rip out their entrails and feast on them for dinner. The old punishments still appeal to me.

I turn toward Astaroth, giving him a look that says I trust him completely. Even if I'm furious that he lost her.

Another lie.

"The Righteous," he says, as if I'd ever believe that a group of pathetic, hate-fueled misogynists could ever get the one-up on me.

Not without divine help, of course.

I glance toward Gabriel. "You'll understand if the delivery of Dad's redemption trophy need wait for a few hours."

Gabriel smirks. Contrary to popular belief, my Father's angels are no less wicked than me. No better either.

I'm simply the fool who was brazen enough to act on what the rest of us were already thinking. The one faithful enough to believe that Father would still love me. Forgive me for my rebellion as He would His humans.

I won't make the same mistake twice.

"Take me to him," I say to Astaroth. "The Handler." I sneer at the nickname.

Astaroth nods, like this is exactly what he expected of me.

Torture. Manipulation. Bloodshed.

Until I get the answers I need. To find the woman he's stolen from me.

But I've yet to show my full hand. Play my ace.

The three of us step through the ether together, me dragging Astaroth along beside me. He's not nearly powerful enough to manipulate time and space on his own. Within seconds I find myself standing inside an abandoned subway tunnel beneath the city. The air is filled with petrichor, the scent of damp concrete, and the stale stench of humanity's unnatural and disruptive innovations fallen into inevitable disrepair. Just as they will no doubt return to the earth.

To my Father. Given time. Even when only the ruins of their civilizations remain, my siblings and I will still be here. And I look forward to bearing witness to it.

The Handler waits on a chair in the middle of the tracks, where he's been tied. Not rope or even chains are good enough to hold him. Only my power will do.

Two of my demons flank him, standing sentry.

They step back as soon as they see me.

I turn toward Astaroth. "Get my trunk," I order.

He nods, then disappears.

The Handler perks up, smirking a little at the sound of my voice. A voice that's no doubt familiar to him.

Astaroth returns with my trunk in hand at the exact moment our captive's wings unfurl.

"Brother," he says, greeting me, just as my demons begin to pull the blindfold from him.

"Hello, Michael," I say tersely.

CHAPTER FORTY-SIX

Charlotte

I'm still tied to the chair. My arms ache as a slap comes across my cheek. The next lands across the other just as quickly.

Like Mark thinks if he beats me enough, he can somehow stamp the wickedness out of me.

I woke from the first round of his anger only moments ago, and already I'm struggling to stay conscious again. But what he doesn't realize is that he was the one who made me this way. Who pushed me to the point of fury.

Enough fury I was willing to run into the devil's waiting arms.

That thought pains me. The thought of Lucifer and what he now means to me. More than any of the blows against my broken and bruised body ever could. But Lucifer taught me more than how to endure pain . . .

He made me crave it.

I crave that pain now more than ever. Not the one he gave me with his hands, but the one he created the moment he ruthlessly stole my heart right out of my chest.

His is a destructive love. A cruel thing.

But even after everything he did, I still want him. Need him.

I think that would have been true, even if the Righteous hadn't struck first.

The power his love creates in me. The adrenaline. The way it makes me feel like I'm falling apart and coming together all at the same time.

It's intoxicating.

And I think, not for the first time, that I might be a little addicted to him. Obsessed.

With his love. With the power it gives me. And with the twisted, wicked games we play.

I lied to him about my marital status for nearly as long as he lied to me. I've spent enough time tied to this chair, lost in the silence of my own thoughts and the blur of pain as Mark attempts to break my body, to realize that now. Even if my reason for lying was somewhat more . . . benevolent.

But the devil is in the details, I suppose.

As Mark lands another blow, I laugh, this time coughing up blood.

I spit, spraying some of it onto his shoes and across the floor as it continues to run down my nose, pouring over my face and into my gasping lips until it coats my teeth, the metallic taste faded because my mouth is numb by now.

But still, I continue to laugh at him.

The chair topples sideways with his next blow, sending it and me to the floor.

"Stop laughing, you worthless cunt!" he roars.

I've learned that's the worst thing you can do to a man like him.

Laugh at them. Humiliate them. Make them feel small.

Smaller than he already feels.

But I won't give him the satisfaction of my fear. I can't. I'm too delirious. Too busy choking on my own blood as the now-garbled words leave me. "Don't you see?" I hiss, my voice nearly as snakelike as Lucifer's.

From the power he gifted me by loving me, allowing me into his life.

Cruel as his world may be.

"Don't you see? You can't hurt me," I whisper. I shake my head at him, smiling through bloodstained teeth. "I'm the queen of the damned," I rasp, using the nickname they've given me in the papers. "And no matter what you do, he will *always* come for me."

I only wish I had recognized that before.

How he'd destroy anything that stood in his path. Or mine.

All to prove his twisted version of love to me.

CHAPTER
FORTY-SEVEN

Lucifer

"I hate to break up this touching little angelic family reunion, but this trunk is fucking heavy," Astaroth drawls.

I nod for Astaroth to drop the wooden trunk only a handful of feet away from Michael. The sound echoes through the abandoned tunnel, the wood smacking against the broken glass and gravel beneath our feet.

My angelic brother has looked better, all things considered. Of course, Astaroth *has* been keeping him down here on ice for me for the last several days. Though it's not as if angels need to eat, drink, or piss. Not with any regularity.

We're immortal, after all.

Unlike humanity in every way.

"A little something I captured for myself back at Sodom and Gomorrah." I nod to the trunk, where I know Michael can sense the plague it contains. A touch of my Father's power that now belongs to me. "Fucking chaos, that. Most fun I'd had in ages."

Michael rolls his head in my direction. "What's your point, Lucifer?" He never did have much patience for me.

I sweep my jacket aside as I place my hands in my pockets. "The point is that even when you and Father choose to play your tiresome little games with humanity, it's *me* who cleans up the mess."

"And?" Michael looks at me like he can already see where this is headed.

We've been having this same argument for all of eternity.

But *this* is the first time I've had something at stake.

Father's redemption. The one thing that can set me free. And now . . .

The one thing that can make me deserve *her*.

"And I find that role no longer suits me."

Michael starts to laugh. "So, what? You're just going to abandon Hell? For good, this time? Even if that works while Father's off on His fucking vacation to . . ."

He shakes his head, highlighting that none of us can even begin to know where my Father disappeared to. Nor if He'll ever return. Especially in the little time that remains of humanity's existence. Though Michael wouldn't dare utter such blasphemy.

"To, well, wherever He is . . . ," he continues, making an annoyed sort of face. "As soon as He returns, you know He'll shove you right back down where He wants you."

"No. No, that's not the plan at all. Not now that I have Father's redemption, anyway." I cast an amused glance toward Gabriel, who leans against the tunnel's graffitied wall as if he's infinitely bored with this. He never had quite the same taste for theatrics as the rest of us. Not unless he's center stage. Thank God Mammon snatched that bloody horn of his and hid it from him centuries ago. Otherwise, we'd still all be hearing it every time he felt the need to make an announcement.

Which is anytime his perfectly square jaw opens.

"The plan was to bring Hell to Earth, you see. Turn Father's own precious creatures against Him." My lips twist into a crooked sneer. "A feat I might have accomplished if you hadn't sent bloody Charlotte to ruin me."

"Charlotte?" Michael says. "Is that the name of the little human I hear you're keeping these days?" He chuckles like he's even more amused than Azmodeus was by the idea of me being in love with a human, the very creatures I waged a rebellion against Father over. "I didn't send her, Lucy. And neither did Father."

"Then who?" My gaze darts toward Gabriel.

He shrugs, flicking a bit of something from beneath one of his nails. "Wasn't me."

Hellfire sparks in my eyes. "So, you mean for me to believe that it *wasn't* Father who sent her?" To ruin me. To destroy me. To create this endless black hole I feel inside my chest whenever I'm not with her. Before her, I never needed anyone, nor anything.

But now . . .

Loving her has unleashed me.

To the point I feel unhinged. Untethered from this Earth. From the heavens. From the fucking ground beneath me. I'd raze any city. Destroy any creature. End the whole of fucking humanity if they so much as looked at her wrong.

And now . . .

Save them. Spare them.

If that's what she asks of me.

Michael smiles like he has a secret he can't wait to share, and it's at that moment I realize he's been playing both sides from the beginning. "Mother."

The moment the word leaves his lips, it makes perfect sense to me.

Lilith. Mother of demons. The first scorned woman.

The stories always got it wrong, of course.

Calling her the first wife of Adam, rather than the ferocious divine goddess who birthed my brothers, my sisters, and me. God's first and only love, and His greatest adversary.

"Leave Mother out of this," I snarl, teeth bared.

"She always did favor you, Lucy. Her first and favorite child." Michael's gaze flicks over me, like he can't possibly begin to see why she does. "Seems she might feel a bit differently these days."

Considering she sent Charlotte to undermine me.

And it almost would have worked, in any case.

Had Charlotte not gone and ensured I fell in love with her.

Vicious and cruel as that love may be.

Perhaps she should have chosen a woman who hadn't endured nearly as much abuse at the supposed hands of my Father as I have.

"Now that you know that I'm not working for Dad, are you going to let me go?" Michael nods to the chains that hold him, reinforced by my power. "I would have told you several days ago, if you'd have bothered to come and see me. Of course, you were too busy fucking about with your human. You always did have a soft spot when it came to women. Lord knows we all remember the cosmic fit you threw over Eve."

Gabriel snorts.

I shoot a glare toward him, then Michael, letting the power in my gaze do the work for me. "The only chance you have of me releasing you, brother, is after I've already dragged you down to Hell and back."

I step forward, turning only at the last second to gut Astaroth, who stands behind me. His heart thumps, only inches away from where I now grip his spine from the inside.

"Lucifer," he rasps, no longer able to breathe.

"You didn't think I wouldn't recognize a snake in my own garden, did you?" I tighten my fist, causing him to writhe. "You disappoint me." I circle my hand around the stringlike tissue of his spine, the body he's wearing convulsing. "I'll deal with you later. In Hell." I rip the spinal bone and tissue from him, snarling ruthlessly before I drop his mutilated corpse onto the subway track.

"Obviously, you still have a flair for the dramatic." Michael wrinkles his nose at the corpse and viscera that lie at my feet.

As if any of us would dare to believe that he isn't equally bloodthirsty.

Turning back toward my brothers, I face Gabriel first. "I believe Father and I had an agreement."

Gabriel tilts his head, inhaling sharply through his teeth in an expression that says *eh, I wouldn't be so sure about that.* "Technically the offer wasn't extended to you, but Father never was one to split hairs on the details." He shrugs. "He's a man of His word. Always has been, Lucy."

"Perhaps when it came to you," I say bitterly, "but with me . . ." My voice trails off. "Well, let's just say the apple never did fall far from the tree."

I snap my fingers, and Michael's bindings drop to the floor.

"Run back to Daddy now and tell Him what you've seen."

"Even *I* don't know where Father is this time, Lucy. This time, He's well and truly gone." Michael stretches his wings. "I'll be in touch, brother." He gives the white feathers of his wings one generous flap before he's gone, disappeared into the ether.

I turn to Gabriel as my gaze flicks upward. "I'll deal with Him later."

"And Mother?" Gabriel asks, grinning. Like he's infinitely pleased he gets a front-row seat to this whole little charade.

"She'll have to wait for another day, I suppose." I grip the handle of my unopened trunk, hoisting it into my hand with ease. "For now, I have places I need to be."

CHAPTER FORTY-EIGHT

Lucifer

It takes only a moment of searching through the ether, the massive, spiraled scrawl of time and stars and space, before I find the Kansas-based church where Charlotte's father is located. A tiny pinprick of a building amid the vastness of the universe with an ethnically incorrect statue of Christ nailed to the cross hanging from the ceiling, his head adorned with a crown of thorns.

I step out of the fold, standing in the middle of the aisle as I stare up at it.

Even *I* can admit he always was the best among us.

Even if he was Father's favorite.

"I'm sorry you have to see this," I say to the effigy of my youngest, and only human, brother. As if the man himself can hear me.

It doesn't take long for the human knelt in the first-row pew to notice me. I could have tortured the information out of Astaroth, I suppose, before I sent him back to Hell, but that wouldn't have been nearly as diverting. Or satisfying.

Besides, I've been waiting for an excuse to do this from the very beginning.

From the moment I first realized I was in love with her.

The man's eyes grow wide at the sight of me, and it strikes me then that he looks more than a little like Charlotte. How she looks whenever she's angry with me.

The muscles in my right hand clench as I lick my lips eagerly.

Somehow, that only makes me want to punish him all the more.

"You—" He sputters, glancing between me and the statue of Christ mounted on the wall like a fucking trophy of his salvation.

My Father was never much a fan of idolatry.

"I thought . . . But you can't—"

"Be in here?" I finish.

He glances around the church helplessly.

"Urban myth, you see." I set my trunk on the floor with an audible thud.

His eyes fall to it.

Something about the sight of it must alert him to exactly how much danger he's in.

Not that he'd ever have the balls to actually face me.

No. Instead, he sent his little hate group to do it for him.

My lip curls. Cowards, the whole lot of them.

My Father's always attracted his kind easily. Lured them in with His false promises. Well, false for men like them, at least. My Father is an unforgiving god.

And He leaves their punishment to me.

I step toward him, and immediately, he starts to pray.

"Our Father who art in Heaven," he starts, beginning the Lord's Prayer.

But it's already too late.

My Father's no longer listening.

". . . hallowed be Thy name . . ."

I join him. "Thy Kingdom come. Thy will be done on Earth as it is in Heaven."

His clasped hands start to shake, and he squeezes his eyes shut. "Give us this day our daily bread. Forgive us our sins, as we forgive those who sin against us. And lead us not into temptation, but deliver us from evil. For Thine is the Kingdom, the power, and the glory, forever and ever."

Our words echo throughout the sanctuary together. But to his credit, his voice doesn't waver. Even as he trembles.

"Amen," I finish. "Who do you think helped translate the original to Greek and Latin?" I lift a telling brow. "That was back when I was still trying to earn His love again." Fire sparks in my eyes. "Now I know better."

"I always knew that girl was wicked to the core," he mutters, still so quick to damn his own daughter for his transgressions.

"Once a misogynist, always a misogynist, I see." I sigh. "Too bad that where I'm sending you, it's women who inflict the torture."

He pales. "What?"

"You'll make a nice offering. Keep my Mother appeased." I shrug. "For now, at least."

I bend and open the trunk at my feet, reveling in the wet stain that forms on the front of his pants as he watches the white light of my Father's plague emerge. "Consider it a gift from my Father. Only a biblical death would do for you."

"Father?" he says, glancing up toward the heavens.

As if that somehow might save him.

"I think you'll find He won't answer these days." I step toward him. "Now, the world answers to me." I lift a hand, some of my Father's power twisting between my fingers. I flex as if to grip the writhing light inside my waiting palm.

Charlotte's father convulses, his body jerking as he drops to his knees, eyes bulging as he begins to choke on his own blood.

"Where is she?" I growl.

He shakes his head.

"Too bad you didn't listen to the part of your little book where it tells you to paint lamb's blood over the door." I wrinkle my nose. "The smell always did nauseate me."

I tighten my grip more, and it sends him careening forward, vomiting blood onto the altar.

"I said, where is she?"

"Mark," he barely manages to rasp.

I tilt my head to the side. "Her ex-husband? He has her?"

He nods weakly.

I flash a cold smile. "Shame that he didn't cherish her from the start. Before she became mine."

I clutch the light inside my closed fist, and Charlotte's father convulses violently. His still-pumping heart bursts forth from his chest a moment later, flying into my now-outstretched hand.

His blood slips down my fingers and wrist to stain the white cuff of my shirt, his heart giving one or two beating pulses where it sits in my palm.

I lick some it away from where it drips, reveling in the metallic taste, before I drop the stray organ onto the sanctuary floor. "Now to retrieve my queen."

CHAPTER
FORTY-NINE

Charlotte

I'm barely conscious, barely clinging to life by the time Mark finally unties me.

The chair has splintered into dozens of pieces beneath me, and I let out a weak moan, trying and failing to use my elbows to crawl toward the door. I try not to notice the wrong angle one arm bends at. It's clearly fractured halfway to the wrist. From here, I can see a rusty old sign on the wall. I can just make out the words **BROOKLYN NAVY YARD**. But knowing where I am doesn't do me any good. Already, Mark's broken me. My body, at least.

But never my spirit.

I, Charlotte Bellefleur, was raised to know how to bend to a man's will.

But never break.

With my one good hand, I clutch one of the splintered chair legs, pulling it underneath me to shield it. Like I'm clutching at my own heart. But the move is only to hide it from him. I don't think Mark ever intended for me to die here. But my laughter has pushed him into a blind fury.

And if it's going to be one of us . . .

Like hell is it going to be me.

I shake my head, what I'm able to move of my neck, anyway. My whole body hurts like I'm one large wound—at this point I might be. A dull ache shoots down between my shoulders, and my face throbs like it's swollen beyond recognition.

But still I force myself to let out a delirious, scratchy laugh.

He wrenches me back by my hair, forcing my spine to bow unnaturally.

"You filthy little slut," he growls, a bit of spittle hitting me.

I grin up at him as I rasp, "He calls me the same thing when he fucks me."

The rest of it is implied as I cast him a deranged smile.

And I fucking love it.

I'm not ashamed, and Mark can't make me be.

The realization that he's lost, that he has no more control over me, plays out on his face. His twisted sneer goes still, but there's visible tension in his jaw before suddenly the veins in his neck strain. He forces me to roll onto my back by the root of my hair, but that's exactly what I was anticipating.

As I roll, I bring my foot up and into his balls. Hard.

It's the weakest spot on his body, but somehow, it's also the part that makes him think he's justified to hold power over me.

But my power is my own.

To give and to take.

Not even the devil himself can keep it from me.

I use the last ounce of my strength to pull the splintered chair leg forward just as Mark topples down onto me. Between the weight of his average five-foot-nine frame and the momentum of him falling, it's enough.

He impales himself on the wooden shard, right in the chest. Not deep.

But it doesn't need to be, to make him bleed.

He rolls onto his side, gasping and panting, his eyes frantically searching for another one of the Righteous to help him as I shove him off me and stagger to my feet. But it's just him and me.

Exactly how he wanted it when he and my father forced me down the aisle.

"You . . . you fucking stabbed me," he says weakly.

Like even he can hardly believe it.

Clearly, he doesn't know how I've been learning in therapy not to bottle up my resentment anymore. I stare down at him, swaying a little as the room spins.

But that doesn't stop me from placing my foot on the splintered chair leg as I use all of my weight to shove it farther in.

"I hope Lucifer fucks you every day for the rest of eternity," I spit onto Mark's now stilling corpse.

"That particular punishment is yours alone, I'm afraid."

I turn just in time to see that he's come for me. To watch the horror in his eyes as he sees what Mark has done to me, the way it melts and heats to an inferno of fury. To see that he really does love me in his own messed-up way, after all. I breathe, "I'm sorry."

Not to him. But to humanity.

For what he'll do to them when I'm gone.

Everything fades to black as I fall into his waiting shadows once again.

CHAPTER FIFTY

Lucifer

My shadows catch Charlotte as she falls, and I'm at her side just as quickly, combing over her, searching for any sign of blood beyond what I can already see smeared all over her arms and face. But internal bleeding doesn't always show through puncture wounds, and it's the moment the light leaves her eyes that truly terrifies me.

My nostrils flare as I clutch hold of her. Crumple to the ground.

She was wrong, in any case. About my abilities.

I can control both.

The light doesn't exist without shadow, but I . . . never got the chance to tell her that before . . .

Death's shadow engulfs her face. Steals her from me.

Pressure builds inside my chest, a pulsating burst of power, and I feel myself begin to shake. My human form is barely able to contain me. Fire blazes inside me, igniting the very ground where I stand as I battle the irresistible urge not to abandon her here.

I have every intention of eviscerating the entire world beneath my feet.

Every last one of them.

"You're fucking hard to keep up with, you know that?" Gabriel's voice has me jerking my head up with a snarl. "Gallivanting all over the place."

The furious sound that tears from me is pure animal.

He sighs, shaking his head at me, as he glances down at Charlotte's corpse that I'm still clinging to. His expression falls. "Oh, that's unfortunate, Lucy."

As if she's little more than a toy. I suppose I might have treated her as such. Initially. All this time I planned to have her. Planned to keep her.

I didn't once stop to fully consider the meaning of her mortality.

That I might lose her. Or worse . . .

That she'd be taken from me.

Because she's good. Pure, through and through. She won't end up in Hell with me.

My own foolish pride got in the way of that, it seems.

Yet another one of Father's cruel lessons.

"It'd be just like Him," I whisper, barely able to breathe, "to give her to me only to cruelly rip her away."

"I thought we'd already established it was Mom who sent her?"

"Dad. Mom. It doesn't matter. Don't you see? It all comes down to Him." I point toward the heavens, snarling. "To His fucked plans. Whatever they may be." Gently, I lay Charlotte down on the dirty concrete floor, standing as I face my brother. "Well, not this time."

I have Gabriel up against the wall within seconds, coaxing my Father's forgiveness from him, as if sucking the light out from his body. He lurches, his mouth falling open as the light spills from inside him, and I reach into his mouth to tug against it, struggling to grasp the whole of it in my hand. I tear it from his body like a long rope that's attached to his entrails, until the last of it spills from his lips and into my now-glowing palm.

Done with Gabriel, I release him, and he drops shakily back to the floor, swearing at me. "Fuck, Lucifer," he growls. "You could have just fucking asked for it. It's already yours."

I shake my head. "But you wouldn't have given it to me if you knew what I was going to do with it, would you?"

A beat of silence follows.

Gabriel glances to where I now stand over Charlotte, my Father's redemption clutched in my now-closed fist. A choke of realization tears from him, then a hiss. "Lucifer, no." His eyes go wide, exactly as they did when they all learned what I did with Eve. "You can't."

I smirk. "You'd think He'd have learned His lesson after clipping my wings, wouldn't you?" Before Gabriel can stop me, I plunge my Father's redemption into Charlotte's chest, reaching inside her to where her heart no longer beats.

Unsurprised that mine still continues.

Even after she stole it from me.

CHAPTER
FIFTY-ONE

Charlotte

I stand in the middle of the empty terminal, not surprised that there's no one else here with me. I've been on my own for as long as I can remember. Long before I ever left Kansas for New York City. I glance down at my now-restored dress, one of my favorites from my walk-in closet in Lucifer's penthouse. A black vintage Prada. Much to Lucifer's disappointment.

"Grand Central Station?" a voice sounds behind me. "Interesting choice, if a little cliché."

An achingly familiar voice.

I find him standing there, hands in his pockets, looking as devilishly handsome as ever. His hair is a bit mussed, and his tie is loosened from where he's stripped off his suit coat to reveal the trim cut of his vest underneath, but I prefer him this way.

Relaxed. Unguarded. Undone.

I wet my lips, feeling lightheaded and fuzzy. I'm unable to shake the feeling that this is all a dream.

"Based on what I'm wearing, I'd say I have some reason to worry." I glance toward the gates, to where the train should be. I don't know how

I know, but . . . I think I'm . . . supposed to get on it and go wherever it leads.

"It looks like whatever you want it to here," Lucifer says, taking a small step toward me.

"And where's here?" I rub my arms apprehensively.

"The in-between," he says slowly, carefully. He's never slow or careful. "Your kind might call it Limbo."

I go still, blinking rapidly.

Limbo.

I'm dead?

I should be concerned, but instead a drowsy sort of . . . peace settles over me.

Like all the tension and stress I've ever felt has melted away.

I feel the unmistakable urge to move toward him then. To tell him I'm sorry for what I did, to both him and me. For making him fall in love with me. Though even when I feared the worst would come because of it, I . . . couldn't bring myself to regret him. Us.

But my heels won't move forward.

In this place, there's only one path you can take.

Though I don't know which direction I'm headed. Up . . . or down.

After an entire life of working toward up, I . . . honestly hope I go the other way.

"This is where I stepped off the train when I first arrived here, in New York." I glance around at the glittering walls and high-vaulted ceilings of the terminal. "I felt . . . safe here. Like I could breathe for the first time in weeks."

One of the boards beside us flashes, announcing one minute until the train arrives.

I look toward him. "Am I going . . . ?" My voice trails off.

He steps closer. "I'm afraid I can't say until you're already well on your way, considering . . ." He gestures to the splintered chair leg I now realize is clutched in my hand.

Right. Murder. So far things aren't looking good for me.

"I killed Mark," I say.

"Yes." He nods.

I glance to the gate where I'm supposed to go. "He'll forgive me."

Lucifer knows exactly who I'm talking about.

He tips his head to the side, pressing his lips together. Ever doubtful. "How can you be so certain?"

"Because He gave you to me." Suddenly, it feels like a breeze rolls over my feet, releasing me, and I'm able to step toward him then. I slowly close the distance between us. "When I escaped from my old life, I . . . ran into the forest, and the shadows there, they sheltered me, protected me, and I prayed to God that He'd send me someone who would keep me safe, protect me at all costs, who would never raise a hand to me."

Lucifer snorts a little at that, lifting a brow as he smirks at me.

That wicked, crooked grin that tempts me, and has so many others before.

But this one is different. Just for me.

A feeling of warmth, like I'm finally home, spreads through me.

"Well, not without my consent, I mean." I beam at him.

He shakes his head, still staring down at me. "I don't understand, Charlotte. How can you still have faith in Him? After all this?" He gestures to the empty terminal around us.

I wrap my arms around his neck, pulling him down so I can kiss him.

Like always, he takes my gentle movement and twists it into his own. Into something darker. More delicious.

I bury my hands in his hair, moaning against his tongue.

If God has a problem with me fucking His fallen son in the middle of Limbo . . . well, I guess I'm already the queen of Hell, anyway.

I break the kiss between us, gently pushing my hand against his chest to keep him from claiming my lips once more. If Lucifer had his way, I'm not certain I'd ever get to wear any of the clothes he bought me ever again.

"Don't you see, Lucifer? He led me to you. You're the answer to my prayer, which means . . ." I brush a hand over his cheek, hoping he'll understand, but all I see in his eyes is a deep-seated hurt, a resentment for the Father who never loved him in the way he needed Him to. "He didn't abandon you, or me," I whisper. "He's still here. In everything."

"Forgive me if I don't find that revelation as comforting as you do, darling." Lucifer's smile fades, his stance turning stiff as he frowns. But he doesn't try to hide his unease from me. Not this time. "And I'm afraid my Mother might have had something to do with it this time."

"Your . . . Mother?" My jaw pops open a little as he steps back. Giving me the space I need to leave.

"Lilith," he says, smiling at how my eyes go wide.

I reach for him, suddenly craving his touch. But he gives a subtle shake of his head.

"But that's a story for another time," he says.

I glance toward the golden clock above the information desk in the middle of the terminal, just as the sound of the train arriving below rumbles under my feet.

I startle at the sound, my eyes going wide as my breath becomes shallow, quick.

"It'll wait for you. Don't worry," he says, easily reading the panic in my expression. "Tell me something, Charlotte."

"Anything."

"Why did you decide to come work for my company?"

I blink.

It's not the question I expected him to ask. Not at all.

But I answer him all the same.

"I . . . knew it was the one place my father wouldn't come looking for me. You represented a safe haven. Or so I thought." I sigh, realizing how thoroughly I underestimated my own father's hatred.

He inhales a deep breath, his stance widening as he steps back with a knowing, satisfied grin. "If you ask me, it sounds like you saved yourself, then." Behind him, cast as shadows on the wall, I see the light move as his wings unfurl. "I've always fancied the idea of free will, you see."

An announcer's voice comes over the station's speakers, warning that the train is about to leave. Now, I *know* I must really be dead, because no severely underpaid subway attendant would ever sound so . . . happy.

Lucifer and I look to one another, silent for a beat.

"Do you . . . want to go to Him?" Lucifer nods toward the gate.

And I suddenly realize there's a strong chance that where I'm going, he might not be able to follow me. I shake my head. "Not if you can't go with me."

He gives me a sad smile, like he already knows what I'm thinking. "I'm afraid I'm no longer welcome there, darling." But he doesn't step toward me.

He holds himself still, offering the choice to me.

Even though I know from the longing in his eyes that it . . . hurts him.

I swallow hard, surprised when a tear falls from my chin as all the implications rush through me. The options laying themselves out in my mind, a scrolling spread of opportunities.

But in the end, there's really no question of who I'll choose.

My heart already knows.

I belong to him, and him, me.

"I want to stay with you, Lucifer," I say, reaching for him.

He exhales audibly, total utter relief. His mouth parts on a slight groan, a shaky chuckle tearing from his lips before a slow smile lights his face up. Making him glow. He steps into me again, pulling me into his arms as I whisper, "I love you."

His smile widens, and the joy behind it is so bright and mischievous, it feels a little like I'm staring straight into the sun, and I realize it's the first time I've ever truly seen him smile that way. Full-toothed and wide. Without any of the shadows of his past haunting his face. "I love you too, Charlotte. Vicious and destructive as that love may be."

I glance over my shoulder. Downstairs. To where the train waits.

"Are you certain?" he asks. Like he's afraid I might change my answer.

I nod. "Yes, I'm certain."

"Then I'm afraid you're going to have to forgive me one last time, darling." He casts a wayward glimpse toward the ceiling. "Sorry, Dad."

Suddenly, he shoves his hand forward, burying it deep inside my chest like he means to rip out my heart as I choke on the light he's just shoved inside me.

"I'm afraid this one is mine." Lucifer smirks.

CHAPTER
FIFTY-TWO

Charlotte

I surge forward, gasping for breath as if I've been underwater and I'm just coming up for air.

"Breathe, Charlotte," Lucifer growls, his voice a harsh command that vibrates against my ear.

Reminding me of the last time he said it to me.

That first night in his penthouse. After the foundation opening.

The night I fell in love with him.

Though I was already falling from the first moment we met.

After all, temptation is kind of his thing. But so is loving me, which is even harder to resist.

My gaze darts toward him, taking in his appearance. Even with the flecks of someone else's blood coating his face, he's still beautiful. Exactly the same as he was only moments ago, and yet it . . . feels like a lifetime since I've seen him.

Or at least, my last lifetime, anyway.

I glance down at my body, no longer broken and bruised, even if still a bit sore, before I take in the setting around me. We're still in the abandoned office inside the old Brooklyn shipyard, but the early morning sun has begun to creep in. Mark's body lies a short distance away, and yet . . .

"Who's he?" I say, watching the angel leaning against the far wall. Based on the massive pair of white-feathered wings that have unfolded behind him, he's clearly one of Lucifer's siblings, but not one of the Originals. I'd recognize them.

"Gabriel," Lucifer says. "One of your numerous future brothers-in-law."

"Dad is going to be so pissed at you for this," Gabriel mutters.

I glance between him and Lucifer, my mind struggling to process what's happened. A manic wave of horror at what I've taken from him rolls through me as I desperately touch my lips, mouth, and face as if to check that they're still there. The last few minutes come back to me, like my life flashing before my eyes. Or the end of it, anyway . . .

The train station. The choice I made. That pulsing beam of light.

And the burning sensation that followed . . .

Like I was being torched from the inside out.

I lift my shaking hands tentatively, examining them.

But there's not so much as a scratch on me.

"Your redemption?" I finally breathe, my mouth falling open.

Because what else could it be?

I glance between Lucifer and my now-healed body as if in search of answers. "You . . . gave it to me?"

Lucifer shrugs. "Not exactly what Father had planned, I think, but I never was one to ask for permission." He smiles first. "I take first and ask for forgiveness later."

Exactly like he did when he sent my press release.

The sparkle in his eye, his happiness, soothes me.

"And I'm asking for yours now, Charlotte." His voice grows softer. Like he's less sure of himself.

I smile at him then. Unable to stop the wide, goofy grin that crosses my face at the euphoric tingling in my head, the surge of joy that starts in my chest and spreads outward, before I'm kissing him. Kissing every part of him I can get my hands on.

Anything and everything.

"Ugh. Someone gag me." Gabriel makes a disgusted choking noise before the whoosh of his wings marks his exit.

Not that I bother to look in his direction.

Lucifer snaps his fingers, and suddenly we're inside the penthouse. In his bedroom.

I'm still too busy kissing every inch of him to be surprised.

He pulls his mouth from mine momentarily. "Had I known that's all it took to get you to ravish me this way, I might have done it a bit sooner," he says, gripping a bit of my hair in his hand as I feel him nod to his lower half. "Though move south a bit more quickly, darling. I'm an impatient bastard."

"Lucifer." I pull back from where I was busy kissing his neck, gripping both sides of his face. "Lucifer, you did it, don't you understand?" I can't stop myself from beaming at him. My eyes fill with tears. "You let me choose. You were selfless. In your love for me."

I kiss him again before he can protest, though he still purrs against my probing tongue, his fangs nipping at me.

"Don't you understand what this means?" I whisper against his lips.

"That I'm going to get to sheathe myself inside your delicious cunt?" His voice drops low, instantly making me wet as I climb onto his lap, pulling him down and onto the floor on top of me.

"No," I say, at first.

He pulls back only to lift a brow at me. "That's not our safe word, Charlotte," he reminds me before his hands and tongue start exploring again, making their way down to where I truly want him. "And I'm not asking."

"No, well, I mean . . . yes. Yes, that, too, of course, but . . ."

He glances up from where his head's now positioned between my knees and looks at me.

"You said you poison everything you love, but that's not true. You can change. You have already," I whisper to him. Like him realizing the goodness that's still inside him is the deepest longing of my heart.

And it is. Teaching him all that love can be. Exactly as he did for me.

"And if you can change, you can still be . . ."

"Redeemed?" he asks, finishing the words for me. His forked tongue probing my pussy is what stops me from finishing them myself.

"And if the devil can be redeemed . . . ," I say, sighing as his tongue starts to circle my clit.

"Well, then I suppose humanity can as well," he says, hitting that spot deep inside that he knows makes me come.

EPILOGUE

Charlotte

Three days later . . .

Much to my delight, Lucifer and I don't stray far from his bedroom or the playroom for the next several days. Every touch, every kiss, every stroke of his tongue is suddenly heightened in the face of our infinity. We're both riding an intoxicating high. One of pain turned to pleasure that feels like it'll last for all eternity. If we only allow it to.

I sigh a little, melting into where he holds me, the unshaved scruff on his cheek brushing against my neck as we lie tangled in his bedsheets.

I don't think either of us is fully prepared to face the outside world just yet.

The mess the Righteous left in our city. The media.

Or what it means for us, for the world, for humanity, and the possibly impending apocalypse to follow, now that he's gifted his Father's redemption to me.

We both want to hold on to whatever this feeling of . . . peace is a little longer.

Before divine reality comes crashing down on both him and me.

It isn't until the morning of the third day, both of our phones turned off and all our team communications silenced, that an unexpected knock at the door forces me to finally separate from him.

I lift a brow. "Did you call down for food?" I ask, throwing back the covers and quickly using the top sheet to cover my nudity as my stomach growls.

Lucifer shakes his head lazily. "Leave it, dove. They'll find an excuse to barge in here eventually," he grumbles as I slip away from where I've been practically encased in his arms.

Like a tomb of my own making.

"You're not *always* the boss of me, you know." I toss a playful smirk over my shoulder at him, watching as he lifts onto one of his elbows.

From the aroused gleam in his eye, I know I'm going to pay for that little bit of rebellious teasing the moment I return to his bed.

My ass has already been deliciously and continually red for the past several days.

And I love it.

I pad toward the door, still holding the top sheet clutched to my chest, but when I pull it open, expecting to find Ramesh or another one of the staff, I don't find anyone waiting for me.

I glance down the hall, anticipating seeing them make a hasty exit, but the hall's empty. Instead, all I find waiting is an expensive-looking bottle of wine placed just outside the doorframe, a smooth, sleek envelope attached.

Hmm. Some kind of immortal honeymoon gift, maybe?

From Az, would be my guess.

I pick up the bottle by its neck, bringing it back into the room with me as I bump the door shut with one sheet-covered hip. I set it down on a small table near the fireplace, on top of some of Lucifer's sheet music.

As I turn to head back to the bed, I do a double take, surprised that the card attached bears my name scrawled in impressive-looking script.

I pause, turning it over in my hand, admiring the quality before I use a nearby letter opener left on the fireplace mantle to open it.

Immediately, a cloud of white dust pours out and onto my hands, causing me to cough.

I stumble back.

What the fuck?

"Did that lust-filled lothario you call a brother just send me a freaking envelope full of drugs?" I snap, now trying and failing to brush some of the powder off myself and the sheet.

Lucifer saunters over to my side, as naked as I am, but unashamed, naturally.

With a body like his, why would he be?

"Where did you get that?" he asks, clearly suspicious. He dips his pinky finger into the small mound that's now poured out onto the table, then licks it, his expression shifting from mildly amused to grave. "That's not cocaine, darling." He snaps his fingers, and abruptly the substance and all its particles are gone.

My stomach drops.

"Then what—?"

Suddenly Lucifer catches my chin in his hand, roughly forcing me to look him in the eye. "*Never* open anything that hasn't been scanned by the mail room or the security team, do you understand me?" All relaxation is stripped from his face, his voice harsh, cold. But it's the fear in his eyes that shocks me.

I nod timidly before he releases me, watching as he drags a rough hand through his hair. "That could have taken out the whole bloody building," he mutters, more to himself than me.

What in God's name could scare Lucifer?

And if it wasn't cocaine, then what . . .

I'm still standing there processing exactly *what* kind of threat was inside that envelope that he just magicked away, when the grim look on Lucifer's face as he glances toward the air vents seems to answer it for me.

Anthrax.

My skin crawls. *No.*

No. No, no, no.

My head shakes back and forth of its own accord, in denial. Only Lucifer and Gabriel know I'm immortal now. We haven't told anyone else yet, which means whoever sent this thought I would . . .

I swallow.

I can't even bring myself to think it.

And not just me.

All the waitstaff. The whole building . . .

I shudder. Thank God Lucifer was with me.

"Who . . . who would do this?" I stammer.

At first, Lucifer doesn't answer me, but the mixed expression of concern and fury on his features is more than answer enough. "My enemies are now your enemies, Charlotte," he says slowly.

The color drains from my face, my palms shaking and clammy.

"But I'm safe, right? I . . . I thought that now I can't . . ."

"I'm afraid there are other ways to kill an immortal, darling."

Thank you for reading!

If you enjoyed *Original Sinner*, you're just one click away from FREE bonus content and deleted scenes featuring Charlotte and Lucifer, plus . . .

- Exclusive giveaways and NSFW character art
- Being the first to hear about new releases
- Sneak peeks at Kait's newest titles

Sign up for Kait's newsletter and receive your free *Original Sinner* bonus content now! www.kaitballenger.com

ABOUT CONSENSUAL KINK

The depictions of BDSM in this book are for fantasy entertainment purposes only and are not intended as an accurate representation of the BDSM/kink community. For many, BDSM and its queer history is sacred, hallowed ground, but I hope readers feel I've used it to appropriately and thematically fuck with the power structures that be.

For those interested in learning more, please seek out resources on risk aware, consensual kink.

ACKNOWLEDGMENTS

To my agents, Nicole Resciniti and Lesley Sabga, thank you for championing this book and so many others and loving it as much as I do. I can't imagine being on this journey without you. I'm so fortunate to have you both in my corner advocating for me.

To my editors, Maria Gomez and Sasha Knight, thank you for believing in me and this series, for asking good questions, and for empowering me by trusting in my vision. I'm so grateful for your guidance, enthusiasm, and expertise.

To my beta readers and brainstorm besties, Abigail Owen, Jax Cassidy, and Kim Rust, thank you for always making yourselves available for a plot chat, for the early reads, and most importantly, for being there through all the highs and lows. I value your friendship more than you know.

To my husband, for always being my first and favorite reader, even if I do affectionately roll my eyes at all the *Godfather* references.

To my boys, for their innocent enthusiasm. I hope you don't read this book until I'm very, very old. Or dead, actually.

To all my readers, loyal and new, for making this and so many other books a success. I could not do this without you. I am forever grateful for your support.

And lastly, since Lucifer would approve, I want to thank me for believing in myself, even in the face of others' doubt, for choosing to write for my own joy no matter where it led to, for being fearless and courageous in pushing boundaries . . .

I'm so proud of you.

ABOUT THE AUTHOR

Kait Ballenger is an award-winning author of dark romantasy and para-normal romance. She is obsessed with tales of morally gray, sometimes villainous heroes and can't resist a spicy redemption arc. When Kait's not busy writing kinky paranormal fantasy, she can usually be found with her nose buried in someone *else's* naughty books. She lives, unfor-tunately, in Florida's Bible Belt with her husband and two adorable sons—and will gladly use that belt to whip you.

You can find her on TikTok @kaitballenger and Instagram @kait.ballenger or sign up for her newsletter at www.kaitballenger.com.